LiT
Part III – Pure Heart
2024 Edition

I0615848

Maxwell F. Hurley

.

LiT
Part III – Pure Heart
2024 Edition

FICTION4ALL

This book is dedicated to anyone who has
battled or supported the fight against cancer

Introduction

"WILL YOU JUST STOP?!" Alex screamed as she chased the Host through the park. She and Komptin have been chasing this Demon for over an hour and she was getting tired. This stubborn and relentless creature of the Dark got a couple of good hits on her, giving her a small cut on her eye, but she managed to overtake him in the beginning. She would have diminished him, but she got distracted when a teenage couple started walking by holding hands. They had no idea Alex just saved their lives by instigating a foot pursuit. She now regretted that decision because this Host could run...and run. She tried shooting her Lite Beam at it, trying anything to slow it down, but it seemed to dodge every shot.

The Demon turned around and gave her a stare of hate. "You will not see the morning light you…"

Alex caught up and held up her hand to the Host. She motioned to hold on a minute as she tried to catch her bearings. "Yah, yah, I know, you Lite harlot." She straightened her posture with her fists ignited before walking towards the Demon. "Seriously, you guys really need to come up with a new insult towards me."

She had been in this position way too many times before. This hunt led her into the wrong part of town, surrounded by old office buildings. She could almost sense what was about to happen. The air had a sense of tension to it. Then she heard the

Demon start to move. He had the stance that showed he was going to attack but decided to run into the building instead. Alex just closed in her eyes in disbelief and chased it into the structure.

Alex didn't know why she bothered to try to turn the lights on; they never worked. Just once she would have liked to be on a hunt where the lights would brighten her hunting grounds. A punch was her greeting, knocking her to the floor as the Demon snarled.

The feeling of a combat boot kicking into Alex's side sent her flying onto the top of an old desk and then she fell to the floor. Alex held her side as she thanked God it wasn't the side that Sanah had stabbed her on. She stood up with her fist ignited, looking at the pair of glowing red eyes in front her. It opened its mouth in a hiss showing off its massive teeth. It charged Alex at full force flying over the desk. Alex grabbed the Host in mid-air, tossing the dark creature through a window back outside.

Alex immediately regretted her decision for doing that, as she now had to pick up the trail and go after it again. She walked back outside and to her surprise was the Demon stuck on a piece of rebar that was hanging out of a dumpster.

"Oh, nice." Though impaled with a metal rod, it continued to try to swipe at her with his sharp claws. She closed the lid to one side of the dumpster and sat down next to the Demon. "You're kind of in a predicament," Alex told him.

The Demon studied his situation. "I kind of am."

She never had this opportunity of such an advantage over a Demon to talk to one. "Can I ask you a question?" she tested, pulling out a piece of gum. She offered one to the Demon, but he just shook his head.

"I'm not going anywhere," he said, looking at the rebar, no doubt trying to think of a way to get out of this situation.

"Why did you accept Infiltration?"

"Absolute power over the primates," he told her. "You all need to be harshly ruled."

"Yah, I know what you think, but why did you do it?" She stole a quick glance down the alley to see if anyone was coming. "Doesn't it ever get lonely? This war, this fight."

"I hate you, Sentry," the Demon coldly stared at her.

"Try to have a civil conversation." She hopped down onto the ground and ignited a Lite Spear. "You want anything before you are diminished?"

"Just to kill all that you love," he hissed.

Alex sighed and shook her head in disbelief before she thrust her Lite Spear into the Host. The Demon's body melted into the dumpster. It was sad to see that one could not reason with Demons or Infiltrators. All they want is death and power over the people of earth in this life then into the next. Alex couldn't let that happen. An overwhelming surge to stop them filled her heart, but she feared for the safety of her family. It started to snow. It was so rare to see such fluffy flakes this time of year. A sense of nostalgia overcame her as the snowflakes fell before her, then many started to follow. One snowflake was caught with her hand open. Alex just took a moment in time to watch it melt away before heading back to the church.

Chapter 1

Anne was deep into her research project that Cardinal Frank assigned to her late last week. She thought she was under higher scrutiny from Father Tom because she was the first Council Historian that wasn't a Catholic priest and was a woman on top of that. Even though she was inducted into the Catholic Council, it still didn't give her much room for failure. She knew she was being judged by Father Tom and he wasn't afraid to show it.

Although the work was hard and the pay was just enough for her and Kale to get by, she always thought she was lucky. She enjoyed her job. Father Tom had made it known that he knew she just got the job because she was attacked by a Demon surrounded by Infiltrators and lived to talk about it. It was truly amazing though that she had not told Kale about her true work here. Also, Alex had not told him either about the pivotal role she plays in all this. She always suspected he knew more than what he let on though. Kale Moler always portrayed something different than what was going on inside his head.

Her phone vibrated as she looked to see a text message from him. "Lunch at 11:30?" the message asked.

Anne regretfully replied, "I have to work through lunch today, sorry."

Kale responded with a sad emoji face and a broken heart. Anne knew she was spending a lot of time at work, and bless Kale, he was being patient about it. She could tell he was starting to miss her. Her attention turned to Alex when she walked into Anne's office in the basement of the church.

"Hey, I'm hungry, let's go get lunch," Alex said, sitting in a chair with her feet on top of Anne's desk.

Anne had to turn down another person she cared about. "I can't. Father Tom wants me to investigate the Council's past records on pre-host conditions. And there isn't much there."

"What's he wanting?" Alex said, looking at an old book sitting on Anne's desk. Alex opened the book and realized it was an ancient Bible that was unreadable to her. "What language is this?"

"Italian," Anne said, still looking through an old-looking book and comparing notes she was holding.

"Where did it come from?" Alex asked, thumbing through it. She looked at a picture of Christ performing an exorcism on a poor village peasant.

Anne continued her work. "The Pope gave it to me when I completed my studies in the Vatican."

"The Pope?" Alex said. "I knew you met him, I thought it was just in passing."

"He actually sat me down for a good hour discussing historical issues within the Councils," Anne said, still sifting through her work. "Ugh!" She flung her wavy brown hair behind her shoulders before sitting back. It felt good to remove her glasses for a bit. "How was your night?"

"Komptin and I ran into a Host last night." From her chair, Alex peered out the window of the old brick church. "It was weird, he ran and ran, really good too. I was having trouble catching up to him."

Alex heard someone coming down the hall.

"But then it seemed like he just gave up," Alex turned to Anne, who had resumed studying. "He just turned around, gave a real minor fight and then I diminished him."

"How come that wasn't in the report?" Father Tom said, coming into Anne's office.

Alex's long, black-weaved hair hit the ground when she tilted her head upwards to see him looking down at her. "Wasn't a fact, just an opinion," Alex told him. "Do you have anything to drink?" Alex asked Anne.

Anne pointed to the fridge where she always had a supply of Apollo Energy Drink for Alex.

"I thought you wanted only facts."

Father Tom went to his paper folder and opened Alex's report. "Chased down Host from Welsher St. to Francis Ave. Diminished Host. A little bit more effort on your part would be nice to see once in a while," he insisted.

"Tell you what, you can go risk your life every night hunting Infiltrators, Hosts, and oh yeah, running into Dark Demons while still trying to maintain our little secret here, and I will spend a little bit more time on your reports," Alex told him while sitting in a chair in front of Anne's desk.

Father Tom just bit his lip and went to Anne. "Get me your findings on the pre-Host conditions in South Africa by the end of the week."

"South Africa?" Anne said. "I've been working on South America."

"Well, I need South Africa," Father Tom said. He turned to leave and stopped himself. "Oh yeah, we are getting a new secretary for the Cardinal. She is arriving tomorrow." Father Tom added, "She is not a member of the Council so remember—" He pointed to Alex. "Stick to your cover."

Alex gave him a thumbs up as she continued to drink her energy drink.

"Yes, Father," Anne told him. Anne watched Father Tom walk away. "You know, when you agitate him, he takes it out on me."

"I thought priests were supposed to be somewhat compassionate," Alex said. "Come on, I'm hungry."

"I really can't, plus I already turned down Kale's invitation," Anne told her. "We were going to go over plans for the wedding. We're getting so far behind on that." She shook her head out of frustration.

"You sound stressed." Alex went back to flipping through another book on Anne's desk.

"Not as fun as I dreamt as a kid." Anne nervously laughed. "But it's coming along."

"I'm assuming the wedding will be here," Alex prodded.

"Yes, and I finally asked the Cardinal if he would perform the ceremony, which he agreed," Anne said.

"He's a good man," Alex admired.

Alex remembered how he had helped her through her little misuse of church revenue when she was with Gastrix. He had such a loving, caring affectation as he was getting her out of her situation. The Cardinal protected her from the Council finding out about her reckless spending and helped her get on track with her life before she started making some real major poor life decisions. Alex thought back on how those decisions could have contributed to her death.

Anne nodded. "Yes, he is a good man," she said going back to her studies.

"So, you got the venue, you got the priest, Dan is going to be Kale's best man; sounds like everything is on its way," Alex was observing Anne's reaction, awaiting a response which seemed to take forever.

"Well, it's a start," she replied, putting together the archives of South America.

"Yep, sounds like Kale's got his groomsmen all ready," Alex hinted.

"Not really, just the best man," Anne corrected.

"Sounds like the wedding party is all picked out." Alex raised her eyebrows at Anne.

"Just about," Anne said. "I still have a lot of work to do for my side." Anne continued to read some of the books she had open. Anne's face had a bit more concentration to it. Alex snuck a view of the book page about on a man who became possessed and then committed suicide prior to the exorcism.

Alex just tapped her can with one of her rings, waiting for Anne.

Anne looked up at Alex through her glasses. "What?"

"So..." Alex wanted Anne to finish up her sentence.

"So… what?" Anne said.

The two of them just looked at each other. "Do you know who your Maid of Honor is going to be?"

Anne was shocked, "I thought that was obvious." Anne smiled at her.

Alex straightened up in her seat while smiling back with excitement.

"My mother," Anne quickly replied.

Alex sat there, a little heartbroken. "Oh…" She tried her best not to sound disappointed.

"Of course, it's you," Anne smiled at her.

"You have been hanging around Kale too much, doing that to me." Alex got up, went behind Anne's desk, and gave her a hug.

"I didn't think I had to ask; I just thought you would know it." Anne returned the hug.

"A girl still wants to hear it," Alex told her.

***

Kale came home from work and placed his keys on his dresser. It felt so good to change his clothes out of his shirt and tie into something free.

16

He was glad to be home, he hated his job, and even though he was good at it, today was a day he didn't particularly care for. The only comfort he had was hoping to have lunch with his fiancé, but that got taken away from him as well. There was a continuing nagging in the back of his mind about cleaning the spare room. He thought the room he was going to was occupied by Alex, but she wanted to stay at the church. It was a weird arrangement, but she seemed at peace staying there. If it helped her heal after her brutal mugging a couple of years back, then he had no complaints. Her excuse was she insisted that he and Anne needed to start their lives together. The sentiment was nice, but he knew she was hiding the fact she felt safe in the church. However, there were times he missed having her around like when they were in college, and she was Anne's roommate. The room just became symbol of what was about to eventually come.

Even though they never really talked about it, he knew this room would eventually have a crib in it. The thought of himself waking up to go to the gym, not finding Anne next to him, and then checking on the baby to see Anne rocking her in a chair feeding their child, gave him a bit of anxiety. That was beaten with a small smile on his face but quickly returned as terror. The thought of the horrors of the world entered his mind—the murders, the political and environmental climate, the rampage of drugs as they make their way into people's lives. How could he bring a child into this world with it being in so much turmoil?

He had to shake those negative views out. They were not even married yet. The wedding was coming up next spring. He was going to be Anne's husband. He flashed back to the night, when Anne said they met. Even though they went through grade school together, he and Anne never really talked.

In fact, Kale thought Anne pretty much didn't like him up to that night at the lake. He wouldn't have thought in a million years that he and Anne McClure would be getting married. But that night, something special happened.

At the time, Roger had a pretty bad thing for Alex. He constantly hounded after her, and for some reason, he had approached Anne. He saw Roger making Anne feel uncomfortable. So, in Kale's infinite wisdom, he thought he just had to say something to him.

He walked over to Roger and pretty much scared him away from Anne. He remembered how scared Anne was sitting in the brisk lake air that night. It wasn't life or death, but more of general fear of the situation she was in.

Her big brown eyes had met with Kale's. That picture would forever be in his mind. She had him hooked from that moment on. He could tell she was shivering so he gave her his sweatshirt to warm up in. His mind went back to that sweatshirt—on how he never got that sweatshirt back. He liked how she wore it from time to time.

The sound of keys rustling by the door meant Anne was coming home. He watched her come through the door with the mail in her hand. He could tell she had a rough day.

She met him with a beautiful smile. "Sorry I couldn't do lunch."

"No big, I get it," Kale replied, greeting her with a small kiss.

She stopped going through the mail. "You know, you actually do," Anne said, putting the mail on the table.

"Do…what?" Kale asked, not knowing what she was talking about.

"You really do understand. Your patience, your love, your dedication." Anne shut the door and locked it. She walked by Kale, grabbing his hand and leading him into the bedroom.

Kale followed his future bride to the bedroom with a smile on his face. Not because of what was about to happen, but because he knew they would be spending the rest of their lives together.

***

It must have been just good luck that she decided to grab a snack at the deli that she happened to come across on one of her hunts. Upon her order for a sandwich, she turned around to see Greg behind her, checking her out. She remembered smiling at him and then they ended up back at his place. It led to Alex and Greg on his couch kissing. Their faces hidden by her long hair extension when she was facing him on his lap. She could feel his hands start to go up the back of her shirt. She saw the face twitch of Greg when he started to feel her scars on her back. There was fear he was going to find her repulsive from the scars with multiple Demons and infiltrators. She needed to make sure he didn't see them, so she escalated the night quicker.

Working in a church didn't really make it easy to find guys, and her hunts have been really frequent. She hadn't had any real time to wind down. Alex knew where this was going.

She asked him while she was kissing him, "Shall we take this somewhere more private?" She wiped off some her lipstick off his face.

Greg nodded. "We don't have that much time before my wife gets home."

"Wait, what?" Alex stood up off the couch. The only thing she could do was shiver. "You're serious." She started gathering her belongings, so angry with herself. She turned to a mirror hanging on the wall. Her pale white face stared back at her. The dark makeup around her eyes was a little bit smeared but she didn't care. She wanted to get out of there.

"Where are you going? We can finish this quickly." Greg unbuttoned the rest of his shirt.

"Yeah, not happening. I gotta go to work," Alex told him as she looked in her bag for her wallet. She just felt dirty, and extremely shameful of her actions even though she knows she is not entirely to blame. It was obvious she was a key player in this scenario. The only thing she could think about was how she could be an instrument for God when she gets herself into situations like this.

"Isn't this your job?" Greg looked at his watch. "We can meet at a hotel if you are worried about my wife," Greg offered. "I'll just tell I have to work late."

"I'm not a pro!" She had to take a moment before she did something rash. "Oh my God, you're nauseating."

He looked back at her in complete amazement. "Right, look in the mirror, lady. You came home with a man ordering a ham on rye." He turned on the television to the news where they were talking about a recent fire at a church.

Alex shook her head and put her leather coat tying it tight around her tiny waist. "Wow, just…wow."

"Well, if you're going to leave, be quiet when you go. You know…neighbors."

Alex quietly exited the door and shut it behind her. She turned to the door and yelled, "Okay, Greg, it was nice seeing you again, just call the agency and ask for 'Mercedes'. They will send me right over."

Some of the doors opened and an older couple looked at her with disgust as she blew the gentlemen a kiss and winked at him. That probably wasn't her best move, but it beat her initial feeling of sending Greg through a wall.

She decided to head to the roof to overlook the city. The air was brisk for early October as she could see a faint distinction of her breath. She heard some people yelling at each other nearby. Sometimes she wished she could get involved in everyday matters. She kind of laughed how easily she could become a living superhero of the city. Praise wasn't something Alex required for what she did on a nightly basis, sometimes though, it was hard for her to risk her life night after night without any "thank you" from the commoners. She knew the church appreciated what she did.

Well, maybe not Father Tom, but the Council appreciates it.

Alex looked down at her feet, kicking around some rocks that were on the roof. The steam from the exhaust pipes covered the ground into a fog. Alex stared out into the distance, thinking about her altercation with Greg.

If she had had any clue he was married, she wouldn't have gone to his apartment. The fact that he thought she was a professional escort didn't much help matters. Maybe she *was* a harlot? There were a lot of guys in her past. A lot of them never lasting more than a weekend.

All her personal excursions were whirling through her mind. Why would He empower the Lite with someone like her who had such loose morals? Osiah's purple star seemed to twinkle a little brighter this night. Almost telling her that he was far from perfect himself.

Her thought was interrupted by the sound of someone sneaking up on her. The faint sound of crunching on the roof was too quiet. This clued her in that whatever it was, it was supernatural. She closed her eyes as it approached. This was just another night of her life.

The sound got closer and closer, and she could feel the presence getting stronger. She slowly took her hands out of her pockets. Soon she was going to pounce on her stalker, making them regret the unprovoked attack. She closed her eyes, showing a faint glow of neon blue from underneath her eyelids before she turned to attack.

Alex supernaturally turned in an instant, pushing on the massive head of a purple gargoyle with glowing neon blue eyes. She tried to push him back but couldn't move the massive creature. She wrapped her arms around his neck still trying to move the massive creature, but it turned into a laugh while giving him a hug.

"Hey, boy. Give up?"

Komptin snuggled up to Alex, giving her a loving hello.

"I know, I know, you want to go hunting."

He jumped onto the edge of the roof, smelling the air for a scent of the Dark.

"What do you say we go for a walk in the southeast section tonight?"

Komptin's body grew fur as he became a German Shepard. Alex gets told by random people that he was extremely huge for that type of dog. It was always humorous that they didn't know what his true state actually was.

"I'm hungry, maybe we can get a double cheeseburger before we head out."

***

Father Tom walked into the Cardinal's office with what information he had from Anne. It wasn't as much as he had hoped. He couldn't help but think that if she was Catholic and, not to sound misogynistic, but a man, because she could have been a priest. That way she could have been molded into the position from the Council. But this is what he got, a non-Catholic, non-denomination, non-priest female who was getting married. And to put the icing on the cake, she was marrying the brother of the Lite Sentry, and the Lite Sentry was a whole other story herself.

He knocked on the office door to the Cardinal's office. "Cardinal, this is all we got on the pre-host conditions."

"Thank you, Father Tom," the elderly man said. He thumbed through the report.

Father Tom watched Cardinal Frank hands shake a bit as he read the paper file. His pure white hair was combed perfectly, and always the same every day. His glasses were a bit out of date, but it fit him appropriately. Father Tom found a place to voice his concern, "I apologize that it's South America and not South Africa. I tasked Anne to get it to me by the end of week."

The Cardinal continued to read the report. "And how did she respond to that?"

"She accepted it; she didn't really have a choice," Father Tom was confused at that question. He didn't understand where the cardinal was going with this. They were in a battle to keep the Dark in balance. He always found it difficult to be a priest active in this war but also to remember to care for his flock.

Something in the report caught the Cardinal's attention. "You know, Father, she has a fiancé and a wedding to plan. If her home life isn't stable, she's not going to be much good to us." The Cardinal looked up at him. "We are in a marathon, not a sprint. Try to ease up on her."

Father Tom could feel himself get a little agitated. "Yes, Cardinal."

The clicking sound of the locked box where the cardinal put the report represented the night was ending. His mentor sat behind his desk with nothing but a desk lamp making the prestigious man glow in the dark. It made the situation much more uncomfortable. "Something on your mind?"

"It's Anne, sir."

"Is she not performing?"

"She's working hard and has a great eye for research, but I don't understand why she is here. Is it because she witnessed the Sentry and a Host with a bunch of Infiltrators?" Father Tom asked. "She's not even Catholic, plus you are going to marry them in our cathedral. It seems like we are losing our values of the church. How are we supposed to be a strong organization to fight the Dark if we don't stick to our foundations?"

"She is still God's creature, Father, regardless of whether she attends this church, a Lutheran church, or even decides to praise Him in the living room of her apartment," the Cardinal stated. "We all appreciate Him in our own way. It just matters where one's heart lays."

"Yes, Cardinal," Father Tom reluctantly agreed.

"Try to ease up on her. She's a fine young lady." He reached into desk to grab a walnut from his bottom drawer. He struggled to crack it open with the nutcracker. "Plus, it must be God's will because she happens to be good friends with the Lite Sentry."

Father Tom had to prevent himself from rolling his eyes. "She's a whole other story,"

"Problem with Alexandria?" the Cardinal asked, almost full well knowing the answer.

"She's not disciplined. She's very mouthy and, again, she's not even Catholic." Father Tom seemed to have his emotion of disparagements come out a little bit more than he wanted to. "I don't know why God would choose her for such responsibility."

The cardinal laughed. "Yes, she is certainly a unique one, Father." He tossed the walnut shell in the garbage. "He has chosen her. Now, for the life of me, I don't know why. You are correct, she is undisciplined. She's also got a very strong heart. She is mouthy; she also needs that confidence to survive. Remember, He asked her at 17 years of age to risk her life every night to balance the Lite against the Dark, which is growing. If you need a reminder of what we ask of her, just take a look at the scars on the side of her face and neck. Lord knows what the rest of her body looks like.

Remember, she almost died fighting a turned Lite Sentry that was disciplined, obedient, and dedicated his life to the cause. It almost cost us the Conduit," the cardinal reminded him.

Father Tom could feel his humility. It seemed as if God had to give him a constant reminder of the whole picture versus what Council had asked him to do. He felt embarrassment and couldn't think of anything for him to reply with.

The Cardinal came out from behind his desk and escorted Father Tom out of his office. "You are doing a great job keeping the support of the Council with everything they ask. Maintain your faith in His decisions."

"Yes, Cardinal," Father Tom replied to him. He glanced over at the clock as he was meeting his sister for a wine and painting party.

"I have a meeting tomorrow with the leader of the Islamic Council," the Cardinal said.

"Oh?"

The Cardinal had a hint of worry in his voice. "We need to discuss the way ahead because no replacement for Sanah has been activated and they are deeply ashamed of his actions." The Cardinal looked over at his bodyguard in a black suit standing by the door. "Tony."

"Cardinal, are we retiring for the night?" he asked.

"Yes, give me a couple of minutes," he replied.

"Of course," he acknowledged stepping back into the background maintaining vigilance.

"Father, the report can wait until the end of next week," the Cardinal said. "Get some rest. Go relax. You do know how to do that, right?"

"Yes, of course." He grinned.

"Go, go relax," the Cardinal stated.

"Well, my sister and I are going to a wine-and-paint get together," Father Tom admitted.

Cardinal tapped his hand on Father Tom's shoulders. "We all have our guilty pleasures." He put his hand on his shoulders. "Good night, Father."

"Good night, Cardinal," Father Tom replied as he watched the Cardinal walk away with his bodyguard. Father Tom looked at his watch. "I can still make it!" Father Tom headed out, grabbing his coat.

***

Warcourt sat in the chair waiting for the meeting to start. He hated waiting, even during his fully human days, he hated waiting. Now that he was infiltrated and full of power and clarity, he sure as hell didn't have the patience.

"We need to get this meeting started, who are we waiting on?" he asked the group who was sitting in the conference room.

This sure beat the other meeting places where the Hosts and Infiltrators normally hung out in. It was clean, it was big, and it was located out in the country in a mansion outside the Lite Sentry's senses. It truly was free. He looked around the room at the mixture of Hosts and Provisionaries. He never

28

understood how the Dark has gone from hiding in the shadows, hunting for kills and hosts, to having full-blooded humans working for them in hopes of becoming Hosts. He just didn't understand why they just couldn't be Infiltrated and become a more powerful army to take over the balance of power in this war.

"I think we are waiting for our host?" Barbara interjected. This Provisionary was pretty for human standards. It was understood that she would use her attractiveness to get some of the male Provisionaries to come to the Dark.

"This is stupid," Warcourt was getting more and more annoyed by just sitting there. "I've got better things to do."

"Oh, what is that?" Gron said, walking into the room with Salamor floating at his side.

"Gron," Warcourt said, standing up. He looked around the room and noticed no one else was standing. He backhanded one of the Provisionaries that was sitting next to him. The human fell backwards, bleeding on the floor. "Show some respect and stand up."

The rest of the room stood up out of fear. Gron looked around the room and noticed a young 17- or 18-year-old girl standing near the table. He walked up to her. "What's your name?"

"Samantha," she said, surveying the position she was in.

Gron could see her trying to hide her trembling. The Hosts were watching where Gron was going with this. "Who brought you here?"

She pointed to one of Hosts.

HullMore stood up. "I did." He was fishing for Gron's approval.

"You brought her here?" The room seemed to darken as Gron took the long way around the table. "All, we are steering towards a critical junction in this war. We delivered a major blow to the Lite with the mass Infiltration a couple of years back. Since then, we have gained power, wealth, momentum, and placed spies within human society." He stopped in front of Barbara to eye her with his intentions without saying a word. She seductively smiled at him, acknowledging.

"Gron," Salamor hissed.

"Of course," Gron said, kissing her before walking away. "Like I was saying, we are at a critical junction as we are about to start the offensive against the Lite." He continued to walk around the table. "We must make sure we all know who we serve while we are here."

"And who is that?" Samantha asked, trying to hide her fear.

Gron could tell she was getting really scared. Even a simple primate could see the fear she was protruding.

"My child, why do you think you are here?" A pale-faced man walked in with long greasy hair and blackened eyes wearing a big black hat. The stench of death filled the room.

Gron bowed and the rest of the room followed suit. Everyone but Samantha; she screamed as he walked in.

"Oh my God!"

"Shhh," Vandor said, putting his finger to his mouth. "God, no my dear. Far from it." Vandor motioned towards two of the Hosts and they grabbed Samantha, covering her mouth. "We cannot afford any leaks; the Sentry is getting more and more powerful. Only the ones true and pure can be here." He looked over at the Host who brought the girl in.

Gron ignited his fist and shoved them through the chest of HullMore. The Demon screamed as it burned from the inside, causing the shell of the human collapse, it then disappeared into the floor. "Only the true and pure," Vandor said. He pointed to Samantha. "This one is not, dispose of her."

Warcourt saw the girl's eyes grow big as the Infiltrators pounced on her, ripping her body apart. All that remained of the girl was torn up clothes and chunks of bones, flesh and pools of blood.

"Only the pure," Vandor said as he walked out of the room. Vandor turned to Salamor who was floating behind him. "Go, now."

"As you command," Salamor said as he floated into the wall to the outside.

Gron looked around the room. "I have a job for you." He pointed to a Provisionary. "But first, everyone leave." All the people started to leave until Gron grabbed Barbara's hand. "Not you."

Warcourt turned around as he walked out of the room. He couldn't help but admire what power Gron had. He could do what he willed and to whom without any consequence. He needed to find a way to achieve such strength. The door slammed shut and Warcourt turned to the rest of the Provisionaries and Hosts. "That, that is what we should all strive to become! That is what true power becomes!"

Chapter 2

The sun was starting to peak on the horizon when Alex returned home. The church was definitely a happy sight. She and Komptin just got into one altercation with a random infiltrator, but it still managed to give her a bloody lip. So, the church was a welcome sight to the eyes. It was safe since no Dark could harm anyone on holy ground of any kind. With the Cardinal's good heart, he set it up so she could stay in the rectory. Alex was uncomfortable at first, but now she found it to be a nice sanctuary. It was just big enough for her stuff, a bed for Komptin, and a bathroom that was decent in size. Komptin jumped into his bed to curl up in a ball and fall asleep. Outside of the door, to the right, was the painting of what Alex thought was a past Sentry with Osiah and Komptin in the background. She remembered seeing it first in Father Carl's office as she was lectured at. She took a second to admire the painting. In each corner, were four Roman Numerals, "III, I, XVIII, I." Alex looked at the girl in the center of the painting as she pulled out her keys to the door. She truly looked noble.

She came into her room and turned the light on. The blood from her lip fell onto her leather coat. That coat had seen its own fair share blood on it, mainly hers. The cold washcloth she got from bathroom felt good on her lip. It pulsated a bit with every pump of blood through her body.

During her shower she noticed she had a small cut on her leg. "Now when did I get that one?" she thought to herself. After drying off, the darkness of the makeup she applied around her eyes was emphasized by her pale white skin. Her extensions reached down to the middle of back; she was going to see if Anne could braid it really quick. Listening to her music loudly was the most relaxing part of her day. The only time she could listen to it this loudly was during nights she didn't hunt or just before Father Tom got in. Occasionally he would come in early so she would have to turn it down even though he didn't say anything. He would just give her that look. She put on a black skirt with a grey shirt with a black suit coat. Alex grabbed a dark grey scarf and tied it around her neck to hide a scar. She turned her head to look at the scar on the side of her face that she couldn't hide.

She did a final look in the mirror as she said good-bye to Komptin. She opened the door to see the young-faced Father Tom with a brown goatee, coming down the hall. "Ugh," Alex said to herself. No escape was possible, she was going to have to walk with him.

"Good morning, Alex," he said, looking up and down at her.

"Good morning, Father," she replied. She double checked that her room was locked.

"Did you have a good hunt last night?"

"I came home alive." She saw that Father Tom looked at the scar on the side of her face. Without even realizing it, she moved her hair to cover up the scar. She checked her lip to see if it was bleeding. It was obviously swollen, but no blood.

"Yes, well," the Father said. "I need you to come upstairs with me to meet the new secretary."

"Do I have to?" Alex asked with a sneer.

"Yes, you do," he said, pointing down the hall.

Alex walked with Father Tom, neither of them saying two words to each other. Father Tom unlocked the door to the rest of the church. "Where is she supposed to be?"

"Cardinal's office." The two of them walked into the Cardinal's front lobby where a short girl with an obvious red wig was sitting in one of the lobby chairs. "Megan?"

"Yes," the girl said, standing up. She had bright red lipstick and was taller than Alex, but then again, most people were. There was slight hint of ethnicity that Alex couldn't place. Alex was horrible at determining if someone had Latin, Mexican, Arabic, or Native American descent.

"Megan, hi, I'm Father Tom. I'm the Administrative Support Priest who oversees ensuring the operations of the church are in smooth order."

"Nice to meet you," Megan gave him a friendly smile. "I'm looking forward to working with you."

Alex didn't like her. Couldn't place it. Maybe she should give her a chance? Nope, didn't like her.

"This is Alexandria," Father Tom motioned to Alex. "She is our Administrative Assistant. Where you will be mainly taken care of the Cardinal; Alex supports me in operations."

"Hi," Megan said.

Alex put out her hand for her to shake it. She could tell Megan did not want to but did it out of kindness. "Nice to meet you."

"Yes," Megan turned to Father Tom. "So where do I sit?"

Father Tom showed her a desk on the other side of the office across from Alex, facing each other. "The Cardinal will be in shortly."

Alex went to her computer to start her day.

The Cardinal walked through the door with his escort. "Good morning all."

"Good morning, Cardinal," Father Tom said. "Sir, your new secretary Megan has arrived."

"Hello, I'm Frank Thomas," the Cardinal said, shaking her hand. "This is my driver, Tony."

"I'm Megan. I guess we will be working pretty close together," Megan had a hint of excitement to her voice.

Alex took it as if she was really motivated to get to work, which might be a good thing. The feeling of fear overcame her as she was worried her role in the church was going to change. "Stupid," she thought. She was one hundred percent sure Megan couldn't do what she did. She was just being paranoid.

"Yes, give me a couple minutes and we'll talk," the Cardinal said, walking into his office. "Tony, around ten?"

"Yes, sir," Tony acknowledged. "Ladies, Father."

"See ya, Tony," Alex sat her desk. "Father, I'll have this report ready before the Cardinal leaves." Alex picked up her pen to start it.

"I should look at it before he reads it. Proofreading and such," Megan chimed in.

Alex really didn't know how to respond to that without sounding snotty. Luckily, Father Tom chimed in, "Alex's two-sentence summaries are far from needing proofreading." He continued to look at the day's itinerary.

Alex had to do a double take and thought, "Did the Father just slam me while defending me at the same time?" Alex didn't know to be offended or impressed. "Well, I need to get going on that massive summary."

Alex opened her email and wrote a message to Anne complaining about her new coworker.

Anne's reply was just as Alex thought it would be: "Give her a chance."

"This is going to suck," Alex instantly wrote back.

"I'm sure it will be fine," Anne answered with a smiling emoji.

Megan came out from the Cardinal's office. She looked right at Alex and said, "The Cardinal will see you now."

"What a tool," Alex thought as she rolled her eyes. The door seemed to squeak as Alex peaked around the door. "You summoned me?"

"Please shut the door, would you, Alexandria?"

The door shut and Alex went over to the couch and took a relaxing position with her feet on the couch next to the window. "What did I do now?"

Cardinal Frank laughed. "What makes you think you're in trouble?"

"It's rare that I come in here without being in trouble," Alex adjusted her hair to flow over the couch so she wouldn't sit on it.

"Yes, I do remember having to justify why you bought certain devices to the Council," the Cardinal remembered back. He had saved her from falling into a bad position. She was had entered an abusive relationship and the Cardinal was instrumental to getting her on the right path. She will forever be grateful for his kind old heart.

Alex just raised her eyebrows and gave a quick little smirk. "Yeah, that one was my bad."

"But no, you are not in trouble," he got up from his desk and got some tea. It seemed he had a small limp to him but managed to walk it off. "Want some?"

"No, thank you." She was studying him. There definitely was something on his mind.

"Of course." He went into a small refrigerator and threw her a can of Apollo.

Alex caught it and opened it. "Thank you." The sweetness of her energy drink seemed to taste extra comforting today.

"Alexandria," the Cardinal started, "I wanted to talk to you about something that may affect you a bit."

"I'm listening." Alex's interest piqued.

The cardinal sat back down at his desk. He took a breath before mustering up what he wanted to say. "I'm going to retire next year," he announced.

"What?" Alex said, sitting up. "What brought this on?" A sudden rush of shock overcame her body. It almost came to tears hearing those words.

The Cardinal adjusted himself in his seat. He opened his drawer to a bag of nuts and picked up his nutcracker and tried to break open a walnut. "Well, for one thing I'm going on 73 years old." He was having a hard time trying to crack it open. "In my younger days, I could open these with my bare hands."

Alex got up from the couch. She gently grabbed the walnut from his hand. She took the nutcracker and cracked it open for him. She gave him a loving smile before heading back to the couch.

The cardinal smiled back out of appreciation. "It's time for some new blood."

"Oh, God, please don't tell me it's going to be Father Tom!" Alex pleaded to him.

"Father Tom is a good man; you should cut him some slack. Try to ease up on the sarcasm," he inputted to her. "He has a lot to offer." He popped the walnut into his mouth and tossed the shell in the garbage.

"Yeah, like giving me crap half the time," Alex told him. The thought of Father Tom becoming the Cardinal was terrifying.

"Alexandria, I don't know who the Council will be choosing," the Cardinal told her. He looked at his watch. "I have a meeting I have to get to." The

Cardinal got up and Alex ran over to him for a big hug.

"I'm going to miss you," she told him. She felt him return the hug. It felt so genuine, Alex didn't want it to stop.

"Please walk this old man out," he asked of her.

She extended her arm, and he wrapped his arms around hers as they walked to the door. Alex never got to meet her grandfathers as they both died when she was a baby. She liked to think of Cardinal Frank as what having a grandfather would be like. "Will you still be performing Anne's and Kale's wedding?"

"Of course." The Cardinal opened the door for Alex. "Actually, it will be my final act as a member of the cloth. Sending two people out in the world with love and God on their side."

She patted him on his arm before she returned to her desk.

The Cardinal turned to Megan. "I'm going to my meeting now." The Cardinal's bodyguard arrived. "Are you ready to go, Tony?"

"Yes, sir," Tony said as he pulled out keys to the car. "The car is right out front."

"Foresee any complications?" The Cardinal asked, putting on his coat.

Tony adjusted the Cardinal's jacket. "The Secret Service will be sending out a small detail after the meeting. I guess the First Lady wants to visit all the major religious worship centers in the city to get a better perspective on their views."

"Sounds good," the Cardinal said. He made it a point to give Alex another smile. "I'll see you both after lunch."

"Later," Alex replied sitting back at her desk. The thought of how much she was going to miss him was all that she could concentrate on. She sent a text to Anne to tell her what she just found out.

"Yes, Cardinal," Megan replied, making home at her desk. "Do you want me to have lunch ready for you upon your return?"

Cardinal Frank zipped up his coat. "No, I will grab something on the way, thank you."

Alex was in a blank stare in Megan's direction. She was mainly thinking about the news the Cardinal dropped on her. He was leaving. This just sucked. Her thought process was interrupted by Megan.

"What happened to your lip?" Megan finished setting some ugly figurines.

Alex didn't know how to reply. "Cold sore." That sounded legit.

"It looks like you got punched," she told her.

Megan wasn't far off from that. The infiltrator Komptin and her came across last night was at a railroad station. When Komptin alerted to it, Alex sent him off down the rail cars to pick up the scent. Alex could have sworn it would be in the railroad cars, preying upon some poor homeless person. But she was wrong. It got the drop on her from above the rail car. It pinned her down with its massive claws as its bear like face got closer to Alex. The breath of the beast smelled so bad that it seemed to

41

trickle down Alex's throat. Before it was going to tear out Alex's throat with its power jaw, Alex head butted the creature. The creature just got mad and returned the head butt causing Alex's lip to bleed. It was just lucky that the sound of another infiltrator being diminished by Komptin caught its attention enough for Alex to push it off her with feet. It charged Alex as she got to her feet. Out of pure instinct, she stepped to the side and clotheslined the creature, causing it to flip in the air before crashing to the ground. She grabbed the creature by the leg and swung it to side of the railroad car. The infiltrator was stunned enough for Alex meet it with a series of punches from her lit fists. The final blow before it was weak enough to diminish came from an upper cut to its face. It fell to the ground face first. Alex jumped in the air landing on its back with her knee. She grabbed its jaw from behind to lift its head up. She formed a small, pointed spear with her Lite and shoved it on top of its head. The body melted away to show her victory.

Alex didn't know how to reply to Megan's punch comment but with, "Looks can be deceiving."

An hour went by before Anne finally made it up to the office to see Alex's new coworker. "Hey," she said to Alex as she walked up to the coffee maker and grabbed a cup of coffee.

"Hey, you have some extra glow to you today," Alex smiled at her. Anne was such a heartwarming site whenever she came to visit.

Anne just smiled back. "Is the coffee from this morning?"

"Yep," Alex said, drinking her energy drink.

"Hey, anything is good right now," Anne motioned to Megan. "Is that her?" she mouthed.

Alex just rolled her eyes.

Anne hid her laugh behind her cup as she drank the old coffee. The polite person that Anne was, she walked up to Megan. "Hi, I'm Anne. I'm the church historian."

"I'm Megan, the new secretary," she shook Anne's hand. "What brings you up here? I don't see you on the schedule with the Cardinal. If you want to make an appointment, you can email me."

Anne just replied, "Well, I'm going to see if Alex wants to go to lunch." She faced Alex again. "Kale is going to meet us at that deli you told him about," Anne told her.

"Actually, let's go somewhere else," Alex quickly suggested. "I think I had some bad meat there and it didn't go well with me."

"Okay, I'll let Kale know," she said, pulling out her phone texting him the change of venue.

"Who's Kale?" Megan butted in, listening to their conversation.

Anne smiled. "He's my fiancé."

Alex chimed in, "And my brother."

Megan went back to her computer and turned on some wooden flute music.

"Let's do an early lunch," Alex said, gathering her stuff. Alex gave a loud whistle and Komptin came into the office lobby.

Megan's eyes grew big as she looked at the massive German Shepherd. "I don't remember seeing where pets were allowed in the church." Megan pulled out the church policy book.

Alex grabbed the book out her hands and highlighted the section "Except Service Animals" and handed it back to her. Megan's constant challenging of anything Alex does was getting annoying, and this was just day one.

"I'm in the mood for a burger and shake," Alex said. She knelt down, giving Komptin some scratches behind the ear.

"Max's Diner?" Anne suggested.

"Yeah, sounds good," Alex said. "I'm going to take Komptin for a walk and I will meet you there." Alex grabbed her coat. She fixed up her hair in the mirror.

"Okay, I have to finish some things up before Kale picks me up," Anne said. "It was nice meeting you."

"Yep," Megan replied to her.

Alex just rolled her eyes as Komptin led them out of the office.

***

The Cardinal walked out of the mosque with Imam Mahamed after a very productive meeting. The Cardinal believed that he eased the worry of his comrade regarding the actions of Sanah and the state of the Islamic Council. The Imam was worried about the repercussions of Sanah's actions. The

Cardinal had to reassure him that it was not the fault of his faction what Sanah had done and become.

"I want to thank you, my friend," Imam Mahamed said as he kissed the cheeks of the Cardinal.

"Of course, my old friend." The Cardinal came outside admiring the sun. "We truly need to thank God for such a beautiful day."

Iman felt the warmth of the rays from the sun. "It really is a wonderful day."

"How are Neha and boys doing?" The Cardinal was watching a group of secret service men congregate in front of the Mosque.

Iman Mahamed answered with a smile, "The boys are driving Neha crazy, but what do you expect from twin boys hitting puberty?"

The Cardinal laughed. "I will pray for her, give them my love."

"Of course," he told him in return. "And congratulations on your retirement. Well deserved."

"Thank you, are you up for golf this weekend? We got to get in a couple rounds before the snow starts coming down?"

Imam Mahamed looked to the sky. "Good call, Frank, but loser buys lunch."

"How's right after morning prayers?"

"Sounds like a plan," Iman Mahamed agreed.

They looked around at the group of men in dark suits with earpieces in their ears overlooking the area.

"The Secret Service has been all over this street looking at the route for the First Lady," Iman said to his Catholic friend.

"Well, they have a hard job." The Cardinal pointed as he waved to Tony that he was ready. Tony returned the wave and walked up to him.

A loud noise came from across the street and the next thing the Cardinal saw was Tony's forehead explode, splattering blood all over him. Tony's body dropped to the ground. People from across the street screamed and scattered as a group of militia-looking members came running across the street with rifles and pistols. The commotion confused Cardinal Frank as he fell to the ground. He watched the Secret Service return fire. One of them turned and shot back killing two of the hostiles.

That same agent came running up to the Cardinal. "We got to get you inside," he said in a relatively calm voice as gunfire and screaming seemed to be overpowering all other noises.

"I... I can't walk." The Cardinal looked at his leg and saw that blood was dripping from it. He turned to see the body of his good friend Muhamed. "No." He tried crawling to his friend who laid there lifeless before him. The only thought that was racing through his mind on how his family would be without him.

A bullet gave a high screech before shattering the glass doors to the mosque. "Cardinal, he's gone! We've got to get you inside," the agent commanded.

The agent quickly turned and shot his pistol at one of the militia, shooting her twice in the torso and then once in the head. The agent lowered his weapon in shock as he stared at the young teenager as she laid there motionless.

The Cardinal saw the girl was no more than sixteen years old, holding a rifle with grenades strapped across her chest. She wore an upside down four on her arm covered in blood. The agent's face was one of disbelief on what he just did. Time seemed to stand still in this chaos but was quickly brought back to reality as people's screams were suddenly silenced.

Amidst the gunfire, the agent dropped to the ground as a bullet pierced his body. The Cardinal tried climbing up the stairs, but the feeling of hot lead stopped him as he felt another bullet enter his other leg. Even though he was in tremendous pain, the Cardinal had a surprising sense of peace to him as he accepted that he was going to die. He managed to turn around to see his attackers. One of the militia walked up to him, kneeling by his side. He stuck his finger in the wound of the Cardinal as he shouted in pain.

"May God forgive you for what you have done."

"God?" the young boy said. The boy took his finger full of blood and drew a symbol on the Cardinal's forehead. "You are missing the point of all this." The boy stood up and drew his pistol with police sirens in the background, ending the Cardinal's existence.

***

Warcourt watched from the rooftop across the street. There was much admiration at the massacre from the view above, quite pleased at what he had accomplished. Being a Host meant he couldn't cause any harm to anyone on sacred ground, even if it was initiated from across the street. He tried it once, but the bullets just dissipated before impact.

"Pretty cool, isn't it?" Gron said, coming up behind him.

"Yeah, it is," Warcourt said. "Looks like we lost six of the members." He pointed to the agent lying next to the Cardinal. "That one there shot three of them."

"Really?" Gron gazed down at the agent lying in blood. "Impressive."

"Yeah, it was something to watch," he commented.

Gron kicked a rock off the building ledge. "Too bad I missed it."

Gron and Warcourt walked towards the other side of the building where the young female Provisionary, Barbara, was cut and bruised with a distant look in her eyes. "How ya doing?" Warcourt asked.

"She's fine," Gron answered for her. He ran his finger down her face and then her arm. He gave it a little squeeze before turning his attention back to Warcourt. "This was a pretty big step in our mission." Gron turned to overlook the city. "This will look like a human radical political shooting and the Lite Sentry should have no idea it came from us." He put his arm around Warcourt. "That is why we cannot get involved directly. We are just the puppeteers."

"I understand," Warcourt said, still feeling a bit left out.

Gron recognized Warcourt's desire to get involved. "Tell you what, why don't you take my Provisionary, find a room, and, well, let out some of your frustration."

"Really?" Warcourt said, looking at her. "You won't mind?"

"Nope, she is my gift to you," Gron offered to her. Warcourt grabbed the Provisionary by the arm and escorted her away. "Oh, Warcourt," Gron yelled.

"Yes?"

"I'm bored with her, dispose of her after you're done," Gron said, waving them off.

Warcourt smiled and as he dragged the Provisionary down the stairs. Warcourt could see she had no will to fight, she just wanted to die. After he was done with her, he was going to grant her wish.

***

Alex walked into the diner with Komptin at her side. She was glad she remembered to put his "service dog" vest on him, otherwise he would have to go make himself scarce. She always knew he would be close by, though. It was rare that he would stray away from her.

She scanned the diner for Anne and Kale. She found them in the corner where they had already started to eat beside each other, backs to the door. Anne knew Alex always liked to see who was coming into places. Alex just assumed it was part of being Sentry, no matter where she was, she was always on the lookout.

The host came up to Alex. "Can I guide you to a seat?"

"No, thank you," Alex informed him. "I know where I'm headed."

Alex just wanted to watch them for a second. Anne placed her head on Kale's shoulders as he leaned his head into hers. Alex thought they were a typical Hallmark couple. She went and joined them at the end of the diner. She sat down, grabbing a fry from Kale's plate.

She ate it, instantly spitting it out. "Gross, what was that?"

"Zucchini strips." He laughed as he ate one.

Even though Kale wasn't racing anymore, not by choice, he still maintained eating healthy. He found his groove after falling hard a couple of years back that almost cost him his relationship with Anne. Luckily, Anne has a stronger will of the heart than Alex ever wished she could have. "Wanna bite my boneless chicken as well?"

"Too healthy, plus I need some comfort food," Alex said to him. "That new secretary for the Cardinal came in today; she's a real tool."

"Alex, give her a chance," Anne said. "You never know, you two just might hit it off."

"Nope," Alex said, handing Komptin a zucchini strip. He just sniffed it and pushed it away with his nose. "See, it's pretty bad if Komptin doesn't want any of it."

"More for me," Kale replied with a mouthful of the strips.

The waitress came over after noticing Alex had joined them. "What can I get you, hon?"

"I'll take a double cheeseburger with everything on it, one slice American, one slice Swiss, large fries, and a large chocolate shake," Alex said.

"Anything else, dear?" the waitress continued to write on her ticket.

"Yes, I would like an order of mozzarella sticks as well," Alex was particularly hungry today. She noticed that when her body is healing, she tends to eat a lot more.

Anne wiped her mouth from her vegetarian pita. "We need to get the final list for the wedding invitations."

"Ah," Kale said, swallowing his food. "I have my list on my work computer." He wiped his mouth with his napkin.

"You do your wedding planning at work?" Alex asked him. Her mozzarella sticks came in and Alex started to eat one. "I'm so hungry."

Kale grabbed a mozzarella stick and bit into it trying not to get the grease to fall onto his shirt and tie. "Yep, it gives me a sense of relief." He dunked the other end into the sauce and took another bite. "Anne told me that Cardinal Frank is retiring."

"Yeah, can you believe that? He told me just before he left for the mosque," Alex dipped took another stick. There was a girl sitting next to her with cocky smirk on her face staring at the table.

"WHAT?!"

"I can't believe you fall for that garbage mind filling propaganda," the girl arrogantly said. "The only power is the one within."

"O-M-G!" Alex spelled out. "What is it with people today? There's like a sense of confrontation in the air." She turned to the girl who was eating a piece of cherry pie. "How about this…mind your own business."

"If you want to be that ignorant of the truth is, go ahead, follow that storybook indoctrination," the lady said, going back to reading an article on her phone.

"You know, I think I've matured," Alex said looking out the window at some cop cars going somewhere in a hurry.

"Why do you say that?" Kale asked her, sneaking the last mozzarella stick.

"Because normally, I would have beaten the daylights out that girl over there," Alex said. "But I think I'm going to let it go." Alex noticed everyone looking at her direction. "Why is everyone looking this way?"

Anne pointed up behind Alex. She turned around to see the news of a mass shooting at a local mosque. The news report stated there were many casualties and the names have not been released yet.

"The comments on the news media's website are stating that the F.O.R. is behind this." Kale showed it to Anne.

Alex and Anne quickly looked at each other, fearful of the possible truth. Then their fear was verified by a text from Father Tom reading, "Get to the church ASAP." Alex put her phone away. "I gotta go." Alex dropped some money on the counter. "Anne, do you mind?"

Anne finished swallowing her sandwich. "No, not all. I'll bring it to you."

"Minus the shake," Kale said, grinning.

"Knock yourself out," Alex looked to the television screen. He can't be hurt. No, she wouldn't allow it. "This is bad."

The girl sitting across from them watched the news report on the massacre at the mosque. "Guess there are a couple less spreaders of lies out there," she winked over at Alex, going back to eating her pie.

Alex grabbed Komptin's leash. "Come on, boy." Alex put on her jacket and started to walk out of the diner. As she passed table, Alex put her hand on the back of her head and shoved her face into the girl's pie. Alex didn't even break stride as she walked out of the restaurant.

Kale just handed the lady a napkin as he continued to drink his iced tea. "She actually has matured since high school," he said to Anne.

Alex got to the church to report to Father's Tom office. She didn't really come into his office that often. She noticed some paintings on the wall that were quite good. She noticed he had a glass with some sort of alcoholic drink on his desk that he was nursing.

"Five o'clock somewhere, huh?" Alex was uncomfortable. Now was not the time for sarcastic remarks. The news about the Cardinal was about to drop, she had to, but didn't want to, hear it.

Father Tom didn't even acknowledge Alex's comment. He got up from his desk finishing his drink. "Follow me."

Alex shook her head to herself as she followed him into the congregation where it was mostly church employees. Alex sat down in the back pew with Komptin at her side. Anne walked in and sat on the other side of her. She handed her the double cheeseburger she ordered from the diner. "Has he announced it yet?" Anne asked.

"No," Alex just sat there petting Komptin. "Thanks for bringing me my food."

"No problem, by the way, the manager said you are not allowed in there anymore," Anne whispered, looking to Father Tom as he was about to address the congregation.

"All, we all heard about the tragedy at a mosque that happened just a bit ago," Father Tom started out. "I have the unfortunate burden to inform you the Cardinal was among the wounded. He was fatally shot at the scene." Father Tom stopped his message to let everyone gather their thoughts. "He and Iman Muhamed were walking out of the mosque when they were gunned down by the assailants. Please let's take a moment for quiet prayer and reflection."

The congregation was quiet minus the tears that people were trying to hold back. She looked down at him as he flashed his eyes. Alex just nodded in agreement. Anne wiped away her tears as she got up with the rest of the congregation.

Father Tom came to Anne. "Anne, you can take the rest of the day off."

"What about the report?" Anne asked.

"It can wait," Father Tom said. "Take time to gather your thoughts. Now is not a time we can make mistakes." Father Tom turned to Alex. "Alex, can I talk to you for a second?"

Alex hugged Anne before she went to her office to close it up. "Yes, Father." Alex followed Father Tom back to his office where he poured himself another drink.

He looked at her. "Want one?" he asked, lifting the bottle in her direction.

"No, thank you," she said. "Alcohol makes me sick to my stomach."

He just nodded as he put the bottle down. "Alex, I just need to say this to clear my conscience. I know nothing I say will prevent you from going out tonight to explore this. I just need you to remember; if it is not Dark affiliated, we cannot engage," Father Tom had to reiterate, probably to clear his conscience. "If the F.O.R. is being influenced by the Dark, which I really think it is, we need proof before..." Father Tom was swirling his drink as he tried to formulate his words. "...you are...released."

"I understand," Alex said. And it was true.

She was entrusted to act as a balance, not become a vigilante of the night. Alex went to gather her belongings at her desk.

She knelt to pet her faithful hunting companion. "We go out tonight after supper, when things calm down."

Komptin gave a dark bark in acknowledgment.

Chapter 3

Alex didn't want to stick around the church while Father Tom was preparing for the Cardinal's funeral. It was way too uncomfortable around there without the Cardinal. She almost felt cold and empty. The atmosphere within the church was darkened with sadness. So, she decided to stop by and see how Anne was doing before she went out on her hunt. She was about to knock on the door when Kale and Anne opened it.

Kale had a look of urgency on his face.

"What's going on?"

"We have to get to the hospital," Kale said. "I'll get the car." He kissed Anne and took off.

Alex looked to Komptin. "I don't like the feeling of today; can you please make sure he gets to the car, okay?"

Komptin acknowledged with a flash of his determined eyes and took off into the darkness. Alex had full confidence Kale wouldn't see Komptin following him.

"What's going on? Everything okay?"

"Yeah, I guess. Remember Kale's old roommate in college?" Anne asked her while she was digging in her purse.

"I don't think I ever met him, but you mentioned him a couple of times, why?"

"Well, he put us down as his local emergency contact in case something happened before his parents could make it down," she continued to scour through her pockets. "Of course, Kale has the keys to get the car." Anne closed her purse to start heading downstairs. "Anyway, we were asked not to say anything about it because he works for the government."

"Doing what?" Alex could see a little movement that only her training would pick up on. She knew that Kale was coming back with the car.

"Secret Service," Anne told her. "Please don't say anything. He doesn't like to advertise where he works. Anyway, he was at the mosque during the attack, and he got shot. He should be getting out of surgery soon."

"Oh God," Alex said. Alex couldn't help but think that Kale's old roommate survived the attack and maybe he saw something. "Do you want me to come with?"

"No, it's okay," Anne said. "We are just going to go to see what we need to do before his parents get here." Anne rubbed Alex's arm before meeting she went to meet Kale at the car. "Thanks though."

Alex watched them leave for the hospital before heading off into the night city to battle the Dark.

***

Anne gathered her belongings to go into the hospital. There was no movement from Kale. He just stared at the hospital illuminated by artificial light. "You okay?"

He just continued to stare, "I hate this parking lot when it's dark out." He just moved his big dark brown eyes towards her. "It just reminds me of Joseph."

She knew it was a hard memory of losing his Iron Man training mentor while in high school. Anne felt a bit of guilt because she had always hidden the truth from the man she loves. It was reported that he was lost by a vicious animal attack. She knew the truth. That was the night Alex killed her first infiltrator. She hunted it down after it killed Joseph and avenged his death.

"Come on, honey." Anne put her fingers through his brown hair. "Let's go see what we can do for Kameron."

Once they got the information from the charge nurse and they sat down in the waiting room. Together they watched TV until the nurse came and talked to Kale about how Kameron was doing. She told him that he was now located in his room, and he had to stay there for about a week. Kale and Anne walked down to his room where he was bandaged and bruised.

"Oh God," she said as she covered her mouth with the tip of her fingers.

"He looks awful." Kale looked down to see Kameron move his hand. Kale snickered as Kameron a thumb's up. "Save your strength, buddy." Kale laughed. "Do you need anything?"

A tall, bald, dark-skinned man walked into the room. He was wearing a black suit and holding a vanilla envelope with a White House logo on it. "Can I help you?"

"I'm Kale Moler, this is my fiancé Anne McClure," Kale said. "Who are you?"

"Special Agent Grossman, I'm Agent Dutcher's supervisor. I was hoping to run into you," he said. "How is he?"

"We just got here," Kale told him. "But he seems to be doing okay."

"He's a tough cookie," the agent took a glance over at his subordinate. "One of the most dedicated I've seen come through the doors." Agent Grossman handed Kale a packet. "I need you to sign this Non-Disclosure Agreement. It's to do with anything you will hear regarding this matter."

"What?" Kale asked in confusion.

"Well, frankly, you are his first care. Since he has no family in town, you will be tending to his care. It's what you signed on for."

"Of course," Anne quickly stepped in.

"Anything he needs," Kale said. "What are we not saying to anyone?"

"Just standard protocol, just in case you happen to hear something; if you do, we will debrief you at that time," the agent said.

"As far as I'm concerned, I don't know anything," Kale told him. "But I will sign it." After all the paperwork was signed, he looked over at Kameron who was fast asleep. "I owe him."

Anne put her arm around Kale's arm. "We both do."

Alex didn't really like rooftop hunting. She felt like it was too distant to be effective. She liked to be in the weeds, to get a feel for where the scent of the Infiltrators and those possessed had been. This really wasn't a hunt; this was a scouting mission. She couldn't get close to the scene because it was cordoned off by police and FBI.

Alex noticed three elegant women looking over the rooftop down at the scene. She walked up to the right side of Devine who didn't acknowledge her presence. Alex looked over at Celestial whose sad face just stared down at the crime scene. There were a couple minutes of silence before Alex spoke.

"He was a good man."

"They all were," Celestial said, continuing to stare.

Alex felt ashamed she forgot about the Iman and others that passed away from the shooting. "Yes, of course." Alex turned to Celestial. "I've been asked to see if the Dark was behind this attack."

"And if it isn't…,what do you plan to do?" Celestial asked her, now looking at her direction.

"Nothing I can do," Alex told her. "I'd be no better than Sanah if I did."

Celestial gave her a quick smile. "Good." Celestial walked by her.

Alex could see she was not herself. This blatant attack must have really upset her more than Alex initially thought it would. "Celestial, may I ask you a question?"

"Of course," she answered, heading back to the rooftop access door with Ariel and Devine following closer than usual.

"How is he?"

Celestial closed her eyes, and a slight glow came from her eyelids. She smiled. "He is at peace but disappointed he did not have a chance to say good-bye."

"I wish I could have said good-bye as well." Alex had a half-heartedly smile. "It seems like I never get to say good-bye to the ones I love." Alex took a moment and remembered the deaths of Sara and Osiah. "But I guess that's life."

Celestial stopped in her tracks, turned to Alex. "Do you think that is what life is?"

"I have all these powers; all these abilities and it seems like I can't be there for the ones who matter. All my loved ones die alone, just once, I would like to make it in time for someone who needed me there," Alex said, fighting back tears. One had escaped Alex's eyes as it dripped down her cheek. "Damn it, I cry a lot," she wiped her tears while trying to force a laugh.

Celestial looked to the purple star in the sky. She gazed upon Alex who was still wiping tears. "Alexandria." Alex looked up at the blonde angel. Celestial just put her hand on Alex's cheek and smiled. She put her finger on Alex's chest. "He was right, rare as Blue Gold." She pointed to her heart. "I have to go."

Alex just nodded. She watched Celestial go behind the massive furnace leaving her behind. The two hands on Alex's shoulders in a supportive double tap was all she got from Ariel and Devine as they left to protect their mistress.

Alex noticed Komptin didn't go up to Celestial on this visit. She looked for him and saw he was standing on the roof ledge staring down at the crime scene. Something had caught his attention. Alex needed to get a closer look so she decided to go for a walk and maybe stroll past the mosque to see if she could see anything.

***

Salamor stayed hidden in the shadows staring at the Sentry. The remembrance of her causing him physical harm made him leery to approach her. No Demon Myst had ever been diminished. He didn't even know what would happen to him if it had happened. For the first time in his existence, he felt fear. He was ashamed of it. He couldn't even bring himself to tell Vandor of the Sentry's ability to harm him. He had to focus, he had other things he had to take care of for his master. Salamor checked his surroundings and left to report his findings to Vandor. He looked around to left and right before he floated out of the shadows to find his prize.

***

Anne changed into her pajamas but decided to put her bathrobe on because she just couldn't shake the shivers since leaving the hospital. It was sad to see Kameron all bloodied and bruised. She came down the end of the hall to see Kale staring at the guest bedroom. "What's wrong?" She asked him.

"Nothing," Kale said. "Just had a different idea about this bedroom." He turned to Anne who was looking over the bedroom as well. "But we need to help him."

Anne kissed Kale. "That's why I love you and why I want to marry you Kale Moler."

He smiled. "I love you, too."

"Are you going to come to bed?" she asked him. "We have to get ready for Saturday."

"Yeah, I'll take Friday off to get it all ready," Kale told her. "I can skip my meeting after work if you want me to help you on Thursday?"

"No, you go, I'll get Alex to help," Anne said. "Now come on, I need the big guy to snuggle up to tonight," she playfully toyed with him.

"Okay," Kale said, smiling. "I'll lock things up and I'll be there."

***

Alex was sitting at her desk writing up the report for Father Tom about her lack of findings from last night. The office had not changed in feelings of being empty with the Cardinal not being there. It didn't help that Megan didn't show up yet either. Alex was annoyed because the phones were ringing off the hook. She even got stuck talking to the Council itself, which really wasn't the thrill of her life.

It was late morning before Father Tom came into the lobby.

"Morning," Alex said to him.

"Good morning," Father Tom said without breaking a stride. He took the keys and opened up the Cardinal's office. He went in and sat down at the Cardinal's desk and logged into his computer. Alex sat there dumbfounded how he acted like it was his office. "Alex, can you come in here?"

Alex got up from her desk and grabbed her an Apollo drink from inside the Cardinal's office. It felt wrong to do this without him. She normally would have made herself comfortable on the couch, but today, today she would just stand in front of the Cardinal's desk. "Yes, Father."

"I need you to get me some packing boxes, supplies, and have them ready for the movers by Wednesday," Father Tom told her. "This office and his private room."

Alex didn't really want to do that. It was more of a task for the Cardinal's secretary that didn't show up. "Where's the secretary?"

Father Tom looked up. "She said she had migraine."

Alex found herself quite happy about that. She wasn't going to come in and ruin her day. Alex acknowledged the priest's request. She sat at her desk and turned her music on.

Anne came up stairs to get a cup of coffee from the lobby. Alex was on the phone but gave her smiling wave to her best friend. "Okay, I'll have the supplies by the end of the day? Okay, thanks." Alex hung up the phone and wrote down the information.

"Where's your coworker?" Anne asked, pointing to the empty desk.

"Migraine." Alex did a minor happy dance at her absence.

"That's too bad, those are not fun." Anne leaned on the heater trying to get warm.

"Made my day," Alex had a bit of chirpiness to her voice.

Father Tom came out of the office and grabbed a cup of coffee. He sat down on top of Megan's desk. "I'm glad you are both here." Alex and Anne got situated. "Alex, any news from your excursion last night?"

Alex shook her head no. "Something caught Komptin's attention, but we couldn't find anything."

Father Tom just stated, "Keep me updated." He turned to Anne. "I need you to look into any information on the Dark influencing humans?"

"Like a Dark Myst? There isn't much there," Anne informed him. Anne never confessed this to anyone, but she remembered her own personal encounter with a Dark Myst. It was trying to influence her to do something tragic when Kale and she were going through some hard times.

"No, I'm looking for direct influence for actions," he told Anne. "I want to see if the Dark

66

had influenced people for actions, if there is any evidence we can link?"

"Any particular sanction?" Anne asked him, sipping her coffee.

"All of them," Father Tom said.

Anne nearly choked on her drink. "Father, I don't know how long that will take and some sanctions are quite tenuous. There's not much to them."

"Impress me," he told her. He got up from the desk and walked back into the Cardinal's office. The door seemed cold as it shut.

"How long do you think before the Council selects a new Cardinal for the position?" Alex stared at the closed door to the Cardinal's office.

"Don't know. Usually, the Council has time. No Cardinal within the Council has died so suddenly," Anne informed her.

Alex lowered her voice. "Do you think they will promote him to Cardinal?" Alex pointed to the closed door.

"I don't know, he's pretty young." Anne refilled her coffee.

"Plus, he's kind of an ass," Alex added, getting back to her report.

***

Kale had taken the day off to get the room prepared for Kameron's stay. He washed the bedding, ran to Kameron's apartment to get some things, and did a quick grocery trip. It was uncomfortable when he met with his mom at Kameron's place to go through some of the things he needed for the stay.

She was a small woman but strong willed. She held in her emotions and did what she needed to get done. Kale admired that. It was too bad she had to get back to their farm, but she was content that Kameron was going to be in good hands. He got a text from Anne apologizing she wasn't there to help but she got caught up at work. Kale understood; with the Cardinal's death, a lot was going on with the church. There really wasn't a lot left to do.

Kale's mind wandered to the wedding. They didn't have anyone to marry them. He was hoping this wasn't a sign or anything. The night he crossed the finish line of the Iron Man race and saw Anne standing there with a flower, he knew right there that he was going to be with her forever. It was fortunate on how it all worked out. His fiancé and sister had become extremely close since their senior year of high school.

There were some roadblocks, or maybe they were tests, with the situation a couple of years ago with Alex's boyfriend. Kale hated him. He never knew how someone could manipulate his sister to become so heartless. His thoughts were interrupted by a knock on the door. He opened it up and saw Agent Grossman in front of him. "Agent Grossman, how can I help you?"

He handed Kale a sealed envelope. "I need SA Dutcher to fill these out as soon as he starts to recover." Kale could see he was peeking around the apartment. He wasn't being very subtle about it. It was probably intentional to let him know that he would be watching Kale and Anne while Kameron recovers at their place.

"Do you want to come in?" Kale asked him to show him into the apartment.

The agent gathered his composure. "No, thank you. No rush on those. Tell Agent Dutcher I will be back the week after next to pick those up."

The agent turned around to see a young lady with pale skin and long, black, weaved-in, hair. She wore a black leather collar around her neck and was dressed in dark clothing. Her dog was a massive German Shepherd who looked well trained as he sat down at her side staring at him. "Miss."

"Mister," she replied without skipping a beat as she entered the apartment.

"My apologies, I didn't hear you coming," he told her.

The young lady just smartly winked at him as she passed him without saying anything else.

**

Alex walked into Kale's apartment, and he was coming out of the guest room. "Who was that?"

"Kameron's supervisor. I think he just stopped by to see where Kameron would be staying," he said closing the door behind Alex. Komptin ran to his favorite chair to jump in it and fell asleep.

"Yeah, I heard he should be getting out of the hospital soon," Alex mentioned sitting on the couch turning on the television to some reality show.

Kale sat down. "My house, my choosing the channel. How can you watch this stuff?"

"Ugh, man of house speak," Alex said putting her arms like a gorilla. Alex knew the answer to his question was since she doesn't sleep. She gets sucked into the void of reality drama on nights she doesn't go for a hunt.

Kale smirked as he turned his attention to Alex. "So sis, had some bad meat at the deli?" A commercial came on for a medicine for someone with Herpes. "Here, you may need to watch this," he told her as he turned up the volume.

"Kiss my ass," Alex said, throwing a pillow at him.

"Guilty conscience, have we?" Kale laughed.

"Okay, jackass, how'd you know?" she asked him as she was straightening up the pillows on the couch.

"I know you," Kale told her. "I had a feeling since you never give alternatives to places to eat. You're a human garbage disposal." He got up and held out his hand. "Come on, I'll treat you to a movie." Alex grabbed his hand and as she got up, she threw Kale to the couch. "Ow."

"And whatever I want to eat," Alex said, slapping him playfully while he put up his hands protecting himself.

"Okay, okay." Kale got up and threw her the keys. "You're driving. Come on let's go." Both

Alex and Komptin walked out the door. Kale looked to the sky as he was locking the door. "What did I ever do to deserve this?"

"I ask Him that every night," Alex yelled from down the stairs.

***

It was about a week since Cardinal's murder had taken place by the F.O.R. Alex had no luck finding anything that linked them to the Dark. She was out almost every night hunting and investigating but there was nothing connecting them. In fact, she hadn't run across any Infiltrators while out scouting for any information. As far as she knew, the police hadn't come up with anything.

Alex sat at her desk where it was almost ten in the morning when Father Tom came strolling in. It was weird that about once a week Father Tom wouldn't come in until late morning. It was sporadic and never on the same day. He looked as if he had a lot on his mind.

"Morning, Father."

"Morning, Alex," he said. "Is your summary on my desk?"

"Yes, but it was the same as the last couple of weeks," Alex told him.

Father Tom didn't give any expressions. In fact, he was stone-faced, and Alex couldn't read him at all. He just turned to Megan. "Good morning, Megan."

"Good morning, Father. I would have given you a summary myself, but she still refuses to give it to me for proofreading," she mentioned to him while giving her a look of disbelief.

"Alex is my subject matter expert, she's been doing it for years," Father Tom said as he was looking at his phone, walking into the office shutting the door behind him.

Alex blew kisses at Megan while flipping her off. Megan bit her lip as she went back to work on her computer. "I really should review everything prior to him seeing it to make sure it's correct," Megan told Alex.

"Get right on that," she told her as she got back to her computer. Alex turned on her music and Megan opened the policy book from the Human Resources department.

"It says here that your music is offensive to me and causes me to have anxiety," Megan told her. "Please shut it off."

Alex bit her lip and shut her music off. She walked up to the fridge to get an Apollo drink. She opened it up and it made a noise. Megan stared at her with complete disgust.

It was well into the afternoon. The office was quiet; Father Tom was behind closed doors all day. Megan was working on, well, whatever the hell she did, Alex didn't know. Alex continued to read the websites that supported the F.O.R.'s actions.

Something caught Alex's attention.

A smell of stale air filled the room. Sometimes she wondered how no one else could sense it.

She walked towards the window and opened it. She scanned the street even though she knew they were not close. What she did know though, was that some got infiltrated. Someone just gave themselves to the Dark.

"You can shut that, it's cold enough in here," Megan said to her, putting on her coat.

"Shhh…" Alex put up her finger silencing her.

Megan got offended but Alex didn't care. Even though she had a point, Alex kept the window open. Komptin came into the room and Alex made eye contact with him. Alex just nodded. Komptin turned back around and went back to wherever he was resting.

Anne walked into the lobby to get a cup of coffee. "Hey, I was wondering if you wanted to come over for dinner tonight?" Anne just watched Alex stare out the window. "Alex."

Father Tom came out of the office. "Where's that draft coming from?"

Megan pointed to Alex who was staring out the window.

Father Tom watched her stare out the window. "Alex, you okay?" He then looked to Anne, and she just shrugged in return.

Father Tom and Anne both yelled, "ALEX."

Alex jumped. "Huh, what? Oh sorry."

"Are you on drugs?" Megan asked before getting back to her work.

Alex nodded at Father Tom telling him nonverbally what he suspected. He just frowned and turned back to his office and shut the door.

Anne full well knew why Alex was staring out the window. She asked in a worried compassionate tone, "Hey, hon, do you want to come over for dinner tonight? Kameron is actually up and moving around quite a bit and he has no idea who you are." Anne always tried to give Alex a secure place for a bit of normalcy from the life she had chosen for herself. Anne never talked about it, but she was worried about Alex whenever she went hunting, or even that it kept her up nights when she would be out.

"How did my name come up?" Alex asked as she shut the window.

"Kale was telling him how we got together," Anne told her, getting a refill on her coffee. "It was definitely a night he wouldn't forget."

"Why, what happened?" Megan asked all up in Anne's conversation.

"Kale doesn't like to talk about it, and I want to respect his wishes by not talking about it," Anne quickly said. She felt guilty that she let that slip out in front of Megan.

"Do you know, Alex?" Megan asked her.

"I was there," Alex directly told her and then turned to Anne. "I would like to, but I can't. I have to take Komptin out for a walk."

Anne got the message. "Okay, maybe next time." She quietly said a little prayer to herself when she turned to go back to her office.

***

74

Alex and Komptin decided to walk through the park. It was a cloudy night and it seemed as if it was on the verge of snowing. There tended to be less homeless in the park this time of year due to the cold coming in. That usually meant the Infiltrators would take more victims living in abandoned buildings. Alex was going to have to go through some of those buildings tonight. She was glad she wore the right boots for the hunt. She continued to walk through the park when a group of guys were coming up in front of Alex.

"Hey, little thing, you lost?" asked one of the bigger ones. He must have been the leader because all the other little suitors were laughing and congratulating him on his attempt at being cool.

Alex sighed. "No, I know exactly where I am." She looked around taking in her surroundings.

"We said, are you lost?" One of the other guys was attempting to walk around her.

"Do I look lost?" she asked. She sat down on a nearby bench. Komptin was beginning to get on edge as one of the members of the gang was now behind Alex.

"Someone is on the wrong side of town at the wrong time," said the short skinny one.

"I don't have time for this." Alex sighed, putting her hands on her knees as she got up. "Look I know that you are trying to act tough in front of all your little buddies here, but I really have to get going."

"Hey, listen up here, you little—" one of them said grabbing her arm.

Alex interrupted him, "Don't say it." She lifted her finger in warning. "And let go of me."

Komptin came up by her side and was starting to get agitated. He barked at the guy grabbing her arm. The guy let go while staring down at Komptin who was keeping an eye on the guy.

She made eye contact with the leader of the group. "Look, I really have to go. Go out and do whatever it is you do." She started to walk away.

"Man shut this crazy skank up," said one of the guys to the leader of the group.

She turned around to see the man attack her. She grabbed his arm and flipped him over her back, twisting hard. She put her foot onto his throat and pressed down as he slammed into the ground.

She held his hand in the twisting position with one hand while looking at her fingernails with the other. "Damn it, I broke a nail." She turned to the rest of the group. "Are we good?"

Komptin gave a low, dark growl to the group. It looked as if he wanted them to try something.

"Yep, we're good."

"All good, we're leaving anyway."

"Crazy bitch," the small one said.

"Excuse me?" Alex sharply turned her head to look at him.

Komptin barked again, ready to attack.

"We cool." He quickly cowered.

"Glad to hear it," Alex said. "Have a good night now."

The guy below her foot started gurgling and slapping Alex's leg.

"Oh, my bad." She let him go as she wiped some of the dirt off her clothes.

The man got up, watching Komptin who was staring at him the whole time.

"I don't know what's scarier, that dog or you." He brushed himself off and to his surprise Alex was helping him.

"You got a little dirt in your collar," she said, wiping it off.

"Ah, thanks." He turned to her. "What are you?"

Alex just raised her eyebrows and gave him a half frown. "Can you please tell me if you have noticed anything strange going on?"

"Besides what just happened?" The guy was straightening up his clothes, making sure no one else saw him get manhandled.

"Yeah," Alex said, putting her collar up.

"Some of the regular beggars have been disappearing, but I just figured it was because it was getting cold out."

"Where at?"

The guy pointed in the direction of a dark alleyway. "Three blocks down."

Alex sighed, "Always a dark alley. Why can't it ever be a day spa or something?" She caught the person staring at her perplexed. "Okay, thanks."

"You're going alone?" the guy asked.

"No, silly," she said. "That would be nuts. I have my dog."

She whistled as she started walking towards the dark as Komptin came up by her side. She made it through the alley without any incident, which was fine with her because she was on high guard. She felt the presence of the Dark, she just couldn't pinpoint where they were.

She knelt to Komptin. "Why do I have a feeling we are going on the opposite side of the infiltration?"

She heard some voices coming down the street, so she hid in the shadows of the buildings. A group of F.O.R. members were walking on the sidewalk. Alex could feel her blood start to rise as flashes of memories of the Cardinal came to her mind. She still didn't have any proof that the Dark was behind the militia group's actions.

She sat back and watched them enter the building that was heavily armed at the door. What she could tell, it seemed to be well maintained. They had security badges, scanners, and the people guarding the door had computer tablets checking everyone credentials.

"That's a lot of tech for a small little radical group." Alex was about to follow them until she caught a feeling of evil and cold. Alex closed her eyes. "Damn," she said as Komptin morphed into his Gargoyle state with his glowing eyes. Alex ignited her fists as she turned around to fight three incoming Infiltrators.

Komptin rushed one of them and the two started to fight.

"I guess that leaves me the other two." Alex ran to them.

She shot a beam at one of them, knocking it over into some garbage, giving her some room to fight the other one. It growled and swung at her as she ducked the massive claws. She punched the one in the ribs and it howled in pain. The other one came attacking her as she kicked it in the chest knocking it into the railing. It fell down a staircase to the basement.

The first one she attacked came running at her as she punched it across the face. She heard the other one come up from the bottom of the staircase as it took off down the alley. "Damn it," Alex couldn't let it get back to whoever was leading them now that she was on their trail. She had let her guard down from the other as the Infiltrator swiped at her, cutting her on the upper part of her back. She dropped to the ground as she yelled in pain. "Son of a…"

The Infiltrator grabbed her and swung her around throwing her into the brick building. She hit the back of her head on the brick. Alex knew she had broken skin as the faint feeling of blood trickled down her neck. The Infiltrator lunged as Alex dropped out of the way causing a cloud of broken bricks to fall on the black creature. She formed a spear with her Lite Force and jabbed it at the back of the Infiltrator's neck. It howled in pain before dissipating into the ground. She turned to check on Komptin as he just ripped the head off the other.

"Come on," Alex said, running after the other. "We can't allow it to let anyone know we are on their trail."

Komptin flashed his eyes and took off into the dark with Alex. They managed to chase it up a fire escape of a building. Komptin climbed up the wall as he dug into the brick of the building to meet Alex on the rooftop. They carefully scouted the rooftop for any sign where the creature had disappeared. She motioned for Komptin to go one direction while she went the opposite. She continued to walk as her lit fist illuminated the blackness of the rooftop.

She grabbed her side, wincing in pain. She bent over putting her hands on her knees. She turned around as the Infiltrator came to attack her at her weakened state.

Komptin lunged onto its back, biting into the back of its neck. It howled in pain as Komptin continued to latch on. Alex straightened her posture as she walked up to the creature.

"Gotcha." She shoved the Lite Force through the bottom of its chin coming out the top of its head before it disappeared.

Chapter 4

Alex just happened to gaze at the clock on her desk when Megan finally decided to come into the office. Alex thought to herself that it must be nice to make up her own hours. She felt annoyed that she goes out and risks her life most nights, battling Demons and Infiltrators, and yet she still managed to come to work on time. She watched Megan sit down and turned on her wooden flute music. Alex just looked at her from the top of her computer screen as she held a wet, cold, washcloth full of ice pressed against her head. The pulsating pounding of her head was exemplified with every heartbeat.

Megan warned Alex in an annoyed fashion, "I woke up with a headache this morning, so don't give me any crap today. Plus, I slept on my shoulder funny, and I haven't had time to go to the chiropractor to get adjusted."

Alex took the wet, cold, washcloth and switched it out with another one soaking in ice water. "Yeah, rough night, huh?"

Megan jumped at the opportunity to talk about her night. "You don't realize what I go through if I sleep wrong. My neck is out, and then I have trouble getting up in the morning. It's just rough."

"Yep, just sucks," Alex commented as she felt the cold ice water drip down her back from the washcloth.

Anne walked into the room to get her cup of coffee. "You look like crap."

"I didn't sleep well last night, and I have a sinus headache coming along," Megan jumped in before Alex could answer.

"Oh, I'm sorry to hear that," she said looking over at Alex giving her a wink. "How about you?"

"Took Komptin out on a walk," Alex said. "It was just so much fun." She showed Anne the bloody washcloth.

"Shouldn't you see someone about that?" Anne made a face of pain as she watched Alex put the bloody rag back on her head.

"I'm going to the chiropractor at my lunch hour," Megan told her, adjusting the volume to her flute music.

Alex rolled her eyes. "I'm good."

Father Tom walked into office behind Anne. "Good morning, Anne." Father Tom stopped in his tracks to see Alex holding the rag to her head.

"Father," Anne replied. "I'm having trouble with that report, but I do have some information."

"Okay, let's go over it," Father Tom said, opening the office. "Come on into the office, Alex, you can give me your report as well." Alex got up from her desk and Anne followed Father Tom into the office. Megan got up to follow them into the office with her notepad. "Megan, please watch the phones."

Megan got mad and turned around. She sat at her desk, throwing the notebook down. Alex whistled at her as she closed the door waving to her in a sarcastic "bye-bye."

"Alex," Father Tom quietly scolded her. "Anything happen last night?"

Alex showed him the bloody washcloth.

Father Tom threw her some Motrin. "What did you find out?"

"I came across a F.O.R. meeting place. They had some pretty high-tech gadgets," Alex told him. "I was about to follow a group of them until we ran into three Infiltrators. I think they were there guarding the place."

"Or perhaps they were going to pounce on the group of F.O.R. members. That still isn't enough proof that the Dark is behind their actions," Father Tom gave an unwanted point of view. "Anything else?"

"I'm pretty sure someone got Infiltrated yesterday," Alex said, checking her bandage.

"But you couldn't find them?" Father Tom asked her as he was reading something on his computer. He had a look of concern before he turned to look at the girls.

Alex just shook her head no to Father Tom's question. Father Tom who sat there expressionless turned to Anne. "Anne, do you have any good news?"

"Not really," Anne shamefully admitted. "I got a reference to what people who wish to be infiltrated are called."

Father Tom sat back in his chair. "And they are?"

Anne's gut was not to say anything, but she did anyway with the false confidence. "Provisionary."

"So, let me get this straight," Father Tom said. "The Lite Sentry assigned here has had no solid proof of the Dark infiltrating the F.O.R. and the Council's Historical Researcher spent days researching with an outcome of a nickname used for someone who wants to be Infiltrated, while the F.O.R. continues to grow with a stunning coincidence that a fire has taken down a Jewish Temple downtown this morning. We are losing this fight."

Megan came onto the intercom, "Father, there is a Father Partinello on line one."

He hit the transmit button. "Of course, he is."

Alex looked to Anne to see if she knew who that was.

"Council interpreter."

"Ah," Alex said, turning her attention back to Father Tom.

He looked to Alex and Anne. "I need more from you two." He picked up the phone. "This is Father Altomer."

Alex got up and threw her blood-soaked washcloth into the trash next to Father Tom in a silent statement that she was trying her hardest to stop the Dark. Anne followed Alex out the door. Megan sat back in her chair and smirked as they walked by.

"I swear, I'm going to knock one of those damn ugly wigs off her head," Alex said, walking out of the lobby.

Anne rubbed her arm in a support. "You should go see a doctor."

"I'm good, are you?" Alex asked her. She knew Anne took her work personally. Anne always thought her work performance was direct reflection onto herself.

"I'm fine, I need to get to work," Anne said, walking down the hall.

***

It was about a week since Anne and Alex got a talking to from Father Tom. He's been on both their cases every morning about progress; Anne sat back in her desk chair and stared out the window up in the sky.

Alex and Komptin walked into her office. "Let's go get some lunch, we're hungry," she said sitting in the chair in front of her desk.

"I really shouldn't. Father Tom is expecting more information," Anne said going into her computer.

Alex walked up to her computer monitor and shut it off. "No, you need a break."

Anne knew that look when Alex was determined on something. "Okay, where?"

"Let's just walk until we find something," Alex suggested, grabbing Anne's coat and throwing it to her.

"Sounds good." Anne gathered her purse and jacket. She then stopped and started reading something that caught her attention.

"Anne!" Alex smiled at her. "Come on."

"Sorry," she said, zipping up her jacket.

Alex straightened up her jacket and looked in the mirror to make sure none of her scars were showing. She covered her neck scar with her scarf and put her hair down to cover the other. "Let's go."

They walked down the hall and saw Megan coming towards them. Anne and Alex both ignored her as they continued to walk down the hall. Anne softly spoke to Alex so no one would hear, "Don't you think that Father Tom has been a little bit more agitated than normal?"

"It's a power trip," Alex said. "He's a fast burner and he wants that position and make Cardinal."

"He's a priest, I thought they frowned against that kind of action?" Anne asked. Anne stopped in her tracks. "Wait, yeah, I locked my office." Anne started to walk towards the side door.

"He's still human," Alex said. "You need a day off."

"I'm fine, just a lot on my mind," she finally admitted.

They walked down the street to a spot near the college where a bunch of food trucks parked in the street. "You wanna eat here?" Anne asked her, worried about the answer.

"Yes, I want the greasiest Mexican food I can get," Alex said, scouting the food trucks. "And I found my target." She pointed to a health hazard of a food truck.

Anne just shook her head in disbelief. "Okay, I'm going to get a garden salad from over there," Anne told her. "Meet you on the library steps?"

"Sounds good," Alex answered. "Come on boy, I'll get you a churro."

Anne got her salad right away. There was no line since most people who eat at the food trucks got more of the greasier food. She put down her iced tea and sat down on the steps trying to enjoy what little sunlight was illuminating. She closed her eyes trying to relax when she felt the sun being blocked. She opened her eyes to a rather rough looking homeless man staring down at her. She got a pit in her stomach as she started to look for Alex.

"Can I help you?" she asked him.

He just stared at her.

"Sir, if you don't mind, you are making me feel uncomfortable," Anne informed him. "I don't have any cash on me."

He just continued to stare.

Anne was getting upset. She was hoping Alex would be coming to join her soon.

***

Alex just got her food from the vendor when she caught sense of something. She scanned the crowd because she knew someone here was infiltrated. The problem would be that if she got into a fight, she couldn't use her powers in front of all these people. The Demon had the advantage. She would hope she would lure him away so she could vanquish the creature. She looked down at Komptin who was on high alert. She grabbed her food and saw a homeless man standing in front of Anne. Alex got a sour pit in her stomach.

"Komptin." Alex motioned to him to get to Anne quickly. Komptin took off and ran towards Anne. No one in the crowd would look twice at a dog running through the area.

***

Anne was thinking of anything she could do for a weapon in case this guy decided to do something. The only thing she had readily available was the plastic knife and fork that came with her salad. She didn't know if she should look away from the man or continue to stare at him. She hated confrontations.

She heard a massive dog bark and felt relieved; she knew Komptin was on his way. The protective German Shepherd came onto the stairs and sat next to Anne. His presence alone was enough to drive the homeless man away as Komptin just stared at the man to make sure he wasn't a threat.

Anne closed her eyes as she pet Komptin on the head. "Thank you, Komptin."

***

Alex saw that Komptin was at Anne's side, and she knew that she was safe. He would die before any harm came to her. Alex was watching the homeless man between the crowds. She needed to verify if he was infiltrated or not, because if he was, lunch was going to be interrupted. She continued to weave through the people, as she never kept her eye off her target. She needed to make contact to make sure. She circled around the front of him and came face to face with the man.

"Do you have a couple of dollars?" the man asked Alex, holding out his hand. "I just want to get something to eat."

Alex just confidently stared at him and stared hard. She could tell the man was getting nervous with her standing in front of him. Alex handed him a five-dollar bill; he took it. Alex grabbed his hand and pulled him in closer to her. She couldn't sense anything in him. He wasn't infiltrated.

"My apologies," Alex said, letting him go. "I thought you were someone else." She handed him another 20-dollar bill. "Sorry again."

The man just nodded and grabbed the money and left.

Alex could still feel the faint distinction of someone that had been infiltrated in the area. She did another look around before she decided to join Anne and Komptin over on the steps. She tried to give Anne a relaxing lunch while still overlooking the crowd to see who the Demon among them was.

***

Warcourt watched from the other side of the road. "She doesn't seem like much."

89

Gron joined him eating a burger. "Trust me, she's a fighter. And see that dog, it's like something you've never seen before. It's always by her side."

Warcourt looked over the situation. "Who's the girl next to her?"

Gron looked over to see Anne laughing with Alex. "I can't believe they're still friends." Gron saw a sparkle on Anne's hand. "If she is still friends with Alex, then that can only mean that he is here as well."

"Who?"

"Her brother," he said, biting into his burger.

"Is he as powerful as she supposedly is?" Warcourt asked scouting the Sentry. He couldn't understand how that little thing had the power Gron was talking about.

"Kale? Not even close, but I may have some unfinished business with him," Gron said, wiping his mouth. "I just got to think on how I'm going to do it." Gron smiled. "I think I want to marinate on that one for a while."

***

Alex was finishing up her work. The end of the day wouldn't come by fast enough. Her stomach was letting her know that she shouldn't have eaten that food from the truck. Komptin was laying down by the side of her desk, sleeping as usual. Father Tom came out of the office putting his jacket on as he was heading out.

"Have a good night, Father," Alex said to him as she held her stomach as it started to make some noise. She shifted a bit trying to get comfortable.

"Good luck tonight on your hunt," he stopped dead in his tracks as he winced at what he just said. He must have forgotten that Megan was still there. "Have a good night, Megan."

"Oh, I will," Megan said in return. She watched Father Tom leave the office. "Is that what you call going out to the bars, 'a hunt'? Finding your next victim?"

Alex shifted in her seat as the gas in her stomach was moving around. Alex didn't even want to warrant her comment with a reaction. She watched Megan shut her computer down.

Megan grabbed her coat and as she was putting it on, she told Alex, "I'm afraid of your dog, I don't think it should be in the lobby. I can't get any work done because it's in here."

"He's my service dog," Alex said just staring at her computer screen trying to fight the gas forming in her stomach. "So, that's not even an option, so get that out of your head."

Megan got frustrated and took off for the night without saying anything to Alex. Anne walked into the lobby. "Good night, Megan."

"Oh, I will," she said as she walked out of the office.

Alex looked over. "I really wonder what she does when she goes home." She just shook the thought off. "Taking off for the night?"

"Yeah." Anne just stood next to her desk.

Alex could see that something was on her mind. "Everything okay?"

"That guy at lunch, kind of freaked me out," Anne confessed. "The way he just stared at me."

"He wasn't infiltrated, if that's what you're worried about," Alex reassured her.

"I know," Anne said. "But still."

Alex smiled at her future sister-in-law. "How about I ride home with you. I have to hunt that side of town anyway. Saves me the walk."

"Thanks," she said, taking her keys out of her purse.

"I just need to change into some different clothes." Alex gathered her things.

She got up from her desk and Komptin joined her to escort Anne home. The whole ride to Anne's apartment Alex was fighting her stomach. She knew she should have gone to the bathroom prior to leaving the church.

"Are you all right?" Anne asked her.

"Bad Mexican," Alex admitted to Anne.

They made it back to Anne's apartment where Alex bypassed Kale who was sitting on the couch and went straight to the bathroom. She was pinching because that food was going to come out. She couldn't get her pants down fast enough. She made it to the toilet and managed to relieve the pressure in time. Alex had a small sense of relief as she took a moment to relax.

She finished unloading her temporary burden as she looked around for some aerosol or something to cover the smell. She couldn't really find anything.

She decided just to wash her hands and then grab something to eat before her hunt tonight. After drying her hands, she opened the door as a man stood in front of her about to come into the bathroom.

He was tall, built, he had light brown hair and a kind, gentle, eyes. He smiled at her as she looked up at him. Alex felt her face turn red standing in front of him. "Hello," he said to her.

"Hi," she said in return. She just stayed in the doorway, not knowing what she should do next.

"Are you the toll clerk for the bathroom?" he asked her.

"Huh, oh, sorry," Alex told him. "I wasn't expecting someone to be there on the other end." Alex couldn't believe she said that. She adjusted her collar on her neck and cleared her throat. The smell from the bathroom snuck up behind Alex coming out into the hallway. She closed her eyes and tightened her lips. "If you will please excuse me."

"Of course, my apologies," the man said, stepping to the side before going into the bathroom.

Alex walked down the hall with her hand over her face. She came into the living room to see Anne and Kale sitting on the couch together. Kale was holding Anne as she was curled up in his arm. The two of them stared at Alex. "Who was that?"

Anne looked confused; she gazed up at Kale who looked down the hall. "Oh, that's Kameron, he is staying here while he recovers from surgery, remember?"

Kale went back to watch TV. "You feeling all right? You look a little flushed," he snickered.

Alex gave him an evil look. "Kale," was all that she could say. Alex sat down on the chair as Komptin lied down at her feet.

Kameron walked down the hall into the living room. He walked behind the couch to see what was on the television. "I'm sorry, I didn't mean to startle you."

Alex continued to read her phone unable to look at him. "Oh, no big." She tried playing it off.

Anne spoke up, "Oh, I forgot you two actually never met; Alex this Kameron, Kameron, Alex." She pointed to the two of them.

Komptin immediately stood up and checked out this guy walking up to her. Alex shook his hand. He had a firm and confident grip. "Alex." She patted her chest with her other hand.

"Kameron," he replied. "Alex? Is that short for something?"

"Alexandria," she told him.

"I like that. That's really nice," he said. He looked down at the big dog scoping him out. "And who is this?"

Alex knelt to Komptin's level. "This is my dog, Komptin."

Kameron moved his left hand to let Komptin smell the back of his hand. Alex watched him give a small wince as he moved his arm. Even though Komptin wasn't a typical dog, he smelled it anyways. He licked his hand in acceptance.

"He's a big boy." He started to scratch the side of his face and underneath his chin. Komptin was enjoying every minute of it. "Well, if you excuse me, I'm finishing up dinner." Kameron smiled at her.

"You're cooking dinner?" Alex asked him.

"Yes, as a thank you to Anne and Kale." He was checking his watch. "Will you be staying?"

Alex caught Anne waiting for her answer with some raised eyebrows. "I really should get going," she commented. She took a smell of what Kameron was cooking. "What are you making?"

"Just some vegetarian lasagna," he said. "There's enough for you if you would like to stay."

"I really can't," Alex said, getting up. Komptin ran to the door. "If I don't take Komptin for a walk, there will be hell to pay."

"Okay, well maybe a raincheck," Kameron offered. "Dinner should be ready in about 20 minutes," he told Anne and Kale as he walked into the kitchen.

"I'll see you tomorrow, Anne," Alex said to her.

"Have a good walk." Anne got up and gave Alex a big hug. "Thanks for coming home with me."

"No problem," Alex told her. Alex just shook her head out of embarrassment thinking of coming out the bathroom. Anne caught Alex looking in the direction of the kitchen. Alex quickly recovered. "I gotta go. Luv ya."

Anne smiled, "Love you too sweetie."

***

Anne came out of the bathroom from taking a shower. She saw Kale was already in bed, reading a lifting magazine. She was proud of him for having a hobby he could jump into. It was nice to see that he was focused on something he enjoyed. It seemed like he was more acceptable to anything when he had his outlet. She knew his true passion was running and biking, but this was a good substitute. Plus, she was impressed by how big and toned he was. Anne would be lying if she said she did not enjoy it when he plays around by posing for her before he jumps into bed sometimes.

She fluffed her hair in the mirror and crawled into bed next to him. He immediately scooted over to her without stopping his reading of the magazine. She loved that, even when he was doing something else, he made a point to be closer to her. She kissed him on the cheek.

Anne reached over to nightstand to open the drawer to grab a book she picked up on religion theories regarding the Middle East. There always seemed to some truth in the writings but others were way off kilter. She often thought maybe she was the wrong in her thinking and maybe they knew something she didn't. Either or, she enjoyed reading about it. Let her mind think outside the box.

She put down her book and turned to Kale. "That was a good dinner."

"It was," Kale answered her. "For a second there, I was debating thirds. I'm not a big fan of vegetarian foods, but that was really good."

"He's a good guy," Anne commented. The thought of how embarrassed Alex was when she was introduced to Kameron stuck out. She never seen Alex flustered like that before.

"Yeah, he's genuine," Kale flipped through his work out magazine. "If I ever get this big, you have my permission to shoot me." He pointed to a guy with his veins popping out of his arms.

"Promise," Anne said. She tapped her pen on her teeth. "What do you think of Kameron and—?"

Kale put the magazine down. "No!"

"Why not? She's been with his type before in high school," Anne reminded Kale.

"No, she had made out with his type before and then she wants nothing to do with them," Kale reminded her.

Anne thought back to high school. Kale was right; Alex really didn't have a good reputation when it came with being with guys.

"I like Kameron," Kale said. "If she hooked up with him, she would just dump him immediately after. I really don't want that to happen. I love my sister, but she doesn't know what she wants with a guy. Plus, they are total opposites."

Anne was shocked. "So are we." Anne could see that Kale felt like he was about to eat his own words.

"We're special," Kale said as he went back to reading his magazine.

Anne just shook her head and went back to her studies.

***

It was Friday afternoon when Alex walked down to see Anne in her office. She sat down and looked at Anne who was in the middle of some research. "How are things going?" Alex asked her.

"Not bad," Anne answered her as she was filing some reports that Alex had written in the church safe. "I reached out to my counterpart in the Middle East in the Islamic Council for any information." Anne took her glasses off. "He said he would get back to me. So that's good." Anne sat back in her chair. "How was your night?"

Alex didn't understand why Anne was looking at her like she was a one of her projects. "It was okay. Komptin and I went back to that house where we saw the F.O.R., but the only thing we saw was a security guard sitting outside." Alex looked outside the window. "I hope that there wasn't another Infiltrator that saw us that night."

"I'm sure not one of those creatures knew you were there," Anne reassured her. She was so glad she had never run into one of those creatures since high school. "Then it looks like you had a pretty quiet night."

"Yeah, it was pretty quiet," Alex said. "Nothing much happened." She continued to look out the window, drinking her Apollo.

Father Tom walked into Anne's office. He looked horrible. "Father, are you okay?" Anne asked him.

"Just funeral prep," Father Tom told her. Father Tom did something that Anne and Alex had never seen him do—he pulled up a chair and sat down. "I just got word that the Council will be sending a new Cardinal up sometime next year."

"Do you know who it is?" Anne asked him.

"Yes," Father Tom said. "It's actually somebody you both know." Alex and Anne looked at each other and shrugged. Father Tom then stated, "Cardinal Joe."

"You mean Father Joe?" Alex said, straightening up in her seat.

"Yes, I thought that would make you two happy," Father Tom said. He gave them a quick little smile before getting up from his chair.

"I'm sorry you didn't get it, Father," Anne told him.

Father Tom turned around to look at them both. "I never applied for the position."

"I thought you did," Alex added as she turned to him.

"No, I'm not ready, plus, at that level, it's mainly management and politics. I wouldn't be able to watch over my flock, especially my two little black sheep." He smiled.

Anne and Alex were shocked that Father Tom was goofing around with the two of them. They just looked at each other and replied with a sheep's "Baaaa."

Father Tom did something else the two of them had not seen for quite a while, he laughed. "Look, I would hate to ask this of you since it is your day off tomorrow."

Anne eased his burden. "What do you need, Father?"

"I'm having trouble with the eulogy for the funeral, and I'm falling behind on the final coordination of the funeral and set up..." Father Tom was saying.

Anne politely interrupted him, "I'll be here tomorrow after breakfast." To Anne's surprise, Alex nodded and agreed to come and help as well.

Father Tom forced a smile. "Thanks." He turned to walk out of the office as if something heavy was on his mind.

"How about that?" Alex asked Anne.

"No kidding. I thought for sure he would have applied," Anne answered her.

"I think that is the first time I ever saw him laugh." Alex was thinking back to all her interactions with Father Tom.

***

Anne was coordinating the flowers in the chapel for the funeral while Alex and Megan were in their offices printing off the brochures. Anne got a text from Kale saying he was going to bring lunch for her and Alex. Anne replied with a thank you and heart emoji. She put the phone in her back pocket and walked up to the Cardinal's office.

She opened the door and saw Alex's hair pulled back into a ponytail. She wasn't wearing her collar like she normally does. Alex's scar from her first battle with a demon was showing on the side of her neck. Anne felt sad for all that Alex goes through and only a few people know of it to show their appreciation. Alex dropped her pen and when she picked it up the scar on the left side of her face was noticeable. Anne turned to Megan who had a look of compassion as she saw the two scars. If she only knew of the other scars on her body from her battles. Anne smiled at Alex as she sat on the couch by the coffee maker.

"I got a text from Kale, he said he is going to bring us lunch," Anne said, drinking some coffee.

"Oh good, I was getting hungry, what did he order for me?" Megan asked her.

Anne was kind of stuck because she didn't have Kale pick up anything for Megan. "I didn't know what you would like so I told him to pick something." Anne quickly picked up her phone to tell Kale to pick up something for Megan.

He replied with, "Who?"

Anne just texted him back, "Just pick up something extra." Anne put her phone away. "How are things going?"

"I'm almost done," Alex said, getting some paper for the printer.

"What are you doing anyway?" Megan asked as she put together the brochures.

"I'm going over the itinerary for the entire day," Alex told her. Alex opened an Apollo drink. "Anne, I could use a second set of eyes on this."

"Sure." Anne got up and leaned over Alex who was now sitting in her chair at her desk. They were working on the itinerary when the door to the lobby opened, and Kale walked in with the smell of food filling the lobby.

"I have an order for a Ms. Anne McClure," Kale playfully said.

"Ah, that's Mrs. Anne Moler," she replied with a playful smile.

"You're not married yet," Megan said while folding brochures.

"Hi, Kameron," Anne said.

Anne felt Alex's arm hit her body as she pulled out her ponytail. Alex shut the computer off so she could use the reflection in the monitor to fluff her hair quickly and cover her scar on the left side of her head. Anne tried her hardest not to smile as she rubbed her friend's back in support.

Megan got up from her chair and adjusted her top to emphasize her cleavage. "I'm Megan," she said, going up to Kameron.

Alex rolled her eyes as she turned on her computer to review the itinerary.

"I'm Kameron," he said. "I think Kale has your chicken pita."

"Oh, you guys are so kind, how'd you know that was my favorite." She put her hand on Kameron's arm.

"Well, I like them." Kameron gave her the box with her food in it. "Good post-workout meal."

"I like to eat healthy when I work out as well," she interjected. "I can see you take very good care of yourself."

Anne looked to Alex who was staring at Megan the whole time. Alex looked up Anne and gave a fake vomit into her mouth. Alex's attention turned back to Kale as he brought up Anne's salad and Alex's lunch. "Here is your salad, and, Alex, I got you a double cheeseburger with fries." Kale held out the greasy bag.

Alex snatched the bag from Kale's hand. "Thanks, Kale." She put it down next to her.

"No problem," Kale told her. He turned to Anne. "How are things going here?"

"Stressful." Alex had a hard time waiting for everyone else to start eating because that cheeseburger was looking especially tasty.

It was obvious that Anne was forcing not to smile. "We are managing." Anne held her fiancé's hand. "I really could use a night out." Anne knew that was something to ask for because Kale didn't like going out too much.

"Done," Kale assured her. "Do you want to have a relaxing dinner or go bar-hopping?"

"Let's go do dinner and then bar-hopping," Anne suggested. "Make a night of it. Sweetie, are you free?"

"Yeah, that sounds like fun," Alex said, leaning on her hair to cover her scars.

Anne looked over at Kameron. "Are you free Friday night? Do you want to come?"

"Yes, sounds like fun. I haven't been out in quite a while," Kameron told her.

"Oh, I was hoping you'd go, I didn't want to be a third wheel," Megan somehow invited herself.

"Okay, I guess we'll meet at our place at seven?" Anne looked at a message on her phone. "Oh, the flowers are on their way."

"Sounds good to me." Kale leaned in and kissed Anne. He whispered, "I love you."

She whispered back, "I love you, too."

He walked over behind Alex and gave her a hug. "You okay, sis?"

She pat his arm. "I'm fine," she told him as she leaned into his chest, closing her eyes.

Anne was reminded how those two used to act in high school together. Alex and Kale always had a connection. It was sweet to see that it was something she hasn't seen in quite a while. Kale gave her a quick squeeze and a kiss on top of her head.

"Ready to go?" He looked over at Kameron who was drifting through a book that was on the table.

Kameron nodded. "Yep, it was nice to see you again, Alex." He smiled at her and gave her a small wave.

Alex looked up at him. "Nice seeing you too."

"I'll see you Friday," Megan told Kameron.

"Yes, it should be fun," he replied to Megan. He adjusted his shoulder as he and Kale walked out of the church.

**

Alex was going to take the night off from hunting but for some reason she wanted to go for a walk. It was a windy and brisk night. It was cold but for some reason it felt good going across her face. She put her scarf on and tucked it into her jacket before heading out for her walk. She and Komptin walked down the street. It was late; the bars were closed and that meant this was prime time for Infiltrators to take a kill if they wanted one. She was hunting, but it wasn't a serious hunt. She halfway hoped she wouldn't run into anything Dark related. She was enjoying the night thinking about everything yet nothing in particular.

Alex walked with her hands in her pocket admiring the night. She found herself coming to an elementary school. Schools always seemed creepy at night. Such a big building blacked out and so many places for the Infiltrators to hide. The playground reminded her of the night she killed her first Infiltrator. It was a tough fight, but she prevailed in the end. She played with the swings before she decided to sit down on one. She slowly started to swing back and forth as Komptin sat down on the grass seeming to enjoy the night as well.

She viewed the sky at the shining purple star shining among all the other stars. Some of them were actual stars, others were placed there in remembrance of all the angels that had fallen in battle. She watched police cars go racing across the street. Then it was quiet. She was thinking of the Cardinal's funeral tomorrow. She missed him; he was a sweet old man who looked out after her. It seems like she was doing a lot of funerals for her lifetime. Maybe she was the cause of it all, maybe she was putting her friends in harm's way. She couldn't handle losing someone she loved to the Dark again. What good was she doing?

Komptin turned his head as someone was approaching. Alex looked to see who or what was coming. To Alex's surprise, it was a little girl. Alex got scared as she didn't know what she was going to do if the Infiltrator's had found a way to inhabit children. She wouldn't know what to do in that case.

"Why, hello, there. What are you doing out this late and alone?"

The little girl had tears running down her face. They were almost freezing to her face from the cold wind. "I'm running away from home."

Alex got up and knelt down to the girl. She zipped up her jacket, fixing her coat to ensure she was warm. "Why?" Alex flipped up the young girl's hood.

"My parents don't love me anymore," the little girl said, wiping her nose.

Alex could see that the little girl was shivering in the cold and from being scared. "Why do you think that?" Alex took off her coat and wrapped it around the little girl.

The little girl tightened the coat up closer to her. Komptin came in closer to offer some of his body heat to her. They little girl jumped at the fear of the massive dog.

"It's okay, he won't hurt you. Why are you running away?" she asked in fear that her parents were Infiltrated and that she was going to have to diminish them right in front of the little girl.

"Because they got a new baby in the house and they love him instead of me," the little girl cried.

Alex smiled at the girl while looking around. "Tell you what, why don't I bring you home and you can see how much they love you?"

"I'm not supposed to go with strangers," the little girl said, wiping her tears and hugging the jacket.

"Well, that is a very good rule," Alex said standing up. She looked down at the little girl. "How can we fix this? I know, how about I tell you my name?"

The little girl nodded.

"Alexandria, but you can call me Alex," she told the girl.

"That's pretty," she told her.

"What's your name?"

"Natasha," she answered. "But you can call me Tasha."

"Natasha, that's a pretty name as well," she told her. "This is Komptin."

"He's big." Natasha was petting Komptin.

"Yes, he is," Alex told her. "He's also my best friend." She pet him. "We are going to make sure you get home safe." Alex stood up and held out her hand. "Would you like that?"

"I'm scared; it's dark," Tasha admitted as she stood closer to Alex.

Alex put her arm around Tasha. "I promise you, Komptin and I will do everything we can to ensure nothing happens to you," Alex assured her.

The little girl sniffled as she grabbed Alex's hand. "Do you know where you live?"

Natasha looked around and shook her head no.

"That's okay, can you pet my dog?"

The little girl pet Komptin as he sniffed her hand. "He's silly."

"Yes, he is, and he's going to bring us to your house," she said.

The little girl turned to Alex and smiled. The sign that Komptin found the trail was verified by the sudden burst of lite in his eyes before heading off to Tasha's home.

**

Salamor floated over a rooftop of one of the buildings watching the Sentry with a young child. He watched her escort the child towards the home from where she came. Salamor was mad at the opportunity that was thwarted by the Sentry. If the

Infiltrators had a chance to kill the little girl, then the parents would feel such a loss. Salamor could have taken advantage of their grief and pounced on their sorrow. He decided to follow the Sentry but being careful to keep his distance since she is the only living creature that could actually cause him harm.

***

Alex rang the doorbell and a man in his bathrobe cautiously answered the door. Alex saw that the doggy door was open and that was probably how Tasha got out.

"Can I help you?" He looked down. "Natasha!" He knelt and hugged his little girl. "Oxana! Come here!" he yelled to his wife.

A lady came from down the hall to see Alex at the door with her daughter. "Oh my God, Tasha!" She came running down to the door hugging her daughter crying.

"I'm sorry, Mama," the little girl cried. "I'm sorry, Papa."

"It's okay, honey," she cried. She looked up at Alex. "Who are you?"

"We just crossed paths and figured she needed to get home safe," Alex told them. "My name is Alex."

"Alexandria, she's not a boy," the little girl told her dad. "That's Komptin." She pointed to the dog.

"How did you get out?" He looked down at the dog door and it clicked. "How can we repay you?"

the father asked. He grabbed his wallet from the counter.

Alex smiled. "Don't worry about it."

"Please let us give you something," the lady said in a Russian accent. "My name is Oxana."

"And I am Matfei," the father said. "Please let us give you something for taking such good care of our little Tasha."

Alex felt like if she didn't accept anything, she would insult the family. So, she thought of the first thing that popped in her head. "Do you have an Apollo energy drink?"

"Sorry, no," the man sadly admitted. "But please, give me your address so I can send you something. Please," Matfei pleaded.

Alex went into her wallet and gave her a business card. "This is where you can reach me."

"A church?" Oxana asked. She said something in Russian to her husband.

"That's where I work," She knelt to the child's level. "See, I told you." She smiled as she took off one of her bracelets. "Here, you can have this, and anytime that you have doubt, just look at this bracelet and remember this night."

Matfei commented, "You truly are a gift from God." He smiled at her. "Thank you, again."

"Thank you." Tasha hugged Alex.

"Thank you again so much," the Oxana said. "We cannot repay you."

Alex just smiled when she was met with a hug from Oxana upon standing up. "Have a good night." Alex walked out of the yard and looked to the sky.

"Thank you for that." She looked down to Komptin. "Come on, let's go home." They started to walk out the yard and they stopped in their tracks.

***

The gargoyle creature stared in the general direction where Salamor was hiding in the shadows of the tree from across the street. The creature flashed his glowing blue eyes signaling he knew Salamor was present. The Sentry turned her face from happiness to one of determination. She too must have known he was near.

The Sentry scanned the area around the area to see if she could find anything to attack. Salamor could feel his nerves heightened from remembering her promise to him that she would kill him if she got ahold of him again. Like the coward he was, he decided to leave the area to ensure he was not seen.

Chapter 5

Alex stopped off at a bakery after bringing sweet little Tasha home. The walk back to the church was calm and relaxing as the morning sun started lighting the area. Her morning bliss was halted when she saw Father Tom sitting on the steps overlooking the street. This was not how she wanted to start her day. Then she thought that an opportunity to clear some tension between them seemed to present itself, so she joined him on the stairs. She offered him an olive branch by reaching into her bag and split the Danish she bought in half offering it to Father Tom.

He took it and dunked in his coffee. "Thank you."

"You okay?" she asked him, looking in the direction he was. She was making sure there wasn't something there. Alex reached over and scratched Komptin behind the ears as he was seated next to her.

"It just hit me why I was having so much trouble with this eulogy," he admitted, taking a sip of his coffee.

"Why is that?" Alex asked him, taking a bite of her Danish chasing it down with an Apollo Energy Drink.

"It's the job," Father Tom admitted to her. "When I became a priest, I wanted to help people. I know this is going to sound crazy, but I really wanted to make a difference in people's lives." He took another bite of his Danish. "I can't believe those kids were so easily manipulated to do what they did. The death, the murder, and those are just poor kids who caused that damage. They are at the bottom of the totem pole, that's not even counting the Infiltrators, the Demons, the…" He just shook his head as he took another sip of his coffee. He turned to look at Alex. Her scar on the side of her head showing. "I want you to know that I'm not blind. I do see you come home morning after morning. You think I don't see the blood, the scars, the fact that I send you out there risking your life night after night and there is nothing I can do about it?"

Alex didn't know what to say; she just stared out on the street.

"You know what the most stressful part of my day is?"

Alex shook her head. "Dealing with me?" she softly asked him.

Father Tom took a sip of his coffee. "No, it's coming to work in the morning to see if you are going to be there or not."

"Father, I chose this. This is my choice and mine alone." She tried to alleviate some of the burden he put on himself.

"Doesn't prevent me from worrying," he told her, staring at a cat that was walking into an alley. "I know I have been hard on Anne and especially you."

"Well, I didn't really give you the greatest first impression either," Alex half joked. She thought

113

back when she was being interrogated by Father Tom in front of Cardinal Frank back in college from her reckless spending.

"Yes, I remember reading your credit card statement," Father Tom reminisced. "But the Cardinal, he handled it like a champion. He knew exactly what to do. He was a great man. Did you know he recruited me into the Council?"

"No, I didn't." Alex took a bite of her Danish.

"I jumped at the opportunity to fight against the hate, the evil… the Dark." Father Tom watched a person who was on some sort of chemical substance walk by in front of the church. "I just don't see a difference being made; I feel like I'm not only failing the Cardinal, but God as well. I really don't think we are doing any good in this world."

Alex never thought what the Cardinal's death was doing to Father Tom. She had a sense of guilt come over her. It didn't even dawn on her that he had lost his mentor. She knew what it was like losing a teacher when Osiah was killed by Vandor. There wasn't one time she had asked Father Tom if he was doing okay. "You wanna know what happened to me tonight?"

Father Tom nodded.

"A sweet little girl, no more than five years old, was out on the streets running away from her parents because she thought they didn't love her anymore," Alex started to tell the story. "This little girl was in the heart of Infiltrator territory and managed to come across my path. I was somewhere I would have never thought I would be."

"Where were you?" Father Tom inquired.

"Southside Elementary, sitting on a swing," Alex admitted. "Komptin and I escorted her home. I was halfway expecting these parents to be drug using, alcoholic, and generally mean people; but when that door opened, they were good people, full of love for their little girl. God put her in my path to escort her home. Just as He put me in your path for you to guide me." Alex stood up. "You can't tell me we are not doing any good." She playfully kicked him. "Now get your ass up and let's send off the Cardinal in the way in which he deserves."

Father Tom smiled as he stood up. "Sounds good, I just have some tweaks to my eulogy I need to do," Father Tom said.

Alex headed towards the rectory as Father Tom headed into the church.

"And Alex?"

"Yeah?" She turned around.

"Thanks." Father Tom smiled.

"You got this." Alex gave him a thumb's up. She couldn't help but smile for some reason. Sudden rush of emotion rushed over her. Seeing him have a spark of relief gave Alex a sense of hope that things were not going to be that bad.

***

The church was beginning to fill with multiple groups of people. There were leaders from the other councils, local politicians, and friends and family of Cardinal Frank. The church was packed but Alex

115

found a spot in the back of the congregation. She saved a spot for Anne and Kale while Komptin laid at her feet. A group of people came in together in dark suits with Kameron among them. He saw her from across the congregation and gave a subtle wave. She smiled back with a small wave. She thought he was coming over to say hi, but a bunch of priests and Cardinals came to shake his hand. They were no doubt thanking him for risking his life trying to save the Cardinal. Father Tom was sitting in the front of the church looking a bit nervous. There was a lot he was carrying. She hoped she could relieve some of that burden.

A tap on her shoulders startled her as she turned around to see a group of older Cardinals. "Ms. Johnson," a priest said in an Italian accent.

"Yes?" she looked up to a middle-aged priest in front of three older cardinals.

"I'm Father Partinello. I'm the official translator for the Catholic Council," he told her.

Alex's eyes got big as she stood up. "I'm sorry."

"No need to apologize, we did not tell anyone we were coming," he told her. "This is Cardinal Berchella, Cardinal Liminadi, and Cardinal Tetalio."

Alex shook all their hands. "So nice to meet you."

Cardinal Berchella spoke something in Italian towards her.

Alex looked over to the translator.

"He just wanted to say it was an honor to meet you," he translated.

"Grazi," Alex hoped she didn't offend them by her poor attempt at Italian.

The Cardinals smiled. Then Cardinal Tetalio spoke. The translator nodded in agreement. "Cardinal Tetalio said that they are proud of the work you are doing here and that if you need anything, don't hesitate to ask."

"Thank you." Alex told them. Alex hated talking to the council let alone in person. She never knew what to say. She was kind of hoping for an escape from talking to them.

Anne came in behind the Interpreter and the three Cardinals. "Father Partinello."

He turned around to give Anne a hug. "Anne, so nice to see you. How are you?"

"I'm fine thank you," she replied. She started speaking a little Italian to the Father and Cardinals. They said their good-byes and went to go sit down in the front of the church.

Father's Tom's eyes grow big as he saw the members of the Council sat in the front pew. He stepped down to greet them, adding more pressure on him that he probably didn't want.

Kale came into the church and sat next to Anne. He was here to support Anne no doubt about it. "Sorry, couldn't find a parking spot."

Anne just tapped him on his leg.

Alex watched as Megan made her way up to Kameron and was laughing and dancing in the church aisle. "Are you serious? This is a funeral, for God's sake," Alex said to Anne.

"That's a little inappropriate," Anne said, watching her.

Komptin got up in an alert position and looked outside the church. Alex peeked behind her and saw a group of F.O.R. members walking up the stairs to enter the church. "Son of a bitch," she said getting up.

Anne turned to Alex. "Alex!"

"Anne, I'll be right back. Komptin, stay here and make sure no one gets hurt." She walked out to the front of the church to meet the members of the group. "I really don't think you guys should be here."

The leader of the group spoke, "Just paying our respects."

"Not welcome or appropriate," she told him.

"Doesn't your little fictional story teach forgiveness," he smartly asked her.

Alex quickly replied, "Are you saying you have something to be forgiven for?"

The group started taunting the leader that Alex got one up on him. "Look, bitch, we're going in." He started to walk towards her.

Alex started to feel tense because no harm could be done by the Dark on holy ground, but in turn she had no power either. However, that wouldn't stop her from getting hurt by everyday humans. She hadn't been in a fight without her power since high school. Little her was about to take on five guys. Standing her ground, she stared at the leader as he walked up to her. This fight was not going to be won by her, but she wasn't going down easily.

"I believe she asked you to leave."

Alex looked to see Kameron, walking down the stairs behind her.

The leader motioned for his crew to go in.

"You are not welcome here," Alex told them, ready to take them on.

"Shut up, goth whore," one of them said. He started to walk up the stairs, and before Alex could react, Kameron grabbed him by the arm, twisting him to the ground while simultaneously drawing his weapon as the leader of the group reached into his pocket.

"Don't," Kameron said, pointing his weapon at the leader. "Move your hands slowly and they'd better be empty."

The leader looked at him. Alex could tell he was debating on trying something.

"Come on, come on, nice and slowly," Kameron instructed him with his weapon steady at the leader of the group. Kameron's stone-cold face meant he would shoot this guy with the slightest wrong movement.

The sound of a group of people came up from behind. Alex slightly turned to see the rest of the agents that Kameron was with coming outside, all of them drawing their weapons. The Secret Service commander was coming out from behind telling them to settle down.

The leader of the F.O.R. stayed still as the group took off running. The rest of the Secret Service chased after the group. Alex turned around to Kameron who was holding the F.O.R. member on the ground while the leader still had a gun pointed at him.

"Stay still," Kameron reminded him.

"You're going to kill me in front of this church?" the leader asked him.

"I'm not Catholic," he quickly quipped back.

Alex prevented a smirk from forming at Kameron's comment, but then it quickly turned to anger. "What the hell do you think you're doing?" Alex yelled at Kameron. She watched as some of the Secret Service team took the two F.O.R. members Kameron had under his control.

"Excuse me?" Kameron asked her bewildered.

"I don't need your protection," she snapped back at him. Alex had a feeling as if she were damsel in distress. It wasn't something she was used to.

"I didn't come out here for your protection, I came out here because..." He stopped himself. "Okay, you're right. I'm sorry."

Alex gave a low growl as she shook her head as she walked away. She turned around to see Kameron sit down on the church steps, putting his face in his hands as the cops came to take the F.O.R. members away. Alex watched him for a moment until she went back into the church.

***

The office was uncomfortable all week. The fact that Alex's stomach was upset since the funeral didn't help matters. Even the sight of food wasn't appealing to her. The thought of having Father Tom to call the doctor was an option she wasn't going to ignore. She and Komptin tried hunting one night, but she made it a block before turning around to go back to the church. The problem of being a Lite Sentry was that they didn't sleep, so if she was sick, she was awake and sick. It was Friday and she was supposed to go out with Anne and Kale tonight. Throwing up all over the dinner table wasn't particularly appealing to her. The only thing that seemed good was an Apollo but when she went to go get one, she was out.

"Damn it."

"Your language isn't appropriate for a church," Megan mentioned to her. She seemed more dressed up today than usual. She had on a blonde wig today and was wearing some pretty nice clothes for just a normal day at the office.

Alex shut the door. "Sorry," she sarcastically said. "Come on, Komptin, it looks like we got to go down the street to the market." She started getting her coat on when someone with a clipboard came into the office.

"Excuse me," a deliveryman said. "I have a delivery for a Ms. Alexandria Johnson."

"That's me." Alex signed for the delivery. "You can just bring it in here."

"I'm sorry, ma'am, but it won't fit in here," the man told her.

"I wonder what it is," Alex said.

Komptin followed her out of the church. A pallet of Apollo Energy drink sitting on the sidewalk with the deliveryman patting it. "All yours," he told her.

There was a card on the pallet that read: "Thank you from Tasha and her family." There was a picture of a Crayon drawing of her helping a little girl, which must have been Tasha. Her stomach actually started to feel a little bit better reading this. She read the business card and it read Matfei Stratovich, District Manager, Super Quality Foods.

Anne joined Alex outside. "What is this from?" she asked, looking at the pallet.

Alex smiled. "Just someone showing appreciation."

Father Tom came from walking down the street when he was staring at the pallet. Stopping in his tracks, he stood there studying the pallet full of the Apollo Drinks. Alex handed him the note. He smiled as he gave it back to her. "Well, where are you going to put it?"

"It will be a tight fit in the room," Alex said.

Anne laughed. "You can make a chair out of it."

"We have that extra room down the hall from Anne's office you can have for storage," Father Tom said, trying to pull on the straps. "Anybody got a knife?"

Anne offered, "I'll go get one from janitor's closet."

Alex snickered, "No need." She pulled the straps off, ripping them with ease.

Father Tom just looked at her.

"What? We're a couple feet off church property."

Father Tom shook his head as he grabbed a box. "Come on."

Megan came outside to see where everyone was. "Where did that come from?"

"Ah, good. More hands. Grab a box," Father Tom said, walking by her.

***

Alex decided to go join everyone at dinner even though she didn't feel like going. Of course, she sat next to Anne but then got stuck next to Megan on the other side. It felt that Megan managed to weasel her way to sit next to Kameron. The feeling of being annoyed by this confused Alex.

Surprisingly, it was a nice evening. Kale and Anne were telling the table how they were engaged. Alex had never tired of hearing that story.

Anne continued, "So I opened the box on the date we officially started dating."

"The day I finished my Iron Man, she was there waiting for me with Alex and my mom," Kale butted in. "I'll never forget it. It was also our first kiss."

"And there was this beautiful ring, with a note saying, 'There's something I want to ask you'," Anne said. "I couldn't wait until he was up, so I called right away."

"I wasn't sleeping anyway," Kale interjected.

"Yeah, I remember you wanted me to stay home and watch movies all night with you waiting for the answer," Alex added to the story.

"I was crying so hard, I couldn't say yes," Anne admitted to the group.

"That's a nice story," Kameron said. "You two are lovely together." He raised his glass. Kale and Anne raised their glasses along with Megan and Alex. "Here's to many wonderful years ahead of you." They all drank to their future.

"You are so nice for saying that," Megan said, touching Kameron's arm.

Alex turned to Anne. "Oh, Kameron." Alex started touching her arm, mocking Megan. "I swear."

Anne patted her hand on top of Alex's. Alex felt there was tension between Kameron and herself. He said hello and that she looked nice, but not that much more. It must have been obvious because Anne asked what was going on between the two of them. Alex didn't really know how to answer that question because she didn't really know.

They all finished their meal and then decided to walk down the street to find a bar. They finally came across a bar they all agreed on. Alex caught the feeling of the Dark nearby. It didn't really surprise her since they ended up in an area where they tend to congregate.

She saw Komptin on the roof keeping an eye on her. She looked up and smiled at him, giving him a little wave. He just turned around to leave her to a night of relaxation.

Kale ordered everyone drinks and handed them out. He made sure to give Alex an Apollo drink without alcohol because it made her sick. They were all in a group looking over the crowd. It looked like it was mostly college students in the bar with the typical forty-year-old man dancing by himself on the dance floor, holding his drink in the air.

"You know, that could have been me in seventeen years," Kale said as he looked at his Coke.

"No way," Alex said to him.

Kale smiled at her. "Ah thanks, sis."

"You're not that good of a dancer," Alex told him.

"Oh, Alex," Kale said to his sister, giving her a gentle hug.

Megan was dancing in front of Kameron as she slowly backed up to him. "I love this song."

Alex watched as Kameron just smiled and took a drink from his glass. She couldn't tell if he was enjoying it or was being polite. "Forget it," Alex accidently said out loud.

Anne and Kale were staring at her.

"Forget what?" Kale asked her.

Alex quickly came up with, "Nothing." She took a drink, scouting out the room. "He's cute," she said about some random guy to Anne.

Anne just nodded and agreed, "Yes, he's okay."

"So, Alex, are you dating anyone? Because you sure do go out a lot at night, and most of the time don't come home until the sun comes up, wearing the same clothes," Megan asked her as she got closer to Kameron. She grabbed Kameron's glass and took a sip. "Mmmm, that's good. What is that?"

"Jack and Coke," he said, giving it to the waitress as she walked by.

"Excuse me," Alex said to Megan. "How would you know this?"

"You're joking right? With all these attacks on churches, I'm not getting blown up. So, Father Tom asked me to review the church security feeds the night before to look for anything suspicious," Megan said. "Almost every night, you go out all dolled up and then come home in the morning. It looks like you had to pick up your clothes in the dark from the bottom of the floor."

Kale's eyes were getting big. He whispered to Anne, "Are we going to see 'high school' Alex before the night's end?"

Anne whispered in my ear, "I hope not." She kissed him on the cheek.

Alex couldn't think of an excuse. She just couldn't say she was hunting Infiltrators with a gargoyle dog. "I like to go for walks," is all she said as she looked over the crowds.

"All night? You do that pretty much every night and then work all day, when do you sleep?" Megan inquired. She looked over at Kameron. "Or with whom?" She winked at him.

Alex thought the best thing to do would be say nothing. She just took a sip of her energy drink and gazed over the crowd. She didn't know how she didn't notice, but somebody came up behind her and put their arms around her.

The touch seemed familiar. She turned around to see Gastrix.

"What's up, babe!"

"Of all people," Alex thought to herself. "Gastrix." Alex tensed up. "Get your hands off me. What are you doing in D.C.?"

"Mixing my beats," he said, putting his arm around her. "Where's your dog?" He nervously looked around.

Alex turned to him after pushing his arms off her. "Why?" Hoping he wouldn't say anything to jeopardize Komptin's identity.

"You are never without him," Gastrix said. He looked over at Kale and Anne. "Hey, man, we cool?"

"No," Anne sharply said to him before Kale could answer. She turned to her fiancé. "Kale, dance with me."

"Glad to," Kale said, giving Gastrix a dirty look. "Jerk," he softly said as he walked away.

"Hey, jackass, I didn't force you to drink those," Gastrix yelled. Some of the bar patrons turned to look at Gastrix.

"Some things never change." Alex mumbled. She shook her head out of disbelief that she ended up with someone like him. "What do you want?"

"Don't I know you?" Gastrix looked over at Kameron.

Kameron went to shake his hand. "I brought Kale to the hospital when he got hurt."

Gastrix was trying to remember. "Oh yeah." He shook his hand back, but Alex could tell he didn't want to.

"How come I don't remember that?" Alex asked Gastrix.

"You were taking a crap," Gastrix told her.

Alex got embarrassed by thinking back at the first time she met Kameron as she came out of the bathroom. Alex didn't know if the bathroom incident was anything or was it all in her head. "Thanks for that," she sarcastically said to him.

"How do you know Alex?" Megan asked him.

Alex stared at her because she knew Megan had a pretty good idea who Gastrix was. "We used to hang out together."

"Yeah, naked most of the time," Gastrix said, patting her on the butt.

"Stop it." Alex pushed him. "Ugh." She shivered at the thought.

"Come on babe, we should get back together, we had some fun," Gastrix told her.

"No," Alex said.

Gastrix grabbed her by the shoulders. "We need to go talk."

"No," she backed off.

He grabbed her by the arm and tried to drag her off to talk. Alex was about to show him how strong she actually was until Kameron came up to him. "I believe she stated she didn't want to go with you."

Gastrix stared down Kameron at first and then let her go. He turned to Alex. "You flat chested gutter whore." Gastrix walked to the bathroom line.

He turned to Alex. "Are you okay?"

"He's an ass, but he can't hurt me. Again, I don't need your protection," Alex said to him as she scouted around the bar. She turned from Kameron to make sure he did not see that Gastrix upset her.

"I can see that," Kameron said, backing off. Kameron watched Gastrix head outside as he couldn't wait in line for the bathroom. "If you will excuse me." Kameron walked away.

Alex watched Kameron walk away to the bathroom line. That nauseating feeling came back into her stomach. She tried everything she could do to prevent herself from vomiting all over the floor.

Megan was leering at Kameron like a piece of meat. "It's amazing how much your family and friends like me. Especially Kameron. I think we make the perfect couple."

Alex continued to watch the crowd dance as she sipped her drink. "You two are dating?"

"Well, no, but I can tell he wants to," Megan told her. "It's so obvious. Do you have a glow light in your hand?"

Alex looked down on her hand. "Damn it," she said, putting her hands in her pocket. "No, it's my key flashlight. Must be broken." She walked over the garbage can and acted like she threw it away. "I have to go to the restroom."

***

Gastrix found a dumpster near the back entrance of the bar because he didn't want to wait in line for the bathroom. There was amusement as he pissed on a dead rat lying next to some cans. After finishing, he turned to see Kameron staring at him. "What do you want?"

"You should really go in there and apologize to Alex," Kameron informed him. "If you really care about her, that is."

"What business is it of yours?" Gastrix asked, leaning on the wall. "Oh, I get it. You have a little goth fetish curiosity."

"Please," Kameron said. "You should really apologize to her. It's just the right thing to do. You hurt her." he genuinely expressed. Kameron turned around to go back into the bar.

"Hey, Kammy," Gastrix yelled.

Kameron stopped and turned around. "Yes."

Gastrix walked up to Kameron. "Let me tell you what it feels like when she was sucking my—"

The next thing Gastrix felt was a sharp pain in his nose. With his eyes watering causing his vision to blur, he barely saw the blood was dripping from his face. Another blow come across his face as he spun around and landing in his own urine next to the dumpster. Kameron stood over him shaking his hand.

"Come on." He extended his hand out to help him. "No one saw this. There's no embarrassment that has been made. It's okay, we're the only ones who know this happened."

Gastrix grabbed his hand.

"Go on, go home, shower. I swear, no word of this will ever come out of my mouth," Kameron assured him as he brushed off some of the dirt on Gastrix's jacket.

Gastrix agreed before he walked down the alley to find his way home.

***

Alex returned from the bathroom to see that Anne and Kale finished their dance as well. She noticed her drink was gone and just sighed.

"Is he gone?" Anne asked her, looking around.

"Yeah, I think he went to the bathroom or something and then probably got distracted by all the pretty lights and colors," Alex commented.

Alex could see that Kale was about to say something cocky, but he refrained and just asked, "You okay?"

Alex nodded. "I just see him, and I just feel ashamed."

"No need." Kale looked around. "Where's Kameron?"

Alex immediately looked to see where Megan was. To her relief, she was at the bar getting another drink. Alex just shrugged her shoulders. Megan bought everyone of drinks and passed out everyone

131

their drinks except to Alex. "I didn't know what you wanted."

Alex looked to Anne and just rolled her eyes as she walked to the bar.

"Where were you?" Kale asked Kameron as he came up to the group.

"I was just getting some fresh air," Kameron said as he grabbed a drink from Megan. "Thanks."

"Not a problem, I got us another Jack and Coke." She sipped it, looking at him.

Alex turned her attention to the bartender "Can I get an Apollo, please?" The bartender handed her the drink. Alex thought she should have gone hunting. She would have had a better time fighting Infiltrators and Demons than sitting through this night. Megan's back was to Alex as Kale, Anne, and Kameron were facing her listening to her talk. Alex got up to the group where she heard what Megan was talking.

"I'm telling you, she is not all that. I have to cover for her all the time at the church. She thinks she had all these special privileges with the Cardinal and now Father Tom. Why does she get a room in the church free of rent? And this is the first time I've ever seen her without that dog."

Alex sat down in the booth watching the people, still within earshot. She was listening but not trying to listen to what Megan was ranting. Alex just wanted to keep her hands hidden in case they decided to start lighting up again. She didn't understand why she didn't have control over it.

Megan continued talking, "You know, she's going to end up back with him. I wouldn't be surprised if he is the one she is sleeping with every time she leaves the church. She deserves him."

Anne and Kale's eyes grew big as Alex jumped onto the table. Alex lunged at Megan but was caught midair by Kameron with one arm. Alex was flipping off Megan behind her back as Kameron carried her to the dance floor. On the dance floor, in typical movie cliché fashion, the song turned into a slow beat.

"I hate slow songs," Alex admitted. She was amazed how strong he was to catch her in midair to bring her out here.

"Well, I think it is good timing." He smiled. "Besides, it's better slow because now two people could actually talk," Kameron said, adjusting his shoulder. "You seemed pretty upset."

"Why do you say that?" Alex asked him as she turned her head to Megan. Alex thought about how much trouble she would get in if she shot a Lite Beam to knock off that wig of hers.

"I'm no detective, but the fact that you were flying through the air was kind of my first indicator." He laughed.

Alex embarrassingly put her head on Kameron's chest. "I'm sorry." There was contentment as the music played. She closed her eyes to savor each second. This was something she had never experienced before.

Alex felt Kameron's hand on the back of her head in a supportive squeeze, even thru the

133

thickness of her hair extensions. "Nothing to be sorry about," Kameron assured her.

"No, there is. I'm sorry I snapped at you at the church and back there with Gastrix," Alex admitted. "It's just a situation I'm not used to." Alex kept her hands on Kameron's arms.

"I get it," Kameron comforted her. "I hate confrontations like that." Kameron adjusted his shoulder.

"Hurting?" Alex found herself gently putting her hand on the spot where he was shot.

"It's just a bit uncomfortable at times," he told her as they continued to dance. "Who knew that getting hot lead lodged into your body isn't the most pleasant feeling?"

Alex just lifted her eyebrows, thinking back of being stabbed with Sanah's Lite Spear. She turned her head to the side as she leaned back into Kameron's chest. "I can relate," she told him as they continued to dance. Alex felt Kameron hug her as she closed her eyes enjoying the sudden sense of nerves mixed with serenity.

The two of them finished the dance and pulled away from each other. They just smiled at each other, not knowing what to do next. Alex was amazed how solid Kameron felt but still had a gentle touch to him. Her heart was beating has if she was closing in on her prey during a hunt. With her mouth suddenly going dry, she told him "I need to get something to drink."

Kameron motioned to her to the area where the group was standing. "Hey, Alex?" Kameron said.

"Yes?" she said, turning to look at him.

He leaned in; at first, she thought he was going to kiss her, but he whispered, "Look behind on my right side next to the back wall."

Alex was confused but then she saw three members of F.O.R. on the back wall. "They are growing, aren't they?"

"I know they have the attention of the FBI now," he admitted. "The worst part is that I bet ninety percent of them do not know the consequences of their actions."

Alex inquired, "And the other ten percent?"

"I do believe there is true evil in the world," he told her. "But there are certain moments in life that are proof He exists, and that is why we fight it."

Alex looked at Kameron intensely in the eyes, studying him.

"What are you doing?"

Alex grabbed his cheeks, pulling him closer, and made him look at her in the eye. "Hold still."

Kameron's squished cheeks made his lips pucker up. "Okay, what are you looking at?"

She twisted his head to make sure she covered all angles while she was studying his face.

"Do I have something on my face?"

Alex wanted to double check to make sure her suspicions. "How many hours of sleep do you get a night?"

"That's not really a question I was expecting; I don't know, six to eight hours," he admitted.

Alex let go of Kameron's face. "Sorry." She straightened up her shirt. She looked at him intensely again. "Are you for real?"

"What?" Kameron was completely confused now. "Are you okay?"

"Yeah, where are you from?" she continued to interrogate him.

"Upstate New York," Kameron told her. "My parents are corn farmers. We should really go join the others." He was studying Alex as she was walking towards the group, and she stopped to turn around again to him.

"You would tell me," Alex turned to ask him.

"Tell you what?"

Alex couldn't sense any presence of Lite or Dark in him. Could he just be a nice guy with good intentions? Alex just shook the thought out of her head. "Nothing, sorry about that. I'm just messing around with you." She smiled as she joined the group.

***

Anne was rubbing Kale's back as he leaned over the banister overlooking the dance floor. "Are you okay?" she asked him.

Kale winced as he turned to look at her. "Yeah, I'm okay."

Anne dug in her purse and handed him some Motrin for him to take. She handed him a glass of water that she ordered earlier. She smiled at him as

136

she continued to rub his back. She mouthed, "I love you," as he returned the same to her.

"Where is she at?" Alex asked Anne as she and Kameron came up to them from the dance floor.

"She claimed she was getting a headache and then took off," Anne told her. Anne felt Kale try to get up off the banister. Anne knew his back was getting stiff, but he would never openly admit it. Anne smiled at Alex, "Have a nice dance?"

Alex just said, "Yep."

"I'm ready to call it a night," Kale told everyone. "One can only have so many sodas."

Anne too was feeling as it was time to go. She grabbed Kale's hand and interlocked fingers. Anne rubbed her fiancé's arm. "I'm tired as well."

"I'll get us a ride," Kameron said. He left the bar to find a cab.

"Let me walk out with you," Kale said, hoping walking would loosen up his back.

Anne watched Kale walk to the door all stiff. "It's going to be a restless night tonight. He's hurting."

Alex felt saddened seeing Kale limp over towards the door. "I really do hope to get even with Roger, or Gron, or whatever he is calling himself these days. Do you ever think of ever telling Kale about what we actually do?" Alex asked her.

"I signed a nondisclosure, I can't," Anne admitted. "Plus, I swore on the Bible I wouldn't."

Alex took one last look to the dance floor. "Come on, let's go home."

***

Anne's apartment was the first stop. Kale was in the front seat of the cab as Kameron was in the middle of Anne and Alex.

"This is comfortable," Kameron joked, trying to get himself situated.

Alex was crunched against the door of the car. "Really, a Mini Cooper was the only one you could find?" she teased Kameron.

Alex opened the door quickly, desperate to escape the close quarters. Anne followed suit as Kameron got out on Alex's side of the car. Kale just sat there in the front seat clenching his jaw.

Anne turned to look at Kale. "Alex," she called for her.

Alex turned to see Kale just sitting there with his eyes closed, breathing heavily. She knew that look of pain.

"Anne," Kale softly called out her name.

"You okay, honey?" Anne opened the door.

He was embarrassed for asking. "I need help getting out," he whispered.

"It's okay," she patted his leg, kissing him on the cheek. "I'll get Alex and Kameron to help while I get the door upstairs."

Kale closed his eyes and nodded.

"Alex, Kameron," Anne called for them. They came straight over. "Guys, he's hurting pretty bad."

Kameron replaced Anne by standing in the car door. "Okay, come on, big guy, put your arm around me and I will lift you out."

Anne was getting upset at the fact that the man she loved was in so much pain. She watched Kameron lift Kale out of the car.

Anne went to Alex. "Can you get the door?"

Alex had the door opened as Kale and Kameron reached the top. Anne went to start the shower. A hot shower always seemed to ease the pain enough to get him into bed and take some medicine. Kameron helped him all the way into their bedroom. "Do you need anything else?"

"No, I'm good, but I think our gym time is cancelled for tomorrow," Kale joked to him.

"No problem," Kameron told him. "Just take it easy."

"Oh crap, I think I left my purse in the cab." Anne turned her attention out the door.

"The cab is waiting for me anyway, he should still be there," Kameron told her. "Come on, I'll walk you down." He turned back to Kale. "Let me know if you need anything."

Anne turned to Kale. "I'll be right back."

Kameron and Anne walked out to the cab.

Kale nodded as he tried to bend over to pick up his shoes. He knew he couldn't do it by himself. "Alex, do you mind?" He pointed down to his shoes.

"Yeah, no problem." She turned to see Kale staring right at her with a stern look.

"He's a good guy, Alex," he told her.

Alex helped Kale take off his shoes. "And?" She got one shoe off and tossed it in the corner of the room. "Man, your feet stink."

"You know I love you, right?" Kale asked her.

"I know, you big ape," she said, trying to get the other shoe off.

"I say this with love then," he told her. "Don't. Just don't."

Alex could feel herself getting a little upset. "Don't what?"

"Don't turn Kameron into another deli sandwich," Kale pleaded.

Alex found herself either offended by Kale's statement or angry, or maybe a little of both. She prevented herself from tearing up as she nodded at him. She finished helping him with his shoes and socks. She found herself unable to look at him as she said good night.

She walked out of the hall and saw Komptin sitting on his favorite chair. "Give me a minute," she said, walking by without missing a beat as she went into the kitchen.

***

Anne had to help Kale shower and get into bed. There was little hope of him having a good night's sleep tonight. She kissed him on the forehead before stepping out of the room. Alex must have gone out hunting already since Komptin wasn't in his normal spot. In the kitchen, she saw Alex at the table drinking her energy drink while Komptin had his head on her lap.

Alex had tears dripping, but she wasn't making a sound. She looked at Anne coming in as she tried to wipe her face.

"Hey," she said to Anne. She took a sip of her drink, trying to mask her tears.

"Hey," Anne replied to her. Anne got a glass of water and sat down on the table across from Alex. "What's wrong, sweetie?"

Alex shook her head as if she did not want to talk about it.

"Okay," Anne patted her hand. "Okay."

They sat there for a couple of minutes before Alex looked to Anne. "Do you think I'm a slut?"

Anne immediately replied, "If this is what Megan was talking about tonight, then to Hell with her."

Alex had more tears forming but she quickly wiped them away before answering, "That may be some of it." Alex got up, went to the faucet, and splashed her face with water. She looked down at Komptin. "You ready?"

Komptin looked at Alex.

Anne could almost see that he was just as worried about her. "Why don't you stay the night?"

"No," Alex instantly replied. "I need to get out of here. I need some fresh air."

"Okay, be safe, sweetie," Anne said to her out of concern. She watched Alex leave the kitchen. "Komptin." He came up to Anne. "Do me a favor, please? Lead her away from anything tonight, okay?"

There seemed to be confirmation from Komptin before he left to join Alex.

***

Alex had been walking for about an hour. She stopped and looked around the rooftops and down darkened alleys. There was a feeling that she was being watched. There was no strong sense of the Dark. "Sense anything?"

Komptin put his head down, telling Alex he couldn't sense any Infiltrators or Demons in the area.

Alex gazed up at the stars. "Clear night." She tightened up her coat. "Where do you feel like going?"

Komptin pulled on her pant leg, going the opposite direction of where the Infiltrator's main territory was.

"We really should go that way."

Komptin barked at Alex.

"Okay, okay, we'll go your way," Alex told him. The two of them walked into the night.

***

"We could take her easy." Brian stared down at the girl. "She doesn't look like much."

"Our job is simply to watch her and report to Warcourt on her actions and who she interacts with," Ken told him. "Do you really want to go against Warcourt's wishes?"

142

"Nope," he told his friend. Brian got on his radio. "She's heading east on 47th Ave."

"Copy," a voice came over the radio.

"The ground unit should be able to catch up to her. Hopefully they won't be spotted," Ken said. "Come on, let's go see if we can make it ahead of her."

Chapter 6

Alex was thrown against a wall while the Infiltrator held her by the throat. It swung one of its massive claws at her face. She was able to smash the arm of the Infiltrator prior to his claw connecting. That loosened the grip and Alex was able to duck out of the way. She managed to give a devastating blow to the dark creature. It stumbled back as it regained its composure. Alex formed a sharp Lite weapon and stabbed it through the neck. The Infiltrator howled in pain as it disappeared.

She looked to see how Komptin was doing. Komptin was tearing into an Infiltrator on the ground as another was clawing on Komptin's back. Alex ran and tackled the one on top of her friend's massive back.

Sparks flew as she hit the ground with her fist lit as the Infiltrator managed to avoid a deadly blow. She managed to get up and grab the Infiltrator's leg before it had a chance to run away, she swung it around and it landed against the wall. She ran full force and jabbed it with a spear into his chest. It found a way to claw her stomach prior to dissipating into the ground.

"You are a royal pain in the ass!" A demon came charging at her from the darkness.

It dug its sharp claws into Alex's shoulder blade. She dropped to the ground and swung around knocking it back far enough for her to gain some much-needed counterattack room. She shot her Lite Beam, throwing the demon into a pile of pallets. Alex instinctively jumped on the demon as she continued her assault.

"Warcourt!"

Alex turned to see a girl and boy running towards her.

"Get her off of me!" he yelled.

Hearing that, Alex turned into a fit of rage and tossed Warcourt into the two humans running towards her causing a collision of bodies. The two humans were hurt but Warcourt stood up and took off running. Alex picked up a pallet and flung it at the Demon. It smashed onto his body knocking him down.

The Sentry ran to Warcourt when he barely got up. Warcourt managed to punch Alex across the face, causing her lip to bleed. She returned the punch and then grabbed his head to smash it against the wall of the building while she was screaming. She formed a Lite Spear and shoved it through his back and shoving it upwards coming out the top of his head.

"You truly are a whore," he said as he crashed to the ground, joining it forever.

"Piece of crap," she said in return.

Komptin joined her side with blue blood dripping from his nose and scratches on his back.

Alex checked her stomach wound. "Well, there goes bikini season this summer." Alex looked around for those two humans. "Slimy little devils got away. Come on, let's go look for them."

Komptin didn't budge.

Alex turned around. "Come on."

She continued to walk towards the direction that the Provisionaries took off. Komptin ran in front of her blocking her view. He pushed her in the opposite direction.

"Let's go find them," Alex told him.

Komptin growled at her and gave a deep gargoyle bark.

Alex found herself getting mad. "We have a chance to find out if they are F.O.R. or not."

Komptin put his massive paw on Alex's stomach. The pain caused her to scream as she staggered her back.

"I'm fine."

Komptin flared his eyes to show anger as he growled at her.

"Fine, let's go home. I'm going to be late for work anyways."

Gron looked down from the rooftop at the result of that battle. "She just killed Warcourt." He turned to Salamor who was hiding in the shadows of a rooftop shed. "She just killed Warcourt."

"She is growing stronger." Salamor made sure he wasn't seen by the Sentry.

"I told him not to engage her," Gron said as he walked away. "Damn it."

***

Anne pulled into the parking lot on this nice morning. She liked the mornings when she got to

146

the church to see the sun peeking out from behind its tall steeple. It made her feel content. She closed her eyes and smelled that brisk November air. Her moment of Zen was interrupted by the sound of Komptin barking from across the street.

Anne turned around to see Alex coming home holding her stomach with blood dripping between her fingers. Her mouth also had blood coming from it as she angrily walked to the church. "Alex!" Anne came running up to her.

"Hey." She just bypassed Anne, heading towards the church rectory.

"Are you okay?" Anne gazed over Alex's wounds. Her eyes got fixated on the blood dripping in between her fingers as Alex was holding her stomach. "Let me see that wound."

"I'm fine," Alex told her.

Komptin jumped in front her and barked.

Alex rolled her eyes and lifted her hand from her stomach. Blood started to ooze out.

"Alex, this is bad," Anne said, putting her hand on it. "Come on, let's get you inside." Anne started to guide her friend to her room.

Father Tom stepped outside to enjoy the nice morning with his cup of coffee when he saw Anne escort Alex up to the rectory. He dropped his coffee on the ground to help Anne get Alex into the church. "What happened?"

"There are four less Infiltrators and one less Demon out there," she said, coughing. She spit a huge amount of blood on the ground.

They managed to get her to her room. "Anne, go call Dr. Smithon. Tell him that Father Tom needs him here ASAP."

Anne ran to her office to call the doctor.

Father Tom looked at Alex. "Alex, I need to clean this wound," he told her as he examined her.

She sat up to remove her top. She winced as she moved her arms to remove her top. Father helped her remove it while holding a towel on her stomach he got from Alex's closet. She couldn't hold in her scream as she took her top off.

"It's okay, Alex," Father Tom assured her. "Anne," he called.

Anne came rushing in with bandages and hot water. "He's on his way."

"Please wet some towels and let's try to clean these the best we can and keep pressure on these wounds," Father Tom calmly instructed her.

Anne was surprised how composed he was handling this. "Okay."

"Damn it, Megan." Father Tom looked at his watch.

"What about her?" Anne asked.

"We can't let her see Dr. Smithon or Alex like this, I need to cut him off before she sees him. Stay with her and keep her awake," he said as he got up.

"Well, you know what happens if I do sleep?" Alex reminded him.

"I know, that's why you are not to fall asleep," he said, walking out.

Alex looked at Anne. "Is it me, or was he actually concerned about me?"

Anne started to clean the wounds the best she knew how. "Honey, what is going on with you?" She hit a spot that made Alex wince. "Sorry."

"What do you mean?" Alex said, looking into her mirror all bloodied and torn.

"For the last three weeks, you have been coming back more bloodied than usual. You're distant, and you haven't said anything to anyone for days," Anne said. "Did I do something?"

"No, of course not," Alex said, wiping her lip.

"Did Kale say something to you?" she asked, grabbing another washcloth wiping the blood from Alex's shoulder.

Anne could see a tear form up in Alex's eyes. "Not directly."

Anne faced Alex. "What did he say?"

Alex tried again to look at herself in the mirror, but this time couldn't bring herself to do it. "Anne, do you think I'm a slut?"

Anne's eyes grew big. "Did he call you that?!"

"No," she defended her brother. "You know Kale. He worries about losing things that are important to him, but you never answered my question; do you think I'm a slut?"

"No, I don't, but honestly speaking," Anne started to say, and she stopped herself. It wasn't like Alex to dwell on what other's thought of her.

Alex pushed her. "Please, Anne, I really want to know what you think."

Anne stopped wiping her wounds and came to sit down in front of her on the bed. "Honey, I think you need to look in here." She pointed to Alex's

149

head. "And here." She pointed to her heart. Anne smiled at her. "And whoever the lucky guy is where those two agree on, you will experience something, like something you can't explain."

"What if they never agree?" Alex had started to have tears dropping from her face.

Anne wiped them with a bloody wet washcloth. "I think they are starting the early phases of negotiation."

Father Tom knocked on the door. "Alex," he said softly. "Dr. Smithon is here."

Alex nodded as an older priest walked in carrying a medical bag. "Well, Ms. Johnson, I'm Dr. Smithon, I understand we have a couple of scratches." He turned to his assistant. "Can you please help me remove her clothing? We need to clean her up."

"Yes, doctor," the older female nurse said.

He did a preliminary scan of her and looked at her stomach. "Father Tom, if you will excuse us."

"Of course." He complied by leaving the room. "Come on Anne."

"Okay," she said, patting Alex's hand. "Love you."

"Love you, too," she replied.

***

The doctor finished patching Alex up. She looked at her stitches across her stomach. She frowned as she looked at them.

"Don't worry," the doctor said, cleaning his hands. "The scar will be minimal." The doctor looked over scratches on her shoulder. "This one might be a little more noticeable but not too bad." He gently rubbed the scar on her face. "Any issues with your eye near this wound?"

"No," Alex replied.

"How about this one on your neck?" He pressed around it.

"No, it's fine," Alex told him.

"How about on your side?" He pressed down on it as she winced.

"It still burns every time someone touches it," Alex said.

The doctor studied the wound. "I'll have to do some research. I don't know of any cases where a Lite Sentry or even non-Sentries have ever been stabbed by a Lite Weapon and lived. It's probably an after effect from the stabbing."

"Honestly, that one really sucked. I could live without feeling that again." Alex looked at her scar.

The doctor smiled. "I'm glad to see you have a sense of humor. That's good." He turned to his nurse. "Can I get my prescription pad?" He filled it out. "Okay, get this filled and then take a couple of weeks off from any hunts."

Alex agreed, "I guess it's late-night movie time."

"Take care, call me directly if you need anything," he said packing up his gear. "God bless."

"Thank you, Father," she said.

After they left, Komptin jumped on the bed and licked her face.

"I guess I owe you another for saving my life again, this time from my own stubbornness." She looked through his fur at his wounds. "You okay?" He nestled up to her and fell asleep. "Show off."

***

Anne was up late reading European Christian history. She had a hard time concentrating as she kept thinking of Alex and how hurt she looked; not just physically, but emotionally. Kale was sound asleep, so peaceful, so content. She jabbed her finger into his side.

"Ow," he said. "What's wrong, what's going on?"

"Oh, you up?" Anne said, shutting her book.

"I am now," he said, looking at the clock. "It's one in the morning."

"You know, Alex asked me something yesterday out of the blue," she told him.

Kale put his head back into his pillow. "Yeah, what was that?"

"She asked if I thought she was a slut."

Kale lifted his head up. "Why would she think that?"

"Do you think she is?"

"No, of course not," he said, sitting up. "But you have to admit she's always jumped from guy to guy," he commented. "The only steady guy she was with longer than a weekend was that numbskull."

"Ever ask yourself why she was so determined to make that relationship work?" Anne asked him as she put her book in her nightstand.

"No, even in high school she went through guys. You know that. Some of them wanted to get close to her but she wouldn't let them. She may have dated Gastrix, but do you think she even came close to letting him get close to her?" he told her. "Of course, he was so self-centered, he probably didn't even think or care about her feelings, probably explains why she stayed with him."

Anne thought back at all the men Alex was with and Kale did have a point. "Do you think she deserves a chance at finding someone special?"

"Deserves, yes. Wants? I think she wants it, but she gets tired of the guy so fast and then throws them away, no relationship building," Kale said. "Look how long it took us to finally reach where we are."

Anne smiled at Kale remembering that night. "I think she is feeling pretty down about herself right now."

Anne could tell Kale was feeling guilty about something. "She is?"

Anne nodded yes. "I caught her crying in the kitchen the night your back went out."

Kale just nodded. He scooted over to Anne, and he put his arms around her. She snuggled into his body and closed her eyes. Anne fell asleep in Kale's arms as he just stared at the blank television.

***

153

Alex checked her wounds while sitting in her recliner. One of the privileges of being a Lite Sentry was that she healed rather quickly compared to human counterparts, but she still hurt. It was early, about three in the morning.

Alex decided to go for a walk around the church. Being the caretaker of the church at night allowed her to appreciate the beauty of church in her own way. It was so peaceful, quiet. The top balcony of the church led up to the bells of the church. They were massive and powerful.

Back inside the church, she decided to sit in her favorite spot, the front pew. The moon made the stained-glass window glow. It must have been over an hour of her just sitting there. How many guys had she gone through and tossed them away? Did she miss good opportunities to be happy? For some reason her mind went to that dance with Kameron. Alex started to stare at the crucifix.

"What are you praying for?" Celestial said, sitting the pew next to her.

"You know." Alex smiled at the sound of her voice. It was amazing how she knew exactly when Alex needed to see her.

Celestial turned to look at Alex who gave her a forced half smile. "How are you, Alexandria?"

"I'm fine," she answered.

"And your wounds?" Celestial examined her stomach.

"I've had worse," She turned her attention to a statue of Mary. "What's she like?"

"There is a reason He chose her," the smiling Conduit of Lite answered her but then turned her attention back to Alex.

Alex turned around to see Ariel and Devine with their heads down giving thanks. "I've always wondered, do you three actually stand in His presence?"

"Yes."

"What does He think of me?" she queried.

"What do *you* think of you?" the angel was waiting for Alex's answer.

"Well, I'm powerful, I don't fear much, I have good friends and would die for them," Alex told her.

"You are telling me what you have, not what you think of yourself," Celestial countered.

Alex found herself unable to answer. "Celestial, can I ask you a personal question?"

"Of course," she said.

"Do you think the reason you and Osiah were never together was because he didn't like himself for his past and it caused him to miss out on something special before he died?" Alex asked her. "Please forgive me if I overstepped my boundaries."

"My child, you are fine," Celestial said. She got up from the pew. "Walk with me," she held out her hand.

Alex grabbed her hand and walked out of the main worship and outside on the steps. Ariel and Devine followed them out. Komptin joined them on the front steps. Celestial sat down on the steps and looked to the sky at Osiah's star. "What one thinks

155

of themselves is quite powerful. It is what forms you to become who you are. Not even God can change that; only the individual has that power. You, yourself need to answer that question you are asking, it is something I or even God cannot answer for you."

"Somehow I knew you were going to answer that in that way." She sat down next to Celestial. Komptin came and sat down in between the two of them. Alex laughed at him. "I guess he wants some love." The two of them scratched Komptin's ears into the early morning.

***

A F.O.R. member was in the room across the street from the church scouting for their potential next target. He wrote down what he witnessed; four girls and a dog were coming out of the church so early in the morning. There was no reason why they should be there. Their body language stated they belonged there. It wasn't his place to question his observations, just to write them down.

***

Kale was feeling guilty all morning. It even affected his workout. He had just stepped out of the shower as he looked at his phone sitting on the shelf of the locker. He texted his boss and told him he was going to be a couple hours late and he needed to take some personal time off.

Kameron came up to Kale with a towel around his waist. Kale could see the scar from the bullet entering his body. "Hey, do you mind giving me a ride to work? I have to drop my car off at the shop."

"No problem," Kale said. "Where's it at?"

"The BMW dealership on this side of town," Kameron told him as he was getting dressed.

"No problem, but I have to do something before I drop you off at work," Kale said looking at his watch one last time.

"No big," Kameron said. "One nice thing about being on light duty is that they really don't care what my hours are." Kameron put his suit on and finished looping his tie. "I'm ready."

Kale walked over to Kameron's BMW, he popped the trunk and opened his locked weapon's case. He put his pistol in the shoulder harness and then another one on his belt. "Jesus, enough fire power?"

"These are mandatory for light duty, you should see when we are actually on security detail," he admitted. "Ready?"

"Yeah, I'll meet you at the dealer," he told him. "Text me the address."

They stopped at a convenience store after Kale picked up Kameron. "This was the one stop you had to make?"

"No, I have to get a peace offering," Kale said as he left the car running. "I'll be right back." Kale came back out with a brown bag and got into the car. He put it in the back seat.

"What is it?"

"An Apollo Energy Drink," he said as he put the car in reverse.

"Okay," Kameron said. Kale watched Kameron look in the mirror and checked his hair. "Do you have any gum?"

"Glove compartment," Kale said, studying his friend.

Kale and Kameron walked into the church through the Annex. He stopped by Anne's to drop Kameron off there so he could go talk to Alex. "She must be upstairs talking to Alex," Kale said as he peaked in her office. They walked upstairs to the main office where Anne was leaning on the wall talking to Alex who was sitting at her desk.

"Kameron!" Megan said, running up to him giving him a hug. Kale saw that he returned the hug but didn't look quite comfortable.

"Hi, Megan," Kameron said. "How are you?"

"Fine, thank you. I can't believe you came up here," she said, fixing her wig. "I look like a wreck."

"You look nice," Kameron assured.

"You're so sweet," she said, touching his arm.

Kale looked over to Alex who was whispering something to Anne. Anne walked up to Kale. "Hey, honey." She kissed him. "What are you doing here?"

"I need to talk to Alex," Kale said to her.

Anne looked over at Kameron. "Hey, Kameron, how are you doing?"

"I'm doing well. How are the wedding plans going?" he asked her.

"Ugh, don't get me started," she said. She grabbed his arm. "Let me tell you about them." She walked out the door trying to rescue Kameron from the clutches of Megan.

Kale walked up to Alex who was still sitting down at her desk not looking at him. He faced her but she turned her head to face the other direction. So, he moved to the other side, and she moved again. He took out the Apollo drink and covered his face with it. "Can we go for a walk?"

"You're such a jackass," she stood up grabbing the drink out his hand. "I need some fresh air anyways." She grabbed her jacket off the coat rack without breaking stride to the door with Komptin at her side.

***

Alex walked down the street taking a sip of her drink. Kale didn't say anything and neither did she. Alex knew he was trying to come up with the words. There were a couple of times he was going to say something but stopped himself. She was going to let him suffer and make him talk first.

"I don't think you're a slut," he told her.

"Wow," Alex said. "That's one hell of an apology. Hey, sis, you're not a slut."

Kale's face turned red. "Look, truly, I'm sorry. Last thing I would want to do is hurt you."

Alex couldn't torture him anymore. "I know." She turned away to look away from him. "I get it. I

159

really do. I knew what you were saying. It just hurts hearing that come from you."

"Never my intention," Kale said. He adjusted his coat to keep him warm.

"I know you would never deliberately do that, you big ape." She turned around to hit him in the chest.

"Are we good?" he asked.

"Of course, you dummy," she said, giving him a hug. Alex stayed in her brother's embrace. "Do you think I'm a good person?"

"Alex, we've been best friends since grade school, I think you are truly a wonderful person." Kale kissed her on top of her head.

Alex and Kale returned to the church where Kameron was in Anne's office talking to her about church history. "Hey, you two," Anne said.

Kameron stood up and offered Alex his seat.

"I'm good, thank you," Alex said, covering up her scar on the side of her face with her hair.

"Kale, since you're here, I'm wondering if you would like to ask Father Tom to perform the ceremony," Anne asked him.

"You think he would? He's not that big of a fan that neither of us are Catholic," he reminded her.

"Never know unless we try." She dragged him out the door.

Alex and Kameron were left in Anne's office looking at each other.

Kameron was looking at her intensely.

"What?" she asked. Alex felt Komptin lay down by her feet.

160

"You okay?" he asked her.

"Fine, why?"

"Just seems like you are walking around a little stiff," Kameron noticed.

"Oh, I spent all night in my recliner," she told him. Alex thought it wasn't a lie.

"Been there," Kameron admitted to her.

There was an awkward silence before Alex spoke up, "So, what've you been up to?" Alex was thinking how dumb she sounded.

"Mainly work," Kameron stood so majestic.

Komptin got up and went to Kameron so he could scratch him behind the ears.

"How ya doing boy?" He looked up at her. "Does he stay here with you at the church?"

"Never leaves my side," she said. "He's my big protector, mainly from myself." Komptin joined Alex by her side. She scratched him behind the ears. "I wouldn't be here today if it wasn't for him."

Kameron smiled at her. "He seems like a good dog."

"The best," she corrected him.

Anne and Kale returned to her office. "That was unexpected," Kale came in with surprised look.

"What did he say?" Alex asked.

"He'd be honored to." It seemed Anne couldn't believe it either.

Alex was shocked over that response. "Really?"

"Yeah, he caught us in the hallway and asked us how the wedding plans were going, if we had everything done. I told him that we've done very little, didn't even have time to go dress shopping yet," Anne told her.

"I told him I felt awkward because of how the Cardinal passed away to find another person to officiate the wedding," Kale mentioned.

"What did he say then?" Kameron asked just as his phone started to ring. "Oh, I have to take this, excuse me," he put the phone to his ear, "Hey what's up…" as he walked out of the office.

"Doesn't sound official," Alex was watching him leave the office.

Anne nudged Kale and motioned over to Alex. Kale just shook his head. "Anyway," Kale emphasized. "Father Tom then said that it was going to be the Cardinal's last act as an official member of the cloth, so he would be honored if he could do that for him."

Anne still had a surprise look on her face. "He actually asked us."

Kameron came back into the room from his phone call.

"Everything okay?" Anne asked him.

"Sorry about that, it's just that I've this function I've got to go on Saturday and my date can't make it," Kameron said, looking through his phone for potential dates.

Alex sensed something strange in the air. Her stomach was in knots and the feeling of hot flashes started to overcome her. She was worried if anyone was noticing, even down at Komptin who was sleeping on the floor.

Anne nudged Kale again, gave him a look, and spoke to him without saying a word. Anne got annoyed that Kale wasn't responding, so she poked him in his side.

"Ahhhhhh... How about you take Alex?" Kale told Kameron rubbing his side from Anne poking him.

Alex's eyes grew big as she looked at Kale and Anne.

"Would you like to go?" Kameron shyly asked her.

Alex's stomach was turning. She looked over at Anne who raised her eyebrows at her to answer him. "I can help you out."

"Okay, well, that just happened," Kale said to the group.

Anne elbowed Kale's side. "You be good."

"I'll pick you up around five on Saturday." Kameron nodded his head at her. "Social starts at six and dinner starts at seven." He looked down at Komptin and then back at Alex. "This is going to sound insane, but I'm going to need the paperwork for this service dog status to get him through security."

"He can stay with Anne that night, if that's okay." Alex turned to Anne. "Can he?"

"Of course, sweetie," she answered her.

Kameron knelt to Komptin. "Well, I'm not going to take Alex unless it's okay with Komptin. May I have permission to take Alex out on Saturday?"

Alex was really concerned; she really didn't know how he was going to respond. All she thought was, *please, please, don't flash your eyes.*

Komptin walked up to Kameron and licked his hands.

"I'll take that as he's okay with it," Alex told him.

"Great," Kameron said. "See you Saturday."

Alex tightened her lip. "See you then." She waved. She turned to Anne who was smiling ear to ear. Kale had a worried expression on his face.

"Come on, Kameron, I'll bring you to work, and we can pick out your outfit for Saturday," he sarcastically said to him.

Kameron stopped in his tracks. "Thanks for reminding me." He turned to Alex. "It's black-tie formal. See you then." He smiled and walked out the door with Kale.

Alex felt as if all her blood left her face. "What did he just say?"

***

Alex sat at her desk not getting any work done. She just sat down staring at her computer screen. She didn't even realize the screensaver was on as she was just staring at it.

"Alex…Alex…hey, Alex," Father Tom called her name.

Alex shook her head. "Huh, what, yes Father?"

"Can you make a copy of these for the Council before giving them to Anne for filing?"

Alex looked at it, it was the medical report from her injury on her last hunt. Alex responded in short, quick nods.

Megan stared at Alex as Father Tom went back into his office. "Why does he give you certain things without me looking at them?"

"Huh, what?" Alex asked her, tapping her pen radically on her desk.

"Are you on drugs or something?" Megan asked her. Megan rolled her eyes as she continued typing. She looked back at Alex. "Isn't it sweet how Kameron came to see me today?"

Alex looked in her direction. "Excuse me?"

"He finds any excuse to come here," she told Alex. "I think I'm going to drop a hint that I'm available this weekend if he wants to do something."

Alex's nerves shot up; she wanted to say he already had plans, that those plans were taking Alex to a dinner, a formal dinner—a dinner where she needed a dress, a formal dress. "Damn it," she said, getting up from her desk.

She knocked on Father Tom's door. "Father, can I ask you something?"

Father Tom sat back in his chair in shock. "You have never knocked on that door."

She looked at him. "I really need to ask you something."

"Yes, of course," he said. "Please." He motioned for her to sit down.

Alex turned around and shut the door.

"Wow, closed door." Father Tom got up and walked around his desk to sit on the other side of the couch. "What can I help you with?"

"Father." Alex sat down on the other side of the couch sitting upright.

"Alex, are you all right, you look…scared." He started getting nervous. "Is there something going on with the Dark or F.O.R.?"

"What? No," Alex assured him. "This is a personal problem."

"Oh…OH!" Father Tom straightened from his relaxed state. "Are you pregnant?"

"What… no," she quickly defended. "Trust me that is the one thing about me you don't have to worry about."

"Then what is it?" he asked her.

"Father." She looked at him. She tapped her hands on her lap a couple of times. "Father, do you mind, if, well, you know how—remember the whole credit card incident thing?"

"Yes," Father Tom said in caution.

"Do you think, if you don't mind, you see, someone just asked me to this formal dinner and I was just wondering, if you don't mind, if I can buy a dress for that?" she asked him.

Father Tom smiled as he sat back on the couch. "Alexandria Johnson, are you asking me permission to go out on a date with a boy?"

"No, I'm asking for permission to buy a dress," she defended. "But if I was asking you permission to go, what would you say?"

"Alex, you are twenty-three years old," Father Tom said. "Officially, I only look out after you when it comes to Lite Sentry duties."

Alex nodded and started to get up when Father Tom stopped her.

"But unofficially, I will tell you this. There is no reason you cannot go. There is no point in protecting people's lives if you yourself are not able to enjoy it from time to time," Father Tom told her.

Alex gave a nervous smile as she got up. "Thank you."

"Alex." Father Tom got up to go to his desk. He shuffled through a bunch of calling cards. He wrote something on the back of the card and handed it to Alex. "Take this to Romero's on the Upper West Side. Ask for Leslie."

Alex took the card. "Thank you."

Alex left, reading the back of the card. *Leslie, take care of this special girl, Tom.* Alex could feel herself blush as she looked at Father Tom who was deep into his work.

***

Father Tom had given Anne and Alex half the day off Thursday to go out and take care of any errands they needed to take care of. They knew that was code for going shopping for Saturday night.

They arrived at the store where they both looked instantly at each other. "This is way out of our league," Anne said. "Are you sure we got the right address?"

167

Alex looked at the card. "This is Romero's."

The host at the door came to greet them. "Good afternoon, ladies, welcome to Romero's. I'm Francis, how may I help you?"

Alex looked around feeling completely out of place. She tightened her jacket to give a small sense of security. "I was told to ask for Leslie."

"Ah, you must be Ms. Johnson and that must make you Ms. McClure, or should I say soon to be Mrs. Moler."

"Anne, please." Anne shook his hands.

"Ms. Anderson is expecting you. Please come with me." Francis politely showed them the way.

"Is my service dog, okay?" Alex asked him.

"Oh, yes, we have people bring their dogs in here all time. Most of the time they fit in their purses and not as big as yours, but we'll make it work." He brought them to a room with mirrors, and multiple dresses. There was a bottle of wine and an Apollo Energy drink waiting for them. Francis served Alex and Anne their drinks as they sat down.

"Ms. Anderson will be right with you," he said. "Will there be anything else?"

Alex and Anne looked at each other. "No, thank you."

"Enjoy, ladies." Francis left the room, came back with a couple of blankets, and put them in a pile. "I hope your friend can make himself comfortable with these."

"Yes, thank you," Alex said.

Komptin walked over to the blankets and adjusted them before laying down. He instantly fell asleep.

"If you will excuse me," Francis said, leaving the room.

"What the hell is going on?" Alex said to Anne.

"I have no idea," Anne replied. Anne walked up to the look at the price tag of the dresses. Her eyes were about to come out of her head. "Alex, you can't even come close to affording these dresses."

The door opened to a sophisticated woman in a very expensive outfit. "Ms. Johnson, Ms. McClure, I'm Leslie."

"Anne, please." Anne extended her hand.

"Please, call me Alex," Alex said, shaking it politely.

"Anne, Alex, I understand you have a special date coming up?"

Alex was still very uncomfortable in her surroundings. She felt as if she was a peasant in a gown room meant for princesses. "Well, I have a formal black-tie dinner on Saturday," Alex said.

"And you have a wedding?" Leslie asked.

"Yes," Anne had a sense of caution in her voice.

"Well, Tommy asked me to take care of you two personally," she said smiling.

Now Alex was in another dimension. She had no idea what was going on. "Tommy?"

"You mean Father Tom?" Anne seemed as if she was putting it together.

"Yes, I'm here to help you with your date for Saturday and I understand that you need to still need to pick out a wedding dress?" she seemed as if she was studying them.

"Yes, but I think it's a little out of our price range," Anne had to admit.

"Don't worry about that." Leslie chuckled as she waved her hand. "Tommy asked me to take special care of you and that's what I'm going to do. It's all covered," Leslie assured her.

Both Anne and Alex chugged their drinks out of shock.

"Ermond, can you please come in here?" Leslie was spinning Alex around.

"Are you ready ma'am?" a Latino looking man asked with a tape measure around his neck.

"Yes, can you please bring me the first set of wedding dresses and the first set formal wear?"

"Of course, ma'am," he said, leaving.

"Who are you?" Alex asked her.

"I'm Leslie Anderson, I'm the owner."

"How do you know Father Tom?" Anne asked.

Leslie laughed as she now spun Anne around getting a good look at them. "Tommy was right, you two are very pretty."

"Why do you call him Tommy?" Anne took a sip of her wine.

"Tommy is my baby brother," Leslie told them. "Now let's get you ready for your special days."

***

170

Gron sat back in his chair looking at the dead girl lying in the corner. He just stared at her. She wasn't going anywhere.

"Something on your mind?" Vandor approached him with Salamor at his side.

"I just got bored with her, so I killed her." Gron looked up at his master. "I saw the Lite Sentry the other night. She killed Warcourt."

"I know this," Vandor said looking over at the dead body. He motioned for the Infiltrators to dispose of the body. They mauled the girl until there was no trace of her.

"I want you to know, the feeling for that bitch is over. I saw her, nothing, especially when she killed Warcourt." Gron's eyes flashed red. "I don't know what to do next?"

"I think it's time to begin a public relations program," Vandor said, sneering.

Gron looked at him in confusion.

***

Anne and Alex returned to Anne's apartment where Kale was in the kitchen, eating an apple, reading a magazine.

He looked up at Anne. "Get over here," he playfully said.

Anne walked up to him. "What's up?"

"I just missed you." He smiled as he kissed her. "Did you find Alex a dress?" He turned the page to the magazine.

"You could say that," Anne answered him, taking a bite of his apple.

Kale looked up. "Let's see it."

"They are tailoring and cleaning it," Alex said.

"Saturday is only the day after tomorrow," Kale said. "You think it will be done in time?"

Anne gave Alex a smile. "They are delivering her the dress here on Saturday morning."

"To the apartment?" Kale asked.

"Yep," Alex said.

"And I found a wedding dress," Anne said.

"How much is that going to cost?" Kale said, going back to his magazine.

"Not a thing," Anne told him.

"You're not getting it?"

"Oh, I'm getting it," Anne said. "Father Tom's sister is the owner of the store. We're not paying anything for those dresses."

"Father Tom?" Kale said. "You need to give him one hell of a thank you. I thought he hated you two."

Alex and Anne looked at each other. "We have to do something," Anne told Alex.

***

The next morning, Anne met Alex by her desk. Megan looked like she was in a particular bad mood. "Is he in?"

"Yes," Alex said, locking her computer.

"You sure this is what we should give him as a 'thank you'?" Anne asked.

"No doubt," Alex said.

They got up, went into Father Tom's office, and shut the door behind them.

He looked up. "Ladies, something wrong?"

Anne and Alex looked at each other and ran to Father Tom. Alex on one side and Anne on the other. They both gave him an embracing hug and kissed him on both sides of his cheeks. "Thank you," they both said.

Father Tom sat back in the chair and took in the appreciation. He smiled out of embarrassment and put his hands on the girl's arms in front of him. "You're welcome." He patted their arms as he started to get choked up. "Now, go get back to work," he playfully told them.

***

"Come on, Alex," Anne told her. "Kameron is here waiting for you."

"Anne, what the hell am I doing?" Alex said from the bathroom. "Do you think he would mind if I didn't go?"

"Get your bony butt out here," Anne yelled at her.

Kale walked into the room. "What is taking so long?"

Alex walked out to look at Anne who was holding her hands over her face. Alex was wearing a white formal dress, with a high collar, and a matching scarf. The dress emphasized her dark makeup around her eyes and black hair woven and tied in the back with a white bow.

"You look beautiful," Kale told her. He shook his head. "I'll go tell Kameron you're ready."

"Thanks, Kale." Alex smiled.

Anne snuck a picture with her phone. "You look amazing." Anne walked up to her, looking her over. "I'm sure you will have a good time."

Alex looked to Komptin. "What do you think?"

Komptin flashed his eyes in acceptance.

Alex smiled at him. "Thank you." She sighed. "Okay, let's do this." Alex walked out of Anne's bedroom down to the end of the hallway where Kameron was talking to Kale.

Kameron stopped his conversation to pay attention to Alex as she walked into the living room, "Wow, you really look beautiful," he said. He walked up to her and handed her a corsage.

"Thank you," she said as he pinned it onto the strap of her dress.

"Okay, you kids, don't be too late and remember—" Kale pointed at them. "No hanky panky."

"I'll be a perfect gentleman," Kameron assured him.

"I was talking to Alex," Kale corrected him.

Anne smacked Kale on the arm. "We'll be here, take your time."

Kameron knelt to Komptin's level. "I promise, I will protect her with my life."

Alex watch Komptin snuggle up to him and then sat down on his favorite chair. Kameron and

174

Alex took his arm to head out the door. Anne jumped up and down like an excited little girl. "Oooo."

"So, this is good-bye to Kameron," Kale said as he sat down on the couch.

Anne knew he wasn't keen on Alex going on a date with Kameron. She leaned over the couch so she could put her arms around Kale. "You know, all my friends sat me down and told me not to date you."

Kale looked at her. "Really?"

"Really."

"Are you glad that you didn't listen?" Kale tilted his head back looking at her.

Anne stood up. "Kale," Anne called to him as she started to walk towards the bedroom.

Kale hopped over the couch as Anne ran to the bedroom laughing.

***

Alex was sitting at the table with Kameron listening to the agents talk about different subjects using a bunch of acronyms. She was trying to keep up with the conversation but couldn't do it. The room was full of people in tuxedos and fancy dresses.

"Are you lost?" the girl next to her asked.

Alex nodded. "Yeah, I have no idea what they are talking about."

"Neither do they, they like to use acronyms more when they are in front of guests. It makes

175

them think they are being all important," she replied. "I'm Rebecca."

"Alexandria, but please call me Alex," she said, shaking her hand.

"Nice to meet you," Rebecca said. "Let me give you a low down to make you feel at ease a bit."

"Okay," Alex said in caution.

"You got lucky, all of us here are not like others, not like the other tables," she told her. "All the other tables use their wives to get ahead. They have their noses so far up the politicians and leadership asses that you can pick the corn off them," she warned them.

"Agreed," the other girl, said to her on the other side. "I'm Jennifer. When you start coming to these you learn to eat prior to coming. Don't ever come hungry. They are sooo dreadful to sit through if you haven't eaten."

A girl from across the table spoke up, "And they feed little, tasteless food that is so God awful expensive, you need to go up four times to get full. We usually go out to eat afterwards. You are welcome to join us," the girl said. "I'm Nadine by the way."

"Alex," she replied. "What are we having?"

Kameron whispered in her ear, "Fish, broccoli, rice, and for dessert, a fruit salad."

Alex looked to the girls to see if he was joking. They all nodded in agreement. "Yummy," Alex thought to herself.

"And then POTUS decided at the last minute that he needs to go to Florida to look at the

176

hurricane damage, and I came close to saying, 'Are you out of your damn mind?' because the VP is already heading down there!" The older men were laughing.

Kameron leaned into Alex. "It's not normal practice for the president and vice to be in the same place at the same time. It becomes a logistical and security nightmare."

"…but then the Chief of Staff comes out and says, 'Darren, the president wants to go to Florida.' And I just said, 'Yes, sir.' So, I had to coordinate VP out of there and POTUS in, then he didn't even go!"

The table laughed.

Alex looked over at Kameron. "Have you ever guarded the president?"

"Once on a motorcade, three times on the perimeter," he told her. "I prefer FLOTUS."

Alex connected the two and for some reason it just hit her why he was at the mosque the day that the cardinal died. "Why?"

"She's pretty easy going, really down to earth," Kameron said, taking a sip of his wine.

"Plus, she makes the best brownies," another person at the table said. The table laughed again.

"She makes brownies?" Alex said. "I just assumed she had staff for that."

"FLOTUS likes to personally make brownies for the new members of her detail to tell us that she is just a person just like everyone else," the older man said.

The people at the table paid attention to the man coming up to the table. "Director," one of them said.

"How are you doing? Enjoying the evening?" he asked.

"Really nice, thank you," was the consensus of the table.

"Good, Kameron is this Michelle?" he asked him to walk up to Alex.

Alex felt a bit out of place and uncomfortable with the fact that he knew that she was an alternate choice.

"Oh, excuse me. Alex, this is Director Morkin. Director, this is Alexandria Johnson."

They shook hands.

"Nice to meet you," he said, studying her. "You work at the same church the Cardinal did."

"Yes, how'd you know?" she asked him.

"I was there at the funeral when you confronted those tyrants, you would have made a good agent." He smiled. "Ever think of protecting lives for a living?"

She gave a half smirk. "It's crossed my mind from time to time."

"Well, I can get you in touch with a recruiter," the Director told her.

"Thank you," she replied to his offer. "I'll think about it."

He turned to Kameron. "Kameron, it's almost time. Just go to the side when I call your name and meet me on stage."

"Yes, of course," he said wiping his mouth.

Alex could tell he was getting a bit uncomfortable.

He turned to Alex and put his hand on top hers. "I really appreciate you coming tonight. Thank you for this." He smiled at her.

"I'm having a great time." She smiled at him putting her h and on top of his. She realized what she was doing so she quickly pulled it back.

"Can I have your attention please?" the Director said. "Thank you for coming this evening. You all know that a couple of months ago we had a vicious attack by a small group of malicious radicals. Even though the FBI eradicated this small group, unfortunately it wasn't in time before they murdered members of the clergy and six of our very own agents. Can I please get a moment of silence for those who were lost in the tragic event?"

After the moment passed, he continued, "But our story came with a small victory. One of our very own prevented an explosion at the mosque where there were children learning about their faith. His training and quick reactions prevented the death of innocent children. Special Agent Kameron Dutcher, please come up for the Jon Levits Award of Honor." The crowd cheered and clapped as he went up to accept his award.

The rest of the evening was a peaceful night. Kameron and Alex were talking about all types of different topics. The night was coming to close, and Kameron went to get their coats. He returned with them as they said good-bye to the people at their table and walked out of the banquet hall.

Alex looked up at the big purple star in the sky and smiled. Kameron tried to see what she was looking at in the sky as well. "It's a beautiful night, the perfect amount of crisp on the air."

"Yes." She turned to look at him. "I had a wonderful time."

"I did, too," he admitted to her. He turned to look around. "How about we get a cab from the other side of the park? I could go for the walk, how about you?"

Alex smiled. "That sounds nice."

The park was busy with bands playing in the park with food vendors. The smell of their food was making Alex hungry. There were children laughing and playing. Alex found herself being escorted by Kameron by wrapping her arm around his. They reached a small bridge coming over a creek. Once on top, the two of them stared at the water.

Alex could tell Kameron had something on his mind, but she didn't want to pry. Kameron reached into his pocket and stared at the medal in his hand. "You know, Alex, tonight they gave me an award for killing a sixteen-year-old girl."

Alex did a quick glance around as she had a small sense of the Dark. It was either a Demon or some Infiltrator quite far from her position. Either or, Alex was in no way prepared for a hunt. She wanted this evening to end on a good note. Alex leaned on the bridge with him looking at the medal. "You saved the lives of children," she tried to support him.

He straightened his posture to adjust his shoulder. "I tell myself every day that I look in the mirror." He grabbed her hand and gently moved her hair out of her eyes on the side of her scar. Her body automatically flinched from embarrassment of her scar.

"Alex, thanks for coming tonight," he smiled at her.

She looked at him and her stomach started to turn as she could feel herself breathing heavy. She was sure she was starting to sweat. She turned away from Kameron to prevent him, or her, from kissing because she felt that was the direction it was going. Something caught Kameron's attention as someone was coming up the bridge.

"Alexandria," a female voice came from behind her.

She closed her eyes. Normally she welcomed a visit from Celestial, but she knew what she brought with her. She was not going to live this down from the twins. She turned around to see Celestial walking on the bridge with Ariel and Devine each eating out of their own greasy brown bag.

"Celestial." Alex nodded as a bow.

Celestial smiled at her. "Nice to see you."

"You as well. Kameron this Celestial, she's my...my." Alex was trying to think of something.

Celestial filled in the gaps. "I am her Godmother."

Kameron shook her hand. "Nice to meet you. So nice to meet someone from Alex's childhood."

"Thank you." Celestial smiled as if she was studying Kameron.

Alex looked at Ariel and Devine who, ironically, had devilish smiles on their faces. "Alexandria," they both said at the same time.

"Kameron," Alex said in a worried voice and then quickly added, "This is Ariel and Devine." She paused to see what the reactions from the Guardians of the Conduit would be.

The two of them looked at each other and then stepped in front of Celestial to get a better view of Kameron.

Devine said, eyeing him up, "Déjà vu."

Ariel followed suit. "We have a sequel."

"Ariel, Devine, be nice," Celestial instructed them.

They both held up two greasy brown bags. "Cheese curd?" they both said to Kameron and Alex.

"No, thank you," Kameron said.

"Gimme," Alex said as she reached into the bag. "Oh, that's bliss." The curd seemed to melt ever so nicely in her mouth.

Kameron laughed. "Yeah, the menu really wasn't all that exciting."

They both looked at each other than back at Alex eating their cheese curds.

"Yes, our little Alex does have an interesting taste for food," Celestial stated.

"Yes, she is full of surprises." He gave Alex a little playful nudge.

Alex gave a shy smile and spoke with a mouthful of fried cheese. "Stop it."

Celestial smiled. "Oh, I think there are plenty of surprises in store for you."

Alex turned to Celestial with a look of shock on her face.

"Alexandria, do you have a second, I need to ask you something," Celestial said. "Kameron, do you mind?"

"Please." He motioned to her.

"Excuse me, Kameron," Alex said, smiling at him. Alex grabbed one more cheese curd from Ariel's bag.

"We will keep him busy," Ariel and Devine both said as they stepped up to him.

"Be courteous," Celestial warned them.

Alex walked with Celestial. "Is everything going okay? There is a sense of the Dark in the area. Are you going to be safe here?"

Celestial looked around. "I'm always near the dark. I am the Conduit, remember? I will be okay."

"So, what did you need to talk to me about?" Alex asked her, looking around.

Celestial hugged Alex as Alex sat there shocked and returned the hug. Normally, it was Alex who initiated the hugs with her. "You look so beautiful," she said. "I just wish Osiah could see you. Are you happy?"

"His date had to cancel on him. I'm just filling in for her. We're just friends," Alex informed her.

"Of course, you are, dear." She kept her arm around Alex and turned her to Kameron who was talking to Ariel and Devine. "We better go save him." Celestial and Alex walked up to the three of them.

"I'm telling you the truth," Kameron was insisting.

Ariel shook her head at him. "It just sounds …wrong."

"I'm dead serious," Kameron told them again.

"No," the two of them said at the same time in disbelief.

Devine asked cautiously, "You just dunk the French fry in the chocolate shake?"

"Trust me." Kameron smiled at them. "You will not be disappointed."

"I've come to rescue you," Alex said, wrapping her hands around Kameron's arm.

Ariel and Devine smiled at Alex as Celestial called to them.

"It was nice meeting you," Kameron told them as they left.

"You as well," both Ariel and Devine told him.

"Wow," Alex said looking at the trio as they were leaving.

"What's the matter?"

"Nothing, I've just never seen Ariel and Devine do that before," Alex admitted.

"Do what?" Kameron asked.

"Be civil." Alex looked up at him and smiled. The two of them walked down the bridge and through the park remaining interlocked with each other.

"Looks like she has a boyfriend." A member of F.O.R. member was looking on. "Boy, this is exciting," Brian, said sarcastically. "I didn't join F.O.R. to watch some little girl."

The other one stared her down. "Shocking that little thing is so tough," Saclure stated. He sat there studying her. "But I don't think she's dating him."

"Why do you say that, Saclure?" he looked at her. He turned to his overwatch partner. "What kind of name is 'Saclure' anyways?"

Saclure glared at the primate with disgust. "Shut up and do your job." Saclure watched the Sentry walk away. "She hasn't kissed him yet."

The two of them walked over to the bridge.

"Who were the three girls she was talking to?" Brian asked.

Saclure knew exactly who they were. This was an unbelievable opportunity. If he destroyed the Conduit, the Dark would put him in power, perhaps over Gron or even Vandor. "I don't know, but I'm going to find out," Saclure told him. "I will follow those three, you get the little one."

"That's not fair, I want the hot girls," the boy said.

Saclure punched him across the face as the other crashed to the ground. "I'm in charge, I get them."

"Fine," Brian said, rubbing his jaw. "But you better get some action from one of them."

185

Saclure followed the scent of the Lite and was watching the Conduit from the darkness of the alley. He heard stories of the Guardians of the Conduit, but they didn't seem like much. He followed them to a small little park that was only lit by the perimeter lights.

He watched the Conduit walk down the path towards some thicket of trees. Saclure knew that if he could get ahead of them on that path, he could pounce and his status within the Dark would be unprecedented.

Saclure stalked them as he made it to his spot where he was going to attack. He lost sight of them for a quick second. He regained his position where he saw the Conduit by herself walking. This was it, Saclure had her alone and vulnerable. He turned his head to make sure he wasn't going to be ambushed.

He was all clear; he turned his attention back to the Conduit where he was face to face with the purple haired Guardian. She grabbed him with force and threw him out in the open. He flashed his red eyes as his demon teeth showed, ready to fight.

"She's dead, you…" The purple haired one showed her skills with her bō staff, and she spun around and quickly thrusted her bō staff through Saclure. Blood dripped from his mouth as the green haired Guardian approached Saclure with the Conduit.

The Conduit just shook her head with sorrow. "I am sorry. I am truly sorry the Dark has consumed you." The Conduit approached. "It is not too late."

Saclure was still impaled with the bō staff. He screamed in anger as he swung with his demon claws to try to kill the Conduit. They were met with the green haired Guardian's Lite Sword slicing his arms off. The green-haired angel spun her sword around before beheading Saclure.

Chapter 7

Gron sat with Vandor in his new office discussing the next actions of the F.O.R. Gron knew the Sentry had located the F.O.R. position. "We need a location that we can operate but from underneath the public's eye."

"Walk with me," Vandor commanded Gron.

The two of them walked down the hall to an empty room. On the far wall was a man chained trying to break free. He had a couple of bruises and scratches but in good shape nonetheless.

"If we operate underneath the public's eye, people tend to look harder." Vandor looked outside to the moon. He stepped sideways to the man chained to the wall. The unidentified man begged to be let go but Vandor just continued his conversation with Gron.

"The Sentry takes two to four Infiltrators every time she engages with them," Gron told Vandor.

"She's either very powerful or very lucky." Vandor turned and studied the man on the wall.

"She had her opportunity," Gron mentioned.

"There are other options." Vandor turned to Gron. "It would just take a little bit more time than planned, but there is always a contingency. How many Infiltrators do we have available for infiltration?"

"Twenty-three," Gron said. "Why do you ask?"

Vandor supernaturally grabbed Gron by the neck. "What did you say?"

"Twenty-three," Gron managed to get out.

"That's it?" he yelled.

"She's killing them and my Demons," Gron said. "We need more."

"They don't grow on trees," he yelled. "We need to push certain Provisionaries," Vandor told him.

Suddenly Vandor staggered back as if he was being pulled by an unknown force. Gron immediately ran over to the man chained to the wall and pulled out his heart. He handed over the bloodied steaming heart to Vandor and he consumed it. Vandor stood up and adjusted his black coat.

"Master," Gron came to him.

"Salamor," Vandor called for his Demon Myst.

"As you command," he floated in.

"Go, come back with your findings," Vandor commanded.

He bowed as he floated out of the building through the wall.

He cleared his voice. "It's time to help the community," Vandor told Gron.

***

"How'd it go?" Kale asked Kameron as he was spotting him on the bench press.

Kameron shrugged his shoulders, "I had a good time," he said. "Come on, push it, push it. Good job." He grabbed the bar and placed it on the holder. The two of them switch positions. "I mean, she's like nobody I've met before," Kameron told him. "Every time I think I get her, she does something that completely blows my mind." Kameron lifted his set and then moved his shoulder around where he got shot. "I think I overstepped my position though."

Kale helped Kameron off the bench. "Why do you say that?"

"She's your sister, I don't know if it's appropriate," Kameron told him.

"It's fine, trust me, I know a lot of Alex's…life. More than I care to," he told him.

Kameron sat up. "There was a moment I thought we were going to kiss." He stopped to look at his reaction. "She read it, and then turned away."

Kale found himself in actual surprise. "You two didn't…ya know, make it a night?"

Kameron shook his head. "Even if I had a chance to do that, I wasn't going to, not on the first date, but she turned away before I could kiss her. So, I just walked her up to your apartment, gave her a hug, and left," Kameron told him. "I guess we'll just be friends."

Kale looked at Kameron's disappointment and tried to cheer him up, "I love my sister, we've known each other since grade school, and I will tell you this. From what I have witnessed, Alex is dedicated to her friends, and if she calls you that, then it's something to cherish."

"What about people she's dated?" he asked him.

Kale knew Alex's past with boys was always something short of questionable. He wanted to warn his friend but still protect Alex. "From what I see, if I were in your shoes, I would take Alex as a friend over anything else."

***

It was the middle of the week, and it was a long week for Alex. The clock wouldn't move as she kept on checking her phone. There was no word from Kameron, no 'had a good time', no 'thank you,' nothing. Now granted, she never texted him either, but she thought it was customary for the guy to at least contact their date three days later, today was day four. Alex pounded her keyboard. "UGH!"

"Please, I have a headache," Megan told her.

Alex got up, irritated. She couldn't sit still. She had a feeling to go out for a hunt. For some reason, she wanted to diminish an Infiltrator or Demon. She was walking back and forth and didn't know what to do. She sat back down and tried to work; she checked her phone again. Nothing. "I don't care," Alex said, throwing her phone on her desk.

Megan looked at her, "You may not care about my health, but I still have a headache."

Alex glared at her from her desk, "FYI...I wasn't talking about you; not everything is about you."

191

Megan was upset as she continued to work on whatever it was she did during the day. Alex didn't know. Anne walked into the room to get a cup of coffee. She looked over at her friend who was clearly had something on her mind. "You okay?"

"I'm fine," she sharply answered. She pounded her keyboard again. "This damn password locked me out again. It's such a piece of junk," she expressed her frustration underneath her breath.

Anne walked up to her keyboard and hit the CAPS Lock button. "There you go, sweetie," she said, rubbing her back.

"Thanks," she embarrassingly said. She checked her phone again and threw it down.

Anne smirked while drinking her coffee. "Waiting for a phone call?"

Alex shot her a dirty look. "Isn't customary for a guy to call to at least say that he had a good time, even though it was a lie?"

"Normally, unless they had an absolute miserable time," Anne pointed out.

"Thanks for that." She tossed her phone again after checking it.

"Honey, I'm pretty sure he had a good time," Anne said, smiling.

Alex annoyingly looked at Anne. "And how do you know that?"

Anne pointed to the door as Kameron was coming in with a big box on a cart.

"Kameron!" Megan said going up and hugging him.

Father Tom came out of his office as he heard the commotion from Megan's screaming. He walked out and saw Alex's fist clenched. "Good thing we're on church property," he told her, leaning on the doorway drinking a cup of coffee.

Alex closed her eyes and took a deep breath. Anne rubbed her friend's back. "Easy." Alex looked up to see her friend almost laughing at her.

After Kameron was done appeasing Megan, he walked up to Alex and Anne. He petted Komptin as he approached him. "Hey, Alex. How are you doing?"

"I'm all right, just working," she said, going back to her computer that hasn't been unlocked yet.

"Hi, Anne," he said.

"How are you doing, Kameron?" she asked him not to smile too much.

"Been busy." He took off his trench coat. He was wearing a suit underneath.

"What's with the box?" Anne said knowingly that Alex was curious but didn't have the nerve to say anything.

Kameron tapped on it. "Well," he nervously said. "I have something for Komptin."

Komptin perked his ears from lying on the floor. Alex's curiosity peaked but tried everything to act like she didn't care. "Komptin?" she asked, looking up at Kameron.

"I just wanted to thank him for trusting me on Saturday night," he smiled at Alex. He lifted the box and there was a beautiful wooden bed with a mattress. "I just thought he would like a mattress next to your desk while you work."

"Wow, that's nice," Father Tom said, getting up from the doorway. He walked up to the bed and studied it. "Did you make this?" He was rubbing his hand across the wood.

"I dabble in carpentry as a hobby, I rent a warehouse room on the west side for all my tools and everything. I use it as a stress reliever," Kameron admitted. "I'm Kameron."

"Tom," Father Tom and Kameron shook hands.

"I hope this is okay?" Kameron asked him.

"I don't have a problem with it," Father Tom said, still admiring it. "What kind of wood is that, maple?"

"Walnut," he said.

Anne nudged Alex in the back of the chair trying to wake her from her state of shock. "Alex…" she whispered.

Alex stood up to come around her desk. "Kameron, that's beautiful, thank you," Alex said trying to regain her composure.

Father Tom helped Kameron lift it up and place it on the wall next to Alex's desk. Komptin was wagging his tail as he jumped on the bed and made himself comfortable and instantly fell to sleep. Alex wanted to go over to Kameron and tell him thank you, but the two of them just looked at each other saying nothing.

Kameron finally spoke, "Well, it's the least I could do." He got a message on his phone. "I have to get work." Kameron just looked at Alex as the

194

two of them stared at each other. "Well, I gotta go." He forced a smile. "See you around."

"Bye, Kameron." Anne smiled. She continued to study Alex.

"Bye." Megan eagerly waved.

Alex just waved at him, but his back was turned before she did it. Father Tom and Anne were watching Alex as she turned around to see them. They smiled at her. "What?"

"He just finds any reason to come see me," Megan told the group.

The group looked at Megan in shock. The moment was interrupted by a special news bulletin over the television. It was announcing the Southside Baptist church exploded. Three ministers and five employees were killed where members of F.O.R. were claiming responsibility.

"Oh my God," Anne put her hand to her mouth.

"I have to make some phone calls," Father Tom said, going back into the office shutting the door. "Alex, Anne, can I see you in my office in two hours?"

"Yes, Father," Alex said, watching the news.

***

Gron sat up on the rooftop watching the church burn.

Vandor took in a deep breath of the smoky air. "Nothing like the smell of church wood burning," he told him. "Last time I got to witness this was in Mississippi." He turned to Gron. "The Lite Sentry will be out tonight. Make sure the Infiltrators lead her away from our new lair. Set up a mock one somewhere in the opposite direction. Tomorrow, we will make our debut in the city, you will be the face of F.O.R."

"What about the Lite Sentry? Won't she recognize me?" he asked.

"I want her to," Vandor said. "She'll be so focused on bringing you down, the organization, that she won't see behind the scenes of what we are actually doing."

"Am I still wanted by the law for my attack on the Moler kid?" Gron asked him.

"No, there is no record of that in any system, it has been all erased, as far as the world is concerned. Roger Somberson is an outstanding citizen that started an organization to help troubled people in becoming a model citizen by thinking of themselves first; no religion and no God," Vandor assured him. "We will grow right in front of their eyes and there is nothing they can do to stop it."

Gron flashed his eyes red. "I wish I could be there when Kale sees my face on television," he laughed.

***

Anne and Alex sat down in Father Tom's office. He was still on the phone with the Council giving them details to what they are to do. "Will do, thank you Cardinal." He hung up the phone, irritated.

196

"What's wrong?" Anne asked him.

Father Tom got up, went into his liquor cabinet, and poured himself a drink. Anne took glass that Father Tom offered. Alex declined a drink but then accepted an Apollo when offered. He sat down behind the desk. "How are you feeling, Alex?"

"A little sore, but okay," she answered him.

"Anne, do you have anything?" he asked her as he took a sip of his drink.

"There's no official evidence on a provisionary prior to infiltration because they become a Demon before anybody could study them," Anne said. "But what I got out of it, only the people have to agree to it for them to be infiltrated."

Alex felt a staleness in the air as she looked out the window. Komptin as well perked up as his eyes flashed blue staring at the window.

"What is it, Alex?" Father Tom asked.

"Someone just got infiltrated," she said. She looked over in Father's Tom direction. "Demons are stronger than Infiltrators, and they can walk among us without the average person knowing."

"Anne, go home tonight, we start again in the morning," Father Tom said.

"Alex, I'm clearing you for recon only, try not to get into an altercation. The Council wanted me to keep you in for another week. If you are not up to it, I don't want you to go out at all," Father Tom said.

"I'm good," Alex said.

"Be careful, I'm not liking this," Father Tom said as he took another sip of his drink.

Alex's walk ended up at the remains of the church. It was such a sad sight to see a beautiful old building to be destroyed by hate. There were still small amounts of smoke showing from the cold air. Alex could feel the presence of Demons in the area or infiltrators in the distance. She looked around trying not to show that she knew they were present in case a Demon was watching her. Komptin knew they were present as well as they walked around the church.

Outside the police tape and fencing, people had placed flowers and crosses on the ground in showing support for the victims of this crime. Something caught her attention. She walked up to a small wooden plaque of an upside down four. "Well, that is just in bad taste," she said, opening the card. It read, "Take ahold of the strength within to get you through this travesty, signed, The F.O.R."

"What are you doing here?" A policeman came over to Alex.

Alex just moved her eyes to see the policeman. "I'm just here looking at the support," Alex told him. She gently placed down the plaque to show she wasn't there to cause any problems, even though she wanted to smash it into many pieces.

"This is a restricted area," the policeman told her.

"I'll leave." Alex turned around and started walking away.

The policeman grabbed her arm. "Hold on, I didn't release you."

"Hey, no need to grab me," Alex said.

Komptin was starting to get upset.

The partner of the policeman came up to him. "What's going on, Paul?"

"This girl was trying to break into the church," he said, holding her arm.

"I was not!" Alex raised her voice.

Alex could have easily broken his hold and get away but then that would start another chain of events that not even the Council could get her out of. She was thrown to the ground planting her face directly into the blacktop. Komptin was getting upset as Alex saw him almost ready to do something drastic. She motioned to Komptin with her face to get out of there. He hesitated and then took off into the dark.

"Was that your dog?" he asked her.

"Yes," she told him.

"Guess we'll charge you with failure to maintain control of your animal as well." He laughed. He looked to his partner. "Call it in, we'll book her downtown." The policeman called it in as Alex was roughly put into the backseat of the police car. It might have been Alex's imagination, but it seemed as if the other policeman didn't feel comfortable with this situation.

Another cop was typing up Alex's name in the system during her processing. She was nice but Alex could tell she didn't take any lip from anyone. "Name?" the policewoman asked.

199

"Alexandria Johnson," she said. "What's going to happen next?"

"I ask you your age," the lady strongly said. "Age?"

Alex liked that response because it's probably something she would have said if the situation were reversed. "Twenty-three."

"Date of Birth?"

Alex gave her the date and answered the rest of the questions. She got placed into a small interview room. It was cold. She sat there as she waited and waited. She didn't know what time it was because they took her watch and there were no clocks in the room. Alex wanted to scratch her nose but found it difficult as she was handcuffed to the table.

A man and girl detective came into the room. They sat down and studied her. The man spoke up in a calming voice. "I'm Detective Flounder, if you don't do any fish jokes, we will get along just fine."

Alex laughed. "Well, I guess that makes you the bad cop." She looked at the female detective.

The lady smiled. "Nope, that doesn't work anymore, too many cop shows out there. I'm Detective Bashford." She un-cuffed Alex from the table. "I'm sure you won't try to escape now?" she asked. "Are you thirsty?"

"Can I get an Apollo?" Alex asked her.

"Right after you answer questions," Detective Flounder stated. "What were you doing at the church so late at night?"

"I was out for a walk and was curious about the incident I heard on the news. So, I took a look," she answered him. She felt a little relief as she was able to scratch her nose.

"The patrolman said you were trying to break in and that you were hostile, resisting arrest," the female detective said.

Alex controlled her temper and calmed herself. She didn't know how to respond so she just bit her lip.

"Talk freely," Detective Flounder told Alex. "Please."

"Look, I get it, cops nowadays have it rough. Being judged even before the truth comes out, but that's a massive pile of hot steamy bull…crap." Alex stopped herself. "I was just reading some of the cards left for the victims. Then he came up and grabbed me, threw me to ground and handcuffed me," she explained.

"What about your dog? He said that you motioned for the dog to attack him," Detective Flounder said.

"Okay, I did motion for him to get out there," Alex told them. "He's a service dog and I panicked. I didn't know how he would react to me being man-handled by someone," she admitted.

"Why is he assigned to you?" Detective Bashford asked, reading over a file.

"PTSD," Alex told her. She showed her the scar on the face and neck. "And there are more if you want to see them."

"I'm assuming it is from your attack a couple of years back." She looked over the file. "Case was

201

closed unsolved. You never saw the assailant and there were no witnesses."

Alex wasn't comfortable having to lie to them. She liked the detectives. They seemed like good people who cared for others. She didn't know what to say. She closed her eyes and took a deep breath.

Detective Flounder patted Alex's arm. "It's okay, you don't have to talk about it." He gave her a kind smile.

There was a knock on the door. "Detectives, the priest is here."

Alex could feel a sense of relief as she knew Father Tom was there to bail her out. The detectives said something to the patrol officer and then returned to Alex. He looked up at the camera and then nodded at the female detective. "I guess we are done here. You are still getting a citation for not maintaining control of your animal.

Alex nodded in agreement. "I understand."

"Come on Ms. Johnson, I'll escort you to your priest." Detective Flounders gave her an expression of friendliness.

***

Father Tom and Alex walked down the steps to the police station. "I always knew I would be bailing you out of jail, I just didn't think it would take this long," he told her, handing her an Apollo.

"Thanks," she said as she took a sip from the can.

They got to Father Tom's car as Alex looked around for Komptin. "Did Komptin make it back to the church?"

"I didn't see him, I left from home. He's probably back at the church," Father Tom said. "Did you find anything out?"

"There were Hosts nearby but I couldn't locate them, and I found a sympathy card from the F.O.R. at the scene," Alex told as she waited for him to unlock the door.

"That's just in poor taste," Father Tom said.

"That's what I said," she agreed.

"Ms. Johnson," a voice came from behind them.

Alex turned to see the Detectives Bashford and Flounders approach them. "Yes?"

"Father," he said, shaking the hands of Father Tom.

"Look, this conversation is strictly off the record, think of it as a confession," Detective Bashford wanted to clarify.

"What about Alex?" Father Tom asked her.

"If she just happens to be in the area and promises she won't say anything." Detective Flounders looked at her.

Alex nodded in agreement.

"Off the record, I want to apologize on behalf of the Washington D.C. Police Department," she told them. "There was no reason for the patrolman to do what he did."

Alex took a sip of her Apollo. "No big."

"No, it was," she replied to her.

"Father, Detective Bashford and I are in Internal Affairs," Detective Flounder stated. "Again, this is off the record, but we have been receiving intelligence that members within the police department have been involved with, let's just say certain hate-groups."

"It's really bizarre. It's like it appeared out of nowhere, and now they made their way to all ranks of the police department," Detective Bashford said.

"Why are you telling us this?" Father Tom asked.

"Frankly, the patrolman slipped up," Detective Flounder said. "Luckily, the arresting officer's partner told us what happened. You just corroborated the story."

"What's going to happen to him?" Alex asked. "I heard police don't like it when they are reported by their own."

"We can't find him," Detective Bashford told her. "It's like he just vanished"

Detective Flounder added, "We have seemed to stumble onto something that we can't explain." He continued, "We need you to be on guard, the F.O.R. don't like anything to do with a higher power."

Father Tom spoke, "They are directly influenced by a higher power, just not the one on our side."

"Be careful, will you, Father? If there is anything you guys see, give us a call. You have our numbers," Bashford insisted.

Alex and Father Tom nodded. They looked back to the detectives, and it appeared they had something else on their minds. "What is it?" Father Tom asked.

"Father, neither of us are Catholic, but there is something wrong about this case, will you, please if you don't mind, will you please give a blessing?" Detective Flounder asked.

"Of course," Father Tom said. "Bow your heads and let us pray."

During the blessing Alex opened one eye as she felt the presence of somebody she hasn't felt since the night she battled Sanah. She tried looking around without causing suspicion. The blessing was completed, and the detectives thanked Father Tom for his services. They returned to their jobs as Alex and Father Tom went into his vehicle.

Father Tom had a smile on his face of pure happiness. "How can you be smiling at a time like this?" Alex asked him.

"That right there is why I became a priest," Father Tom said. "I don't know what is in for those two, but I know God will watch over their souls."

Alex couldn't bring herself to tell Father Tom that their lives were in danger. She knew the presence of Salamor usually had death following.

***

The next day, Alex was working on her report for Father Tom. Megan was across playing some wind chime in the breeze music. Alex kept her headphones on so she could play her music and not deal with her. Her music was interrupted by a text message from Kameron.

It read, "Rough night?" and had a picture of a girl in prison clothes.

Alex texted him back, "How'd you know about that?"

Kameron replied, "Know about what?" with a winking picture following. Then it hit Alex—he probably could not divulge the source of his information. "I'm hungry, do you want to go get lunch?"

"Sounds good."

Kameron texted her the place and time.

Alex agreed as she gathered her stuff. "I'm going to lunch."

"Where are you and Anne going? I could go for some lunch." Megan was being as nosy as always.

Alex didn't know how to answer it. She didn't want to make a big deal she was going with Kameron, so she just said, "I'm going with someone else."

Alex met Kameron at a local diner. He was in his suit, so proper. They found a seat next to the window. He took off his jacket showing his service pistol as a shoulder strap. She never cared for guns, but she understood why people had them. She was just fortunate her weapons were built into her body.

"So, I heard that orange is the new black," Kameron said to her.

Alex rolled her eyes. "Stalking me?"

"Yeah, I guess that came off kind of creepy that I know that," he said, looking at the menu. He glanced around to make sure no one was listening. "We are coordinating with the FBI on these attacks since the initial one happened on the eve of a potential visit of FLOTUS," he said. "My director came across your name in last night's report."

"Too bad, here I thought you had a fetish with me," she teased. The waitress came up to take their order. "I'll have a double bacon cheeseburger with everything on it, an order of onion rings, and an Oreo milkshake."

Kameron shook his head in amazement. "And I'll have a boneless chicken pita with lettuce, tomato, cheese, and a side of ranch. I'll stick with water."

"Okay, it will be right up." She wrote down the order.

"So, minus your little insight into our criminal justice system, how was your night?"

Alex replied, "It was okay. I just stayed in my room for the rest of the night. How about yours?"

"Well, I went for a run and then came back to my apartment. My sister called me, and that's about it."

"I didn't know you had a sister," Alex said.

"Two actually," he added. "How about you?"

"Only child," Alex said.

"What do you mean? I thought Kale was your brother," he asked her as the waitress returned with their food.

Alex started eating her double cheeseburger. "Well," she said with a mouthful of food. Kameron handed her a napkin as she wiped her mouth from ketchup dripping. She went to tell them how Kale and she found out they were brother and sister.

"Oh, that makes sense now," Kameron said. "I was confused by some of the conversations of your families and got lost."

Kameron walked Alex back to the church. They stood outside the steps of the church. The wind was brisk. Alex shivered as she tightened her coat. Kameron flipped up her collar to protect her from the wind. He put his hands in his pockets as the two just looked at each other. "This was nice," Kameron said.

"It was," Alex agreed. She just looked up at him.

"I wouldn't mind doing it again," Kameron said.

"I'll be here," she said. Again, the two just stared at each other not saying a word.

"I see how it is, going to lunch without us," Kale said, walking with Anne.

"Oh, hey, what are you doing here?" Alex asked Kale as she gave him a hug.

"We had a meeting with Father Tom about details on the wedding, which looks like it'll be in April," Anne said. "And then we went to lunch to discuss the plans."

"Then we can send out the invites," Kale excitingly said.

Anne squeezed him. "Then it's locked in, I'll be on my way to becoming Mrs. Kale Moler."

Father Tom walked down the stairs. "Alex, I'm heading to lunch with a representative of the Baptist Council, I'll be back." He waved to them and left.

"All right," she said.

"I have to get going," Kale said looking at his watch.

"Yeah, me, too," Kameron told them.

Both Anne and Alex waved with their same hand and said at the same time, "Bye."

Anne turned to Alex. "So, how was lunch?" she asked, grinning.

***

John was sitting at his desk looking over the case file of the church fire. "You think they are planned or random attacks?" He looked over at Katherine, who was looking over some of the evidence in bags.

"I think they are planning it to look random," she answered him. "There's no pattern."

"They are a freedom against religion group, meaning they don't like religion, any religion," he started thinking, tapping his pen to his face. "Ah forget it," he said.

"No what are you thinking," she said.

"Something the priest said. Are there any highly known Satanic churches out there, do you think they would attack them? I mean, technically, it's a religion," he pointed out. "Those never had any threats against them or anything. The priest did hint the F.O.R. was under some dark influence."

"Good point," she said. "But let's talk about it tomorrow. My husband and kids are waiting for me to get home. We've been working so late a lot, that I promised them a pizza and game night."

"Yeah, I'm taking Nancy out tonight as well, she told me the other day that the mailman was starting to look good to her, so I figured that was my cue to spend some time with her." He laughed.

The door opened and the missing patrol officer came in holding his cap. "Detectives."

"Yes, I'm Detective Flounders, this is Detective Bashford," he said, cautiously. "We've been looking for you. What can we do for you?"

He nervously looked around. "Look, I don't know if I should come to you." He jumped when the radiator started up.

"It's okay, what's wrong?" Detective Bashford asked.

"I heard some news regarding some people in the department going to a F.O.R. meeting...tonight," he said. "They were acting really suspicious. They might think I overheard." The patrol officer then told them, "I had my earbuds in pretending I was listening to music."

"Where?" John asked.

"Here." He handed Detective Flounder a piece of paper. "I can't be seen here. I already said too much." He ran outside of the building.

John and Katherine looked at each other. "I guess we are altering our plans." Bashford grabbed his coat.

***

Alex looked in the mirror at herself. For some reason, she wanted to look good even though she was just going for a hunt. She stepped outside of the church and smelled the air. She looked down at Komptin.

"I have a feeling tonight is going to be a good night, let's go get some infiltrators."

Komptin's eyes flashed blue, and they went off into the night.

***

John and Katherine arrived at what looked like an abandoned house. They pulled up and watched it for over an hour from a darkened alley. Katherine started fidgeting as John just stared at the house.

"John, I don't like this," she said looking back.

"Why do you keep on looking back there? It's a dead-end alley and we already cleared it, there's nothing back there," he insisted.

"I know, but it feels like we're being watched," she said. "We should have brought back up."

"Who?" he asked. "We told the sergeant and he laughed at us and then threatened a reprimand if we continued down this road. The only reason we are still going is because of our supervisor. He told us to keep on going and if it came to light that cops are involved to go to him and then straight to the press." There was general fear in his voice. "Face it, we are on our own."

Some headlights pulled up to the house. "Here we go," she said. "Who is that?"

An older man stepped out of a car as he was greeted by a group of patrol officers and a couple of detectives. "Is that Lt. Lanthes from Narcotics?"

"I can't tell who that older guy is," Nancy said. "What are they pointing at?"

"I don't know," John said. "Who is that?" He tried adjusting the binoculars.

"Who?"

"Look at the top window of the building, left hand side." John grabbed his binoculars. "It looks like a man with a white face and a black hat. I can't tell who it is." He adjusted the binoculars, and the man was gone.

"John, look," Katherine said. "It's that patrolman that came into our office." She looked hard again, "Son of a bitch, he's chained up and gagged." She pulled out her pistol.

John pulled out his pistol. "We wait until they go in, if we go now, we certainly will get shot and along with the patrolman."

"What do you want to do?" she asked him.

***

Alex caught a trail of a Demon that led her to a neighborhood where she heard was a high crime rate. There were people still living there, it wasn't rundown, but Alex knew she wasn't in a good neighborhood. She continued to walk down the alley to find out where the Demon was hiding. Her

212

only fear was that it was hiding in a house and putting a family in jeopardy.

Komptin was picking up the scent as they walked down the alley. Alex could feel the presence of Infiltrators as well. They carefully walked down between the houses. There were a couple of broken door cars in the alley but nothing out of the ordinary.

Two Infiltrators jumped across the alley and took off into the dark. A Demon stopped in the middle of the alley and looked to Alex. He flashed his eyes and took off down the alley away from the Infiltrators.

"Damn it, I hate it when they split up. Go get the black beasts, I'll go get our friend down the alley."

Excitement in Komptin was present when he flashed his eyes and took off after the Infiltrators. Alex lit her fists and headed down the alley.

***

Katherine and John waited as the streets were clear of the people who were attending the F.O.R. meeting. "Are you sure you want to do this?" she asked her partner.

"Want to? No. Going to?" He checked his ammunition and went in the back to put his vest on. Nancy joined him checking her ammo and the rest of her gear. They nodded to each other and were about to go into the house when people started exiting the building and laughing. John and Nancy hid in the shadows of the alley.

"What are they doing?" Katherine was watching them.

"I don't care as long as they are leaving," John said. "I don't see the patrolman."

"You think they killed him?"

"Only one way to find out." They waited for twenty minutes to see any activity before heading into the building.

***

Alex caught sense of the Demon into a worn-down house. She entered the house where it was for sale and empty.

"Why can't these guys stay away from the movie clichés?" Alex said to herself.

She opened the door into the house and walked into the house. There was a set of footprints leading stairs.

She thought twice about going up, but she convinced herself otherwise. The stairs were creaking on every step, so she knew if someone was up there, they knew she was coming. She reached the top of the stairs where the Demon lunged at her as they tumbled down the stairs together.

She prevented his massive Demon claws from any damage onto her. She picked up the demon and swung him through the wall into the living room.

The Demon hissed as he crouched like an animal on all fours. It attacked Alex when she

214

followed him into the living room. It punched her a couple of times in the face before Alex picked a sharp wooden piece from the banister and stabbed it in the eye. It staggered back as Alex regained her momentum as she went onto the attack. They fell through the floor and went into the basement.

***

Katherine tapped John on the shoulder showing him that the basement door was open. She signaled to him to clear it first. He agreed as they headed down some stairs. They walked into a darkened musty basement. The smell of death filled the room. They heard some noise on the other side of the room and headed in that direction.

***

"Oh, did that suck," Alex said, getting up from the floor. She had pieces of wood and dust all over herself. She looked to see the Demon unable to move from being impaled with boards from the fall. Alex got up and looked at it. She formed a spear and jammed it into the neck of the Demon as it dissipated into the ground.

***

Katherine turned the corner with John covering her to shine a flashlight. "Oh my God," she said. "John you are not going to believe this." She put the light on the patrol officer beaten and chained against the wall. They quickly looked around before running to the patrol officer to try to get the chains off. "I can't get them off."

"I'll go get the bolt cutters from the vehicle," John said. He turned around to see they were now surrounded by a bunch of glowing red eyes. John drew his weapon. "Katherine."

Katherine turned around pointing her weapon at the group as the lights came on. They were surrounded by members of F.O.R., some black looking beasts with large fangs, and several detectives and patrol officers. The older gentleman they saw earlier came through them to look at them. The black beasts growled.

"Katherine," John said. "This is not good." John made the sign of the crucifix and prayed that God would take care of his wife.

"John, it's been a privilege," Katherine said. She quickly prayed for her family.

The old man nodded as the black beasts attacked them, screaming into the night.

***

Alex turned to the sound of Komptin coming into the house. He met her downstairs and he looked at her. "Get 'em?" she asked him.

He flashed his eyes.

"Good. I call that a successful night. Let's go home." She scratched the massive gargoyle behind the ears.

The next morning, Alex was in a real good mood. She had a successful hunt; two Infiltrators and a Demon were off this planet. She picked up her phone and texted Kameron to see if he wanted to go to lunch. He immediately answered with a thumb's up. She smiled at the phone and went into the office where Megan was already at work.

"Good morning, Megan," Alex cheerfully said.

"What are you in such a good mood for?" Megan asked with a hint of annoyance.

"I just had a good night." Alex was whistling to the sound of Megan's flute music. "That's all just a good night."

All morning was going smooth and great. She even got her report to Father Tom in time talking about her successful hunt. Anne had been working hard downstairs and Alex swung by a couple of times to bring her some coffee. She just came back from telling Anne that she will bring her back lunch when she goes with Kameron. Anne was appreciative because she couldn't leave. She said she was waiting for something from the Russian Orthodox Sanction.

She sat down at her desk waiting for Kameron to arrive when Father Tom came out of the office. "Hey, look at this." He changed the television channel to breaking news.

"Three police officers were found brutally attacked by what looked like claw marks. Their bodies have been ripped to shreds. The bodies have been identified as Detectives John Flounders and Katherine Bashford along with Patrolman Dan

217

Costes, we now go live to our on-ground correspondence."

Father Tom turned off the television and put his head down in a prayer. He sighed before he turned around to Alex who had her eyes closed by the shocking news.

Father Tom walked up behind Alex and put his hands on her shoulders, as he whispered, "Not your fault." He patted her on the shoulders.

"Kameron!" Megan said, running up and hugging him. "What are you doing here?"

"I'm here to take Alex to lunch," he said looking at Alex. "Are you okay?"

Alex wiped a tear from her eye before it dropped. "Yeah, come on let's go. Father, is that okay?"

"Take your time," he said. "Nice to see you again, Kameron."

"You, too, Father," Kameron, acknowledged him.

Alex didn't say much during lunch. Kameron bless his heart, didn't pry. He just ate his food as Alex played with hers. They were sitting in the parking lot and Alex just stared out the window. "Alex," Kameron said. She turned to look at him. "Alex, if you want to talk about it—"

She shook her head no. "I can't."

Kameron got out of the car and opened the door for Alex.

She got out of the car and Komptin followed.

"If you want to talk, I'm here anytime."

218

She looked down at her feet, she looked up at him with tears running down her face.

He came up to her and hugged her as she broke down in his arms. "It's okay, whatever it is, it's okay." He stroked her hair.

She wiped the tears from her face and realized she left snot on his coat. Alex gave a mixture of tears and laughter as she tried to wipe it and was just actually making it worse. "Sorry."

Alex looked up at him, as he was reassuring, "It's okay."

She kissed him on his cheek. "Thank you for lunch." She shyly smiled. "I'll talk to you later."

Alex walked into the office to see Father Tom watching the news. "What happened now?"

He looked to see if Megan was still out to lunch before he answered. "The F.O.R. have donated $200,000 to each of the victims of the Baptist Church fire and they claimed that a radical group have been using their name in actions they don't condone," Father Tom said. He threw the remote on the chair. "Our job just got a lot harder." He walked into the office.

***

It was the holiday season. Anne sat in her office overlooking some of the reports from the Russian Sanction. She was digging through files and came across some writings of the dark slender spirit. She could have sworn she caught that reference before

219

from one of the other Sanctions, but she couldn't remember which one.

She looked up to see Alex staring at her, she screamed and jumped. "You scared the daylights out of me." She sat back in the chair. Alex handed her some lunch. "Thank you."

"No problem," Alex said, sitting down.

"How was lunch?" Anne smiled at her.

"It was good," Alex said, looking through one of Anne's piles of paperwork.

"You two have been spending a lot of time together?" Anne observed.

Alex peered over the paperwork. "Only lunch a couple of times a week." She went back to reading the paperwork.

Anne reached over her desk and grabbed the paperwork. "Gimme." She put it back in the correct pile. "Alex, what are you doing?"

Alex looked around. "Sitting here."

"We need to have a talk about you and Kameron," Anne was looking at what Alex had brought her.

"We're just friends," Alex swiftly stated.

Anne sat back in her chair and studied Alex. "Just friends?"

"Ah, yeah," Alex sat back in her chair. She bent forward a bit so she could put her hair behind the chair.

Anne tapped her coffee cup with her engagement ring, looking at Alex. "Okay, so you don't mind if I set him up with my indoor cycling instructor?"

220

"Jody?" Alex had a small sense of relief. "I don't have a problem with that."

"No, Samantha," Anne corrected her.

"Samantha." Alex tried remembering who she was. "Wait, is that the one that's on all those billboards for the gym?"

"That's her," Anne said, getting back to her paperwork. Anne peered above her glasses to see Alex's reactions. "Any issues with that?"

Alex got up from the chair and gazed out the window. She didn't understand why Anne would do that to Kameron. They wouldn't be right together. "Why would I have any issues with that?" She turned to Anne. "They would be no good together. She's so flakey. Why would you do that?"

"Huh, I knew it." Anne pointed to her. "You would have a problem with it."

Alex tightened her lip out of anger and embarrassment. "Anne." She turned to her friend. "Anne." She looked around. "…you," She was trying to find words. "You have a messy desk." She stormed out of the office.

Anne just sat back and laughed.

***

Alex knocked on Anne's door and Kale answered. Kale just shook his head as he laughed. "What?" she asked him.

"You're killing me," he said as he invited her in.

221

Komptin jumped on his favorite chair to nestle into a deep sleep.

"Why?" Alex was staring at him out of confusion. "I just want some food."

"Well, we were just on our way to get some dinner. Do you want to come?" Kale asked her.

"Sure," Alex said. She tightened her coat. "I could eat."

Anne came out putting her coat on. "Hey, sweetie, what are you doing here?" she asked her. "Are you coming to dinner with us?"

"I just invited her," Kale said, going to get the car.

"Really?" Anne smirked. "Okay. You better call and tell them there will be an extra person."

"Okay, I will when I go get the car," Kale said, grabbing the keys. "Come on, Komptin, let's go." Komptin jumped off the chair and followed Kale to the car.

Anne came up to Alex and fluffed her hair. "Why are you doing that?"

"No reason," Anne made sure the door was locked. "Let's go."

"You're such a dork," Alex told her.

Kale pulled into an apartment complex and shut the car off. Anne and Kale started getting out of the car.

"What are we doing here?" Alex had a sudden rush of worry.

"Going to dinner," Kale told her.

"Whose apartment are we going to?" Alex asked the question, even though she knew the answer.

"Kameron's." Anne got out of the car.

Alex looked in the mirror quickly. She was in her black hiking boots that were hidden with her black pants. The black leather jacket was hiding her leather vest that was over a dark maroon long sleeve shirt. The black leather collar was still covering her scar on her neck. She got out of the car and walked past Anne, "I hate you." Anne just laughed as she rubbed her friend's back as she walked by.

Kale came up to the front of the car and put his arm around Anne as he watched Alex go up to the apartment door all by herself. Even Komptin was staying with Anne and Kale as if he were enjoying the show as well.

She turned to look at them staring at her. "What? Are you coming or not?"

Kale spoke up, pointing behind himself, "It's that one."

Alex took a deep breath and tightened her coat. She flipped up her coat collar and calmly walked down the sidewalk, passed Anne and Kale. "Not a damn word." She walked to the building across the parking lot.

They knocked on Kameron's door to the apartment. Kameron opened the door and invited them. He had a nice apartment, which he kept clean. "Welcome. I'm glad you could join us, Alex."

"Yes, well I would have brought something, but I thought we were going to a restaurant," she commented, hitting Kale in the arm.

"Oh, don't worry about that, I'm afraid I don't have any Apollo though," he told her.

"Got you covered," Kale said, holding up a bag. "You'll learn; always keep a pack of it in the trunk of your car for such an emergency."

"Why do I have a feeling that I'm a butt of your jokes tonight?" she asked the group.

Kameron smiled as he squeezed her shoulders. "Come on, I almost got dinner ready."

Dinner went smoothly and Alex was having a good time laughing with her friends. They decided to play some cribbage during dessert. The teams were boys against the girls and girls were losing.

"What do you have Alex?" Anne asked her.

"Fifteen for two," she said. Alex picked up the discard pile and looked at them.

"Please tell me we have some points," Anne begged.

Alex laid the cards down. "Nothing."

"I do believe if we get more than 6 points on this next hand, that you would be double skunked," Kale pointed out to Anne. "You see that our pegs are up here, and yours are all the way down here."

"Quiet," Anne teased back.

"So, what're your guy's plans for Christmas?" Kameron asked, taking a sip of his drink.

Kale answered, "Anne and I are going to Hawaii with my mom and her parents, but I think it's going to be planning a wedding instead of scuba diving vacation." He turned to Anne. "But in four months, I will marry the girl of my dreams." He kissed on the side of the head. "By the way, fifteen for two."

Anne playfully shoved him off her. "How about you, Kameron?"

"I'm going to my parent's house in upstate New York," he said. "Our family always gets together and spends it at my parent's house."

Alex laid down her card as she sighed. "Three." She looked over at Kameron who was laying down his card smirking. "Pair for two."

He moved the peg. Two more points, Kameron, and Kale would win.

"What are you doing, Alex?"

"My parents are going on vacation in the Bahamas this Christmas, so I'll just spend it at home," Alex said. She was waiting for Anne to put her card down.

Anne was studying Kale. He confidentially pulled at the card out of hand and tapped on the table, teasing Anne that he was going to play that next card no matter what she chose to play. She lifted up a card but then put it back in the pile. She picked up another card and played the five of clubs. "Twenty-six." She looked at him smartly.

Kale dropped the card he was teasing Anne. "Pair for two, last card, plus thirty-one… Double … skunked."

"What?!" Anne said. "We are not playing this in Hawaii." She sat back and took a sip of her wine.

Kameron looked over at Alex. "Don't you stay in a room at the church? You shouldn't be alone for Christmas."

Alex nodded. "But there will be midnight mass, so I won't be alone."

"Why don't you come to my parent's house for Christmas?" he offered as he was shuffling the cards.

Kale and Anne looked at each other waiting for Alex to answer.

"No, I can't. I don't want to be a burden," Alex told him. That trip would be uncomfortable. They weren't dating, they just barely started to hang out.

"Please, I wouldn't be able to enjoy my holiday if I knew you were here alone," Kameron insisted.

"I don't know," Alex debated to herself. "I should really work those nights and what about Komptin?"

"I'm pretty sure Father Tom will give you the time off," Anne interjected.

He grabbed his phone that was near him on the table to message someone. "My mom just said you are more than welcome to come." He showed her the text message.

A sudden rush of fear overpowered her. Alex was trying to think of an excuse out of it. "I don't know."

"Tell you what, we'll make a bet. You beat Kale and I in the next round and I won't ask you again, but if we win, you're going?" he challenged Alex.

"Done, you guys can't win three in a row," Alex said as she dealt the cards. A sudden sense of relief came to her, as she knew there was no way they could win again.

Kameron laid down the first card. "Four."

Anne shook her head. "Alex, just to let you know, this is not on purpose." Anne laid down the six of clubs.

"Five, that's fifteen for two and a run for three more," Kale slammed his cards down.

Chapter 8

"I'll meet you by the luggage rack," Alex told Kameron as they departed the plane. "I have to go to the bathroom and then claim Komptin. I'm pretty sure he's not going to be too happy."

Kameron pointed towards the end of the hall. "Cargo claim is down the hall; there's a bathroom on your way." He looked around the airport. "I'll get our luggage."

Alex walked down the hallway of the small airport. There were little kid drawings hanging on the wall. They were so sweet and innocent. There was a fear that one would have of a child's interpretation of an infiltrator. They shouldn't be in this area; there was no reason for it. Plus, she was under enough stress. Inside the bathroom, she found herself staring at herself in the mirror. Her hair was tied back, showing her scar on the side of her face. For some reason, she was becoming self-conscious of everything she was doing, and she didn't like it.

After she went to the bathroom, she located the cargo pick up for her dog. "Good afternoon, I'm here to pick up my dog." She reached into her bag and pulled out Komptin's leash. She knew he was not going to be happy with her when he saw her.

"Do you have your ticket?" the big hairy man behind the counter asked. He was a welcoming sight on this stressful trip for some reason. The smile he gave was loving and gentle.

Alex showed him the ticket her name on it.

228

"Alex Johnson?"

"It's the German Shepherd." Alex showed him her ID. Alex sat there and waited, noticing that people were staring at her direction. She knew she clearly stood out in the airport. Her long braids were hanging down against her pale skin. She saw airport security point over to her direction. She was starting to get uncomfortable.

"What's your destination?" The big man behind the counter asked with his teddy bear smile.

"I don't know," Alex told him as she read her ticket.

Two officers were talking to each other as Alex saw Komptin come in the dog kennel. Alex got out her leash and whispered to him, "I'm sorry about this but I have to leash you." Alex opened the kennel to clip on the leash.

"Miss, you can't let that dog out," the guard told her as they approached.

She reached into her pocket and lifted the papers for the guard to read.

He was reading them as Komptin came out of the kennel. His back scraping the top of the roof.

"Just keep him leashed" he coldly told her. His demeanor wasn't so inviting.

Komptin gave a massive deep bark which startled everyone in the room.

"Control your dog," he commanded, as he walked away.

She turned to grab Komptin. She signed the paper. "I'll be back the day after Christmas. I have a reservation to store the kennel here."

"We'll take care of it, dear," the man behind the counter said. He looked over at the security guard, "Don't let that Neanderthal bother you. He doesn't like anyone who he thinks is different. Some people just don't get it."

Alex smiled at the big hairy guy. "Thank you." Alex could tell he must have felt his share of outcasting in his life. His fingernails were polished and had multiple earrings. He wore a scarf on his neck.

"So, you have no idea where you are headed, do you?" he asked as he was giving her a loving smile.

"I really don't know." More fear came from her voice than she wanted to. "I'm going with a friend to his house for Christmas. I'm actually kind of nervous about it."

"Why?" he asked her, stamping some papers, eyeing her.

Alex felt secure in talking to him for some reason. There was just a sense of a caring protection from him. "I don't know," she dropped her guard a bit. "It's just...weird."

The man just grinned at her. "It will be okay, I promise," he told her.

Kameron came down by Alex. "What's taking so long? Everything okay?"

"Yes, I'm just talking to my new friend here," Alex turned to the man. "Thank you."

Kameron's welcoming expression was comforting, "Okay, well the car is ready. They are warming it up for us." Kameron looked over at the man. "Is there anything we need to do, sir?"

The man smiled at him. "Just do me a favor and take care of my girl here."

"My pleasure. Merry Christmas, sir," Kameron told him.

"Merry Christmas," the man told him. "And you have a Merry Christmas, Alexandria." He gave her a loving smile. "You will enjoy your holiday."

"Merry Christmas to you as well." She looked down at Komptin who had one front paw bent and the other forward with his head down. "Come on, boy."

Kameron sat in the driver's seat, trying to get comfortable. Alex could see his shoulder was hurting him from not moving that much on the plane.

"You okay?" she asked him.

"I'm fine, just a bit sore from the plane ride. I never really was much of a flyer," he admitted. He looked back at the massive dog making himself comfortable. "Comfy, boy?"

Komptin found his sweet spot as he let Kameron pet him.

He smiled at Komptin before turning to catch Alex grinning at him from her seat. "What?"

"Nothing," she said. She had always thought Kameron was nice and polite because that is what he thought he should do, almost in the realm of fakeness about it. But now, she was starting to think he truly was sincere in his actions. "How far is it to your parent's house?"

"Just under two hours," he replied, adjusting his mirrors. "Are you hungry?"

"Not really, just a little thirsty."

"Okay, there's a small little mercantile down the road outside of town. We used to go there after football games," he said. "In the meantime, I know it's a little outside your norm, but I have this new drink you should try."

Alex's interests piqued "Really, what is it?"

"Water." He smiled at her as he gave her a bottle.

She grabbed the water. "Ass." She playfully smiled. She looked back at Komptin who was already sleeping in the back seat. "I guess he's ready."

Kameron just chuckled as he went out of the rental parking lot. Alex couldn't believe how peaceful the drive was going to his house. The sun was peering through the trees. Even though the massive pines were blocking some of the rays, it still managed to get through in between and sparkle up the snow. She closed her eyes to feel for Infiltrators or Hosts, but she couldn't feel any of the Dark around her. She just got so used to it in the city that she forgot what an absence of the evil felt like.

She liked it. Even though she couldn't sleep, she kept her eyes closed to take in the peacefulness.

Alex lost track of time before she started thinking of the night Kameron took her to the awards dinner. It truly was a nice evening. She had never gotten dolled up like that before. The dinner wasn't the best but the people who Kameron worked with were really nice for what she thought were the stereotypical government employee. Maybe it was their line of work, but they were really reserved. Even the director was nice to her. In fact, he was really nice to her. He must have had an old man crush on her because he really couldn't keep his eyes away from the table.

"Do you think the F.O.R. is infiltrating government agencies?" Alex caught herself saying.

"I thought you were sleeping," Kameron adjusted his body to get comfortable.

Alex shook her head no. "No, just a racing mind."

"Weird question to come up with," Kameron said. "I think they are gaining momentum, but they are a young organization; hopefully just a fad." He looked at Alex who was still looking outside the window. "Why do you ask?"

"I was just thinking," Alex was staring out the window. "It's so peace—"

"Damn it!" Kameron yelled as he slammed on the brakes.

Alex hit her head on the dashboard as Komptin went flying onto the floor of the backseat. Alex checked to see if he was okay, which was mute because he was pretty much indestructible, well, by human terms. She knew she hit her head, but it didn't hurt.

She looked to see what had happened and she saw a bunch of deer run across the road. "Oh, aren't they pretty." Alex looked to Kameron who was a bit white knuckled with his grip on the steering wheel. "Hey, are you okay?"

He didn't answer her. He just was breathing fast but she could tell he was trying to slow it down.

"Hey, Kameron, are you okay?" She placed her hand on his while on top of the steering wheel. She said in a soft soothing voice, "It's okay."

Kameron regained control of his breathing. He closed his eyes and then slowly opened them. "Yeah, I'm fine. Are you okay?" He turned to her. "I saw you hit your head."

"I'm fine," Alex said, studying Kameron. She noticed the color in his face started to return to normal.

"Let me check your head." He lifted his hand and moved some of her hair away from her eyes. She quickly jerked back, afraid of showing her scar on the side of her face.

"It's okay, I just want to make sure you don't have a concussion," he said, looking into her big brown eyes.

She looked into his eyes to show she was okay. She kind of got an upset stomach as if she was on a dangerous hunt and she was anticipating the vicious attack.

Kameron smiled at her. "Looks good to me."

Alex didn't really know how to take that. Did he just compliment her or just say she didn't have a concussion? All she could say was, "My mom always said I was hard-headed."

Kameron looked back at Komptin who was laying back down on the backseat. "You okay, boy?" Kameron patted his head and Komptin leaned into the scratch behind his ears. Kameron put the car back in gear. "Well, the mercantile is just up the road a bit. My mom texted me and said she'll have dinner ready for us when we get there."

Alex could feel her stomach start to feel queasier. "Nice, I'm hungry."

"Good, you'll love Mom's cooking," he said.

They pulled into the parking lot of a small little market. She got out of the car as Komptin sat up in the backseat. She put her finger up telling him to stay. Komptin acknowledged by laying back down on the chair.

"I can't believe how well you have him trained. I've never seen a dog respond to someone as well as he does to you," he noticed.

"I'm blessed to have him," Alex said.

"You can take him out. Dogs come in here all the time." Kameron opened the door to the car.

Komptin jumped out and ran to Alex's side. He sat down waiting to see what they were going to do next.

Kameron just shook his head. "Wow."

"Now he's just showing off," Alex told him as she roughed Komptin up a bit. Alex walked into the mercantile and it felt as if she went back in time to the mid-1800s. She looked around to see goods in barrels, food in sealed mason jars, and the workers in old clothes. Surprisingly, it was rather clean, and what she could see the kitchen was up to date.

"I have to use the bathroom. If you need to go it's upstairs and to the right of the little flower cart," Kameron said as he scratched Komptin behind the ears. He lightly touched Alex's arm and smiled as

235

he walked upstairs looking at the wall of all the decorations.

Alex could tell he knew the area and was probably remembering some things from his childhood. She decided to take a look at the refrigerator section in hopes that they had an energy drink of some sorts. Nope, nothing.

Alex caught herself looking at some homemade strawberry preserves. She was examining the contents in the jar. She could see it was homemade and not in a factory. Alex's attention was quickly diverted to a woman screaming at her kid.

"Jack and Sarah, get back here!"

Alex saw two kids running up to her. Alex could tell that the boy was no more than three years old, and the girl was about seven. They stopped in their tracks as they looked at Komptin. "Can I pet your dog?" the girl asked.

Alex bent down to her knee. "Of course, you can." She put her hand on Komptin's back. Komptin laid down so the children could pet him.

"He's so big," the little girl stated. "And soft."

"His name is Komptin," Alex told her. She watched the little girl cautiously put her hand out to pet the massive creature. "What's your name?"

"I'm Sarah, this is my brother Jack," she said.

Alex looked at Jack who was staring at her with a smile. Alex smiled back at him. "Well, I'm Alex."

A woman came up to Alex, more than likely their mother. "I am so sorry about this."

Alex smiled and mouthed to the mother, "It's fine."

The little girl grabbed a piece of Alex's black woven hair extension. "You have weird hair."

"Sarah!" the lady scolded her.

Alex laughed. "It's okay."

"Are you a witch? Your skin is so white."

Alex could see the mother's mouth just dropped as if she didn't know what to say. "I'm so sorry," she apologized.

"She's not white, Momma, she's blue," the little boy said pointing at her.

"Jack," the lady said, pushing her son's hand down.

Alex looked to the boy as he continued to stare at her. "It's okay, really." She turned to the girl. "You know my best friend in high school was named Sarah. She was so beautiful, just like you."

"Where's your friend now?" she said, turning back her attention to Komptin.

Alex tightened her lip at the remembrance of her friend. "She died when I was in high school."

"Is she in Heaven?" Sarah asked her.

"Yes, she is," Alex said.

"My Gamma is in Heaven," she informed Alex.

"I'm sure she is looking down at you smiling," Alex told her.

"Come on, Jack and Sarah," the lady said. "Say 'thank you' to the nice lady."

"Thank you," the little girl said.

The mom picked up the little boy and walked away. The little boy turned his head to look at Alex as he waved good-bye. She waved to him, and he buried his head into his mom's shoulders in embarrassment. Alex looked down at her hands to make sure she wasn't glowing, but if she was, she would have thought others would have seen it.

She got up and turned around, jumping at the sight of Kameron sitting down watching her. "You scared me."

"Sorry, I was just watching," Kameron said as he got up.

"Stalker," she said to him as he greeted him. "Shall we grab a desert for your family for dinner tonight?"

"They have great pies in the back, and we'll grab some whiskey for my dad," Kameron said. "That will get you on his good side."

"Should I be worried?"

"No, he can just be a bit..." Kameron was searching for his words. "Hard to take for people who don't know him."

"Great, can't wait," Alex said as she walked towards the liquor portion of the store.

They were driving down a dark road. It must have been cloudy out because Alex couldn't see any of the stars except for the faint glow of the purple star she was fortunate to see. She could feel her stomach start getting a bit uneasy.

"You okay?" Kameron asked her.

"Yeah, why?" Alex asked him, staring out the window.

"You're shifting around a lot," he noticed.

"Just looking around the country," she said. "Reminds me a bit of home."

"Never really thought of you as a country girl. I would really like to see the town where Alex grew up," Kameron said.

"What do you think it's like?"

"Not one clue," Kameron said. "Every time I think I got you down, it's completely wrong."

"Is that a bad thing?"

"Nope," Kameron said. He pointed to a long driveway. "Here we are." He pulled into the driveway where it led up to a massive house.

Alex opened the car door and looked around. She was reminded of what a typical American farm would look like. There was a tire swing on a tree in the yard and a barn off in the distance. The smell of a crisp country air filled her lungs,

"What do you think?"

"Looks... yeah, nothing like what I would expect," Alex commented as she opened the car door to let Komptin out.

He hopped out and looked around as well. Alex could see he was securing the area as he did every time they entered a new area. He couldn't help it; it was second nature to him. She understood that because she was doing the same.

"Come on," Kameron said. "Dinner should be getting done soon."

They stepped onto the porch and Alex could hear a bunch of people talking and laughing. They walked into the kitchen from what was obviously a mud room before coming into the house. Alex removed her shoes and followed Kameron into the house.

"Kameron!" A woman came running up to him hugging as only a mother could do. "Oh, honey, are you doing okay?" she asked, rubbing the spot where he was shot.

"I'm fine, Mom. It's good to see you," he said.

She hugged him again. Kameron towered over his mother.

She peered over to Alex who was standing in the doorway. "You must be Alex."

Alex had never met anyone's parents before. She really didn't know what to do. "Hello, Mrs. Dutcher." She put her hand to shake her hand.

"Oh, please call me, Mary," she said, giving her a welcoming hug. Alex returned the hug in kind. "Are you hungry?"

"I could eat," Kameron said. "We really haven't eaten."

Alex agreed. "I'm pretty hungry."

"Excellent," she said rubbing Kameron's arm. "We're all in the dining room."

"Who's all here?" Kameron asked.

"Your sisters and the family," Mary said.

"So, pretty much everyone," Kameron said.

"Yes," Mary answered her son. "The whole family is here for the holidays. What more could a mother ask for?" Mary looked around. "Where's your dog, dear?"

Alex replied, "He's outside. I didn't know what to do with him."

"Oh, bring him in, the kids are looking forward to seeing him," Mary said. "They made him a bed by the fireplace."

She turned around and opened the door to Komptin covered in snow. "Sorry about that."

He shook it off and joined Alex by her side.

Mary's eyes were fixated on Komptin. "Wow, you weren't kidding, Kameron, he is big."

"If he is too much, I can find him a place outside," Alex insisted.

"Oh, mish mash, dear. He's more than welcome." Mary offered her home to them both. "Come on, everyone is excited to meet you."

They walked into the dining room and all eyes were on Alex. She looked around as if not knowing what to do. A girl, who Alex assumed was one of Kameron's sisters, hit a man next to her as he said something in her ear.

Kameron made his way around the table introducing Alex to the family giving hugs to everyone. They were all nice, but Alex was on her guard for some reason.

"And I didn't forget about you, Dad, we got you some Merchant Whiskey." Kameron handed him the bottle. Kameron sighed before saying, "Dad, this is Alex."

His dad got up. He was a big man who looked like he was not afraid of the work. Alex could tell he had a rough life spending much time in the weather. He looked her up and down. "You're a tiny little thing," he said.

Alex put her hand out to shake it. There was fear that her hand was sweating from nerves. What if her hands started glowing for no reason? What if she crushed his hand?

He grabbed it. "Nice to meet you. Where did you go to college?"

"Saint Michaels, a private college," Alex quickly replied. She just wanted this to end.

He instantly came back with, "What do you do for work?"

She tried to match his speed. "I'm an Administrative Assistant."

"For what company?"

"A Catholic Church."

"Name?"

"St. Thomas Aquinas."

"Your boss's name?"

"Currently, I report to Father Tom Altomer."

"How long have you been there?"

"Since college."

Mary interrupted, "Harold, she's our guest."

"So was the last one," he came back with.

Alex didn't miss the message in his comment. She knew there was something on Harold's mind.

"Dad," Kameron quietly said out of embarrassment. He turned to Alex. "Alex, I'm sorry."

"It's okay," Alex said. She finished shaking his hand.

"Secretary for a Catholic Church, huh?" Harold was studying her.

"Administrative Assistant. The secretary is a different position," she corrected him. "So, what do you do?"

"Farmer in summer, snowplow driver in winter."

Alex squinted her eyes. For what seemed like an eternity, she debated if she was counteract with an integration of her own. Would he take offense? This could ruin the whole trip. Alex cracked her neck, here we go. "How long?"

"30 years."

"County, state, or city?"

"County."

"Who's your boss?"

"In the summer? Me. The winter? Mr. Ron Stirman."

"What do you grow?"

"Corn."

"Field or sweet?"

"Field." Harold pulled her closer to him. "Nice." He winked at her while giving her a small smile. "Hell, of a grip," he said, shaking his hand as he sat back down. "Let's eat."

"I was hoping to see if Michelle was still awake?" Kameron asked.

"I was just about to go get her," Mary said. "We didn't tell her you were coming in tonight."

"I'll go get her," Kameron offered.

"That would be great. Thanks, honey."

Kameron turned to Alex. "Come on, I can't wait for you to meet her."

They walked up the stairs to a room with angels plastered on the front of the bedroom. Kameron knocked on the door. "I'll be down in a second."

"Ah, there's no such thing as a second with you," Kameron said through the door.

"KAMERON!" A young girl sounded excited with a cough. "Get your ass in here."

The door opened to a young girl who was in her mid-teens. She was lying in bed with a bandana on her head, a laptop beside her on the bed. Alex saw a bowl next to her as well. She uncovered herself to get up, but Kameron beat her to the side of the bed. She hugged Kameron tight.

"How are you doing, little sis?"

"Oh my God, I thought you were coming tomorrow," she said, wiping away a tear. "How the hell are you? I'm sorry I couldn't come to see you in the hospital."

"No big, I understand," Kameron told her, putting his hand on the back of her head.

"No, really, I wanted to see how it looked from the other side." She laughed. Then, she got a frown on her face. "Why the hell did you let yourself get shot, you dumb bastard?" She started hitting him. "UGH! You scared me half to death, and you think I have that much time to spare for your stupid ass!"

"Funny," Kameron said. "Michelle, this is Alex and her dog Komptin."

Alex put out her hand to shake but she was greeted with a big hug instead. Alex laughed. "Well, hello." Alex hugged her back and she was surprised at how frail she felt. "I'm not going to get hit, am I?"

"Don't be stupid and put yourself in harm's way, like some other idiot I know," Michelle answered. She pushed Alex back to look at her.

"You weren't kidding, Kameron, she really is beautiful," she told him.

Alex raised her eyebrows over to Kameron who was obviously embarrassed. "Michelle," he said. He looked over at Alex. "Chemo-brain." He playfully pointed to Michelle.

"Ass," Michelle smiled back at him. "Come on, help me up. I don't want to miss dinner." She lifted up her arms. Kameron and Alex both helped her get up as Komptin was overlooking out the window.

He seemed to be on extra look out, but there was no Dark present.

"Can I pet your dog?"

"Of course," Alex said. "Komptin."

Komptin stepped away from the window and gently sat down next to Michelle so she could pet him.

"Damn, he's so big."

"He's a teddy bear," Alex pointed out.

"Could you do me a favor and get my bathrobe?" Michelle asked.

"I'll get it," Alex said.

"Kameron can get it," Michelle told her. "It's in the bathroom behind the door."

"Sure," Kameron said. He let go of his baby sister as she adjusted her stance to stand on her own.

She wrapped her arm around Alex's arm. "I'm glad that you came."

"Oh?" Alex inquired.

"No one should be alone on Christmas. I heard Kameron had to convince you to come," Michelle started to get cold.

"He told you?"

"We tell each other a lot," Michelle informed her. "Sometimes he tells me stuff without him saying one word. Just between us girls, he can be kind of a dumbass." She smiled.

Kameron came into the room with her bathrobe, and after they helped Michelle slip it on, she put her arm back around Alex. "Come on. You are going to love my mom's cooking. On Christmas, her prime rib is to die for. I hope I don't before I can have another bite." She laughed.

"You're warped," Kameron said, following behind her.

***

Alex hadn't had a meal like that for quite some time. She was full to the point that her pants felt tight. She was listening to the family talk about a variety of topics with laughter over the year's events.

"Did you get enough to eat, dear?" Mary grabbed her plate.

Alex replied, "Please, let me get that."

"Oh, you don't have to."

"Please, I want to." Alex got up grabbing some of the dishes.

Janelle joined Alex and Mary in the kitchen.

Kameron sat in the living room as he was caught staring at Alex walking into the kitchen by Michelle. "You should just go for it."

Kameron looked over at his sister. "What are you talking about?"

"Nothing, you big dork." She shook her head. "The worst part is, is that you're not playing that you're that stupid," she said as she was escorted into the living room by her brother.

Alex was drying the dishes and then handed them over to Kameron's sister, Janelle.

"So, Alex, how did you get to know my Kameron?" Janelle asked her.

Alex felt a little embarrassed. "Well, actually we ran into each other at my brother's apartment as I was coming out of the bathroom. I opened that door and there he was."

"I remember how I first met Conner," Janelle said. "He was with a bunch of his buddies drinking—" She looked over a Mary who was giving her a playful scorn. "—soda pop. He was playing some stupid dare game. Conner was up."

"What did they do?" Alex asked her.

"He went to the school from the next town. We were playing basketball at his school, and we got done with the game. They dropped him off in the middle of the girls' locker room. There he was, blindfolded, earmuffed, sitting in the girls' locker room naked." She laughed. "I drew the short end of the stick and had to escort him out the locker room before the coach found him. One thing led to another, and here we are with two kids."

"What was Kameron like when he was younger?" Alex asked his mom.

247

She smiled. "He was much like he is now. Excelled at everything he did. Honor roll, one of the top players in football and track, and very dedicated to his beliefs."

"His only flaw is that he leaps into situations leading with his heart," Janelle pointed out. "It's bit him more than once."

"Janelle." Mary looked over to Janelle. "Looks like we are done with the dishes. Shall we go into the living room with the rest of the family?"

"Sounds good," Janelle said. She closed the last of the cabinets and then followed Mary and Alex into the living room.

Kameron was sitting on the couch next to the fireplace. Michelle was on the floor under a blanket with Komptin laying his head on her lap as she pet him, enjoying the heat from the fire. Komptin has been through a lot and Alex could tell he truly cherished these types of moments. "Come sit next to me, Alex." Michelle scooted over to leave room between herself and the couch.

Alex made herself comfortable. She was all set but realized that she really wanted an Apollo to drink. Then, a glass came in front of her face with her energy drink and ice. She looked to Kameron handing it over to her as he continued to talk to his brother-in-law about the upcoming Giants game.

"He's really intuitive, isn't he?" Alex whispered over to Michelle.

"On most things." Michelle smirked. "But he's really a dumbass on the most obvious," she replied to Alex.

"Michelle," Mary interjected. "Language."

Alex laughed as she was reminded of Ariel and Devine. Alex enjoyed the company of the family. They were laughing and telling stories about their times together.

It was getting late when Michelle turned to Mary. "Mom, I'm getting pretty tired. I'm going to go to bed."

"Okay, honey," she said as she went to get up.

"It's okay. Sit down and relax," Harold said. "I'll help put her down." He set his drink aside.

Alex stepped up. "I'll do it."

Michelle seemed to light up. "Yeah, I will walk Alex through it."

Mary smiled. "Are you sure, Alex?"

"No problem," Alex said. "I got this." She winked at Michelle.

Michelle smiled and grabbed Alex by the arm. They walked upstairs as Komptin ran in front of them to lead them to her bedroom.

"What do you need me to do?" Alex asked, wondering what she got herself into.

"Just sit with me as I take my medicine. Pretty much make sure I don't choke on my vomit," Michelle let her know.

"Oh joy." Alex was looking for the bowl by the side of Michelle's bed.

Michelle laughed. "I'm kidding. The pills are numbered, and they make me a bit loopy. So, you just need to make sure I take them all."

"I can do that," Alex ensured her.

Michelle tried to take her shirt off but was having trouble. Alex quickly got up and helped her.

"Thank you."

Alex smiled at her. "Anything else?"

"My Minnie Mouse jammies are in my second drawer, if you don't mind." She started to get ready for bed.

Alex walked over to her dresser. Michelle had pictures of herself with her friends which must have been before she was diagnosed. She had long, light brown hair, and she looked bright and full of life. "That picture on the left was from my last track meet before I found out about my cancer."

Alex said, "These pictures remind me of my best friend Sarah." She picked up the picture remembering her friend. She put the picture down.

"How'd she die?" Michelle asked her.

"What makes you think she died?" Alex grabbed her pajamas.

"I can tell." After she put on her pajamas, she took the first set of her pills.

Alex knew she couldn't hide the truth from Michelle. She was like Kameron, really intuitive. So, she came up with the best answer she could. "Her father killed her."

"Oh my God," Michelle said. "What the hell happened to him?"

Alex looked in the mirror. "He died." It was awkward situation telling Michelle about the Sarah's dad. She couldn't tell her the truth—that Alex was the one who had to kill him because he volunteered to become infiltrated.

250

"Sounds like the bastard got what he deserved." Michelle slowly got into her bed and pulled up the covers. "Come on, boy." Komptin jumped onto the foot of the bed. He curled up and went to sleep.

"Show off." Alex ruffled up Komptin. She sat down on the bed next to Michelle.

Michelle grabbed a piece of Alex's hair. "You are so beautiful."

"Your drugs must be kicking in," Alex teased her. Alex gave Michelle the last of her medicine. "Sleep tight." She pulled up the covers for Michelle as she got adjusted.

"I can see why he likes you," Michelle said, as she rolled over and went to bed.

Alex stayed with her until she was fast asleep, just watching Michelle sleep peacefully. Alex slowly got off the bed. Komptin lifted his head. "Please make sure she is safe tonight."

Alex knew there was nothing around, she hadn't felt the Dark since they left; it was just peace of mind. Komptin flashed his eyes in agreement and laid his face down on the bed.

Alex walked out of the room and met with Mary, who came out of her bedroom across from Michelle's. "Alex."

"She's sleeping and Komptin is in there, if that's okay?" Alex asked.

"Of course, it is, my dear." Mary peeked in on Michelle. She looked at Komptin, who lifted his head. "She loves dogs and he's all dog."

"He's so much more than a dog," Alex smiled. "I wouldn't be here today if it wasn't for him." Alex tried to cover up her scar on the side of her head.

"I have the two of you set up in the den in the attic." Mary handed her some towels. "Bathroom is down the hall on the left."

Alex looked upstairs. "Den is right up there?" Alex didn't really think about it, but she knew it was going to be a long night if she was just lying in bed with her eyes open. "Thank you." But, the house did have welcoming feeling to it.

"Everyone is leaving if you want to say good-bye," Mary said, rubbing Alex's arm heading downstairs.

"I do, thank you," The sound of everyone getting their jackets and boots on told Alex she'd better hurry.

Janelle and her family left, and Alex went into the den where there were two twin size beds. She put her suitcase on one of them as she unpacked her bathrobe. She turned around to see Kameron looking at her. "You have a lovely family," she said, continuing to get her shower supplies.

"I'll keep them," Kameron said. "I just wanted to make sure you had everything."

"Where are you sleeping?" Alex asked.

Kameron just pointed to the other bed.

Alex could feel herself get tensed up. "Oh,"

Kameron laughed. "Just kidding, my mom still has my old bedroom setup. It's right next to Michelle's if you need me for anything." He turned around and went downstairs.

**

It was late that night, around two in the morning. Alex had her energy drink in her hand looking out the window. The night was clear, and the snow continued to glisten. Alex thought she saw movement near the fence of the field. It was too far for her sense if it was Dark, but she didn't feel any presence around.

She saw the shadow again and this time it was closer. She felt her arms start to tingle. She calmed down after she saw it was just a deer coming out from the field. She heard someone come behind her. It was Michelle coming around the corner in her bathrobe and bandana.

"Hey."

"What are you doing up?" Michelle asked her.

"I'm a light sleeper," she replied to her, looking out the window. Alex continued to scan the window and watch the deer. She turned back around to Michelle. "What are you doing up?"

"My stomach was upset and, not to get too graphic, but let's just say dinner the second time around doesn't taste as good as the first," she admitted. "I just came down to get a glass of water."

"I'll get it, sit down," Alex said. She stopped in front of the cabinets and opened them up to see a bunch of bowls.

"Next one over." Michelle smiled.

"Of course." Alex grabbed a glass.

"Warm tap water would be perfect," she requested.

Alex filled the glass and sat down on the corner of the table next to Michelle. She handed her the glass and squeezed her shoulders. "Anything else?"

"No," Michelle said. She looked at Alex. "I love your hair."

"Thank you," Alex said.

"How long is it without the extensions?"

Alex touched her shoulders. "Right about here."

"My hair used to be in the middle of my back," she said. "I miss it. I don't know any guy who will like this." She pointed to her bald head underneath her bandanna.

"I can kind of relate," Alex said. She moved her hair back to show Michelle her scar. "These are a couple of many." She removed her neck collar to show her the scar.

Michelle put her hand to her mouth in shock. "Oh, damn, can I ask what happened?"

Alex tried to muster up something to tell her, but she couldn't think of anything.

"It's okay, I get it." Michelle took a sip of her water. "Have you ever come close to death?"

Alex played with her glass of Apollo and ice. "More times than I care to admit." Alex looked over at Komptin coming around the corner.

She heard him earlier walking quietly around the house. There was no doubt he was conducting a small patrol as Michelle walked downstairs. He came up and laid down next to Alex. Alex felt secure and appreciative of Komptin's actions.

"Why do you ask?"

"I know I'm not going to see my graduation," Michelle admitted.

"Don't say that," Alex said. "You've got plenty of life in you."

"I'm a realist," Michelle told her. "Do you believe in Heaven?"

Alex took a drink. "Do you?"

"I know there is a God and I know there is a reason He is calling for me to join Him sooner than I wished, it's just…" She stopped.

"Just what?" Alex inquired.

"Just that, I wish I knew what was going to happen," Michelle said. "I've talked to priests and ministers, and they give me the 'Book' answer. I just wish someone could tell me that it's going to be all right. Every night I go to bed wondering if this is going to be the last." She wiped a tear from her face.

Alex smiled at her. "It will be okay." She winked at her. "Come on, I'll help you get back to bed."

***

Alex knew everyone else was sleeping. Normally, she would whistle for Komptin to come out for a walk, but she walked through the dark house to Michelle's room. She opened the door to let Komptin know that she wanted to get some fresh

255

air. Komptin looked up at her as she motioned for him to come along. It was close to four in morning when they got ready to go outside. She saw a figure standing in the living room looking out in the distance. "Kameron?"

He turned around to see him white as a ghost and she could tell he was sweating. "Oh, hey. Did I wake you?"

"No, I was up, just thought I would get Komptin some air," she said. She walked up to him. "You okay?"

"Yeah, I'm fine," he said. He took a tissue out of his pocket and wiped his nose. "I haven't been home for a while and forgot how crisp the air is here." He laughed.

"Do you want to come with me and Komptin for a small walk?" Alex asked him. Komptin came up to Kameron and pushed him towards the door.

"How can I say no to that?" he commented. "Give me five minutes to get dressed. He walked back upstairs.

"Take your time." She watched him go upstairs.

Once Kameron got dressed, they headed outside to the bitter night's cold air. They came to the end of the driveway and looked left or right. "Which way do you want to go?" Alex asked him.

"Straight," Kameron told her. "About ten yards into the woods is a groomed snowmobile trail. I think you would like it."

"Okay," she said. "We'll go straight."

Komptin ran ahead of them into the woods. Alex couldn't help but think he was remembering hunting with Osiah. Alex knew that if Kameron wasn't with them, he would be in Gargoyle state running through the woods. Being in the city, he just couldn't be in that state all the time without somebody seeing him.

The moon provided enough light to see the tree branches making it an eerie beauty to it. Kameron was leading the way holding branches for Alex.

"It's just past those pine trees."

He grabbed the branch of the pine tree and moved it for her so she would have a clear path to the trail. The movement of the branch caused a train reaction of snow to fall onto Alex. It covered her head with snow.

"I'm sorry." Kameron somewhat laughed but more nervous than anything. "Are you okay?"

"Great." Alex brushed off the snow. "Feels especially good as it goes down my back."

"Sorry about that." Kameron held out his hand.

"Oh, I'll get you back." She laughed, easing his nervousness. She grabbed his hand and he pulled her towards him to help her onto the trail. He lost his balance and they fell into the snow with her landing on top of him.

"Does this make us even?" he asked as he moved some of her hair out of the way.

She felt her stomach start to turn as she could feel herself getting a little hot. She looked at him in the eyes which seemed like eternity before she spoke. "Not quite." She laughed.

Alex got up and helped him get off the ground.

"I want you to live in fear for a while." she snickered at him.

They walked down the trail a bit as Komptin was hopping along through the thicket of the woods.

"He seems happy," Kameron observed.

"He likes the woods. Wish I could get transferred back to a rural area," she commented.

"What do you mean transferred? If you want to move, then just move," Kameron said. "It's not like you're tied to the church."

"Not that easy," Alex said, looking up at the sky. She looked at the purple star blinking above her. "Sometimes I wish it was."

"I get it, I just can't quit either," Kameron said. "My integrity won't allow me to." Kameron bent down and looked at some tracks in the snow. "That's a big deer." He got up as the snow started to fall. He looked over at Alex. "Have you ever been snowmobiling?"

***

Mary had cooked the whole family a big country breakfast. Alex had gorged herself with the homemade biscuits and gravy. Kameron had convinced her to go snowmobiling. Michelle had given Alex her winter gear to go out in. Mary was on the porch with a smile on her face.

"Where's Kameron?" Alex had asked her.

"Getting the snowmobile from the barn," Mary said. "You know, there's something I have to tell you."

258

"What's that?" Alex was finishing up tightening her snow outfit.

"Kameron…Kameron's got a big heart, a real big one," Mary said. "I just wanted to tell you that."

Alex nodded to Mary to tell her that she understood.

Kameron pulled up to the porch with the snowmobile. "Ready to go?" He held out a helmet.

Harold came up onto the porch. "Where are you heading?"

"Thought I would take a ride out to camp, my blind, and the lake," Kameron said. "Then come on back."

Harold looked at his watch. "Okay, we are heading into town to do a family shopping trip after lunch."

Kameron looked back at Alex. "You wanna go?"

"Sounds like fun," Alex muffled through her helmet.

"We'll be back for lunch," Kameron said.

"Good, can you also check the cabin windows? The bunk room window was a little rough last time we were out there." Harold asked him as he put his arm around Mary.

Komptin came up on the porch looking to Alex to see what she wanted him to do. Alex motioned for him to stay as he nodded overlooking the porch in an over watch position.

Kameron looked back at Alex. "You have to tell me where you got him trained." He revved up the snowmobile. "Ready?"

Alex slapped him on the top of the head, and they took off into the field.

***

After their snow adventure on that death machine Alex had the privilege of riding, they ate lunch and went to the mall for shopping. It was completely covered in Christmas decorations. The mall had carolers singing in the center of the mall next to the tree where Santa was talking to the children.

Mary and Harold were holding hands ahead of Alex and Michelle as Kameron parked the car. Harold looked back at Michelle. "How are you feeling honey?"

"I'm fine, Dad," she said. "Hey, do you mind if I go to the wig store?"

Mary looked back at her. "Okay, we'll be in Macy's."

Michelle grabbed Alex's hand. "Come on, it's just around the corner."

Alex laughed. "Okay, I'm coming." She held Komptin's leash as he followed them wearing his service dog outfit.

Harold looked over at Mary. "She really likes her."

"So, do I," Mary said.

Harold smiled at Mary. "Come on, let's go get a coffee as we wait for Kameron."

***

Alex was trying on a blonde wig while looking in the mirror. "What do you think of this one?" She turned to Michelle who was wearing a bright neon glittering blue wig.

Michelle looked at her. "Looks like your IQ just dropped 20 points. How about me?"

"You should be singing bubblegum pop music." Alex laughed.

Michelle belted out a popular song in a mocking high screech. "I'm a star," she sang.

"Hi, Shelly," a girl said behind them, holding a phone.

"Oh, God," Michelle said, laughing. "Please tell me you didn't get that?"

"Oh, I got it, and it just made it up to the school webpage." The girl laughed.

"Alex, this is Wendy, Wendy this is my brother's girlfriend, Alex."

"Hi," Alex said, taking off the wig. She shook Wendy's hand and noticed she was studying Alex.

"You're dating Kameron?" Wendy asked as she was checking Alex out.

"We're friends," Alex corrected them both.

Alex caught a glimpse of Michelle shaking her head at her friend.

"We'll talk tonight," Wendy said to Michelle.

Michelle nodded. "We need to go anyway."

"Talk later," Wendy said. "It was nice meeting you."

"You as well," Alex said. Alex turned to Michelle who was putting away the wig she was trying on. "Why was she so shocked that Kameron and I are dating, or not dating but friends, but she thought we were dating—oh you know what I mean?"

Michelle looked over to Alex. "Do you want to get a coffee?"

***

Alex ordered the coffees for the two of them as they sat down over-looking people Christmas shopping. "You never answered my question, Michelle," Alex pointed out, giving her the cup.

Michelle looked down at her drink. "Kameron dated a couple of girls in high school, and they were all the same." Michelle reluctantly looked at her. "I like you Alex; I don't want you to worry."

"Go ahead," she insisted.

"Well, Alex, Kameron always went for the preppy girls. A lot of them were dating him because he was a sure thing, meaning guaranteed for success in life." Michelle looked around to make sure no one was listening. She leaned into Alex's direction. "Kameron fell in love hard with a real bitch. She was constantly cheating on him, easy,—I'm talking she would pick up guys going through the drive-thru window. I'm talking a real ho."

Alex could feel herself starting to feel shameful about herself. "What happened?"

"He bought her a ring, we all warned him not to do it. He was a junior in college, I think. She would have killed his career," Michelle said. "He did it anyway, real expensive. He went to give it to her, but that night, she was screwing around. And the guy she was with convinced her to send him a video of the two of them doing it in the backseat of Kameron's car. The bitch was on all fours while he was behind her. Ever since then, he wouldn't even go on a date or even consider it." Michelle took a sip of her coffee. "I never saw Dad so mad when he saw how hurt Kameron was when he told him."

"Why was the girl so shocked?" Alex said.

"It wasn't shock, it was shame. That girl was Wendy's older sister, that's how we became friends," Michelle said. "She was so ashamed of her sister's actions that she still apologizes to our family now and again."

"He's a good guy, any girl would be lucky to be dating him," Alex said.

Michelle laughed. "You know, I was supposed to be his date for that ball the two of you went on."

"Really? What happened?" Alex asked.

"My body wouldn't really let me travel. I got really sick a day prior to going," Michelle said. "But I'm glad it happened,"

"Why is that?" Alex said, drinking her coffee.

"Because our family wouldn't have never met you," she smiled.

Komptin stood up with his ears perked; Alex looked down at him and she saw that something had caught his attention. Alex saw two kids walking by with F.O.R. symbols on their jacket. She really hoped those kids weren't actual members but just wearing their logo out of pure ignorance.

"I'm glad I met you, too. We should get going."

***

Michelle opened one eye from her sleep. Her room was bit warmer than usual but there was a feeling of comfort to it. The power must have been out because the time on her clock wasn't showing. She went to grab her phone because it dropped on the floor, but it was too cold to get out of bed to get it.

"Michelle," a soft voice whispered.

Michelle's eyes grew big. "Oh damn." She peered above her covers to see a beautiful blonde woman sitting on the foot of her bed. "Am I dead?"

The woman laughed. "No, my dear."

Michelle sat up in her bed looking around. Komptin was near the beautiful blonde woman who had a gold band around in her hair. The majestic lady was petting Alex's dog and then seemed to generate something from her hand to feed it to him. "Did I just see that?"

The woman smiled. "Komptin is very fond of you." She nodded at him, and he walked out of the room.

"Who are you? I mean, I know who you are. At least I think I do. But I don't know you, but I do. This is a very weird feeling," Michelle admitted.

"Who do you think I am?" The blonde woman got up to sit next to Michelle.

Michelle moved over on her bed, and she joined her under the covers. "Peace."

"I will take that." Celestial gave a small laugh. "My name is Celestial."

"Why are you here?" Michelle asked Celestial.

"I thought you may want to watch a movie," she said, picking up the remote. "What do you want to watch?"

Michelle got herself situated. "I don't know what's on at this hour, but there is a really good movie on in the theatre if you want to go when it opens. It's about this vegan guy who gets stuck working on a butcher cow farm and falls in love with a female rancher. It's called, 'Hearty Steak'."

"Sounds good to me, but why wait, we will watch it now," Celestial said. She pushed the remote and the movie started.

"This movie just came out." Michelle looked around. "Aren't we going to wake the family?"

"They are going to have the best night of sleep," Celestial said as she got situated in the bed. "You know what would be great?"

They both looked at each other and said, "Ice cream."

"What kind do you want?" Celestial asked her.

"Chocolate Salted Caramel with marshmallow," Michelle suggested.

Celestial leaned over the side of the bed and pulled out that ice cream. "That is what I wanted as well," she said. Together they shared the ice cream as the movie began.

***

Alex was outside on the porch. For some reason she wanted to stay out in the cold. She could see her breath hanging in the air. She had just finished texting Anne about her day. It seemed as if they were having a good time except that Anne was getting frustrated that both the moms were planning the wedding and she had no say in it. Anne didn't really care though because she just wanted to marry Kale.

Alex found herself a little jealous of Anne since she found her true soulmate. Alex looked out to the field and noticed the moon was quite bright tonight. The stars were out in the open. She caught herself gazing up at Osiah's star, staring down at her all bright and purple.

"Hello, Little Spitfire," a pair of voices behind her said.

Alex turned around quickly out of shock with her fists lit.

"Easy, easy," Ariel said, putting her hands up.

"It is just us," Devine concluded.

"Where did you hear that from?" Alex dissipated the lite from her fists as she looked up at the star one last time before turning her attention to the Guardians of the Conduit.

"The night Osiah was diminished," Devine said.

"In our huddle, he asked us to look over his Little Spitfire," Ariel informed her.

Alex smiled. "Here I thought you just liked me."

They joined her looking out to the field. Komptin came out and morphed into gargoyle state. He flashed his eyes and took off to guard the perimeter since Celestial was no doubt upstairs with Michelle.

"Something on your mind?" Ariel asked.

"You seem not yourself," Devine added.

Alex walked off the porch and went to a tree with the tire swing. She shook the branch and watched the snow fall with some of it landing on her head. "Ever regret your actions of the past, afraid you might have screwed something up in the future?"

The two of them looked at each other. "No," they both said.

Alex raised her eyebrows and shook her head. "Didn't think so."

"Alexandria, your actions of the past are what makes you are today," Devine said.

"And who you are is why you are loved," Ariel finished off.

"You saying you love me?" Alex smirked. The two of them looked at each other and sighed as they joined Alex by the tree. "You don't have to answer that," Alex playfully relieved them of that question. Alex stared at the house.

Both Ariel and Devine smiled at her. "You know the answer to your question that you really want to ask," Devine said.

"But you are too scared to ask it," Ariel concluded.

Alex just continued to stare at the house. "Yeah, I don't think so."

They both slapped her on the back of the head. "You are an idiot."

***

Michelle and Celestial watched the ending of the movie. Michelle wiped a tear from her face. "That was cute."

"It was," Celestial agreed, for some reason her mind raced to Osiah.

"Are you all right? You look sad,' Michelle asked Celestial.

Celestial looked out the window. "There is a lot of hate in the world. Many have lost ones that they hold true to their heart. Losing just one to evil is a pain of sadness." Celestial looked down and smiled at Michelle. "But you should not worry about such things."

Michelle took all her strength to climb up to Celestial and kissed her on the cheek. "Feel better?"

Celestial laughed. Even though Michelle had a slow, painful, dying sickness, she managed to think of others. Celestial wiped a golden tear from her cheek as Michelle sparked a rejuvenation of hope in this war. She just wrapped her arms around Michelle and gave her a hug. "I do."

Michelle yawned. "I'm getting tired."

Celestial adjusted the covers as Michelle snuggled up to Celestial. Celestial put her arms around her in a motherly embrace.

"What's going to happen when the time comes?" Michelle asked as she started drifting to sleep.

"It will be an incredible, peaceful journey," Celestial started to tell her. "You are going to be surrounded by everyone you love." Celestial looked down to see Michelle smiling at that thought.

"I just wish I could have had more time to do something worthy of my life," Michelle informed her.

"Your crossing over will be filled with sadness by your family, but it will bring them stronger together with a bond that cannot be broken," she comforted Michelle.

"I like that," she whispered. "Will you be there?"

"I will personally be there on the other side to guide you on your journey," Celestial let her know.

"I appreciate that," Michelle said. "I know you have done so much for me all ready, but can you do me one more favor?" Michelle was almost asleep.

"What is that, my dear?" Celestial asked, placing her head on top of Michelle's.

"Can you make sure Kameron is happy before I go? He deserves to be happy."

"Honey, you are pivotal to make that happen," Celestial said.

Michelle smiled as she fell asleep on Celestial.

Celestial slowly got out of bed and tucked Michelle into bed. She kissed her on her forehead. "Good night, my child."

Alex sat on the porch with Ariel and Devine. They were digging through a bunch of Christmas candy that Alex had bought at the mall. "You have to try this one." Alex gorged herself with another piece of chocolate. Ariel smacked the hand of Devine as she picked up the chocolate. Devine playfully smacked her hand back.

"Enjoying yourselves?" Celestial came out from the front door. Komptin came up from his patrol and joined Alex by the porch swing. Ariel and Devine both grabbed some more chocolates before joining Celestial at her side. "How are you doing, Alexandria?"

With a mouthful of chocolate, Alex replied, "Okay." Alex swallowed her chocolate with her energy drink. "Sorry about that." Alex stood up and gave Celestial a hug. "Thank you for that." Alex looked up to Michelle's room. "She's a sweet kid."

"She reminds me of you when you were that age," Celestial said.

"She's better than me," Alex said.

"Alexandria, there is something that I have never known about you," Celestial observed.

"What's that?"

"You have never known fear and you have never doubted yourself." She smiled and walked up to her. "You have both, and I could not be happier for you." She gave her a hug before she and her guardians left.

"Well, I'm pretty sure everyone is going to be dead asleep, and nothing is going to wake them, so what do you say we take advantage of it." She leaned on Komptin's massive body. "Why don't we go for a hunt in the dark woods? Just like old times."

Komptin and Alex both flashed their eyes as they ran into the woods in full hunting mode.

***

Alex returned from their hunt and walked into the kitchen where the whole family was up. The room was energized, and Alex could tell the effects from Celestial sleeping aid was in full swing. Alex was smiling at the fact the family was together eating breakfast.

"I guess somebody got up early." Harold reached for the last piece of French toast.

Mary smacked his hand with a wooden spoon.

"Ow!" He shook his hand from the sting.

"That piece is for Alex," Mary scolded him.

"I had to take Komptin for a walk," Alex let him know.

Kameron got up and gave her an Apollo from the fridge. "My mom's awesome Christmas Eve French toast with strawberries and whip cream is pure bliss," he handed her the plate.

"Thank you," Alex said. "Can I sit next to you?" she asked Michelle.

Michelle looked content and peaceful. "Please."

271

Alex knew that Michelle couldn't speak about what happened last night. Celestial let her know without knowing details, kind of a remembrance of a feeling.

"How are you feeling this morning?" Alex asked her.

"Happy." Michelle smiled.

Alex rubbed her back.

"What should we do this morning?" Harold asked, full of life.

"How about a family activity, something all of us could do?" Mary suggested.

"We could go for a walk," Janelle said while feeding her two boys.

"Nah," Janelle's husband said while stuffing his face full of food. "How about we go up to the mountains."

Kameron spoke up, "How about we go play volleyball at the Y?"

Alex kind of perked at that thought.

The family turned at each other. "That sounds perfect," Harold said, finishing up breakfast. "Let's get moving." He got up all energized to go change into his gym clothes.

"I got clothes that can fit you," Michelle said to Alex.

After breakfast, Michelle enthusiastically dragged Alex to her bedroom. There was much digging around and clothes flying everywhere before Michelle found something for Alex to wear.

"Just anything is fine," Alex told her.

272

"Well, I do have a couple of things." She threw her hot pink workout pants and tube top with a tank top over it.

Alex lifted it up. "You really think I can fit into this?"

"Yep," she laughed. "I have to go take my meds, I'll be right back."

Alex closed the door to Michelle's room and started to take her shirt off when she heard Kameron knock on the door. "Hey, sis."

Alex quickly covered herself up. She was hoping to get dressed before anybody saw her scars. "Ah, I'm changing here."

Kameron stepped back a bit. "Oh, my bad, Michelle needs to take her meds."

"She went to take them," Alex said, still covering herself.

Kameron leaned on the door. "So have you played volleyball before?"

"In high school, we played a couple times in gym class," Alex informed him, hiding the fact that her team finished the season undefeated.

"Okay, we can get a little competitive, but we have fun," Kameron said, still leaning on the door. The two of them just stared uncomfortably at each other for a while before Michelle came up behind him.

"God, you two, just do it all ready," she said as she walked by him. "Excuse me," she shooed him out of the way. "My pill bag is downstairs."

Kameron got frustrated and flicked Michelle on the head. "Quiet Q-ball."

273

She hit him back and made chicken sounds. She turned and waved Kameron off. Kameron turned back to Alex who was still covering herself. "We're all ready." He smiled. "Hmmm, that's weird."

Alex looked at him. "What?"

"Thought I heard thunder." He winked at her as he left for downstairs.

***

The teams were divided up and Mary was with Kameron and Janelle's husband, while Janelle, Harold, and Alex were on the other side. Michelle sat down on the bleachers overlooking the game with Komptin laying on her lap. Michelle was more interested in her phone than what was going on with the game, which was understood for a teenage girl.

The game was fun. Alex wasn't going full force; she actually was just setting the ball and lightly tapping it over the net. Kameron just happened to be in front of her.

"Are you ready for the thunder?" he joked as it winked at her.

Alex looked around. "Not too worried, I don't see a cloud in the sky."

Harold served the ball and Mary returned it over to Kameron. Janelle went to block it, but he gently placed it over her head. Harold dove to get it but missed the ball.

"Oooo…. the thunder is rolling in; did you feel the vibration?" He laughed at his dad.

"Funny, good placement, Kam; Janelle, my bad, I should have had your back," Harold said. "Come on, let's get the ball back." He clapped trying to get his team motivated.

Alex walked over to her teammates motioning a timeout. "Time."

"The gathering of the minds, people," Janelle's husband Robert teased.

"You can't stop us, you see that storm coming, dark clouds, the thunder is coming." Kameron started teasing Janelle, "We will make it quick and painless on you."

Alex took her hand and waved him off. In the huddle Alex spoke, "Can I get a good set on the right side?"

Janelle confidently spoke, "Yeah. Dad, can you get a good return?"

"I got your back," Harold said.

"Janelle, make it a high set," Alex requested.

"He'll see it and go to block it," Janelle informed her.

"I'm counting on it," she replied.

"Are you sure?"

"I got this," Alex said, giving her a thumb's up.

Mary served the ball and Harold returned it over to Janelle who set the ball perfectly.

Instantly, Alex saw Kameron prep for a jump to block it, she matched his jump and with a controlled might she hit the ball with a thunderous explosion. The ball broke through his hands, forcing him backwards landing on the ground.

"HOLY SHIT!" Michelle yelled out.

The whole family turned to look at Michelle who instantly covered her mouth.

"Sorry," she softly said.

Mary ran over to Kameron with a mother's love, laughing. "I think the thunder dissipated."

Kameron regained his composure and looked at Alex in her neon pink outfit, over-emphasizing her gum chewing and giving a huge wink. "Our ball," she said to him.

"That's my girl, there!" Harold said running over to Alex and putting his arm around her squeezing. "Shake it off, Kam, we are making our comeback here."

***

Alex was enjoying the hot shower of the gym. It felt good to play volleyball again. She hadn't played since they won that game where she beat up that girl from Westington and then her life took an unexpected turn. She replayed her life; there were some heartaches from losses, but she looked at Kameron and his family, she thought of the future that Anne and Kale were about to have, and she came to peace that what she was and her mission in life was something important.

She walked out of the shower and Mary and Janelle were already dressed. They were obviously waiting for Alex to get dressed so they could walk out together. "Where did you learn to play like that?"

"Our school was undefeated in volleyball, I just forgot to tell Kameron that when he asked if I ever played." She snickered.

She turned around to find her collar, but it had dropped to the ground. Her neck wound was out in the open, she quickly covered her scar on her face and neck with her hair. She knew that Mary and Janelle saw it but, bless their hearts, they didn't say anything.

Her towel dropped from her playing with her hair and her full body was exposed. The scars on her back were showing from multiple Infiltrator attacks and massive burn and fray scars on her side where Sanah had stabbed his Lite Spear. She frantically picked up her towel to cover herself up out of embarrassment. Mary and Janelle had their hands over their mouths in shock.

"Oh my God, what happened?" Janelle asked.

"Janelle! You don't have to answer that dear," Mary said in response to Janelle.

Alex knew there wasn't any hiding it, she was trying to think of a quick cover story. "I'm sorry you had to see those," Alex embarrassingly said.

Alex got dressed as a sudden rush of emotion came from her. There was a tear from dropping from her face. Alex tried to tell them something, but nothing came out.

"Alex, please don't," Janelle hugged her. "I shouldn't have asked that." She handed her another towel to wipe the tears from her face.

"It's okay." Alex blew into the towel loudly. "Damn allergies." She forced a laugh.

"Is that why you have Komptin? Do you need me to go get him?" Mary asked out of caring.

Alex wiped away another tear. "It's why I have him," Alex could honestly tell them. "If I need him, he'll come in full force." Alex laughed while sucking up some of her snot.

"Do you want to wait a bit before we leave?" Janelle asked Alex.

Alex nodded as she tried to regain her composure. "I'm sorry about this," she said wiping another tear. "I don't know what's coming over me." She wiped another tear as the memory of Sara and Osiah flashed through her head. Then another of Sanah standing over her ready to diminish her before Roger stood over her lifeless body asking her to join him or die.

"Damn it," Alex rolled her eyes.

Mary just got done talking to Harold. "I told Harold that we girls are going to go for a coffee and for him and the boys to go home to put turkey going for tonight." Mary joined Janelle in trying to comfort Alex. "Take your time."

Alex gave a breath. "I really should go get Komptin." Alex didn't need him for emotional support, but she needed him there since he was walking around as her PTSD dog.

"Will he come to me?" Janelle asked. "I'll go get him."

"If I know him, he's probably already at the door," Alex said.

Janelle came back from getting Komptin. "Right at the door like you said." She smiled.

He ran and quickly came up to Alex. "I bet Osiah had never done this?" She forced a laugh.

Komptin looked up at her and gave a sad look; this was his confirmation that his former master had his fair share of breakdowns over the past.

"Who's Osiah?" Mary asked her to get Alex's gym bag together.

"A mentor and a friend," Alex said. She got up. "He died the night I got this." She pointed to her neck. "I'm good now," Alex said. "I'm just going to wash my face down and put on makeup."

"We'll be right here." Janelle smiled at her.

"Thank you," Alex said to them both. "I'm sorry again for putting you through this."

***

That Christmas Eve night was out of a Hallmark movie. The family all gathered and laughed, especially retelling the story of how Alex knocked Kameron over during volleyball. Kameron, being a good sport, accepted his defeat with grace and humor. Janelle's kids were begging to open one gift.

"Okay, okay, but Momma and Dada are going to choose which one," Janelle said.

"I hope it's a toy!" the oldest boy, Jerry, said while running into the living room looking over the presents underneath the tree. They went around shaking the boxes.

The whole family sat around the living room. Kameron and Alex were sitting next to each other.

279

Alex closed her eyes for a quick second, enjoying the feeling of a normal family setting.

Kameron leaned over to Alex. "Every year we all open one gift on Christmas Eve."

"Mom and Dad, your gift from all of us is under the tree."

They opened the big box. The two of them opened it to an envelope. "An envelope? Oh, you shouldn't have." He laughed as he opened it. The two of them read it. "Oh, you guys, you really shouldn't have."

Alex leaned over to Kameron. "What did you get them?"

Mary stated, "Plane tickets to Florida for a week's vacation."

Robert said, "I know it's during the growing season, but I had some extra vacation time at work, and I will handle the watering of the fields. It will actually be quite relaxing."

"Thank you, guys," Harold said, hugging his family.

Kameron opened a gift from Michelle. "Cute."

"What is it?" Mary asked.

"Free Volleyball lessons from the YMCA." Kameron showed the family.

Everyone laughed as he head-locked his little sister and kissed her on the top of her head.

"Here's yours." Kameron gave her a gift.

Michelle opened her gift and looked in the box. "Very funny," she said as she pulled out a jar with a label reading "Swear Jar." She looked at her dad. "Dad, can I have a dollar?"

He handed her a dollar and she put in the jar and looked at Kameron.

"Ass."

The family laughed as the two other kids came to Kameron. "Now? Can we now?"

"Okay." Kameron smiled.

The two kids ran underneath the tree and grabbed a bag with Alex's name on it. They ran over and gave it to Alex.

"What's this?"

"This is for you," they told her as they jumped up and down with excitement.

Alex looked to Michelle. "Did you have your hand in this?"

"Nope, I wasn't supposed to keep you busy at the mall." She winked.

Alex opened it to a jewelry box. A sudden rush of emotion starting to overpower her as she looked inside the box. She looked to the boys, "I love it." Then the boys rushed over to her to give her a big hug.

"What is it?" Janelle asked.

Alex turned it around to show a gold necklace with a gold and sapphire angel attached to it. "When I was young, a real good friend of mine, who died, used to tell me I was rare blue gold and the angel, well, let's just say angels are something very special to me." She turned to Kameron. "How did…this is…I really love it."

"Put it on," the youngest boy, Derek, screamed.

"Okay." Alex was having trouble clasping it.

Kameron stood up. "I'll get it."

Alex stood up and turned around for him to put it on. She lifted her hair for him. "Got it."

She turned around and met face to face with him. She stared into his eyes which seemed to last for eternity. "Thank you," she said, as she gave him a hug.

He just nodded and sat back down on the couch.

"Can we open ours now, Mom?" the boy asked.

"You can open these ones from Grandma and Grandpa," Janelle's husband said.

"Awesome!" the other boy said. They quickly unwrapped the gifts. "Captain Buster Blasters!" They went around pretending to fire them. "Can we go outside and play with them?"

"Okay, but you have to get your winter gear on," Janelle said. She turned to Robert. "Let them expend some of that energy before going to bed."

"Agreed," he said.

Alex was feeling the joy of having that necklace around her neck as she played with it sitting next to Kameron who was talking to Michelle. She felt Mary tap her on the leg. "Yes?"

"What's your cell phone number, dear?" she asked Alex.

Alex thought it was a weird question, but she gave it to her. Alex then got a message from a strange number that must have been Mary. She opened the attachment to a picture of Alex and Kameron looking at each other. He had his hands on her waist and her hands around the back of his neck.

"Oh God," Alex thought. "I even have one leg in the air." She looked at Kameron out of embarrassment wondering if his mother sent him the same picture. All she could do in return is smile at Mary who was grinning ear to ear.

"I'll go watch the boys outside," Robert said, getting up.

"I'll do it," Alex said. "I could use the fresh air." Alex got up and got her coat.

"Are you sure?" Robert asked.

"No problem, I like the relaxation of the farm air," Alex said, getting her coat on. She tied her black leather overcoat.

Komptin just lifted an eyebrow while laying on Michelle's lap in front of the fire.

"You can stay," she told him as he went back to sleep.

The boys ran outside after getting their winter jackets and snow pants on. They were pretending to shoot each other with the toy space pistols. Alex flipped up her collar and watched them run off.

"Derek, Jerry, don't go too far," she told them.

She overlooked the field as the big fluffy snowflakes were falling from the sky. She could barely make out the purple haze of Osiah's star, she knew it was up there and that was good enough for her.

"I think I know how you felt there, big guy," she said to the star.

"Who are you talking to?" Kameron said, coming up behind her, handing her an Apollo drink.

283

"Thank you," Alex said, giving him an appreciative smile. "I was just talking to the star."

Kameron looked up at the cloudy sky dropping the snow. "Any particular one?"

"That one." She pointed to Osiah's star. She knew that he couldn't see it, especially behind a bunch of clouds, but it felt good to let Kameron be a small vague part of her little world. "Always that one," Alex informed him.

"Any special story behind it?" Kameron asked her, zipping up his coat.

"The star was named after a Dark Sentry sent to kill the Conduit of the Lite. A beautiful Lite Being sent to balance the war of good and evil." She looked to him to see if she thought she was full of it, but he continued to listen. "He and his Dark partner had her cornered; he went to go kill her and they instantly fell in love with each other. He rescued her from annihilation and inadvertently saved mankind from Hell on earth."

"That sounds nice, I like happy endings," Kameron said. "I'm kind of a sucker for love stories." He stared off in the field as he began flicking the snow off the porch banister.

"It didn't end happily," Alex informed him. "He got banished from the Dark and was constantly hunted. He refused to go to the Lite in fear of what he was capable of. So, he asked God for a companion, someone who could kill him in an instant in case he ever turned to the Dark again. The two of them spent the centuries fighting the Dark wherever they appeared."

284

Just then Alex got a familiar faint feeling that the Dark was present. It was small and not that strong. It seemed way far out in the distance. She just looked to the field and concluded that it was just paranoia because she was so content here. Retelling the story of Osiah probably reminded her of what the Dark felt like.

"Where does the star come in?" he asked about the story.

Alex smiled at him. "When an angel dies, their Lite is diminished and sent to the skies as a star in their remembrance."

"How'd he die?"

She looked up to the sky. "He sacrificed himself to save the Conduit and an upcoming Lite Sentry, who he was training. They were surrounded by the Dark; he ensured their safety with his life." She grabbed her neck remembering that night and then grabbing the blue gold angel she had gotten from Kameron.

"That's a sad story," Kameron said. "You know that story quite well."

"I wrote about it in high school," Alex said quickly, trying to cover her tracks.

"No, there is more to it," he noticed. "The only thing I surmise was that you were there firsthand."

Alex suddenly got a big lump in her throat as she continued to look out at the field. "What do you mean?"

"Well, obviously you are the beautiful Lite Conduit sent down to help mankind," Kameron told her, playfully bumping into her.

Alex could feel herself smile as she turned to him. He, too, had turned to face her. She felt like she was a high school girl falling in love for the first time.

"Kameron…"

He moved some of her hair away from her face. "Alex…"

Alex grabbed a bunch of snow from the banister and threw it in his face. It went down his shirt as he laughed. "Now we're even!" Alex laughed as she hopped over the banister trying to get away from him.

"Oh, it's on now!" Kameron caught up to her quite faster than Alex expected.

The kind playful laughter from him was genuine had Alex giggling until he picked her and started swinging her around. Now she was in full out laughter. "You better stop or you're going to make me puke all over you!" She continued laughing.

The boys came screaming and running from the barn, interrupting their spirited banter. The fear in their eyes was something Alex was accustomed to. "What's wrong?"

"We just saw a bear!" one of the boys said. "He was big!"

"All the bears are sleeping through the winter," Kameron said. "It was probably just a coyote or something."

"Nope," the other disagreed. "It was a bear, it was huge."

"What color eyes did it have?" Alex asked him.

"Glowing red eyes with big claws," he told her.

Alex closed her eyes and sighed.

"Overactive imagination," Kameron told her. "Where are your pistols?"

"In the barn, where the bear is," the boy told her. "I'm not going back there to get them."

Kameron rolled his eyes. "I'll go look for them."

"I'll go," Alex said, looking over in the barn's direction. "I have to take Komptin for a walk anyways." Alex flipped up her collar again. "Take the boys inside, I'll get the pistols. No coyote is going to come near me, especially with Komptin nearby."

"Okay," Kameron hesitantly said. "Come on, boys, let's go get some hot chocolate."

Alex started walking towards the barn and gave a loud whistle.

Komptin came running out of the house in full stride as he joined Alex at her side.

"Light is by the door on the left-hand side!" Kameron yelled to her as the two of them walked calmly out to the barn. Alex just stuck her hand up in the air giving him a thumb's up.

Alex was approaching the barn. The sound of crunching snow below her feet made it pretty much impossible to be stealthy. So, she just calmly walked up to the barn door.

She looked down at Komptin. "What do you think?"

Komptin flashed his eyes in agreement.

Alex nodded. She looked back at the house, and it seemed like no one was around.

Then an Infiltrator jumped out of the other side of the barn running into the woods.

"Go," she told Komptin.

Komptin morphed into his gargoyle state and took off after the Infiltrator. Alex watched him take off disappearing into the woods.

"Damn it," Alex said, opening the doors to the inside of the barn.

She looked for the light switch full knowing that it wasn't going to work.

Alex shook her head. "You know just once I would like to go into a room where the lights worked," she said to herself. Kameron was still dropping the boys off with the parents giving the opportunity to light her fists to see her surroundings. There was nervous rumbling in her stomach, but it wasn't fear of dying, it was fear for the safety of this family.

The barn was full of equipment, but it was quite roomy. That was good in case she had to maneuver in a fight. There was nothing on the other side of the turbine. There was something nearby, the Dark was present. The sound her cracking her neck was all that could be heard as she knew it was approaching her from behind. She closed her eyes and got her body in stance to attack. In a flash, she had the Dark Myst by his throat. "Salamor!"

"Lite Sentry," he hissed out at her trying to pry his hands off his throat.

288

Alex knew the Dark Myst wasn't used to having anyone able to hurt it. She squeezed a little bit more and his legs were flapping in the air.

"I told you, the next time I saw you, I was going to kill you. Why are you here?" Alex demanded.

"I'm not talking, Sentry Bitch," he hissed again.

Alex squeezed a little bit more. "That's not nice. Now, why are you here?"

Salamor was having trouble talking as Alex had a tight grip on his throat. She let up a little so he could talk. "We sensed the Conduit was here, for no reason we couldn't figure out why, so I was sent to investigate."

Alex could hear a faint sound of Christmas music being played in the background along with the sound of the Infiltrator being diminished by Komptin. Alex looked outside to the snow falling and she turned to Salamor.

She extinguished her fists and let go of her grip. "I don't want to kill you, not this Christmas."

Salamor stayed in the spot on the wall while floating in front of her. Alex could tell he was hesitant about her actions.

Komptin came into the barn in full gargoyle mode with eyes glowing staring at Salamor. Alex motioned to him to stand down. Komptin walked around the turbine and positioned himself behind Alex.

"You can go." She motioned towards the door. She flipped her collar up and adjusted her hair to the outside of the coat and tightened her belt on her black leather overcoat. "Go on."

Salamor nodded still in shock.

He slowly started to float away before Alex said, "Salamor."

He turned around to look at the Lite Sentry.

"Not this house, not this family."

"As you command," he said as he floated off into the darkness in the opposite direction of the house.

Komptin's face was one of confusion. She noticed the pistols and picked them up. The two of them walked out of the barn. Alex leaned on the gargoyle, staring at the house. The enormous, purple-skinned friend moved his head over so she could lean on his massive body. She wrapped her arm around his neck scratching behind his ears.

"I just couldn't do it, I didn't want to end this trip with me killing someone." The two of them stared at the house. "Let me ask you something, big guy." She continued to stare at the house as the snow fell. "You weren't a really big fan of Gastrix, were you?"

Komptin growled in acknowledgement.

Alex gave a small chuckle from his reaction. "Asked and answered, got it. What do you think of Kameron?"

Komptin acknowledged his approval of Kameron by a quick flashing of eyes. This gave Alex the final endorsement she was wanting. "Yeah, me too."

"Alex," Kameron's voice came out from a distance.

Alex watched Kameron come to them. She felt Komptin morph back to a dog causing her to fall into the snow. "Could have warned me."

"Oh, there you are. What are you doing in the snow?" Kameron asked, extending his hands.

Alex took his hand and got off the ground. She noticed he was wearing his service pistol underneath his coat.

"I fell," she told him as she looked at Komptin.

Komptin moved behind Kameron, so he flashed his eyes at her.

"Come on, let's go inside," Kameron said.

Alex started walking to the house not letting go of Kameron's hand.

***

Everyone was asleep as Alex was sitting in the living room. The family had left the Christmas lights on, and Alex was enjoying the ambience of the room. Komptin was lying on the couch with his head on Alex's lap. She was drinking her energy drink as she was just watching the Christmas tree. She heard someone coming down the stairs.

Kameron walked down the stairs, still dressed.

"What are you doing up?"

"I told Mom and Dad I would go get the kid's Christmas presents from Santa from the barn loft. They got them bikes and Janelle and Robert will be here around five in the morning before the kids' get up." Kameron got his coat on. "What are you doing up at this hour?"

Alex tried to think of something. "Just soaking it all in." She smiled at him.

"Do you want me to take Komptin out with me in case he has to go to the bathroom?"

Alex kind of snickered to herself, as Komptin never did that. "Do you want to go?" She looked down at Komptin who jumped at the opportunity.

Kameron was roughing him up a little bit, playing with him. "Come on, boy, let's go do man-time." He laughed. "I'll take good care of him."

"It's more that he will take care of you," she told him. "Have fun boys."

Alex took comfort in knowing that Komptin went with Kameron to the barn. Even though she was pretty sure that Salamor and any Infiltrator wouldn't return. It was just a nice comfort. They returned with two bikes with big bows on them. Kameron placed the bikes by the tree for the boys to see as they came down the stairs.

Komptin curled up by the fire to dry off as Kameron poured himself a glass of wine. "Want a refill of your drink?"

"Please." She handed him the glass. He returned with her drink. "Thank you, join me?" She moved over so he could have the side of the couch.

He grabbed a small glass of wine and joined her. He sat down and situated his shoulder.

"Shoulder hurt?"

292

"Yeah, seems like the weather really aggravates it," Kameron told her. "You know I still have the bullet."

"You do? Why?" Alex asked him.

"Just a reminder, more of a humility check," Kameron told her as he took a sip of wine. He grabbed Alex's hand to hold it.

She allowed it and squeezed it lovingly. "I get that." The two of them just stared at the tree. Komptin laid on his side enjoying the fire.

"You know, it's pretty interesting how I've never seen you before the first time we met, even though we were there at the same time in Kale's hospital room," Kameron told her.

"I wasn't in a good place during that time, things went bad, really bad," Alex admitted.

Kameron took a sip of his drink. "Yeah, well I'm glad I got the opportunity to know you now." He looked over at her. "I can't remember a more perfect Christmas than this one."

Alex looked over to him. She felt nerves like she never felt before. Was she supposed to kiss him? Was he going to kiss her?

She didn't want to ruin such a perfect trip by crossing over a line. She liked him, she really liked him, she finally admitted to herself, but she didn't know if he was being nice or did he like her as well.

"Kameron, I..." she tried to say something.

Kameron interrupted her, "Look at the clock, it's a minute passed midnight."

"Yeah," she said, still looking at him. "What does that mean?"

"Merry Christmas, Alexandria," he said, as he leaned in gently kissed her.

The kiss was like nothing she had felt before. She placed her hand on his face as she returned the kiss.

"It's about damn time." A voice came up from on top of the stairs as Michelle walked down in her bathrobe wearing a Christmas bandana.

Alex and Kameron regained their composure, not letting go of holding hands. "What are you doing up?" Kameron asked. "You okay?"

"Not as good as some people, it would seem." She smiled at them. "I just came down to get a glass of water." She walked over to Kameron and punched him in the arm. "You stud."

"Go put a dollar in your jar, will you?" he teased.

She laughed as she walked by Alex. "If I died right now, I'd couldn't be happier." She tapped her on the leg. "Now, I'm going to get my water. If you want, I can take my time."

Mary and Harold followed down the stairs with a bunch of presents. "I see Santa has got a bunch of helpers this morning," Mary said. "What are you guys doing up?"

"I'm getting water," Michelle said. "Those two are making out."

Alex hid her face into Kameron. "Oh God!" She laughed.

Harold looked over at his son in acknowledgement; Kameron nodded with a smile. Harold just smiled. "Merry Christmas, you two."

Chapter 9

"Stupid, stupid, stupid, just stupid," Alex said, hitting the keyboard at work.

Father Tom just stood in front of her desk. "So, you didn't have a nice Christmas?" Father Tom instantly knew not to push the subject when Alex gave him irritated glare. "Okay, Okay." He laughed putting up his hands.

Alex looked down at Komptin laying down in his bed next to her desk. Alex could have sworn he was sneering. "Not you, too." Komptin put his head down.

Alex got a text from Kameron reading, "We just got done ice fishing" and a picture of Kameron holding a tiny fish. Alex couldn't think of a reply, so she just sent him a picture of a laughing face.

She decided to see what happened at work while she was on her trip. She picked some of the mail that accumulated while she was gone. She thought that Megan would have done something while Alex was gone, but no Christmas miracle this year. She saw a card with a return address from the F.O.R. wishing them a Happy Holidays. She initially was going to throw it away, but she thought Father Tom would like to know it came. "Hey, Father, we just got a Happy Holidays card from the F.O.R."

Father Tom rolled his eyes, "Just leave it my inbox and I will look at and then give it to Anne for filing."

"Will do," Alex said as she turned around. She stopped herself, turned back around to Father Tom, but then went to go back to her desk.

"Hey Alex," Father Tom said, writing something in a journal.

"Yes, Father," she looked back at him.

"I'm going to head out before the roads get too bad," Father Tom told her, putting on his coat. "Can you lock up?"

"Not a problem," Alex said. She was looking forward to an empty church. She wanted to be alone to sit in the Cathedral with an energy drink in her hand. Just to sit and think and maybe ask a question.

"Roads are getting bad. I told Megan to stay home. Nothing really is going on here anyways." He continued to write in his book. "Shoot me a text if you decide to go anywhere tonight, okay?"

She nodded in acceptance. "Yes, Father. I'll probably just stay in tonight, if that's okay?"

He nodded as he started his car with his remote. He watched her pause for a second and then turned back around to go to her desk.

Father Tom made sure to shut his computer off. "Hey, Alex, I know it's none of my business, but be sure you take advantage of the open-door God gives you, if you don't, you may not get another one." Alex's text message alerted her. "Hmmm, a knock." He gave her a teasing smile.

Alex opened the message to see it was a video from Michelle. Alex watched Michelle take a video of herself putting a bowl of chocolate pudding on the floor next to Kameron sleeping peacefully on the couch. She slid it underneath Kameron's hand, so his fingers were in the bowl.

Alex was snickering at Michelle who was trying not to laugh too loud to prevent her from waking Kameron. She took a piece of hay from the barn. She started to put the straw across his nose trying not to laugh. This time she took the piece of hay and gently put it up his nostril and he jumped and swiped the straw across his face covering himself in chocolate pudding.

Michelle ran from Kameron loudly laughing as he chased her with his monster pudding hand. "He's such a dumbass!" She busted out laughing and the video ended.

Alex found herself missing Kameron and his family. She didn't reply to the message.

***

Gron sat down in his new desk as the Leader of the F.O.R. He adjusted the chair and turned on his computer. He wanted to see what assets he had at his disposal before launching Vandor's plan. He sat back and watched out of the shadows as Vandor appeared with Salamor at this side. "To your command," Gron got up and bowed.

"How do you like your new office?" Vandor gently grazed the desk with his sharp fingernails. The reflection of the wood shows his pale face with darkened eyes.

"I can get used to it," he said. "We are going to start the public relations portion of the plan after the

New Year. I have the video department putting together the project now."

Vandor smiled as he gave Gron a piece of paper.

"I can get it by tonight. I will send my top Demon," Gron assured.

Salamor interjected, "He will not be an easy grab."

"We will not fail," Gron told him.

"Better not," Vandor told him.

Gron asked Salamor, "Is there any report on why the Sentry was in upstate New York over the holidays?"

Salamor spoke, "As far as I saw, she was just there to get away."

Vandor wanted answer from Salamor. "How'd we lose an Infiltrator?"

"The mutt caught wind of it when she was returning from an eating establishment and hunted it in an alley in town and they distinguished it," Salamor told them. "Then she just stayed in a hotel resort and ate a bunch of food, and then came home the day after Christmas."

Gron contributed to the interrogation of the living shadow. "What about the Lite Conduit?"

"Probably just there to stop by on the holiday, they are close," Salamor pointed out.

Vandor wanted something more, something he could use against the Sentry. "Gron what do you think?

"Sounds like something she would do. Her brother and his girlfriend were out of town." Gron watched as a young beautiful blonde came in giving him his coffee. She placed it on his desk and smiled before she turned around. "What's your name?"

"Lea," she said, turning to him.

"Come back in 15 minutes." Gron waved her off.

"Yes, my leader," she said as she walked out.

Gron studied the backside of the young girl as he talked to the Dark Conduit. "We're going to donate 3.5 million to runaway teens and offer them drug rehab and a place to live, while giving them a sort of education." Gron checked his suit in the mirror. "I'm going to go announce it to the press shortly."

"Good, see you tonight, have it ready," Vandor said.

"It will be here," Gron promised. "Lea, I'm ready now."

Lea entered, undoing her blouse after she shut the door behind her. Salamor watched as the door closed and he floated off to join Vandor.

***

Anne made it back to work halfway hoping all her work was done for her when she was gone. She opened her office, and it was just as she left it. She took a sip of her coffee she just bought on her way into work. She knew she had to go talk to Alex considering they haven't talked since they returned from Hawaii. Plus, she was dying to know how her Christmas went.

She texted Kale, "Hey, I just want to say I love you."

Kale immediately responded, "I love you doesn't even cover how I feel about you."

She smiled at his response when Alex walked in. She texted Kale back, "Alex just walked in, talk later. Luv you!" She put her phone down. "Morning."

"Morning, you look tan." Alex came around her desk and gave her a hug. "How'd everything go?"

"Well, we got a majority of all the wedding plans done, so there's a stress reliever," Anne told her opening her email. She frowned as she said, "Nothing from the Russian Orthodox Council Historian." She sat back in her chair drinking her coffee.

"That's good about the wedding plans," Alex told her.

"Where's Komptin?" Anne was looking around.

"At my desk, sleeping in his bed." Alex opened her energy drink and sat down looking at Anne as if something was on her mind.

Anne wanted to ask her how her trip went, but obviously something happened. Anne resisted the urge to ask so she sat down opening her email. Alex just sat there tapping her can with one of her rings. Anne looked back at her, smiled and then went back to her computer. Alex stared at her, tapping her can.

"Something on your mind?" Anne lost to her urge.

Alex tightened her lip as if trying to say something but was unable to do it.

"How was your trip?" Anne asked.

"I did something stupid, just stupid, stupid," Alex said, rolling her eyes.

Anne sat back in her chair with her coffee. "Did you sleep with Kameron?"

"No," Alex admitted to her.

Anne raised her eyebrows. "Really?"

"Yes, really," Alex said, taking a drink of her Apollo.

"Then what happened?"

Alex stood up and looked out the window of Anne's office. "I had a great time. His family was kind, funny, and basically accepted me as one of their own."

"And so, what's the issue?"

Alex turned to her. "I kissed him, or he kissed me, or I think we kissed each other." Alex got frustrated and sat down back in the chair.

Anne tried not to smile. "Okay, but you didn't sleep with him."

"It would have been better if I did then we could have just gone our separate ways, now there's this thing out there," Alex said.

Anne was genuinely confused. "How?"

"Because, because…because it just is," Alex said out of confusion.

"Honey, do you think you didn't sleep with him for a reason?"

Alex just looked at her.

Anne's phone rang. "Yes, Father, we'll be right up." Anne got up from the desk. "Father Tom wants to see us right away."

***

Kale just finished his set on the bench and moved out of the way for Kameron to take his turn. Kameron sat, grabbed the bar and started lifting, "And then I kissed her."

Kale grabbed the bar, "That's all that happened?"

"Yeah," Kameron said, finishing his set. He sat up taking a break. "I shouldn't have done that." Kameron shook his head from being discouraged with himself.

"What happened after that?" Kale asked.

"Well, frankly, nothing really. We helped my parents put the presents under the tree, she went to bed after helping my sister get to bed, and then we spent Christmas Day together. I drove her to the airport and then dropped her off. We gave each other a kiss good-bye with a hug and that was it. She just turned to wave to me with a smile as she made it through security," he told Kale. "I shouldn't have kissed her. It was unfair to her."

"Unfair?" Kale asked him.

"She was out of her element, and I was her only familiar thing she knew," Kameron said, getting up.

Kale took his place while Kameron added more weight. He lifted his set as Kameron helped him with the last one. Kale stayed laying down. "You

302

don't have to worry about Alex feeling vulnerable or out of place when it comes to guys." He sat up and turned to his friend who was clearly worried that he put his friendship with Alex in jeopardy. "Alex Johnson doesn't do anything with guys that she doesn't want to. Have you contacted her since you dropped her off at the airport?"

"I texted her once, she replied back with a smiling pic, but I didn't want her to think I was some sort of stalker or something," he said. His attention turned to the news. He reached up and turned up the volume.

Kale looked up to see Roger Somberson on the television set giving an interview on a local radio station. "Son-of-a-bitch."

***

"The ignorance thrown out at our organization has just been a scapegoat for the radicals that use our name for their cause," Roger told the reporter.

"So, you're saying you don't condone the actions of the militants bombing religion centers?" the reporter asked.

"Okay, let's get the facts straight here, first, try not to convolute the whole truth because there were only two horrific attacks, and second, these people who pervert and bastardize our mission and ideals are in no way affiliated with our organization. We don't condone violence. I never have, and never will, think violence is the answer."

"Does your organization believe religion should be eradicated from the communities?" the reporter asked.

"Religion has caused so much death and destruction in the name of an 'almighty'. I'm telling you, if you want true absolute power, you need to open yourself to it," he said. "Then, you can accomplish anything. Live in a world without drugs, chaos, and fighting among ourselves over who is right over some absentee ghost."

"But what about the allegations—" the reporter tried to ask before he was interrupted by Roger.

"Look, in the near future, I will make a community announcement which will show our true intentions regarding the F.O.R." Roger said. "In the meantime, only our actions will show you our true intentions."

"Well, that's all the time we have, thank you for your time," the reporter told him.

"Anytime," Roger said.

***

Father Tom turned down the volume of the television. Anne, Alex, and Megan stood behind Father Tom as they finished watching the broadcast. "Thoughts?"

"I don't see the big deal," Megan told the group.

Alex gave a loud sigh.

Father Tom turned to Alex. "Alex, I need all perspectives to understand what they are doing."

Alex turned around and sat back down at her desk.

"Okay, we got Alex's perspective, Anne?"

Anne looked over at Father Tom.

"Anne, you look a little pale."

"Sorry, it's just seeing him again brought back some memories. I just hope Kale didn't see this," Anne said. Then both Anne's and Alex's phone got a text message. "I think I'm going to be sick," she responded, as it was from Kale. Anne looked to Alex. "He saw it."

Father Tom turned to go into his office. "Alex, Anne."

Alex and Anne followed Father Tom to his office as Megan gave Alex a disgusted expression as she walked by her.

"Can we get rid of her?" Alex said to Father Tom. "Why didn't the Council hire a secretary that was cleared?"

"They are working on it," Father Tom answered. "Anne, how are you doing?"

"I'm fine," she answered, taking a drink of water. "I don't think Kale is going to be well."

"I take it that he was the Demon that attacked him that night," Father Tom assumed. "I've never seen him before."

"He's gotten more powerful," Alex told the two of them.

"How are you with this?" he asked her. "The last time you saw him wasn't the ideal circumstance."

"The hardest part of dealing with it was that he actually saved my life, before he left me to die," she said, rubbing her scar on the side of her head.

"Well, we have no doubt now that the Dark is running F.O.R.," Father Tom said. "Alex, you are under strict orders, try your best not to kill any full humans, they are going to be innocent pawns in all of this."

Alex nodded. She understood that she might have to kill a human, but it was a guilt she did not want to live with if she could help it.

"Anne, where are we at?" Father Tom asked her.

"I found two references that might match each other when it comes to Infiltrators. The Russian one talked of the 'walking smell death' and 'consumption of life' and another in South American stating the 'dark lite moon eating'. The texts are vague because they were torn and faded by the time the Council got a hold of them. The Russian Orthodox council is looking into their vaults for any other information."

"Feels like a good path to follow," Father Tom said. "Alex, go out tonight, see what you can find out and if you happen to kill a couple of those black monsters, I could live with that." He smiled.

***

Alex was getting ready for her hunt. She put on her leather pants and boots before applying her makeup. The mirror was reflecting to her a young, pale faced girl who wore dark makeup, didn't really portray a fierce warrior. Her hand grabbed the angel on her necklace. This was the first gift she ever got from a guy before, well besides Kale, but that didn't count. It has been over a week since Kameron had contacted her. She picked up her phone and started writing him a text. There were plenty of drafts before she yielded to her defeat by tossing her phone on her dresser.

"You know, piss on him, if he doesn't want to talk." She turned to Komptin for agreement but didn't get it.

The sound of someone knocking on Alex's door startled her. Alex checked her hair one more time before answering it.

She opened the door to see Kale standing in front her with snow on his jacket.

"Kale, what are you doing here?"

"I was out for a walk and found myself here, can I come in?" He brushed off his jacket. "Going out tonight?"

Alex didn't know how to respond to him. She knew she couldn't tell him she was going to go spy on an organization run by dark demons. "Yeah, I want to go out tonight and see what's happening."

He sat on the bed and petted Komptin.

She turned the mirror and continued to get ready. "How do I look?"

"Pretty as always," Kale said, rubbing Komptin's ears.

Alex knew something was on his mind since he didn't make a smart-ass response. "Hey, you okay?"

"Seeing him today, it brought up stuff that I haven't thought of for years," Kale admitted. "I literally threw up in the bathroom at the gym."

Alex sat on the bed with her brother. "Hey, I get it. I really do. Seeing him again wasn't the highlight of my year."

Kale looked at Alex who was smiling at him as a loving sister would. "We've always looked out for each other through all these years, and we tell each other everything."

Alex looked down. "Mostly everything." She started to feel guilty that she hadn't told him about her true job risking her life night and after night maintaining the balance between the Lite and the Dark.

"To this day, I don't know how Anne and I survived that night. I keep on remembering hearing your voice, a light, and this big, massive purple thing, but then it all gets blurry," Kale told her. "I remember talking to Father Joe about it and he said that it was probably hallucinations from the injuries. My mind made up stuff to prevent me from thinking of my body. I get that, but seeing Roger again, brought up that night over and over again all day."

Alex grabbed his hand and smiled. "Let me know if there is anything I can do. Have you talked to Anne about this?"

"Yes, and she's a great support system, but honestly, that's not why I'm here," Kale told her.

"Oh?" She inquired. "What's going on?"

"What's going on with you and Kameron?"

Alex could feel her stomach get into knots. She got up and grabbed an energy drink. "Nothing, absolutely nothing."

Kale was studying his sister. "Alex, I know you. I got the privilege of bearing the burden of witnessing your dating life since you were 12 when I caught you kissing that kid at camp." He started to get up but winced in the pain in his back. "I knew about every guy you've fooled around with, and they didn't last long."

"What about Gastrix?" Alex reminded him.

"Come on, he doesn't count," Kale told her. "You know that. You really want to have that conversation?"

"What are you getting at?"

"Kameron is a good guy, and frankly speaking, you not sleeping with him, should tell you something," Kale started getting agitated.

"What did he say?" Alex asked out of concern.

"He is feeling guilty because he thought he shouldn't have kissed you because you were not in your comfortable surroundings," he said.

Alex laughed. "That dumbass! That is farthest from it." She looked to Kale. "I was never so comfortable and happy."

"Then why haven't you contacted him?" He got up from her bed. "Look, I'm not going to tell him I talked to you." He put on his jacket. "I didn't want you two to hook up as it is, but I'm going to say this and then I'm going to walk home. I've never seen you act like this around a guy before." He zipped up his jacket. "Just something for you to think about."

Alex nodded as she hugged Kale good-bye. "Are you walking home?"

"Yeah, the air is feeling pretty good," he replied. "I'll text you when I get home."

"Please do," Alex said as she and Komptin walked him out of the church.

She watched him head in the direction of his apartment.

She looked down at Komptin. "Make sure he gets home, okay?"

Komptin flashed his eyes and took off. Alex knew full well that if Komptin wasn't going to be seen unless he wanted to. Alex locked up the church and headed towards the new F.O.R. headquarters.

She knew this mission was strictly recon so she really wouldn't need Komptin. It was still early enough in the night for any Infiltrators not to be out in such a nice part of the city. Alex made it to the shopping section of town where she saw many couples holding hands. She found herself thinking about holding Kameron's hands during her trip to upstate New York.

There was no message on her phone. She clicked on his name and went to write a message but closed her phone. Confusion clouded her mind. The only thing that gave her serenity was being engulfed in the shopping center surrounded by the Christmas decorations. As she was getting coffee, her phone beeped and thought it was Kameron, but it ended being Kale telling her that he made it home safe. She responded to him and then put her phone in her pocket. Alex found herself staring at her reflection from a storefront window. There was no movement from her when Celestial's reflection came to the side of hers.

"What are you looking at?" Celestial asked her.

Alex just continued to look at her reflection. "I don't know." Alex turned to Celestial.

Ariel and Devine were studying Alex.

"What?"

They looked at each other then back at her, "Nothing," they both said softly.

"I'm going to go find out what the F.O.R. are up to," Alex told her in a monotone unmotivated voice. Big fluffy snowflakes started to fall from the sky.

"Are you okay?" Celestial asked.

"I don't know, I just don't know," Alex said. "I need to go; can I talk to you later?"

"Of course," Celestial said, giving her a sad wave good-bye. Ariel and Devine looked to each other and then watched Alex walk off towards the F.O.R. building.

*　*　*

Alex made it near the new F.O.R. building. She felt the sense of Demons but this close to the F.O.R. building it was to be expected. She stayed in the shadows of the alley watching people walk by but nothing out of the ordinary.

She looked at her phone to see if any messages came through, but it was blank. Alex heard some people talking so she hid deeper in the shadows.

311

She wasn't getting intelligence from sitting in an alley. She was done, she just wanted to go home and crawl underneath a blanket and watch movies. She walked down the other end of the alley in a slow manner. She wasn't in a hurry, and she didn't want to draw attention to herself. She reached a fence that was sealing off the alley. It didn't stop her from seeing two demons with glowing eyes staring at her.

She halfway expected to turn around to see her surrounded but there was no one there. She turned back to look at the Demons and more started to move up to the fence which was sealing off the exit to the alley. They watched her as she slowly started walking backwards as they slowly climbed the fence while watching her.

"Damn," she said as she turned around and started running.

The alley was cleared to her left and to the right and she saw more Demons within the crowd of people walking her way. The parking structure had two Demons in her way ready for her demise. Her fists were lit ready for the inevitable encounter. This was not a hunt, this was survival. The only sanction she had was to get to the nearest holy ground, but she didn't know where that was. She took a deep breath before she ran at full force knocking one of them and Lite Beamed the other as it screamed. It shook off the effects of the beam and started to chase her. More Demons came out of the shadows and a mixture of Provisionary people started to join in the fight. The humans were easily manhandled, but she didn't want to kill them unless she had to.

There was a moment to catch her bearing when she made it to the top of a parking structure. There was no escape in sight. If she were to jump, she certainly would die. There were no trees or other structures to break the fall.

"Damn it." All around her were Demons, Provisionaries, and a couple of Infiltrators walking towards her.

They started to charge at her with the Infiltrators leading the pack running on all fours. She stood battle ready as they lunged at her. She managed to knock a couple of them into each other. A Demon somehow got behind her and knocked her to the ground. Another demon, with his eyes glowing red, jumped in the air to land on her. Alex rolled out of the way before the demon landed, causing the concrete ground to break.

A feeling of knowing this was the end came over her as she stumbled back up. A Demon punched her across the face, causing her to fall to the ground, confirming the thought. The only grace she had was a Provisionary thought he could take her, and she managed to grab him throwing him into three Demons, knocking them over. But an Infiltrator managed to get on top of her as she felt others kicking and scratching her.

The sound of thunder came from the sky as a bright light flashed. Alex managed to look up to see Ariel and Devine in full battle gear land on the parking structure and start to fend off Alex's attackers. With what strength Alex had left, she pushed off her assailants. Devine jabbed her bō staff into a Demon as it howled in pain and burnt to ash. Ariel grabbed an Infiltrator flipping it upside down and stabbing it through the neck.

"We cannot keep this up," Ariel screamed to the two of them.

"We have to go," Devine added.

"Not like that thought hasn't crossed my miiiiiiinnnnnndddd…." Alex said as she saw the top of the parking structure from the sky.

***

Gron watched as Alex was carried off into the sky. "Almost had her, and Celestial was left unguarded." He just watched up in the sky.

"Were those angels?" one of the Provisionaries asked.

Gron turned him. "What?"

"Those were angels." He looked around. "That makes you all…"

Gron took his hands and twisted the neck of the provisionary. "Kill all the provisionaries that are here." He told them this as he left for his office.

The Demons and Infiltrators attacked all the humans, devouring their carcasses.

***

Ariel and Devine put Alex on the ground once they knew they wouldn't be spotted. "Where's Celestial?" Alex immediately asked.

"Your church," Devine answered her.

"Komptin is there with her," Ariel assured Alex of Celestial's safety.

That made Alex feel better. "Thank God for that." She looked up at Ariel and Devine. "Thank you."

"No problem," they both said as they looked over their wounds.

"Not like I don't appreciate you showing up, but what were you doing there anyways?" Alex asked them. She took off her leather jacket to see claw marks on the back. "I liked this jacket, too."

"We are just wondering why you are so scared?" Devine asked.

"Scared, hey, I was ready to die over there, I just faced a bunch of Demons and Infiltrators," Alex's voice was growing more intense.

"That was an escape from your fear," Ariel specified.

"Then I don't know what you are talking about," Alex told them.

"Send a message to your friend then," Ariel said.

"If you are not too scared," Devine finished off.

Alex pulled out her phone. "Anne, okay, I'll tell her I'm okay."

"Kameron," they both said sternly.

Alex put her phone away. "Yeah, that's not happening."

"Why not?" Devine asked.

"We know you like him," Ariel said.

Alex put her hands in her pockets. "I can't put him through this."

"Through what?" They both asked.

"This." She pulled out her lit hands. "You guys, Celestial, Infiltrators, Demons, Vandor, all of it."

Ariel and Devine looked at each other and frowned at Alex. "That is crap," they both said.

Alex got taken back. "Excuse me?"

"You are too scared to let him in." Ariel pointed to her chest.

"To be vulnerable to your feelings." Devine came up along Ariel.

"Why?" They both pushed.

"Because I don't want to lose him!" Alex screamed at them. She turned away from the two angels so she could wipe her tears. "I can't lose what I don't have." She turned back to them.

The two of them just looked at Alex before Devine spoke. "Every visit to this place puts us in fear."

"She is hunted continuously, we constantly fear losing her," the green-haired angel admitted.

"It doesn't stop us from letting her, or others, in," they both looked to Alex. "We constantly fear losing those we love," Devine said.

"Our love overtakes that fear so we can be happy," Ariel said.

"Happy?" Alex asked them.

"She needs to interact with primates for her to do her job," Devine checked her armor for damages.

316

"Our love for her gives us strength for her protection," Ariel tried adjusting the protective armor of hers.

Devine came up to Ariel to help. "Her happiness is everything to us."

"It would be useless to walk without allowing love in," Ariel said.

Devine added, "Regardless how scared we are."

Alex looked at them. "You get scared?"

"Every time she walks the Earth," they both told her.

She put on her ripped coat. "But what if he doesn't feel the same?"

"Then you know, and you can move on," Ariel said.

"But any man who is wise enough to dip French fries in a chocolate shake is certainly smart enough to see what a strong, beautiful, caring, brave, young woman you are," Devine told her.

Alex smiled. "You think that of me?"

Ariel lifted her chin up to meet her gaze. "Of course, there is not a night we do not check the stars."

Devine came in on the other side of Alex. "To make sure our little sister is not among them."

Alex didn't know what to say. She had never heard Ariel and Devine speak so highly of her. All she could do was smile back at them.

Ariel and Devine formed out of their battle gear and were in their human clothes.

"Come on," Devine said.

"We will walk you home," Ariel finished.

"Yeah, no more flying," Alex said as she started to walk home with her surrogate siblings. "Hey, wait a minute." Alex stopped in her tracks. "If you are able to fly like that, how come you don't lift Celestial out of dangerous situations?"

Devine looked at her like she said something stupid. "Do you know how heavy she is?"

"We could barely toss her, if needed," Ariel added.

"Oh." Alex never really thought about trying to lift her up. She wanted to try it.

***

Gron got back to his office where Vandor was waiting for him. "Did you get it?"

"As you command." Gron bowed. He pushed a button on the intercom. A Demon came in carrying a middle-aged man bound and gagged. "We found him down by the soup kitchen giving blankets to some of the homeless."

Vandor came up to him and sniffed. "You did well." He looked back at Salamor. "Pick out another. Report back to Gron."

"As you command," Salamor said. He floated out of the building. He came across one before, but he could not bring himself to report it. He decided to find another.

***

Alex texted Kale while he was at work. "I need a favor."

Kale replied, "What?"

She texted him what she wanted him to do, and he replied back to her. "I'll do it, but under protest."

"I owe you," she said back to him.

She put her phone down. She got up and walked into Father Tom's office. She sat down on the couch as he threw her an Apollo drink from his desk as he just continued to work on his paperwork.

"Can I take the morning off?"

"If what you say in your report is true, then I think you deserve it," Father Tom said, continuing to read the paper. "They actually left her side to come help you?"

"Not exactly," Alex said, taking a drink.

Father Tom looked it over. "You didn't put it in here."

"They wanted to give me, I guess you can call it, a big sister talk," Alex added in.

"Oh really," Father Tom said, putting his paper down. "About dealing with the F.O.R.?"

"No," she said.

"The Dark?" he questioned.

"No," she tried hiding her smile behind her can.

"Oh." Father Tom's light bulb just clicked. He sat back in his chair. "I hope their advice was sound."

"It was," Alex admitted as she thought about her upcoming task.

"And the result," he asked.

"I guess we'll find out after lunch," Alex told him after leaving the office.

"Alex," Father Tom yelled.

"Yes," she answered.

"You got this," he smiled at her.

***

Kameron was sitting at his desk going over the security protocols for the FLOTUS visit to a city orphanage. It looked standard as he handed it over to his supervisor. He looked at his watch as he realized Kale was going to meet him for lunch.

He grabbed his suit coat as he adjusted his holsters for his weapons.

"Where are you off to?" his coworker asked him.

"Oh, I'm meeting a buddy of mine for lunch. He said he was in the neighborhood."

"Have fun," he said. "I'll stay back here and cover your work for you," he said as he put his feet on his desk and started reading the newspaper.

"I'm sure I'm leaving it in fully capable hands," he said to him, patting him on the shoulders.

Kameron walked down the hallway and ran into the director. "Director, how are you?"

"I'm fine," Director Morkin said, yawning.

"Late night?" Kameron asked.

"Yeah, I had to run around the whole city last night, wasn't what I call ideal," he told Kameron. "Where are you off to?"

"Going to lunch, a friend of mine is in the neighborhood," he told him.

They both scanned their cards logging their exit time. Kameron saw Kale and Anne standing in the lobby and waved to him. The director followed Kameron to his friend. "Kale this is Director Morkin, Director, Kale Moler," Kameron introduced them to each other.

"You're Kale Moler," the director said shaking his hand.

"Yes, have you heard of me?" Kale asked jokingly. "Should I be scared? This is my fiancé Anne."

"Nice to meet you," Anne said.

Director laughed. "You as well, Anne, No, I just knew you took care of Kameron when he got injured. Nice to meet you Anne."

"Yeah, Kale isn't a common name," he told him.

"Why are you here, it's pretty far from the hospital?" Kameron asked him, adjusting his coat.

Kale sighed. "Yeah, about that."

Anne poked him in the side. "Stop it," she whispered.

He then hesitated before stating. "I'm here fulfilling a debt."

Alex turned the corner and walked up to Kameron.

"Alex," Kameron said. "What are you doing here?"

The two of them looked at each other for a second or two before Alex threw her arms around

Kameron's neck, kissing him in the middle of the lobby. People started clapping and cheering with loud whistling at the two of them. Alex and Kameron were touching foreheads looking at each other smiling and laughing. Kameron turned around to his audience and politely waved to everyone cheering as Alex was hiding in Kameron's chest from embarrassment.

***

The Director came back to his office and pulled a cell phone out from the desk drawer. "It's Director Morkin, get me Gron." He looked out his window at Kameron holding hands with Lite Sentry going to lunch. "Yes, we have an interesting turn of events."

Chapter 10

"This is going to sound silly." Alex was walking home with Kameron holding his hand.

"What's that?" he asked her, staring up at the sky.

"I've never had somebody walk me home before after a…" Alex stopped herself.

"What's wrong?" he asked her.

"I don't think I've ever been on a date before." She laughed.

If she were to die right now, she would die a happy girl as she was walking with Kameron down the sidewalk with Komptin at her side. They arrived on the backside of the church as Alex pulled out her keys.

"Well, I'm home."

"How did you end up with a room at the church?" Kameron asked her.

"Special arrangement. After my attack, I needed a place to live and Cardinal Frank pulled some strings and here I am," she told him.

He pulled back her hair behind her ear and looked at her scar. "Whoever did this better pray to God he doesn't come across me at some point," he told her.

Alex looked up and smiled at him. "He died."

Kameron looked down at her in shock.

"No, I didn't kill him." She eased his worry. "Do you want to come in?"

"I would love to see your place." Kameron brushed off some of the snow off his coat. "I've never been in a church so late at night."

Alex opened the door and Alex led him down the hallway of the rectory. She looked at the time. "Hey, you have to see this, come on," she said, holding his hand leading him to the worship congregation room.

They sat down in the front pew in front facing the stained-glass window.

She whispered in his ear, "Don't make a sound." She laid her head on his shoulder as they sat in the dark. The sounds of a choir were echoing faintly in the room as the moon peaked its way out of the clouds causing the stained-glass window to glow.

Kameron leaned into Alex. "That's amazing, where is that coming from?" he asked her, not taking his eyes off of the stained-glass window.

"The choir practices in the Annex and it carries through the vents," Alex said, smiling. "I like to think it's God's way of letting me know that He is there and it's His little gift to me that only He and I know about, which makes it extra special."

The two of them sat in there for a while before Kameron walked Alex to her room. She unlocked the door to her room. "Well, this is it." She turned around to see Kameron admiring the painting on the side of the door.

"This is really interesting. Who's Cara?" he continued to study the painting.

Alex stood there in shock. "What?" Alex hadn't heard that name since high school. Osiah mentioned her once while they were training one night in the deep woods. Alex didn't want to pry because it seemed like something he didn't want to talk about. All she knew was that he kept her hair braided with a strand of his.

"Where do you see that?" She studied the painting with him.

"In each of the four corners." He pointed to the Roman Numerals. "See, III, I, XVIII, I. Replace the numerals with a letter and it spells, 'Cara'."

Alex didn't know what to say, she just sat there perplexed that he figured that out by just looking at it. She looked at the painting almost every day for two years and never noticed that. "Never noticed that before." Alex opened the door to her bedroom. "Well, this is it."

Kameron peaked his head in but didn't enter the room. "Looks nice, cozy, very relaxing."

"You can come in," Alex said.

Kameron looked a bit nervous.

"What's wrong?"

"Nothing," Kameron said. "Just feels weird coming into your room on a first official date, then being in a church on top of that."

"You think we are going to have sex now?" Alex turned to him as she untied her coat.

"No, not at all," Kameron said, getting embarrassed.

"So, you don't want to have sex with me?" She gave him a surprised look.

"What no, yes. Wait." He was getting flustered.

"I'm just messing with you." She laughed. She put her keys on her dresser.

He looked at some of her other belongings that were out in the open. He picked up a picture of Osiah, Komptin, and Alex. "Who's this? He's got kind eyes," Kameron asked.

"That's Osiah, he was my mentor, I guess you can say," Alex said, looking at the picture. "It's how I got Komptin. He was his dog, and he gave him to me before he passed away, like he knew his time was near."

Kameron placed the picture back on her dresser. "I thought he was your service dog?" Kameron asked.

"He was Osiah's and then it just so happened that after my attack he already had the training, so…" Alex said.

"It's like God had it all planned out for you," he said, looking over the rest of the room.

"Probably had to make a few course corrections." Alex motioned with her hands. She saw him looking at the girl in the dresser. "That was my best friend, Sara."

"Was?" Kameron inquired.

"She died my senior year of high school," Alex told Kameron.

Kameron stared at the pictures. "She looks like a sweet girl."

"She was. She didn't deserve what happened to her." Alex got a moment of sadness.

"I should get going," he said looking at his watch. "I have an early morning tomorrow."

Alex walked Kameron out of her room, and she stayed in the doorway to her room. The two looked at each other. He leaned in and kissed her in a sweet, loving kiss, keeping his hands at her waist and hers on his arms.

"I'll talk to you tomorrow."

Alex nodded and smiled. "Yes." She watched him walk down the hall as he stopped and turned around.

"Alex, I just want you to know, there's nobody else, so what you see right here." He pointed to himself. "It's all here, there's nothing hiding from you." Kameron looked relieved as he said that. "I just wanted you to know that."

"I know," Alex told him. "I trust you one hundred percent."

"And I trust you," Kameron said, smiling and waving. He turned around and headed out the door, checking the door behind him to make sure it's locked.

"Always the gentleman," Alex said out loud. She looked to Komptin who was sleeping on her bed. She sat in the recliner. "Let's go find some infiltrators."

Komptin wagged his tail with excitement.

***

Alex was at her computer trying to find something on the F.O.R. that she could bring out to the public. At face value, the F.O.R. looked legitimate. There was nothing she could find about them. She looked over at Megan who was working on Father Tom's schedule for the week.

Anne walked into the room grabbing some coffee. "How'd your date go last night?" she asked Alex as she put the coffee pot down. Anne turned to look at Alex smiling ear to ear.

"Never experienced anything like it," Alex said. "We just went to dinner and then went for a walk. He walked me home and then he left after kissing me goodnight."

Megan looked up at Alex and shook her head, not approving.

"What?" Alex raised her voice at her.

Anne quickly distracted Alex. "What are you working on?"

"Trying to see if I can find anything about them I can exploit," Alex told them. "But everything on the net seems legit."

Anne's wheels were turning as she asked Alex, "You know, Vicki and Tori moved to D.C.?"

Alex raised her eyebrows at Anne knowing where she was going. Her attention was thwarted at the sound of Megan screaming Kameron's name at a high pitch sound. Alex smiled at him as he walked in, but it quickly turned to a frown as Megan was hugging him.

"What are you doing here?" Megan asked, touching his arm.

"I came to take Alex to lunch," he let her know. "Ready?"

"Just give me a minute." Alex started to lock her computer and gather her things.

"No problem, hey I just wanted to tell you that I have to go out of town for a week, I leave the day after tomorrow," he told her.

Alex knew that because he didn't say where he was going meant that it was work related. "Okay," she said. "Separation makes the heart grow fonder." She winked at him.

"I like to think so." Kameron smiled at her.

"Anne and I have to ask Father Tom something, can you wait for five minutes?" Alex asked him. "Just five minutes."

"Take your time, I'll sit here and keep Komptin company." He knelt and started playing with him.

They walked into Father Tom's office as he started to get his coat. "What's going on ladies?"

"We're heading out to lunch," Alex said.

"Yeah, I have a meeting with the Jewish Council about security protocol," he said, buttoning up his coat.

"I'm not able to find anything on the internet about anything really negative about the F.O.R." Alex started to tell him.

"Why am I not surprised?" Father Tom said, shutting off his computer.

"But we may have an idea," Anne said. "It's a little, unorthodox." Anne continued to tell them about these computer hackers they know and how they may be able to help them, unofficially.

Father Tom looked at them. "You want me to hire someone to break the law?"

The two girls looked at each other. "Well…"

"Stop." Father Tom put his hands up. The girls could tell he was contemplating on the possibility. "I will need absolute certainty that it does not link back to the church."

Anne spoke up. "We will talk to them to make sure so there is no way we had this conversation."

"There is to be no report on this, understood?" Father Tom sternly commanded.

"Yes, Father," the two girls said at the same time.

"Talk to them," he said. "Don't make me regret this."

The two girls walked out of the office listening to Megan talking to Kameron about Alex. "And then she brought her date here to do who knows what. So tacky, in a church."

If Alex could use her powers on church grounds, she was going to throw Megan through the glass doors. Anne grabbed her arm and squeezed. "Do you mind if we stop somewhere on the way and Anne comes along?" Alex asked.

"No, not all," Kameron said, taking his keys out of his pocket. "I'll go get the car."

Father Tom was in the doorway to his office. "Megan, I'm going to my meeting, I'll be back at three."

Megan sat there smiling. "Of course." She turned to look at Kameron leaving. "Isn't it sweet that he came all this way to tell me that he was going for a week?" The three of them turned to look at Megan in shock. "I'll be right back, I'm going to use the restroom," she told them, smiling.

Father Tom tapped Alex on the shoulder. "You really need to tell her, nicely."

Alex sneered. "Do I have to? It's kind of fun watching her make an ass out of herself."

***

The three of them walked into a computer shop where two girls were behind the counter working on some software. They turned to look at Anne, Alex, and Kameron as they approached them.

"Why hello?" Tori said. "Longtime."

"Hi, Tori. Hi, Vicki," Anne said.

The two of them looked at Kameron. "And who do we have here?" Tori asked. "He's cute."

"This is Kameron," Alex said, rubbing his arm.

The two girls looked at each other in shock. "Definitely upgraded." The two said at the same time.

Kameron got embarrassed. He unbuttoned his coat and the two girls saw that he had a pistol. "Are you a cop?" Tori asked.

"No," Kameron said. "But I know who you two are."

Anne and Alex's eyes grew big as they looked at each other in fear as not knowing what Kameron was doing or talking about.

"We were exonerated," Vicki let him know.

"Unofficially, whoever did that, I'm not saying it was you, but whoever did that, far as I'm concerned, they gave those people their money back and poised no immediate national threat," Kameron said. "Officially, I was never here." He grabbed Alex's hand squeezed. "I'll be in the car." He turned to Vicki and Tori and smiled and winked at them. "Ladies." He walked out the door as Alex watched him.

"I like him," Tori said.

"Me, too," Vicki agreed. "What can we do for you?"

Alex was about to speak when their employee walked out with a laptop. "Mr. Gravel's computer isn't taking the new OS, keeps on rebooting itself."

"I'll be right there," Tori said. "In the meantime, work on Mr. Marrion's computer." They watched him leave.

"What is your view on the F.O.R.?" Anne asked.

"Those whack jobs?" Vicki asked.

"Oh, honey, please tell me you're not involved with them," Tori worried.

Alex looked at Anne. "We would like to see if you could, you know, find information that really isn't out there to the general public?"

"Oh, oh," Tori smirked. "Anything particular?"

"Finances and membership names," Alex said.

"It's going to take a while, I mean a while," Vicki said.

"We can't have it come back to us," Anne mentioned.

"If we get caught, I mean big if, I swear, your names will not be mentioned," Tori said.

"You have our word," Vicki said. "We cannot start this until next month to prevent any link to you guys. In the meantime, I suggest you buy something, so you have a reason to come in here."

"I always thought Kale needed a new phone," Anne said, picking out a phone.

"And Kameron needs." She looked around. "One of those."

Anne and Alex got into the car where Kameron was reading a newspaper. "Get what you needed?" He put the newspaper down.

"I got Kale a gift." Anne showed him the new phone.

"Nice," he said.

"And I got you something as well." Alex pulled out the Hello Kitty mouse pad and handed it to him giving him a kiss on the cheek with a smart-ass smile.

"Oh, honey, thank you, how'd you know?" He smiled as he started the car. "Let's go get Kale, I'm hungry."

***

The four of them decided to walk through the park to get to the restaurant since it turned out to be a nice day. Alex and Kameron were walking behind Kale and Anne as they were talking about multiple different things.

"Hey, I wonder what's going on up there." Kale was trying to look. "Might be a concert or something, let's go check it out."

Alex tensed up as she felt the presence of the Dark. They walked up to the crowd where there

333

were multiple TV cameras, reporters, and the general public was waiting. A big sign was promoting the F.O.R. in the background.

Anne tapped on Alex's shoulders. "We should leave."

Alex just put up her finger. She pointed up on the stage.

"Damn," Kale said as Roger Somberson took the stage. Kale squeezed Anne's hand as she leaned into Kale, supporting him.

Kameron leaned into Alex. "I take it that's him."

Alex just folded her arms and stared at the stage. "Yep."

Roger waited for the crowd to stop cheering before he started to talk. Roger was toning down the crowd when he was looking around. Komptin gave a monstrous bark which caught Roger's attention toward the four of them. He just smiled as he got ready for his speech.

"Oh man," Kale said, looking around.

Anne could feel him start to sweat and breathe heavy. "Relax honey; it's okay."

Roger started to speak. "I want to thank you all for coming today and we should remember this day, for this is going to be a good day. Back when man just learned to walk, he believed in an empty spiritual being to help guide them in life; but then, man invented the wheel and his knowledge of how life is actually. The only power comes within yourself." The crowd began to cheer.

Alex just continued to stare at him through her dark sunglasses as he gave his speech.

"Please, please, I'm not telling you something you don't already know. The churches in this town take your money, cover up sexual misconduct on your children, and promote racism and prejudice on those different from their brainwashing rules and regulations."

"We love you, Roger," someone yelled from the crowd.

"Not as much as I love all of you." He smiled at the crowd as they erupted. "There is so much true absolute power you all hold. You all have the capability of harnessing this absolute power. That is why I am announcing that the F.O.R. will be opening a 3.5-million-dollar facility in an effort to help homeless children get off the drugs, give them food, shelter, and most of all education." The crowd cheered. "This effort is a direct positive influence in our communities to show how religion does our communities no good. We must positively rise above these religious organizations. There have been many bombings by militants using our name and I condemn these actions," he screamed. He looked over at Kale. "I hate violence, I never believed in it." He winked in his direction.

"That piece of…" Kale started to say.

"Kale," Anne warned him.

Alex just continued to stare at Roger on stage.

Roger then continued, "I want a community where we don't give the religions any more power to ruin your lives and start taking actions into your

335

own hands. Let's start by getting our teens off the streets, bring them to the F.O.R. to teach them the true meaning of absolute power." He looked over at Alex as he addressed the crowd. "Can you imagine what we can do with all those people who are infiltrated with true power?" The crowd cheered as Roger exited the stage. The crowd was cheering his name when he came in front of Alex.

Alex didn't budge as she stood her ground.

"Alex, been awhile. You didn't look well the last time I saw you." Roger was looking down at her.

"Roger," Alex said, keeping her arms crossed staring at him. Alex was stone cold, as she didn't let Roger phase her.

"Still sporting the Goth look I see, things haven't changed much since high school," Roger eyed her up and down. He snapped his fingers. "Speaking of high school; how's the back Kale? Still limping along, I see?"

"You son of..." Kale started to walk towards Roger but Anne and Alex both stopped him.

Alex turned to Roger. "You still are the weak, little man from high school, Roger."

He leaned in over to Alex. "That maybe, but I still saved your ass," he whispered.

"Leaving me to die if I didn't join your pathetic organization." Alex got up close to his face.

"Alex, this is not the place," Kameron said, grabbing her hand.

Roger turned to Kameron. "You must be Kameron Dutcher."

"I am," he cautiously admitted.

He turned back to Alex. "You don't have a chance—" He gave an evil grin. "—in Hell." He then whispered to her, "And it's coming."

Alex pushed him into the crowd. Roger laughed as he turned back to the gathering that was supporting by cheering for Roger.

He turned back to his followers, "Come to the F.O.R. HQ to show what we have to offer."

Alex just watched him leave.

"I hate him," Kale said.

Kameron and Anne looked at Kale as Alex just continued to watch him leave.

"Alex," Anne calmly addressed. "Sweetie."

Alex turned to Anne.

"We need to talk to Father Tom," Anne told her.

Anne walked Kale to his office leaving Alex and Kameron alone in the car. Kameron turned to Alex. She was staring out the window with a blank stare. "Are you all right?"

"I'm fine," Alex told him.

"I know we just started dating, but I really hope you don't keep me shut out. I want to share all with you; the good and the bad," he said to her. "I want to support you."

Alex had a teardrop. "The day I got this," she pointed to her scar on the side of her face. "A man who I worked with attacked me, he scared me. He was about to end my life when Roger killed him." Alex thought about it before she decided to speak. "He just started that cult." Alex thought about how

337

she was going to say this next part. "He pretty much said that he would save my life if I joined his organization and sleep with him."

"What happened?" Kameron sympathized.

"I told him 'no' and he left me to die in the mud," Alex said, wiping away her tears.

Kameron handed her tissue. She went to grab it and Kameron put his hand on top of hers. All he did was smile at her reassuring her that he understood.

***

It has been a week since Kameron left and she got a message that he got pushed back two more days. Alex found herself irritated by it, but she understood. She thought it was a weird feeling that she missed him. She got a text message from Michelle. She opened it up to show her new wig.

Alex replied, "It looks great!" Michelle answered back with how her day was going.

Alex continued to text her throughout the day. She ended by telling Alex that she is glad that she and Kameron were together. She had never heard him so happy.

The only thing Alex could reply to that was, "He makes me happy too!"

Michelle answered back with a heart.

"Kameron comes back today, I'm sure he will find an excuse to come and see me," Megan said looking at her hair.

Alex looked up at her from her computer. It was near the end of the day, so now would be a good time as any. Father Tom was out at a meeting, and it was just the two of them so she wouldn't be too embarrassed. Alex was kind of curious how she was going to react to her telling Megan that she was dating Kameron. It was still weird for her saying that. Alex was dating someone. "Hey Megan," Alex came out saying. Well, there was no turning back now.

"Yeah," she said, looking at herself in the mirror.

"I think Kameron is dating someone," Alex sat watching for her reaction.

"Really? He hasn't mentioned it."

"Do you talk to him outside this office?" Alex was really hoping she didn't have to spell it out for her.

"Well, no, but he's shy, he's just getting up the courage to ask," she applied some touch up make to herself.

Alex knew this was not going to go well. "Megan, I'm hundred percent positive that he is dating somebody, exclusively." She was still in shock that it was her.

"Did he tell you that?" Megan said, putting down her makeup.

Alex just tapped her fingers on her keyboard. "Yeah, pretty much."

"Well, who is it?" she asked. "Do I know her?"

Alex studied her. Was she this naive? Can she be this stupid? "Well, you work with her."

Alex could see that Megan was putting it all together. "Wow. Really?" Megan asked her.

"Yes," Alex told her in a sympathetic voice. She felt bad for what Megan was feeling.

"Poor Kale. I never thought Anne would be the type," Megan said in amazement.

"Wait, what?" Alex was completely shocked.

"That poor guy, and they are supposed to get married," Megan said. "I can't believe you're hiding that from your brother."

"Oh my God, Megan," Alex got fed up. She got up and showed her the background to her phone. It was a picture of her and Kameron, cheek to cheek as the snow was falling.

"I see," Megan said, without any emotion. She turned to her computer. "Well, if you're the type he wants to be with, he can get what he wants then."

Alex just rolled her eyes and went back to her computer. She texted Kameron to tell him how she had to pretty much spell it out that they were dating. He replied saying, "Have fun with that." And then sent her a picture of a kissing face. "Dinner at my place after I get back?" Alex immediately answered, "Can't wait!" She hung up the phone and then went downstairs to talk to Anne.

Alex went into Anne's office where she was deep into her work. "Hey, you got a second?"

Anne looked up. "Yeah, what's going on, sweetie?"

"I'm having dinner at Kameron's when he gets back," Alex mentioned.

"Oh, that's nice, he's a good cook," Anne said. "Bring a bottle of wine or something, or even better, make a dessert." Anne looked at her. "But I'm getting the impression that is not why you are here."

"When you were first with Kale, were you nervous?" Alex asked her.

"Extremely," Anne said. "It was both our first time. No offense, but this isn't new territory for you."

"Yeah, and I know he has as well, but this is going to be different," she told her.

"Because you actually care about him?"

"Yeah," Alex admitted.

"It's going to make it better," Anne told her.

"He's going to see my scars," Alex reminded her. "And what about that fact that I don't sleep."

"You are just going to have to tell him something to cover it," Anne said. "Kale is starting to remember more and more from that night. He's waking up telling me dreams he had that are directly from that night. He described an Infiltrator exactly to me a couple of nights ago."

"This has the potential to get really complicated," Alex said.

"When you reach the point where you can't hide it anymore you are only going to have two options, you either tell him or you break up with him," Anne pointed out.

***

Alex's dinner with Kameron was fantastic. There was no doubt he learned to cook from his mother. She helped him clear the table and put the dishes in the dishwasher.

"Do you want to sit down?" Kameron asked, pointing to the couch.

"I do." Alex took his hand and led him to the couch. The couch was soft, and it overlooked the fireplace. The two of them sat down on the couch watching the fire. Kameron took a sip of his wine and Alex held her energy drink in her hand.

"This is nice," she said.

"It is," Kameron said, playing with her hair.

"Where did you go?" Alex asked him.

"North Carolina," he said. "Nothing exciting."

She looked up at him and they started kissing. Their bodies started to lean into each other closer. They put their drinks down and continued to kiss more passionately. His hands passed her lower back and she pushed herself closer to his body. Alex's hands went into his shirt feeling his muscular body. Kameron returned with his hand up her back on her skin and she jumped off him.

"I'm sorry," he immediately said out of fear. "If I went too far…"

Alex knew he was genuinely afraid that he made her feel uncomfortable. "No, that's not it. Trust me, that is not it," she told him. "If we are going to do this, which I really, really, want to, there is something I need to show you."

"Okay," Kameron said, adjusting himself.

"You may want to turn the lights on," Alex told him. "And shut the drapes please."

Kameron got up and shut drapes. He walked over to the lights and turned them on. He sat back down on the couch. "Are you okay, you look nervous?"

"I'm really scared of how you are going to react to these," Alex said. "Your mother or sister didn't tell you?"

"Tell me what," Kameron started getting scared. "You're not going to tell me you're a guy, are you?"

Alex busted out laughing. "No, all woman." Alex got up and unbuttoned her blouse and turned around facing the fireplace. There was worry of how he was going to react to her scars. It might have been embarrassment as well. She took a deep breath and then removed her blouse. The scars on her body from Demon and Infiltrator claws were now evident.

He swallowed hard but other than that remained emotionless. "From your attack?"

Alex removed her collar to show him the scar on her neck. Then guided his hand and placed it on the side where Sanah stabbed her.

"It's radiating heat," Kameron noticed as he was studying her scar.

"It still hurts when it's pressed on."

Kameron looked at her in the eye. "I'll be careful." He kissed her. "I think you are the most amazing, beautiful woman I have ever seen."

There was relief to see how much Kameron cared for her. It was something she had never felt before. That feeling intensified as Kameron led

Alex to his bedroom when she realized she had such feelings for him as well.

***

It was nearing the end of February and Anne was up late looking over the final plans on the wedding. Now everything was done; they were just waiting for the date to come. Anne watched Kale sleep as he was keeping her up from the tossing and turning. There was no doubt that Kale was having a nightmare of some kind. Anne wanted to wake him, but she knew you were not supposed to wake someone who was having such an intense dream.

He suddenly sat up sweating. "Jesus," he said as he looked at Anne.

Anne was almost afraid to ask. "What's the matter?"

Kale looked at her. "I just can't shake that dream of that night. The same dark monster and big purple thing fighting it and then like blue lightning but coming from the ground."

"It's okay, honey," she said rubbing his back.

"I'm going to have to talk to a shrink or something about this." Kale wiped his face from the sweat. "This is getting out of hand."

"Let me find you one, okay?" Anne offered.

"Okay." He crashed back down on the bed. "Since we're both up, you wanna?"

"You have such a great pillow talk baby; how can I resist?" She put her arms around him as she kissed him.

344

***

Salamor was on his hunt for Vandor. He floated all around the city hoping he could catch a hint of his prize. He continued his scouting when he came across a familiar feeling. He came across a young lady crying in her apartment holding a letter.

He could sense the pain the girl was feeling as she forced herself to read the letter. She sat in the corner of the floor in tremendous pain. Salamor salivated as the despair oozed from this girl. He flew up to her face, studying, knowing she was on her final string of hope. All Salamor had to do was push it a couple times and her actions would fulfill his anticipation.

"There will be no one else," he whispered in her ear.

She continued to cry harder as she held the letter to her face.

"End the pain," he suggested to her.

She got up to the bathroom and turned the bath on with hot water. She grabbed her shaving razor and broke it into pieces. She picked up the metal razor and climbed into the bathtub. One final push and Salamor would have accomplished this feat. Salamor studied the girl's face as he came down to watch her slice her wrists. Salamor noticed she had painted her nails a bright blue as she tightly grabbed the razor with fingers. He floated back in as he hesitated and then went back close to the girl.

Salamor leaned to the girl's face. "Stop." The girl dropped the razor. "Call," he whispered.

The girl looked at her phone. "Mom, can you get me in touch with your priest?" the girl sobbed. "And Mom, I really need you to come over."

Salamor floated off to finish the request Vandor had requested of him.

***

Alex and Kameron were walking down the street a couple of blocks from Kameron's apartment. They decided to walk down to a local ice cream shop to grab themselves a treat. Kameron ordered a vanilla caramel swirl while Alex asked for a chocolate with fudge swirls and chocolate chunks dipped in caramel and topped with sprinkles.

Kameron turned to her as he offered her a bite of his cone. "Are you going to spend the night?" He looked around as if he were on edge.

"If you will have me?" She teased back as she took a bite of his ice cream. She offered some hers to Kameron.

He took a bite and shivered at the amount of chocolate. "That is really sweet."

"But so good." Alex laughed.

The two of them continued to walk. They turned the corner and Kameron ran into a group of young kids, knocking a young girl who was around seventeen onto the ground. "Oh, I'm so sorry." He handed Alex his cone as he helped her.

Alex noticed the group had F.O.R. patches on their arms. She could sense a dull sensation of the Dark, but that didn't mean anything. It seemed that feeling was around all the time. She looked to see how Komptin was doing, and he was on alert, but nothing to be worried about.

"That hurt." The girl laughed, while laying on her back.

Kameron seemed to be frozen but suddenly snapped out of the state, extending his hand. She allowed Kameron to help her up. "Sorry again," Kameron said to her. He brushed off some of the snow off her.

The girl's friends started teasing her. "Don't worry about it." She smiled at him.

Alex could see her start to blush as Kameron helped her up. The group of kids started to leave while teasing the girl. Alex could hear her tell her friends how cute Kameron was. Alex smiled as she gave her ice cream cone back to Kameron. "You just have a way with the ladies, don't you?"

"Yeah, I'm a real lady killer," he said, grabbing Alex's hand giving her a loving smile.

They went back to Kameron's apartment where she hung up each of their coats in the closet. Kameron turned on the fireplace and sat on the couch petting Komptin. He just stared at the fire, scratching the dog's head. Alex caught herself smiling at that for some reason. She slowly walked up behind and put her arms around him kissing him on the cheek.

"Move over, you big ogre," she told Komptin.

Komptin made a small, annoyed growl but he moved off Kameron so Alex could sit next him. She hopped over the couch with ease and landed softly on the couch. Komptin jumped back on the couch laying now on Alex's lap.

"He's definitely not a lap dog." Kameron yawned.

"Tired?" she asked him as she scratched Komptin's head.

"Yeah, you?"

Alex got a worried feeling, she didn't know how to answer the question, "I could go to bed," was all she could think of.

"I'm going to shower and jump into bed." He smiled at her.

"I'll meet you in bed," she said, as she watched him get up.

He turned to her. "The restaurant down the street has great breakfast if you want to get up a little early and eat before we go to work?"

Alex didn't say anything. She just stared at him and shrugged her shoulders. She watched as Kameron just nodded and headed into the shower. Alex got into the shorts and a t-shirt and crawled into bed. Komptin was lying near the window, sleeping.

Alex was on her phone just reading about an upcoming concert that seemed interesting. Kameron came into the room rubbing his shoulder. Alex could tell he was hurting. He put on a pair of shorts and jumped into bed. She nestled up to him as he put his arm around her.

Alex didn't know how long they laid like that before he finally fell asleep. All Alex could think of was that she needed to get on a hunt. She wanted to wait a bit before she snuck out of bed to find some Infiltrators. She made sure Kameron was in a deep sleep before she snuck into the living room where she got dressed in her black leather hunting clothes. She realized she left her phone on the end table in Kameron's room, so she quietly walked in to grab it. She watched Kameron toss and turn a bit as she grabbed her phone.

Kameron sat straight up in a cold sweat and pale. Alex could tell he was controlling his breathing before he finally opened his eyes to see Alex dressed ready to leave. "Leaving?"

"Yeah," she reluctantly told him. "I have to be at work early. Are you okay?"

Kameron grabbed his face and wiped off the sweat before he finally got up. He grabbed his bathrobe from behind the door. "I'm fine, I thought we were going to breakfast in the morning." The two of them walked down the hall into the kitchen. Kameron got a drink of water.

"I really need to be at work early tomorrow," Alex said to him trying to figure out a way out of this situation.

Kameron looked at the time on the clock. "It's midnight, by the time you get to room and get ready for bed it's going to be close to one in the morning, don't you ever sleep?"

Alex didn't know what to say, she just sat there dumbfounded.

"Why don't you just stay here?" He just waited for her reaction.

Alex really needed to get out and go for hunt. "I really should get back to my room."

"Whatever," he annoyingly said. He took another sip of his water.

"Look, it's not that," Alex started to say.

"Alex." Kameron put up his hand. "It's fine. If you want to go, then go."

Alex didn't know what to do. She just stood there before saying, "Come on, Komptin." She watched Kameron come to her and he gave her a small kiss before sitting down on the couch with his water.

Alex watched him not knowing what to say.

"Good night." He turned his head to her. The two just stared at each other for a quick moment before Alex went off to do her hunt.

***

Anne got to work early and noticed Alex walking in with Komptin in her hunting clothes. "How was your night?"

"Difficult," Alex snapped. "Yours?"

"Same, you first." Anne took a sip of her coffee.

"Kameron is getting irritated or suspicious; more than likely both." They both started walking up the stairs. "I'm running out of excuses on why I don't spend the night there. He flat out asked me if I

350

ever slept," Alex said. "I don't know what to do." She turned to Anne. "How about you?"

"Kale is remembering more and more," Anne told her. "I think it's time to talk to Father Tom about it."

"Yeah, sounds about right," Alex said as they both walked into the reception area. "Morning Megan, is Father Tom in?"

Megan just motioned that he was in his office.

Anne and Alex closed the doors and turned to Father Tom who looked like he had a rough night. "You okay father?" Anne asked him.

"Just someone called me last night, saying they were trying to commit suicide, but then suddenly changed their minds and just needed to talk to someone," he told them. "What can I do for you?" He started rubbing his eyes after he looked at his watch.

Alex kept on forgetting that Father Tom was an actual priest at times and that he didn't always spend the time on Council issues.

"Father, it's about Kale," Anne said. "He's starting to remember."

Father Tom just closed his eyes. "I thought this day would be coming, but not so soon," he replied. "How much is he remembering?"

"The Infiltrators, he started to remember Komptin in his true state, and some of Alex's power," she said. "I'm running out of excuses."

He turned to Alex. "I see that you and Kameron are getting pretty serious."

Alex smiled. "Yes, we are."

351

"I'm glad," Father Tom said. "Are you spending the night at his place?"

"Do you want details?" Alex asked him.

Father Tom put up his hands. "NO! But what I do need to know is, how are you doing with keeping your secret?"

Alex looked down at her feet. "Not too good."

"You didn't tell him, did you?"

"No," she immediately replied. "But he's a federal agent, a good one. He's starting to get suspicious on why I don't sleep or spend the night there."

Father Tom got up and made himself a Bloody Mary. "I knew this day was coming but I really didn't want it to." He took a sip of his drink. "I guess you two won't make it easy on me and just break up with your guys, huh?" he sarcastically asked.

Anne and Alex both knew he wasn't serious. "No," they both said.

Father Tom finished his drink with haste, and he pushed down on the intercom. "Megan."

"Yes, Father?" her voice came up over the intercom.

"Book me a flight for Venice. I need to leave this Friday and return the following Friday," he said over the intercom.

"Yes Father," she replied.

"Megan, First Class, put it on my personal credit card." He turned off the intercom. He refilled his drink and poured one for Anne and handed Alex an Apollo. "Hey, if I'm going to get my butt

352

chewed off as I go into a losing battle, I'm going to enjoy the trip over. Cheers."

They lifted their glasses to a toast to the impossible when Alex got text on her phone. All it read was, "We need to talk right away, in person." Alex felt her gut drop.

Anne reached over to Alex. "What's wrong?"

Alex showed her the text message. "This."

Anne read it. "It could mean anything." She rubbed her friends back.

Alex replied to him, "Okay, I'm free now."

He replied, "I'm in the parking lot coming in."

Alex could feel herself getting scared. "It's too late," she said. "Do you think I should just tell him now?"

"NO!" Father Tom said. "Alex, please have faith, see what he wants before you do anything rash." He sat back down on his chair. "Have faith, go, go see what he wants."

Alex walked out of Father Tom's office to see Kameron in his trench coat all tightened up and his hands in his pockets. "Alex," he said.

"Kameron," Alex replied as Megan and Anne sat there watching.

"Can we talk?" he asked in a somber face.

Alex nodded, thinking, "Here it comes." She could feel a lump in her throat as he was about to end the relationship.

Kameron nodded. "Thanks." He walked forward grabbing Alex's hand. Alex was shocked because he walked up to Father Tom's office and knocked on the door. "Father, do you have a minute?"

"Of course," he said, motioning them to come in.

They walked in and Kameron shut the door behind them. Now Alex was getting nervous because this was out of the norm. Was he worried that she was going to go psycho on him or something? Did he not trust her? She looked at him and he was upset.

"What's on your mind, Kameron?" Father Tom asked him.

Kameron grabbed Alex's hand as he smiled at her lovingly. He turned back to Father Tom. "I just got a call from my mom; my sister doesn't have long. I have to go home right away." He tried to hold back to the tears.

"Kameron, I'm so sorry." Alex grabbed his hand as she was wiping her tears from her face.

"Before I go, can we pray for her and my family?" Kameron asked.

"Of course." Father Tom came around his desk and knelt. Kameron and Alex both got out of their chairs and knelt. Father Tom finished his prayer. "Is there anything I can do?"

Kameron wiped eyes and blew his nose into a handkerchief that he had in his pocket. "No, thank you." He turned to Alex. "My flight leaves at six tonight. I'm gonna go home and pack."

Alex nodded. "Father, do you mind if I take some personal time?"

"It's okay, go on," he said. "I'll be back next Friday."

"Thank you," she said. "Kameron, I just need to purchase my ticket and pack."

The two of them walked out of Father Tom's office. Kameron leaned to Alex and whispered, "I already purchased your ticket." He stopped to turn to Alex. "Can you meet me at my place at three and then we can go to the airport?"

She nodded. "I'll see you then if not sooner."

He grabbed her hand and squeezed. "Thank you. I don't know what I would do without you." He turned around and left.

Megan just rolled her eyes. "Sappy."

Alex just put her index finger up at Megan as Alex continued to watch Kameron leave. "Don't, just don't."

***

Alex and Kameron arrived late at night at his parent's house. Harold met the two of them at the door. "How was your flight?" He hugged Kameron and Alex as they came into the house.

"Fine, how are you and Mom doing?" Kameron asked him.

"Surprisingly, okay," Harold said. "Michelle's not in any pain. It's a good thing you came when you did, the doctor said she probably isn't going to make it through the night."

Kameron grabbed Alex's hand. "We better go see her." The two of them, along with Komptin, walked upstairs into Michelle's room where the family was at her side.

The doctor had his stethoscope to her chest. She took it off her ears, "It will be anytime now," she said in a calming voice.

Mary leaned to Michelle's ear. "Honey, honey, Kameron and Alex are here."

Michelle could barely smile as Kameron grabbed her hand. "Hey, sis."

"Hey," she barely said.

"I just wanted to say, well…I don't know what to say," Kameron admitted.

"Dumbass." she smiled. "Alex?"

Alex came up to her. "I'm here, Michelle."

"Thank you…thank you for saving Kameron," she barely spoke. She managed to open her eyes a bit. "You're so, so…" Michelle squinted her eyes. "You're so blue."

Alex patted her hand and kissed it as she guided it to Komptin's head for her to pet. He kept his head on her bed with sad eyes looking at her.

She started to fade away as she smiled. "Celestial…you're here…"

The family started to cry as the doctor checked her heart and then recorded the time of death. Alex was sad but was equally as happy as she knew Celestial was on the other side personally escorting her to her new life.

***

Alex sat out on the porch with Komptin at her side. She was sipping her drink as a morning dove landed on the banister in front her. She waved to it as it flew off into the sunrise. Kameron sat down in his bathrobe and jacket as he just stared. "Was that Michelle?" He laughed.

"I like to think so," Alex said, sipping her drink.

He turned to Alex. "I can't tell you how glad I am that you are here."

She turned to him. "I wouldn't have missed it."

Kameron put his arms around her as she cozied into his body. "She was such a sweet kid," he told her. "She hated my ex-girlfriends. Absolutely hated them." He laughed. "I remember one time she had a one-on-one intervention with me. Her first words were, 'Kameron, you're being the biggest dumbass I've ever known'," he laughed.

Alex smiled.

"She saved me from a horrible mistake. The last time I saw my ex, she was dancing at a strip club," he said. "My little sister always looked out for me." He squeezed Alex, "But when it came to you, she didn't even meet you and she liked you when I told her about you."

"She's got a good judge of character," Alex told him.

"Then when I told her we were dating, her words were, 'Don't be a dumbass and 'eff' it up'," he said. "But she didn't say 'eff'."

"I'm more worried about me messing it up," Alex said.

She watched Komptin perk his ears to the sound of animals making some noise. Alex went with her gut, and she was going to tell him. "Kameron, I know this isn't the best time, but before emotions get confusing, there's something I need to tell you."

"What is it?" he said as he moved her hair from her eyes.

"I'm in love with you, there's no doubt about it," Alex said. "You don't have to respond, but I..." She was stopped by Kameron kissing her.

"I love you, too, Alexandria Johnson," he answered back.

***

Michelle wanted an outdoor funeral and upstate New York in the spring proved it challenging. The rain was coming down and it was cold. Alex could feel the dampness reach her bones. Michelle was a sweet girl and her funeral proved that to be true. It seemed as if the whole school shut down and attended her funeral. Alex stayed underneath the umbrella listening to the choir sing Michelle's favorite song.

She caught the feeling of a presence before she saw Celestial with Ariel and Devine in the crowd. They were being inconspicuous as possible; if Alex didn't sense her presence, she wouldn't have seen them. The minister finished the funeral as most of the attendees left. People were walking by her casket, saying good-bye. All that remained was Kameron's family.

"Too young," Mary said. "She was nothing but heart."

"We should get the kids out of the rain?" Janelle said to her husband.

"I'll take them," Robert offered. "Come on, boys, let's go get some food."

They were heading to the town hall where the wake was taking place. Alex watched as the kids were asking their dad what happens when someone dies. Alex looked up to the sky to Osiah's star shining through the clouds.

Kameron pulled out a shiny silver dollar. He showed it to Alex. "The year she was born." He pointed to the date. He placed it on the coffin. "For your swear jar in Heaven, try not to call anyone a dumbass." He snickered. "Love you, sis."

Alex smiled as she squeezed his hand. She walked up to the coffin and knelt to the coffin. "This is the only thing I can think of giving you," she whispered. Alex looked around to make sure no one could see as she opened her coat to hide the lite of the fists. "Just wanted you to know, I will give my life to protect him from any harm." Alex got up and turned to Kameron. The rest of the family said their personal good-byes before going to the wake.

The hall had a memorial table for Michelle as some of her pictures and personal effects were on a table. Alex was amazed to see a picture of Michelle and Alex hugging each other while taking a picture.

Mary came to her. "She really liked you."

"I wish I could have spent more time with her," Alex admitted. "We would have had fun in the city together. Probably would have gotten into some trouble with you." She laughed.

"No doubt about it." Mary rubbed Alex's back.

Alex turned to her. "If there is anything you need, please let me know."

"Honey, I have a feeling you did more for her than I can ever possibly know," Mary said holding her hand. "I thank God He introduced our family to you." She grabbed her hands.

Alex hugged her. "I thank Him as well." Alex wanted to get some air, so she let the kids run around with Komptin in the field. He acted as he was playing with them, but occasionally she saw him in guard mode.

Alex felt Celestial next to her. "How is she doing?"

Celestial smiled. "She brought new life to the place."

Alex chuckled. "She shouldn't have died so young."

"She did not die in vain. She lived life to her fullest and did exactly what she was destined to do," Celestial said.

Alex turned to her. "What was that?" But she had disappeared.

***

Alex and Anne got to the church and met Father Tom in his office. "Have a seat," he told them. Anne and Alex didn't say a word, they both were trying to figure out if Father Tom had good news or bad news. "I went to bat for you two," he said. "It wasn't pretty. Ever have a bunch of Cardinals grilling you for days?"

They both shook their heads.

"It's not fun," Father Tom said. "I argued the fact that no matter what happens, Kale Moler was bound to remember everything. I presented them with multiple cases of civilians witnessing Infiltrators and not living normal lives because of what they have witnessed. Some of them are being institutionalized."

Anne got her nerves up. "I'll quit before they put Kale in an institution for witnessing something that happened. He's not insane."

"I told them that as well," Father Tom said. "Alex, their first question to me was, 'Why doesn't she just break up with the guy?'" Father Tom was choosing his words carefully. "It came down to me stating, that is an option, but he is a member of the Secret Service, he knows how to keep a secret." He sat down on his chair. "Without my knowledge they did an intense background investigation on Kameron; I know about his sister's passing, I'm sorry," Father Tom said.

"She was a sweet kid with a big heart," Alex told him. "What about Kameron and Kale?"

"I found out Kale had an investigation on him quite some time ago, they gave me the decisions on both of them at the same time," Father Tom said, taking a big swig of whiskey.

"And?" the girls said.

"You can tell them," he said.

They cheered and then sighed as they sat back in their chairs.

"There's a condition, I need to be present as a neutral third party to make sure they don't.... overreact," Father Tom said.

"Understandable," Anne said. She turned to Alex. "You okay?"

"Just scared, this isn't going to be easy," Alex told them.

"When and how do you want to tell them?" Anne asked.

Father Tom stated, "Like any story, start from the beginning. I think it's time for you two to go home."

Chapter 11

Father Tom was sitting by the window seat as he was watching the people walk by. He was halfway hoping he would have the seat next to him open. He knew the girls and their guys were in the back of the plane. The window seat was fine, but he preferred the aisle.

A young lady sat down next to him as she double checked to see if she had the right seat. She sat down and took a deep breath as she got herself situated. The young girl turned on her phone as she was receiving a text.

Father Tom noticed the upside down four as the screen background. His nerves went up a little bit. He knew everyone was entitled to their opinion, but he couldn't help but think of a worst-case scenario if she was going to cause trouble on this plane. Father Tom got irritated with himself and started giving a silent prayer for the young girl.

"You know I'm an atheist," the young girl said to Father Tom as he was just about to put his headphones on.

Father Tom was a bit lost for words, since he really wasn't expecting to talk to her considering her phone background. "He still loves you," was the only thing Father Tom could think of as a reply.

"Just wanted to make that clear," the girl said to him, opening her college books.

Father Tom smiled as he felt the plane take off.

***

Alex watched Kameron adjust his body in his seat as he winced from the pain in his shoulder. "You okay?"

"I'm fine," he said, smiling at her grabbing her hand. He looked over at Alex. "How about you? You look really nervous."

"A lot on my mind," she told him.

"Why don't you get some sleep?" Kameron told her. "We have a long flight."

Alex could have sworn he was studying her reaction to see what she was going to say in response. Alex was lucky as the stewardess came by asking if they wanted anything to drink. "No, I'm good." Alex smiled.

"No Apollo?" Kameron looked over at her with a sarcastic confusion.

"I'm good," Alex sneered at him.

"Well, just let me know if you need anything." She touched Kameron on the shoulder and smiled at him.

Kameron smiled back as he turned to see a very unhappy Alex staring at him. "What?"

"Nothing." Alex shook her head and stared out the window.

"Did I do something wrong?" Kameron asked her. Alex felt a tap on her shoulder. "Alex," Kameron said to her.

"What?"

"You have been on edge all week, what is going on with you?" Kameron asked her.

364

"Nothing," she said, leaning back on her chair acting like she was trying to get some sleep.

Alex could feel him leaning over to her as he whispered, "Well, since I finally got you cornered where you can't run away, I'm going to tell you something."

Alex turned around to look at him with spite. "Go ahead."

"Look, you confuse the hell out of me. You make no sense. I told you since our first date that what you see is what you get, nothing hiding. We told each other that we trust each other one hundred percent." Kameron looked around to make sure he wasn't getting too loud.

Alex could tell he was getting angry.

"You come to the apartment, we go to bed together, but you leave in the middle of the night. No explanation, no good-bye, nothing. You tell me you love me, but you keep your distance and then out of the blue, you want me to come to your hometown to meet your parents. And apparently, the stewardess smiles at me, touches my shoulder, and it's my fault?"

"You know, I don't want to do this now," Alex said.

"Do what?" Kameron halfway laughed. Kameron sat back on the chair. He got irritated and got up and headed towards the head of the plane to talk to the head stewardess. He had to act as the air marshal since he was the only federal agent on the plane.

Anne nudged Kale as he was halfway asleep. "What?"

"Look over at Alex and Kameron," Anne told him.

Kale peered over the seat to see Alex and Kameron's body language. "Oh, that's cute, they are having their first fight," he laughed.

"Remember ours?" Anne said.

"Ah, yes, the 'not making the bed' incident," Kale said. "I remember, it was the end of days if the bed wasn't going to be made every day."

"No, I think it was the 'separate your clothes when you take them off' scenario," Anne corrected him.

Kale thought back. "Oh yeah." He laughed. "That was a good one." He went back to try to fall asleep. "Why did we need to come to this trip home anyways?"

"I thought it would be nice to see our parents, plus, wouldn't it be nice to watch Alex squirm as she shows Kameron around town?" Anne pointed over to her.

***

Father Tom opened his book he picked up at the airport. It was a crime-drama book that was poorly written, horrible plot, and the characters were two-dimensional; he couldn't put it down.

"I thought you would be reading the bible," the girl next to him said.

Father Tom put the book down. "Do you think that priests don't have any interests?"

"Never really thought about it," the girl said. "I never thought of you as people before."

Father Tom snickered. "How do you view us?"

"I don't want to offend you," the girl said, going back to her studies.

"You won't," Father Tom insisted. "Please."

The girl hesitated before she finally said, "You preach about a deity that you have no proof of existing. It's just a scapegoat. Murderers and rapists say they found Christ and we are supposed to forgive them. People who claim to be Christian are some of the most despicable human beings out there. They think they are above everyone else. That is why the only true power is the one within."

"Yes, people are flawed, especially the one sitting next to you." He pointed to himself.

"Really?" she looked at him with disbelief. "What makes you flawed?"

"I drink way more than I should," he admitted to the girl. The stewardess walked by as Father Tom called for her.

"Miss, can I get a vodka and cranberry and a drink for my friend here. But it's so good." He smiled at her.

"Certainly, Father." She looked over to the girl. "Miss, what would you like?"

The girl couldn't believe it. "Why are you being nice to me? I'm a member of F.O.R." the girl asked him.

Father Tom smiled. "I'd rather share a drink with someone who is genuine who holds different views, then someone fake that says things because they think that is what they should say."

"Ma'am," the stewardess pushed.

"Make that two," she responded.

***

Alex had been in plenty of fights, usually she would just thrust her Lite through the individual and it was over, but this fight was different. She didn't like it. She had no idea what to do. She looked over at Kameron who was keeping his distance as he was talking to Kale. Alex watched Father Tom talking to the girl who had been sitting next to him on the plane. Alex walked up to the two of them.

"Alex," Father Tom acknowledged.

"Father," she said, looking at the girl.

"Oh, I'm sorry, this is my new friend Lana." He pointed to her. "Lana, this is Alex."

Alex shook her hand. "Lana."

"Alex." Lana looked away.

Alex continued to stare at her. "Father, I need to get Komptin." She turned around to bump into Kameron. "Oh hey, I'm going to get Komptin."

He nodded. "I'll go get the luggage," he said as he walked away from her.

Alex started to walk to the cargo pick up when she saw Anne come join her side. "So, how's it going?"

"Great," she said, gritting her teeth.

"I take it you two are fighting," Anne inquired.

"Yeah, but I don't even know what about," Alex admitted. "One of the stewardesses was flirting with Kameron, or at least I think she was, and I just got mad. And then he started asking me why I don't spend the night, and I think he is starting to question our relationship."

"Oh honey, we all question our relationships," Anne told her.

"You didn't."

"Are you kidding me? Don't you remember when Kale and I broke up for those couple of days when he was drinking again?" Anne told her. "I thought it was completely over." She looked over at Alex. "Do you want it to be over?"

"No, of course not," Alex said. "I love him, this is new to me, and I'm afraid I'm pushing him away."

***

They all got their separate rental vehicles and went their separate ways. Anne and Kale went to his mother's to spend the week there. Alex guessed they alternated places to stay every time they came back home. Father Tom went to the hotel to check in before they were going to meet at the Catholic Church. Alex wanted to stop by there first to see it.

She drove the car to the parking lot not really saying a word to Kameron. She didn't really know what to say. She wanted to tell him all about the church and her mission, but she couldn't, not yet. She pulled into the parking lot to see the church looking dark.

"Looks dark," Kameron observed.

"It does and it doesn't just look it," Alex said, observing the church. She shut off the car and got out looking at the building where she spent so much time. "Komptin." The massive dog got out of the car. She turned to Kameron who was looking at her. Alex smiled at him. "I'm sorry."

"Me, too," Kameron said. "Look, I don't want to pressure you into going to fast in anything. If you are not comfortable spending the night at the apartment, I can wait."

Alex walked around the car. She grabbed him by the coat and pulled him in for a kiss. "I promise you, you'll understand everything by the end of this trip."

Alex could feel Kameron was a little on edge. "Okay, I trust you."

She smiled up at him. "Come on, let me show you around." The two of them walked up to the church but it was locked. "That's weird. It's not that late that church shouldn't be locked up."

"Could be at function, understaffed, or something," Kameron assured her.

"Maybe," Alex said.

They walked behind the church to see the grass overgrown. She looked up to see the crosses on the

370

steeple had been removed. She felt herself starting to get on edge as a feeling of stale air came across her senses. She looked down at Komptin who flashed his eyes and took off into the woods.

"Komptin!" Kameron tried calling him back. "He must have caught wind of something he didn't like."

"Yeah, I think he did," Alex said. She turned to Kameron. "Why don't you go check into the hotel? I'll find Komptin and meet you there." She tried to get him out of the area.

"And leave you here alone? Not happening," Kameron said. "This place gives me the creeps."

Alex watched him unbutton his coat nonchalantly to get easy access to his pistol. Alex knew he wasn't going to go anywhere, but she couldn't protect him if there were Infiltrators around. She would give her secret away before they could plan for it.

Alex tightened her lip. "Okay." She walked up to the church and tried peeking into the window. "It looks abandoned." The sound of an Infiltrator being diminished echoed deep from the woods behind the church.

"What was that?" Kameron started walking towards the woods. He turned to the sound of glass breaking. Kameron turned to see Alex hopping into the church from the broken window. "What are you doing?" Kameron came running up to her.

"Breaking and entering," she said underneath breath. She hopped onto the floor. "I understand if you can't follow me. I'll be right back, there's something I need to check out." Alex walked into the darkness of the church.

"Damn it, Alex," Kameron said, as he watched her walk away.

Alex slowly walked through the church main worship hall. The church was musty, with the smell of abandonment. There was an eerie echo as she walked down the aisle in the middle of the congregation room. She tried to lite her fists but was not able to do so, which was a welcoming feeling. The view of the destroyed alter showed no evidence to what had happened. There was a broken wooden cross laying down in the corner. She walked over and picked it up and ripped one of her extensions out of her head. She wrapped it around the cross putting it back together. A little prayer was given after she placed the cross back on the altar.

"Nobody's home," a familiar voice said behind her.

The smell of rotting corpses came across her nose as she saw a couple of rats run off into the walls. Alex turned around to see Vandor leaning on the entrance to the main hall. He got up and started walking into the main congregation. Alex immediately started looking for Kameron in fear that he fell to Vandor's hand. She tried to light her fist but nothing.

Vandor sneered, "I didn't hurt your boyfriend." He looked behind him. "He's really not your type."

Alex just stared at Vandor. "And you are here, why?"

"Curiosity," Vandor said. "Why are you here?"

Alex sat down on the step leading to the altar studying Vandor. "I suppose you aren't going to tell me what happened to the church."

"No," Vandor told her.

Alex sarcastically nodded at him. "I didn't think so." She got up and walked past Vandor. He grabbed her with white demon hands with long black fingernails. "Let me go, you smelly piece of rotting flesh."

"You had your chance. I want you know the true meaning of suffering," Vandor said.

"Play country music." Alex stared at him in the eye.

He grinned with sharpened black teeth. "I will enjoy every second of watching you suffer, you arrogant Lite bitch." Alex knew this was purely a scare technique since she knew he couldn't hurt her here. On a small scale, it was working.

She punched him in the face, but it had no affect since she was in the church. All he did was smile at her as he came up closer to her.

"Sir, don't you move another inch," Kameron yelled behind her. Alex turned to see Kameron with his pistol drawn at Vandor.

"Kameron." Alex still struggled to get out Vandor's grip.

"So, this is the man that took your heart," the Dark creature studied Kameron.

"You okay, honey?" Kameron asked her, inching closer to Vandor calmly, keeping his pistol fixed on his head.

"Just fine," Alex said, still trying to get away.

"Sir, if you don't let her go, I'm going to put a bullet right through your skull," Kameron forcefully said.

Vandor was grinning at Alex and then to Kameron, and then back to Alex. "He doesn't know," Vandor laughed. Alex saw Vandor as his expression went from laughing to one of worry. Without Kameron's knowledge, Komptin was in his full gargoyle state breathing heavily ready to attack.

"Mister, I will put a bullet in your head and not lose a wink of sleep," Kameron told him. "Now if you don't let her go in the next three seconds, I'm going to…"

"Okay." Vandor let go of her. He grinned down at Alex. He made it a point to get Kameron's attention. "You've got a pure heart; I'll have to remember that."

Kameron motioned for him to leave with his pistol. "I suggest you don't bother her again, got it?"

Vandor laughed as he disappeared into the darkness of the church.

He ran up to Alex and the two of them embraced each other. "You okay?" Alex could feel the warmth that Kameron was embracing.

"I'm fine," she said in return. "Thank you." She hugged him. Komptin made sure all was secure as he was breathing heavy, with small amounts of blue blood dripping from above his eye. "Thank you."

He flashed his eyes and took off to scout the perimeter.

"You look nervous," Kameron told her. "Are you sure you don't want to go to the hospital?"

"I'm fine," Alex said, as they pulled into the restaurant.

"That guy must have really scared you," Kameron said. "Are you sure you don't want to file a police report?"

"Huh, what? No. That's not what I'm nervous about," Alex said, looking at the people going into the supper club.

"Then what is it?"

Alex turned to him and kissed him. "You know I love you." She smiled at him. "But after this weekend, this relationship will not be the same."

"Are you nervous about introducing me to your parents?" Kameron asked her.

"There's a lot I'm going to introduce you to." Alex turned to look at her boyfriend.

"Come on." Kameron smiled. "I'm looking forward to meeting your family."

Inside the restaurant Anne and Kale were talking to Kale's mom at the bar. Alex had invited Father Tom who was listening to the conversation. Alex could feel her stomach intensify as Kale snickered and pointed to Alex. Kate winked, smiled, and gave Alex a thumb's up. She wasn't known for being subtle.

Alex walked up to the group of them as her nerves were rising. Running into Vandor with the smell of Infiltrators was not something she was expecting. On top of everything she just saw her parents walk up and gave them a hug.

"Hey, honey," her mom said.

"Mom, Dad," she said after finishing her hugs. She took a deep breath. "This is Kameron."

"Nice to meet you," Kameron said, shaking her dad's hand.

Her dad was looking at Kameron. "You're dating my daughter?"

"Yes, sir," Kameron said. "I'm lucky to have her in my life."

"Suit, tie; did you just wear this because you were meeting us?" her dad asked.

"Dad," Alex said. "Don't worry about it, Kameron. No, Dad, he wears it for work as well."

"Really, what do you do?" her mom asked.

Kameron was vague with his answer. "I work for the government; Department of Homeland Security."

"Oh, how nice," her mom said. "Come on, let's go order, I'm hungry."

Kameron and her dad went off talking. Alex just sat there watching. "You okay?" Anne asked her.

She turned to Anne. "This weekend is going to change everything."

"Yes, it is," Anne said.

"Don't worry about it," Kale said. "If he can survive your dad, he can survive anything, even dating you." He smiled. "I know I didn't want you two together to begin with, but I can honestly say I

376

was wrong. You two are truly amazing together." He hugged her and went to join the table.

Anne and Alex sat there watching as Father Tom joined the two of them. "Why did you want me here?"

Alex turned to Father Tom. "Father, we need to tell them tonight."

Father Tom downed his drink. "Why?" he asked, wiping his mouth.

"I got a visit from Vandor at the church, Kameron was there," Alex said.

"Did he see him?" Anne asked her.

"He pointed a gun at his head," Alex told him. "Vandor was grabbing me by the arm and wouldn't let me go."

Father Tom inquired, "And Vandor just happened to let you go."

"Well, Komptin was behind Kameron in his gargoyle state. Kameron didn't see him, but Vandor did," Alex sneered.

"Let's see how this evening goes, tomorrow for sure, okay?" Father Tom said.

Alex nodded in agreement.

At dinner they were all talking and laughing; mainly it was Alex's parents grilling Kameron all about him. There was a dull moment when Alex asked, "What happened to the church?"

"It was weird, some organization called F.O.R. bought it along with a bunch of land and abandoned buildings," her dad said.

"They tried buying out this place as well," Kate told her. "I have no idea why, but I've always wondered if they were behind what's been going on."

"What do you mean, Mom?" Kale asked, grabbing a piece of pizza.

"I've been hit with five surprise health inspections this month, my food vendors have either stopped selling to me or raised the prices, even my online reviews have started to drop," she said. "I'm not a conspiracy theorist, but that just seems too convenient."

"I can look into it," Alex's dad said.

"I bet you it's Roger," Kale angrily stated.

"I thought he disappeared after he attacked you?" Kate asked.

Anne spoke up, "He's resurfaced, he's the leader of the F.O.R."

Kale's mom looked to Alex's dad. "How is that possible? Why isn't that son of a bitch in jail?"

"Nothing I could do. They were both juveniles; he basically disappeared up to about a year ago; I can't find any record on him," Alex's dad admitted. "It's as if he was a perfect poster child."

"He makes me sick to my stomach," Kale said. "I haven't had a decent night sleep since he has reemerged."

Alex and Anne looked to Father Tom, he closed his eyes and shook his head. Acknowledging that tonight would be the night the truth would come out.

***

Father Tom borrowed a van from a church on the other side of town. He was in the driver's seat as Alex was in the front passenger seat showing him where to go. It was quiet in the van when Kale voiced his concern, "Why are coming down this way? Really, there was no other way?"

Anne grabbed Kale's hand. "It's okay, babe."

Alex turned to see Kale getting a bit tense.

"Did I miss something?" Kameron asked, looking around.

"Here," Alex said, at the bottom hill. The van stopped and Alex got out with Father Tom.

"This is messed up, Alex," Kale sat there, stern.

Anne turned Kale's head to meet with hers. "Kale, please, you need to do this."

Kale nodded, as he got out of the van.

Everyone got out of the van as everyone scouted the area. Kameron asked again, "What's going on?"

"This is where I was attacked," Kale said, looking over the area.

Kameron acknowledged by just nodding. Alex was by his side as he leaned into her. "Do you think it is wise for him to be here reliving this?"

"This is for you as well," Alex said, grabbing his hand leading him into the woods.

"Kale, what do you remember about that night?" Alex asked him.

"It happened just in front of the van, I saw a small flash of red and then Roger coming over knocking me off the bike." He mustered up the memory of that night. "I managed to limp over

379

here." He walked into the woods and was in the area where he once laid beaten. "I remember Anne coming to help me, and then this flash of blue, a monster fighting a bunch of other monsters; I must be losing my mind."

"The mind can do a lot to keep from concentrating on the pain," Kameron pointed out.

Alex looked over to Father Tom who motioned to her to wait one second. He reached into his pocket and did a small prayer with his rosary, "Okay, go ahead."

Alex cracked her neck. "Kameron, Kale, there's something…I'm…you see…" Alex was trying to say.

Kameron and Kale just looked at her.

"Lite, Dark…you know," Alex tried to explain.

The two of them just looked at her in confusion.

Alex gave a grunt out of annoyance. "Komptin, come here, boy." Komptin came up to Alex and sat down, right next to her looking at Kameron and Kale. Alex looked to Kameron. "Kameron, you have to promise me something."

"Sure, what is it?" Kameron stated.

"Keep your weapon in your holster no matter what, promise me," Alex said, kneeling next to Komptin.

"Of course," he assured her.

Father Tom stepped up. "And I can't emphasize this enough, what you are about to see, you can never say to anyone. Doing so could put a lot of people in jeopardy to include yourselves and the ones you love."

Kale didn't know what to say but "Okay."

Kameron just was stone faced but nodded. "Of course, but short of national security, I won't say anything."

"Fair enough," Father Tom said. He put his hand on Alex shoulder's giving her the permission. "Komptin, is there anything around." He flashed his eyes neon blue, telling her all was clear.

"What the hell was that?" Kale screamed.

Kameron just stayed still, expressionless. "Did his eyes flash blue?"

"Yes," Alex said.

"Why?" Kale asked. He felt Anne's hand hold his.

"Kale, honey, that is just the tip of the iceberg," Anne told him.

Alex backed up a little bit from Komptin, "Hey boy, can you make sure the perimeter is secure?"

Komptin flashed his eyes again as he morphed into his gargoyle state. The massive dog grew into his purple skinned hunting mode.

"What the hell?!" Kale stumbled back a little as he tripped over a log.

Kameron watched him fall to the ground, without expression and then turning his attention back to Komptin.

Alex could see that Kameron flinched for his weapon but stopped himself, remembering his promise. Other than that, he just stayed expressionless.

"It's okay, Kale, he's the same dog you know…just a tad bit bigger and stronger than you thought he was."

Kale got up and Komptin gave him a slobbering lick.

"Okay, he's the same dog."

Kameron finally spoke up in a monotone without expression. "Why is he attached to you?"

Everyone's attention was to Alex to see how she was going to respond. Alex looked to Kameron who she could tell he was studying her deeply. Alex and Kameron just watched at each other, Kameron expressionless, Alex's face was out of fear of revealing her answer. The two just stared at each other.

"She's a Lite Sentry," Anne blurted out. Everyone looked to Anne except Kameron and Alex who were just staring at each other. "What? She wasn't telling him."

"A what?" Kale asked.

Kameron finally spoke, expressionless and monotone. "A Lite Sentry is a, if you will excuse me, a mythical guardian to balance the Lite and Dark to ensure the Dark doesn't upset the balance of life, in return protecting humanity."

Father Tom and Anne looked at each other, shrugged their shoulders and then looked at Kameron. Kameron's cell phone rang as he looked at and answered. "This is Agent Dutcher. Okay, give me 15 minutes and I will call you back." He hung up the phone not taking his eyes off of Alex.

"Are you saying you're this Lite Sentry?" Kale asked his sister.

Alex answered him without taking her eyes off of Kameron. "Yes."

"So, what can you do?" Kale asked.

Alex lit her fists blue and showed her glowing hands without taking her eyes off of Kameron who was still expressionless watching her.

"It turns your hands blue?" Kale asked out of confusion.

Alex turned to Kale and flashed her eyes blue. She turned around and swung at a tree, busting through it knocking it over. She turned her attention back to Kameron who was still without expression.

"You knew about this?" He turned to Anne.

Anne tightened her lips and shook her head.

"And you didn't tell me?" Kale asked his fiancée.

"She couldn't," Father Tom chimed in. "She is part of the Catholic Council."

Anne felt a sense of acceptance. It was the first time Father Tom openly accepted her as part of the Council.

"The what?"

"Put it frankly, a special division among all the religions of the world to monitor, balance, and push back the Dark," Father Tom stated.

"And my attack wasn't imagined." Kale looked down to confirm with Anne.

"I'm afraid not, honey. Roger is possessed by an Infiltrator, those black monsters you are dreaming about, Alex and Komptin saved us from their attacks."

"Where do you two fit in this?" Kale asked Father Tom and Anne.

"I'm the priest to ensure the operation for the Catholic Council goes smoothly," Father Tom told him. "Anne is the Council Historian and Record Keeper."

Anne turned to look at Kameron who was still without expression. Both Alex and he just stared at each other.

Father Tom looked at his watch. "It's getting late, why don't we get out of here." He looked over at Alex and Kameron who were still looking at each other. "Besides, I think it would be best if these two talked. Kale, I will answer all your questions in the van on the way back to your parent's house." The three of the walked to the van and took off. Alex and Kameron just remained staring at each other.

"We're just going to stare at each other all night?" Alex finally broke the silence.

"Forgive me, it's a lot to process," Kameron admitted.

"I'm still the same girl, just a little bit more to answer."

"Fills in some gaps," Kameron said. His phone rang again. "Damn it, excuse me," answering his phone. "Agent Dutcher. Really? I'm on vacation, there's no one else. Fine, I'll be there tomorrow night." He shook his head. "Director Morkin needs me to fly home. FLOTUS is traveling out of the country, and they don't have enough agents to cover it."

Alex just nodded.

The two of them walked for about half a mile before Alex finally spoke. "How did you know about a Lite Sentry?"

"Remember when you told me about that story you did a report on that evil being falling in Love with the Conduit of Life?"

Alex thought back. "Yeah,"

"Well, I was going to surprise you with a book with that story. Funny thing was, every story I found ended with Conduit of Lite and that Dark Angel going their separate ways; nothing about him having an apprentice or him dying to protect them," Kameron admitted. He looked at her with a confident question, "You were the one he was protecting?"

"Yes," Alex admitted. "He died right in front of me by that creature you had the privilege of meeting in the church earlier today."

"That would make him Vandor," Kameron concluded. Alex was shocked on how much information he had. "When do you sleep?"

"I don't. The last time I slept was over three years ago. I almost died fighting a Lite Sentry who turned to the Dark. It's where I got this," she pointed to her scar on the side of her face and side.

"And the other scars?"

"Just regular Demon and Infiltrator fights," Alex told him.

"And the Conduit of Lite?"

"You met her before," Alex told him.

"Your Godmother, and the other two are angels assigned to protect her." Kameron filled in the blanks. Then something came to realize with Kameron. "Now it makes sense why Michelle said you were so blue."

Alex was quite amazed at how he put the puzzle pieces together. "You heard that, huh? Did you know?"

"I had my suspicions something was up," he admitted. "But it wouldn't sound sane of me to ask my girlfriend if she has supernatural powers." They two of them continued walking with Komptin next to Kameron in his gargoyle state.

Alex felt a sense of relief as she looked over at Kameron who was scratching Komptin behind the ears while he was in his true form. "So, where does that leave us?"

He turned to Alex. "Actually relieved."

Alex was confused. "Why?"

"It makes perfect sense why you don't sleep over, instead of what I feared," Kameron told her.

"What did you fear?" she asked him.

"You didn't actually love me, and you wanted nothing to do with me," he admitted.

Alex stopped him, turned him to face her. "Kameron, farthest from the truth."

Kameron smiled. "Good, because I think you are just as strong, smart, beautiful, and special since that day I saw you coming out of the bathroom." The two hugged as he kissed her.

Kameron checked in at the ticket counter as he was ready to be escorted past security. He bent down and patted Komptin. "Take care of her." Komptin licked Kameron. He stood up to look at Alex. "I'm sorry, I have to leave."

"Me, too," she said looking at him. The two of them just stared at each other. Alex didn't want him to go. She just wanted to spend more time with him. She just nestled up to him as he put his arms around her. She was happy and content.

"I have to go," he whispered. "I have to get to my Air Marshal briefing."

She nodded. "I know, but it doesn't mean I have to like it." They kissed each other good-bye. Alex watched Kameron walk through security of the airport. She received a text message from him reading, "Do you hear that?" Alex looked up at Kameron shaking her head.

"I LOVE YOU, ALEX JOHNSON!" he yelled from the other end of the security. Everyone turned to look at Alex who was beat red from embarrassment.

"I love you, too," she softly said.

He motioned he couldn't hear her.

"I love you, too," she said a little bit louder.

He motioned again that he couldn't hear her.

"I LOVE YOU, TOO!" she yelled out as she felt her face get redder. He blew her a kiss as he walked to the plane.

"Never thought I would see the day that Alex Johnson said, 'I love you'," a voice behind her stated.

She turned around to see Shawn standing behind her. "Shawn," she greeted him. "How have you been?"

"Okay," he said, trying to see who Alex was saying she loved.

"What are you doing here?" Alex asked him.

"Work, I'm the assistant airfield manager," he said. "I was on my way to work when I thought I saw you."

Alex grabbed Komptin by the leash. "Well, I'm glad you're doing well." The two of them started walking in the airport.

"I was in some hard times, but an old friend got me through it," he told her. Shawn took a sip of his coffee and bit into his doughnut.

"That's good, glad to see you are on your feet," Alex said, pulling Komptin closer to him.

"So, who's the guy that broke through the Johnson wall?"

"Nobody you know." She tried see Kameron one last time.

He looked again at her. "Oh my, you actually are in love."

"It was nice to see you again Shawn, but I have to go," Alex said, as she started walking away.

"Are you still in touch with Anne, because I would like to get to touch her," Shawn yelled to her.

"Shawn, she is marrying Kale this spring," Alex informed him.

Shawn smirked. "Doesn't mean she still can't meet me for dinner."

Alex turned around. If she could have, she would teach him a lesson right there in the airport. "I swear if I see you near her, you will pay," she warned him. She walked away with Komptin following her.

Alex decided to take Komptin for a hunt since she just got done dropping Kameron off at the airport. It had been a while since he was able to hunt in his full gargoyle mode running through the woods. She put on dark clothes and applied her makeup. She texted Father Tom and Anne that she was taking Komptin for a walk which both knew what that was code for. They both wished her to be careful as they went off to their hunt.

After a late-night burger from Marty's, which tasted exceptionally fantastic, Alex decided to start her hunt at the church. She didn't know why she wanted to go back there, but seeing it broken down and worn out was heartbreaking. Her last memory of the church isn't going to be her in Vandor's clutches. She jumped back into the window which she had broken earlier. The look on Kameron's face was priceless.

The time on her watch told her there were a couple more hours before his plane landed. Alex, with Komptin at her side, decided to walk up to Osiah's old office. To her surprise, his office wasn't that bad of shape. She pulled back the chair and studied it. She missed him. She sat down on the chair with her feet on the desk. She glanced out the window to see the purple star staring down at her.

"I know all that's left of you is that bright burning star in the sky, but I just want you to know that I miss you. I think you'd be proud of me. I have a steady boyfriend who I love so much. He is good to me. Komptin is doing well, I don't know what I would do without him."

Komptin fell asleep in the corner while in his gargoyle state. She smiled at him as she continued to talk to Osiah's star. "I really wish you were here. The F.O.R. is becoming more and more powerful. They are getting their hands into everything. I was activated to balance the Lite and Dark, but I'm afraid I'm not doing such a good job."

Alex got her feet off the desk and the stale smell of air entered the room. Someone got infiltrated. Komptin got up and flashed his eyes. His stance was ready to hunt. Alex nodded to Osiah's star before taking off into the woods behind the church.

Chapter 12

Alex and Komptin were on the hunt. Even though they were risking their lives, she could see a sense of fun coming from Komptin. She could tell he was enjoying hunting in his true state. Alex had to admit to herself, she was having a sense of fun to it as well as she was dodging the tree branches, stumps, and basically running through the forest obstacles as if she belonged there.

Komptin barked and increased his speed as he caught sight of an Infiltrator. Alex lit her fists as she caught a glimpse of the creature. Her eyes flashed blue as she increased her speed. She heard a growl but before she knew, she was side swiped onto the ground.

She was rolling on the ground with an Infiltrator. Alex managed to flip it off her into a tree resulting in a noise of crackling branches when it landed. The black beast was shaking its head. It was in a weakened state, so she jumped over a log kicking the Infiltrator in the throat. Out of pure instinct, it swiped its claws as a last effort causing Alex to duck. On the way, her head was a weapon as she used it to slam it its mouth shut. The creature stumbled back to lean on a tree. Alex grabbed a nearby sick and placed herself behind the beast. The stick went around it's throat as she leaned back to weaken it so she could diminish it.

Another infiltrator tried to sneak up on her, but she used her Lite Beam to give her some room. She knocked it to the ground far enough to finish off the first Infiltrator she was dealing with by shoving a Lite Spear through its chest. It dropped to the ground disappearing as Alex turned around to catch where the other one was. It wasn't around. It was dark, not a sound in the woods. The animals were quiet from the sense of the Dark in the woods. There was no movement in the wood. Not even the sound of Komptin hunting could be heard. Then straight ahead of her was a pair of red eyes walking towards her.

"And who do we have here?" Alex said, looking around to make sure he was alone.

"Fraket," he said calmly walking up to her.

"You look familiar," Alex said to him. She tried studying him before he decided to attack.

"I just have one of those faces I guess." He grinned with his sharpened teeth. "Lite whore, you don't know power like…" He tried to say but was interrupted by Alex shooting her Lite Beam at him knocking down. "Bitch!" he yelled as he got up from some mud on the base of a big tree.

Alex charged Fraket grabbing its head and smashing it against the tree. It swiped its demon claws, hitting the side where Sanah had stabbed Alex. She screamed in pain and stumbled back as the demon grabbed a thick tree stick and smashed it across Alex's face spinning her around. She felt another blow to the back of her head as she stumbled forward. The only reason she didn't fall to the ground was because she grabbed onto a tree.

"You really are not all that," Fraket hissed. "Gron warned me not to underestimate you, but you are weak compared to me."

Alex spit out blood as she turned around to lean on the tree. "Oh, shut the hell up, will you?" she said as she wiped her mouth from the blood.

The demon hissed at her as he charged her. She dropped to her knees punching him in the crotch with her lighted fist. The demon stopped in his tracks as he grabbed his groin dropping to the ground. Alex took a moment to regain her composure as she wobbled to Fraket.

She dropped her knee on the demon's head and continued to pound it until it pushed Alex off it. Alex kicked the creature in the stomach as it turned around, getting a stick jabbed through its chest. It looked at Alex and rolled its eyes as she jabbed her Lite Spear through the throat of the demon. It disappeared into the ground and Alex decided to take a break sitting on a tree stump.

Komptin came up behind her. She looked at him. "And, where were you?" She petted the massive creature on the head smiling at him. Alex saw a couple of scratches on him. "Okay, what do you say we call it a night?" Alex got up and noticed a badge of some sort laying on the ground. She picked it up. It was an airport security badge for one the airlines. "This is the airline that Kameron went on." She pulled out her phone. "Please let me know you landed okay," she texted him.

To her surprise she got a response right away. "I was just about to text you. Just landed, heading home. Luv you."

She smiled and replied, "Love you, too." She put the badge in her pocket. "Probably just a coincidence. Come on boy, I think we've earned the rest of the night off." She checked her wounds as they walked back to the hotel.

***

Kameron got to the luggage rack to wait for his suitcase to come. For some reason he was tired. He could barely keep his eyes open on the plane. The fact that he had to act as the air marshal for the flight really wasn't a thrill. The fortunes must have been favoring him since his luggage was the first one to come down.

"Must be my lucky day," he thought to himself.

He walked outside and saw one of his coworkers, Bob, waving him over. Kameron walked up to him. "What are you doing here?"

"We need you to come to work right away," he answered him. "Here let me get your bag." He grabbed the bag and put it in the trunk of the car.

"Thanks, what's going on?" Kameron said, getting into the car. He adjusted his shoulder since it was hurting.

Bob turned around. "Still hurting?"

"Yeah, flying and weather changes," Kameron said. "Pretty much moving." He laughed.

Bob turned back around. "Hopefully it will stop hurting as time goes by."

"So, what's the rush?" Kameron asked.

"Before we say anything, we need to go black," Bob said.

The agent driving handed over his phone to Bob. Bob shut off his phone along with the driver's. Kameron pulled out his phone and shut it off. He showed Bob it was off.

Bob acknowledged as he quickly drew his gun on Kameron.

"What the hell, Bob?" Kameron felt a pit in his stomach form.

"Weapons, lose them," Bob said.

Kameron hesitated, but complied. He pulled out his weapon with his index finger and thumb.

"The ankle holster; try anything and I will shoot you," Bob said.

Kameron leaned over and unstrapped his ankle holster and handed it over to Bob. The car pulled over and two more agents got in the car sandwiching Kameron. Bob kept his weapon fixated on Kameron. "I suppose you're not going to tell me what is going on?"

"It's the left shoulder," Bob told them.

The man next to Kameron adjusted his body and jabbed a flashlight into the shoulder of Kameron. Kameron tried not to scream as he felt the other agent push him forward. He pulled out his weapon that Kameron had in his belt. The other agent pushed him back to sit up right. He took his weapon and elbowed him in the mouth as the other one took that same flashlight and jabbed again into his stomach.

"Bag him," Bob said.

They put a bag over Kameron's head, and he felt a blow to his head, knocking him out.

***

Anne was checking her email in the hotel lobby as they were waiting for Alex. Kale gave her a cup of coffee. "What are you working on?"

"I got an email from the Russian Orthodox Council Historian; she said she may have found something deep within the vaults and she is sending it to me. Should arrive by the time we get back home," she answered him.

"Why not just take a picture of it and send it to you," Kale asked, taking a sip of coffee. "I hate coffee." He switched with Anne who must have had his hot chocolate.

"We can't send information electronically in fear of hacking, all pertinent information must be by courier, but she was really paranoid even over email," Anne told him. She looked at her phone. "Alex is on her way down."

Anne watched Alex come down the stairs with Komptin. Kale got up and looked at his sister. "You look horrible."

"My walk last night didn't really go as expected," she said. "I'm hungry."

Father Tom walked down from his room. He looked at Alex and threw her a bottle of Motrin.

396

Kale kind of got offended. "She looks like that and all you give her is Motrin?"

He looked at her. "She'll be fine."

Alex just shook her head as if it was common knowledge.

"I don't know if I will ever get used to this," Kale said. "Do your parents know?"

"Nope," Alex told him looking at her phone. "Not a word."

"I won't," Kale reassured her.

"What? Oh, that? Yeah, thanks. No, Kameron hasn't texted or called me since he landed," Alex told them.

"He had to leave early, probably wasn't able to," Father Tom tried to comfort her.

"Yeah, I guess," Alex told him.

Anne got a phone call. "Hello." Anne's face changed to that of nervous. "Hang on, we need to get somewhere a little more private." Anne covered up the phone. "It's Vicki and Tori, they are about to access the information, but they said they only have a couple minutes before the system detects something and locks them out."

"Let's go to my room," Alex said. The group of them moved quickly to the room to move as inconspicuous as possible.

"You're on speaker phone," Anne said.

"This is some sophisticated tech," Tori said. "This is like, really high government type stuff here."

Kale was trying to grasp everything that was going on. He happened to peak into Alex's bathroom where he saw a bunch of bloody towels in the bathroom sink. He looked over at Alex who was now holding an ice pack on the back of her head, listening to the phone.

"We're almost in, we won't have long," Vicki said.

***

Vicki was always impressed how well Tori worked under pressure. Her fingers ran across that keyboard as if it was always a part of her body. The sounds of the keyboard were quite rhythmic. "Look out for the…"

"Got it," Tori said.

Vicki was rubbing the back of Tori to try to ease the tension she was starting to show. "You can get this," she reassured her.

"No," Tori said. She sat back in the chair. "I already got it." She stood up and pointed at the computer screen. "I got you, you bitch!"

They high fived each other. "We only got a short time, who are you looking for?" Vicki said.

"I don't know; anybody with some gout," Alex said. "Anybody look interesting?"

"Random people, the names are not in alphabetical order; there's labels next to the names. Hosts, provisionary, obtainable, unknown; it's really weird," Vicki said.

"Anything else attached to the names, like jobs?" Alex asked them.

Vicki scanned very quickly. "Yes, their professions are attached to their profiles, wait," she said.

"What?" Anne asked.

"The director of the Secret Service, Agent Morkin is listed under 'provisionary'," Vicki said.

***

Alex's stomach dropped as she felt all the blood from her face leave. She knew she was paler than usual. "Kameron," she said. She picked up her phone and texted him. "Can you call me? I need to talk to you."

Anne looked at her. "It's going to be okay."

Tori interrupted. "Stop, wait. There's cops, low-level politicians, government employees, accountants, and…"

Vicki and Tori both stopped and looked closer at the screen. Alex asked over the phone, "What is it?"

Vicki and Tori both looked at each other and then turned around to see their intern with red eyes and sharp teeth drooling at them. Vicki and Tori both looked at each other as they were both consumed by darkness.

***

"Vicki? Tori?" Anne softly called out their names. A faint growl is heard in the background as

399

Komptin ears perked up as his eyes flashed. The sounds of Infiltrators could be heard.

Alex looked to Anne and shook her head 'no'. Anne fought back tears as Kale asked, "What's that noise?"

"Infiltrator's destroying the evidence," Father Tom calmly said as he closed his eyes in a silent prayer.

"How are you guys being so calm about this?" Kale started getting agitated. "You just heard two girls get murdered while on the phone with you. They are being devoured by some creature and something is going on some high government thing."

"Kale," Anne said motioning to Alex.

Kale saw Alex's face look of worry and she continuously kept on checking her phone.

"I'm going back," Alex told him.

"To what?" Kale asked. "To hunt down the director of the Secret Service? You don't even know if Kameron is in danger."

"I'm going back, Kale," Alex said to him with a stern look.

"I'll make the plane reservations," Anne said. "I'll get it for as soon as possible."

"I have to make some phone calls," Father Tom said, getting up leaving the room.

***

Kameron could hear a bunch of people talking. Some of the voices he recognized but others almost didn't sound human. He tried listening in close, but he knew he wasn't going to make it out alive tonight. The only thing he couldn't make out was one, why he was in the situation to begin with and two, why did they need him alive.

He felt the presence of a person come up to him as the bag was lifted from his head. The room was dark, but he could still make out that he was in an empty room with him sitting in a chair with a light on him. He made out about eleven people surrounding him.

"I suppose this isn't a hazing of some sort?" he asked the group.

One of the guys came up to him and punched him in his shoulder and then again across the face. "Shut up."

He spit out the blood and he could feel one of his teeth was starting to come loose. "Noted," he replied back to him.

"Kameron," Director Morkin said to him as he entered the room. "I must apologize for the men, they haven't been quite themselves lately." He wiped the blood from Kameron's face.

"Thank you, sir," Kameron said.

"Always the polite one," the director said. He motioned for a garbage can for the paper towel. "I suppose you have questions."

"A couple," he said surveying around him.

"It's nothing personal, it's just you are dating the wrong person," the director commented.

"Alex?" Kameron acted as if he was confused. "Why her?"

"Don't play dumb with me Kameron; lying is not your strong suit," Morkin told him. "I know she told you about her…job."

"She's an Administrative Assistant to the Catholic Church," Kameron said.

The director sighed and motioned to one of the agents. The agent aggressively came to Kameron and grabbed a knife slicing the top of his fingers and putting a small amount of gasoline on the wound. He tried everything not to scream.

"It's okay to scream, no shame will come to you," the director said. Kameron held it in as much as he could. "Okay," the director commented. "That's a bad cut, we should really do something about that." He lit a match and then slowly put down his finger. His finger blazed cauterizing the wound.

Kameron looked down at his finger. "Why don't you just kill me now?"

The director looked at his watch. "Oh, Kameron, I only need you as a backup."

***

The group of them walked into the church late at night. They seemed to go in their separate directions. Anne went to her office downstairs along with Kale, Alex went to her desk, and Father Tom went into his office. No doubt he had calls to make with the Council regarding the information about the F.O.R.

Anne walked into her office to see a delivery package sitting on her desk. She kind of smiled. "I've been waiting for this."

"What is it?" Kale asked her.

"My package from the Russian Orthodox Council Historian," she opened to find a laptop. "Okay, not exactly what I was expecting." She plugged it in but didn't work. "It doesn't work. It must have gotten damaged in transit."

"Maybe," Kale said. "Can I see it?"

Anne gave it to him. He looked it over and shook it a little. "It's a fake," he said to her. He took it and pried it open and inside where the components should have been, was a stack of old papers and a note. Kale handed Anne the note.

"I love you more and more every day." She smiled at him. She read the note. There was a look of worry on her face.

"What's wrong?" Kale asked her.

"She said she thinks she's being followed. The clergy of her council have been involved in terrible accidents. She's gone into hiding," Anne said. "God, I hope she's gonna be okay."

Anne picked up the papers that had very old blood on them and very old writing. "This is going to take some time."

"I'll leave you alone," Kale said. "Don't want to be a third wheel." He walked up to her and kissed her. "I love you."

"Love you, too, honey," she said.

Kale walked upstairs to see what Alex was up to.

Alex looked at her phone one last time. Time was standing still; she was fed up and walked into Father Tom's office who was still on the phone. She sat down on the couch as he threw her an Apollo to drink.

"Yes, Cardinal," Father Tom said. "God bless you as well."

"That looked serious," Alex said.

"It was, the South American Lite Sentry was killed last night," Father Tom said.

Alex looked up at the sky. "Why doesn't he activate more? Clearly we are becoming overwhelmed." Alex stopped herself. "It's just me isn't it?"

Father Tom slowly nodded. "Alex, I don't have answers for you. All I can tell you is keep faith."

Alex looked at her phone again. "That's it, I'm going to his apartment."

"I'll take you," Kale said. "Sorry, the door was open and I kind of feel like a fish out of water."

"No problem," Father Tom told him. He looked over to Alex who had a look of concern tattooed onto her face. "He'll be okay, Alex."

"I'm sure he is," Alex tried to convince herself. She got up and walked out with Kale to the car. "Because if he isn't, Lord may have mercy, but I won't."

***

Alex and Kale pulled into the parking lot of the apartment complex. Kale shut the car off and they sat in the car while Alex surveyed the area.

"What are you doing?" Kale asked her.

"Looking for anything unusual," she said. She turned to Komptin. "Anything?"

"Can you understand him?" Kale gazed back at Komptin.

"Not directly, it's more of body language and actions," Alex said, not really paying attention to Kale. "Come on boy." Kale got out of the car as well, Alex looked at him. "What do you think you're doing?"

"Look, I'm safer with you and Komptin than I am sitting alone in a car in a dark parking lot. Have you ever seen any horror movie ever?" he pointed out.

They walked into the apartment where it was quite late. Alex knocked on the door, but nothing came from the other side. Alex went to open the door, but it was locked.

"Now what? You're going to do that flashy thing and knock the door down." Alex looked at Kale and flashed her eyes and lit her fists. "No, I'll use the key." She held up her keys. She unlocked the door, and they entered the apartment.

"He gave you a key to his apartment?" Kale asked her, halfway smiling. Kale was shocked as he didn't realize it was getting that serious between the two of them.

She just put her keys in her pocket. They walked around the apartment quietly. Alex walked through the rooms looking for any sign of Kameron. Kale looked around the apartment and picked up a picture of Kameron and Alex hugging, looking at each other next to the Christmas tree. He walked into the master bedroom to see Alex looking through the closet. "What are you looking for?"

"Kameron doesn't leave town on business without his…" Alex stopped dead in her tracks. "Damn it." She picked up a small bag. She opened it up and pulled out a picture of Kameron and her with a girl who obviously had cancer. "The bag is his personal effects he constantly has packed ready to go." She looked outside at the clouds covering the moon. "I sure hope he's okay."

***

Kameron got sliced again on another finger. He felt the gasoline being poured in the wound. He prepared himself as he felt the heat ignite on his finger. He screamed in pain and could almost feel himself passing out. He could barely see the figure that was talking to Director Morkin. It was a floating shadow with red eyes. Any other day, Kameron would think he was hallucinating, but the last couple of days have been more than unusual.

The shadow figure came close to Kameron as if he was studying him. "His heart is pure; he cannot die by your hands."

"He's not dead yet," the Director told him. "Besides, he's only in case we don't accomplish the first operation."

The shadow figure looked to Kameron and floated away. Kameron could see Director Morkin look at some of the agents, but he could not tell what he was saying. He turned to Kameron. "It looks like your girlfriend is out looking for you."

Kameron calmly replied, "You better pray she doesn't find me."

"Pray? That's cute," Director said. He nodded to one of the agents as he began to slice another finger.

***

"I…I don't know what to do," Alex admitted to herself and Kale in the car. "I killed him."

Kale looked at her as if she said something completely outlandish. "How do you figure?"

"If I didn't love him, he wouldn't be in any danger," she told herself. "I will never forgive myself."

"Hey, sis," Kale said in a loving tone. "That is the most stupid, idiotic, thing I ever heard you say. Did those powers take away your common sense?"

Alex got a bit offended. "Excuse me?"

"Do you think Roger beating me like he did was your fault? Sara? Joseph? Or what about any other person who fell because of this horrible thing that is out there?" Kale asked her. "This is not the Alex I know. The Alex I know wouldn't put up with

407

this Darkness nonsense and would kick its ass!" he scolded her. "Now, get that bony butt of yours moving, and find your boyfriend!"

Alex wiped a tear from her face. "You're right."

"Damn right I'm right," Kale said. "I am older than you."

"By three months, you big ape." She smiled.

"So, what's the next move?" Kale asked her.

"I do have one idea, but you are not going to like it." She smiled.

Alex and Kale pulled in front of the federal building where Kameron worked. "You're right, I'm not liking this," Kale told her. "How are you going to get by security?"

"I'm not," Alex said. She pointed to a man breaking away from a group of people. "Follow that car."

Kale sighed. "Okay." Kale followed the car for a couple of miles hoping he wasn't going to get spotted. "Do you think he's one of those Demon things?"

"No, but he might be a provisionary," Alex said. "Not too close."

"I got it," Kale told her. They continued to drive when the car pulled into a parking lot of an apartment complex. "Now what?"

"We are going to have a little talk?" She got out of the car and the three of them walked into the parking complex.

The man got to the parking lot elevator. He didn't suspect anything. Kale walked up to him making sure his hands were showing; he didn't feel like getting shot tonight. "Sir."

The man turned around. "Yes, can I help you?"

"Yes, are you Kameron's supervisor?"

"Why do you ask? Aren't you Kameron's friend?" he inquired, putting his briefcase down and unbuckling his jacket no doubt getting ready to pull his weapon on him.

"Just needed to confirm, for my sister," Kale said.

"Your sister?" Alex grabbed the man and threw him against the concrete pillar.

"Jesus!" the man yelled.

Alex lit her fists and formed a sharp object pointed at the man's throat. "Do you know who I am?" Alex asked him as her eyes were glowing. The man just nodded his head yes looking at the light being aimed at his throat. The man was generally scared. "Tell me where Kameron is."

"I thought he was with you?" he said to Alex.

"Excuse me?" she said putting the Lite object closer to his throat.

"I thought he was leaving to meet your parents. He came into my office all nervous about it. That's the last I saw of him, I swear," he said. "Can you put me down?"

"Sorry." Alex lowered the man off the pillar. "Komptin, make sure he doesn't go for any of his guns." Komptin morphed into his gargoyle snarling and growling at the man.

"I don't know, do you believe him?" Kale asked Alex as he was looking at Komptin keeping the man on the pillar.

"I do," Alex said. "He's wearing a Star of David on his necklace. So that means he's not F.O.R. and I can't sense any creature in him." She looked over at him. "Plus, he's pretty scared," Komptin continued to growl at the man.

"Damn," Alex walked over to the man. "I suppose I can count on you to keep our little secret." She said petting Komptin behind the ears.

"No one would believe me. I'd lose my security clearance and my job," the man said.

"I need your help," Alex said. "Kameron is missing. He said there was an operation that was leaving tomorrow night."

"That's not true," the man started to look around as if someone might see them.

Alex's eyes flashed.

"I swear," he said, putting his hands up.

"I believe you," she said. "Can you help us find him?"

The man shook his head. "I'm going to reach in my pocket and grab my cell phone." Alex nodded in agreement. The man pulled out his cell phone. "There has been some weird stuff going on at work. It's almost as if the agency is being divided by two." The man called a number. "Agent Grossman Security Code: Gamma, Oscar, 3, 2, Papa. I need a track on Agent Kameron Dutcher's phone." He covered the phone so he could talk to Alex. "Kameron is a good man with great instinct. If he truly cares for you as much I think he does, then you can trust me." He went back to his phone. "It was shut off at the airport last night. Thanks. Grossman out."

"Do you think the F.O.R. grabbed him?" Kale asked.

"No way," Alex said. "He'd put up too much of a fight not to make a scene."

"You're right. He went with somebody he knew and trusted," Agent Grossman said. "I do have an idea where he might be, but if he's in there, we are not getting him out easily."

"Where is that?" Alex said.

"If we want to—" The agent was trying to come up with some words. "—have a private conservation with someone."

"Private? You mean interrogate with torture?" Kale chimed in.

The man leered at Kale. "I mean private. There's a place where we take them. It's outfitted so no one can hear anything from the outside."

"Screaming?" Alex asked, tightening her lips.

The man shook his head. "That means no cell phone reception inside either."

Alex grabbed the agent by the tie. "Let's go, you're going to help get my boyfriend back."

***

Alex was sitting in the passenger seat of the car with Kale behind the wheel. Komptin was keeping

Agent Grossman company in the backseat. He kept his eyes fixated on the agent, staring.

"Is he going to bite me?" the agent asked.

"Not if you don't do anything stupid," she said in a monotone voice staring at the building where she was hoping Kameron was located. She pointed over at the roof. "Is there any way to get in from the top?"

"No," the agent said. "The whole thing is cemented in with rebar. Only small ventilation shafts are present."

Alex took a deep breath. She continued to look at the building. She turned to Kale. "I'm going to need you to stay in the car, I don't know what's in there. I can't feel any demons."

"What are you?" the agent asked her.

"Livid," she said, opening the door to the car. She felt Kale's hand on her arm.

"What are you going to do?" he asked her.

"Walk through the front door," she said. "Come on, boy."

Komptin got out of the car as Alex walked behind the car.

"Oh, thank God they're gone." The agent leaned back on the back seat, closing his eyes. All of sudden the door flung open, and Alex grabbed him by the shirt dragging him out.

"Come on, you are going to get me in," Alex said.

"How am I supposed to do that?"

"You have until we get to the front door to figure it out," she told him as he walked towards the house.

"Fine, but you will have to trust me," the agent said, pulling out his handcuffs.

The two of them walked up to the door with Alex handcuffed behind her. The agent was grabbing her by the arm dragging her to the door. The two guards on the door who were dressed in slum clothes approached. "Can I help you?"

"Agent Grossman Access Code Gamma, Oscar, 3, 2, Papa. I need to use room 206-C," he said in a convincing tone.

The two guards looked at each other. "Sir, the second floor is occupied."

"Then L101 will do," he said.

"Sir, the building is occupied with residents," the other one said. "Besides, you can't think of anywhere else to take this little girl or is there a reason you need sound proofing?" he sneered sexually.

"Agent, you better watch that tone. This little girl is known for…" he continued.

Alex got to the point where she couldn't handle it anymore. She flashed her eyes and lit her fists as she broke the cuffs. Komptin morphed into his gargoyle state as Alex easily disarmed one of the guards and Komptin leaped on the other. Alex knocked out the guard with a single punch and Komptin made a guard faint from fright.

Agent Grossman stood in amazement. "The cards should be in their pockets." The two of them dug through the pockets as they grabbed the card keys. They entered the first door which was a normal door that led into an entryway that had a thick door.

"Can you get us in with these?" Alex asked.

"Yes." He went to the door and swiped the card on the keypad. He entered his access code and the door green lit. He turned the knob and stopped.

"What's the matter?" Alex asked with fist lit ready to pounce on whatever was on the other side.

"You tell me what's going on before I enter this building and lose my job," Agent Grossman pleaded.

"I promise to tell you, but first we save Kameron," Alex started, getting irritated.

Agent Grossman opened the door to a group of people in the living room. They all drew their weapons as Alex shot a light beam on the light smashing it. The sound of gunfire and quick flashes of light from Komptin's eyes and Alex's fists were all that the agent could see. The emergency light turned on and all that stood was Alex and Komptin over the bodies of the agents.

"Did you kill them?" Agent Grossman asked, almost afraid of the answer.

"No," she said softly. "Komptin, stay here, cover our backs." He flashed his eyes as Alex walked upstairs to the house.

"Who are you?" Agent Grossman asked again.

***

414

Kameron was trying not to show any pain, but he knew deep down he was failing at that miserably. He had come to the point where he had wished he would just die. He looked at the director who was listening to his earpiece. Kameron couldn't help but think this was God punishing him for killing that young girl. Frankly put, Kameron felt he deserved it. His stomach was starting to feel sick from the blood that he was swallowing.

The director came up to him. "Tell me about your girlfriend."

"Her name is Alex," Kameron said. "She works at a church on the south side of town."

"Hit him," the director told one of the agents.

Kameron felt the blow come across the face.

"Now tell me about her abilities," the director asked him, getting annoyed.

Kameron looked at him. "She's the only person I know who can burn cold cereal."

The director slapped his hands on his laps. "He must like it, hit him again."

Kameron got punched again, knocking him over on the floor still tied to the chair. The big agent picked him off the floor and set him back up in the position in front of the director. The sounds of commotion came from down the hall along with people screaming.

"What's going on out there?" the director asked the big agent.

"That would be my girlfriend," Kameron said to him.

The door was surrounded by bright blue light. It suddenly burst off its hinges with fragments flying into the room. Alex stood in the doorway, breathing heavy with her body protruding a blue light all around it. She had her eyes glowing and fists lit. "Honey," Kameron said. "Can I go home please?"

"Give me one sec," Alex said eyeing up the room.

"Don't just stand there, get her!" the director said pointing at her.

The big agent confidently walked up to Alex. She didn't even flinch as she punched the man directly in the chest knocking him down to his knees. Alex walked by him, pushing on the back of the big man's head. He fell to the ground as she shot a Lite Beam at the director knocking him into the wall. He too fell to the ground.

Alex walked up to Kameron giving him a kiss. "Bastards," she softly whispered as she was untying him from his chair.

"I'm okay," he tried to convince her but his wincing as he moved his finger proved the opposite.

"I'm sorry I got you mixed up in this," she said.

"Alex, it's okay, I don't…" Kameron tried to say.

He suddenly pushed her over as they both fell to the ground as a gunshot echoed through the room. Kameron grabbed a gun that was lying on the floor and shot the director who was holding the gun. Kameron took a second to contemplate what he just did.

The wall busted open as Komptin came running into the room.

"We're okay," Alex said, picking up Kameron. "We need to get you to the hospital." Alex suddenly flashed her eyes the same time Komptin did as they both looked around.

Kameron too was looking around. "What's wrong?" he softly said.

"We're not alone," she said, still holding Kameron up. Alex lit her fist as she looked to the shadow figure in front her with red eyes.

"Lite Sentry," he hissed. "You shouldn't be here."

"Salamor," Alex sneered. She was energizing her fist to shoot him with her beam until he raised his arms up.

"You need to be with the historic pure of heart! That's who Vandor wants," he warned.

Alex took a second. "Historic pure of heart?" she pondered. She took a small gasp of air. "Anne!" she softly cried out. She picked up her cell phone but there was no service.

***

Anne was deep into translating the old written scripts from the Russian Orthodox Council Historian. She was getting tired and even more nervous because she hadn't heard from Kale, Alex, or even Kameron. She looked up to look at the time.

It was getting late, into the next day. She happened to see her notes from the South American faction. Something had caught Anne's eye. She then picked up what she had translated from the Russian Orthodox Faction. She didn't understand why she didn't put it together before. She gathered her notes and went to go see Father Tom.

Father Tom had finished his report to the Council on what they had found out from the two girls that were brutally murdered by the demon. Father Tom silently gave the two girls a thank you while praying for their peace in the afterlife.

He sat back in his chair with a drink in his hand. It was quiet in the church. He looked to his phone to see if Alex had found out where Kameron was. There were no messages. He got up as he heard Anne call for his name.

He left his office as he yelled, "I'm in the congregation."

Anne ran up to the stairs and came in from the side. "Father! Father! The Dark one is mentioned, as Vandor is, in the Russian Orthodox text."

Father Tom met her in the middle of the hall. "Okay, slow down, catch your breath."

"I can't believe I didn't catch it before, but we have a chance to banish him," Anne said.

"Who?" Father Tom said looking at the text.

"Vandor!" she screamed.

"Are you serious?" Father Tom said, looking at the old papers. "What am I doing? I can't read this." He handed the papers back to Anne.

"It's right here in the text. Putting it all together from the texts, each of them are degraded enough not to be complete. But look, this one says 'the

418

Dark one consumes,' while this faction states 'untainted soul feeding,' feeding and consuming are basically the same thing, but this other faction just has the word 'eat' and then a couple of sentences later says 'height of the ball of lite in the dark sky.' That's obviously the moon."

"Anne, calm down," Father Tom said as he held her shoulders. "Put it in layman's terms."

Anne took a deep breath. "Vandor, the dark one, must consume someone of pure of heart on the height of the full moon."

Father Tom's eyes grew big. "That's tomorrow night. We have to find Alex."

The doors flew open to the church as the members of F.O.R. raid the church. Father Tom turned to Anne. "GO! HIDE!"

"But Father," Anne pleaded.

"GO NOW!" He turned her around and pushed her towards the back of the church. Father Tom watched her run off as he grabbed his rosary. He held it tight, and he prayed silently. He calmly walked to the leader of the F.O.R. group.

"Father," the leader said.

"You don't have to do this," Father Tom stated.

The leader of the F.O.R. pushed Father Tom on the pew. He adjusted himself. "Where's the girl?"

"She's out looking for her boyfriend," Father Tom calmly replied.

"I'm not talking about the Goth chick; where's the Historian?"

Anne was hiding behind the organ of the church. She didn't know where else to hide. She could see Father Tom as she was trying to avoid being seen. She was looking around for a way out but couldn't find one.

Father Tom looked to the leader of the group. "I don't know where she is."

"Isn't lying a no-no in your religion?" the leader of the group said.

"I'm not lying, I really don't know where she is," Father Tom told him.

"He's telling the truth," a girl said as she came up from behind. "He doesn't know, we should go," she said, trying to pull the leader away. "Who knows if that girl has called the police or not."

"We have to find her," the leader of the F.O.R. group said.

Father Tom looked over at the girl. "I know you," he told her. He recognized her from the plane as they shared a couple of drinks on the plane.

"Father, please be quiet for your life, please tell us where she's at," she pleaded to him.

"God will forgive you for this," Father Tom told her. "Just accept him into your heart."

"One last time Father, where is she?" the leader asked.

"I don't know," Father Tom reiterated in a monotone voice.

"Fine." The leader of the F.O.R. group pulled out a gun and shot Father Tom in the head. His lifeless body fell over in the aisle of the congregation.

Anne covered her mouth from screaming as she was blinded by tears. All she saw was Father Tom's body lying in the church.

"You didn't have to kill him," the girl said. "He was a good man."

"People like him are the ones pushing that propaganda onto easily manipulated minds," the leader said. "I just saved thousands of people with one bullet."

"I'm done," the girl said. "I'm out of here."

"Lana," the leader yelled out. "Come on Lana." The leader turned to the group of people. "Check every nook and cranny in the church, he wants her tonight."

Anne tried to keep calm and prevent her shaking. She closed her eyes and prayed for protection. She opened them to the leader's face staring at her.

"Hi," he said in a cold hateful tone.

Chapter 13

Agent Grossman was running through the red lights with the siren going. Alex convinced him to get to the church instead of taking Kameron to the hospital. She tried to call Anne and Father Tom multiple times on the phone with no answer on the other end. "I can't believe I let this happen again," Alex was beating herself up.

"What are you talking about?" Kale said, trying to get a hold of Anne.

"First Sara and now Anne," Alex said. "They are using my family against me."

"Come on Anne," Kale said still on his phone trying to get a hold of her. "Alex, you can't blame yourself for Sara. And Anne, it's not going to happen tonight." Kale told her with confidence. "I know you; you won't let it happen."

"Damn," the agent said as he swerved from hitting another car. They came up to the church to see the doors open.

"Something isn't right," Alex said. She turned to Komptin who flashed his eyes as he jumped out the window and morphed to his gargoyle state. Kale and Kameron got out of the car. "Stay in the car," Alex told them.

"Not a chance," Kale said, walking around the car.

"We are all in this now," Kameron said. He turned to Agent Grossman as he got out from the driver's side door. He walked around to the trunk of the car and opened the lock box. He pulled out a small automatic weapon and tossed it to Kale.

"What the hell am I supposed to do with this?" Kale was looking at the weapon.

"Flick the safety off and shoot," he said. He pulled out his pistol and cocked back the handle.

The group of them walked up the church stairs as they were met by Celestial coming out of the front door. Agent Grossman pulled up his weapon to shoot her but was met by Ariel's blade at his throat as Devine stood in front of Celestial.

"Wait!" Alex said, holding up her hands. "Both of you, were all on the same side!"

Ariel and Devine didn't let their guard down with a stone face emotion until Agent Grossman lowered his weapon. "Anything else you may want to tell me before I accidently shoot the wrong being?" Agent Grossman pleaded.

Alex continued up the stairs, but Celestial stood in her way. "Alexandria, prepare yourself," she told her.

Alex nodded as she continued into the church. She walked in to see Father Tom's body laying down in the middle of the aisle. She slowly walked up to him and turned him over to see his eyes wide open, lifeless. Blood from the back of his head covered her clothes as she held him looking up to the ceiling. "Now is not the time for tears," she told herself. Celestial stood behind her and knelt beside her. Alex heard Kale screaming for Anne throughout the church.

"He died trying to protect her," Celestial let her know.

"I'm not going to let his death become a failure," Alex said gently, placing his head on the ground and closing his eyes. She continued to hear Kale scream for Anne.

"I can't find her," Kale said, turning white from panic.

Alex started to head out the door. She was walking briskly towards the door as the group yelled for her to stop. She almost made it out the door when both Ariel and Devine grabbed her by both arms and brought her back to the church. "LET ME GO!" Alex yelled at them.

"Alexandria," Devine said in a stern tone.

"Now is the time to think," Ariel mentored her.

Alex looked around the church halfway hoping Anne would show up. As she looked around, she saw a concerned Celestial, a nervous Kale, Kameron bloody and beat-up, a confused Secret Agent, and Salamor. Alex did a double take at him as she aggressively asked, "What are you doing here?!"

"Lite Sentry," he hissed. Ariel and Devine both surrounded Celestial as she was studying the Dark Myst.

"Let him talk," Celestial said, coming out from behind Ariel and Devine. "Ariel, Devine, please take care of Thomas' body." Ariel and Devine reluctantly obeyed as they gently carried Father Tom's body out of the room.

"Why did they take Anne?" Alex asked him.

424

"She is pure of heart," he mentioned.

"You said that before," Kameron chimed in. "But you said historic along with that."

Salamor looked around before he whispered, "He knows they are here."

"What?" Kale asked him.

"The dark texts," Salamor said.

Alex looked to Celestial whose facial expression turned to shock. "They are here."

"What are the dark texts?" Alex asked as she sat down on the pew.

Celestial spoke, "Text written in the blood of the darkest of demons, written instructions for those who follow the Dark. It is a legend they contain insight into the dark."

Agent Grossman chimed in, "Why don't you know what they are or look for them?"

"We are Lite," Celestial answered him.

Ariel and Devine returned next to Celestial.

Devine was now leaning on her bō staff. "To us it would be as if we were looking at a blank sheet of paper."

Ariel concluded, "Just as the Dark are not able to read our texts."

"If Anne figured it out, then they must be here," Kale said. "What do they look like?"

Alex stood up. "We don't need them." She looked to Salamor. "You know what they say."

"It will not help us." Ariel looked at Salamor in disgust.

"Anything it says is a lie," Devine said.

"It reeks of Dark," they both said.

425

She turned to him. "Salamor?"

"She found out about the Pure of Heart consumption at the high moon," Salamor said.

Celestial chimed in, "You mean, Vandor must consume a pure of heart on the height of the full moon?"

Salamor nodded.

"And if he doesn't?" Alex asked.

"Then he cannot return until the peak of the Darkened Solstice, if the proper ceremony is conducted," he commented as he looked over at Alex.

"When is that?" Kameron asked.

"Seventeen years from this winter," Celestial informed them.

"You mean we have a chance to get rid of Vandor for close to 20 years!" Alex said standing up.

"If he needed a pure of heart, why not just grab someone else? Why is he fixated on Anne?" Kale asked.

"To see if she translated the texts and if she told anyone," Kameron chimed. "If I had a weakness like that, I would want to know who she told."

"They are going to torture her," Kale said out of fear. "I gotta get her out of there."

"Where?" Agent Grossman asked.

"The F.O.R. have buildings everywhere," Alex chimed in. "She could be anywhere."

"Hey shadow thing, do you know where my wife is?" Kale said getting irritated.

"The new F.O.R. HQ just below the top floor."

"It is lying," Ariel pointed out.

"It feeds on misery," Devine continued.

"Ariel, Devine," Celestial said, putting her guards at ease. She walked up to the shadow figure. She placed her hand on the side of Salamor's face. She whispered, "It is okay."

Salamor floated off to the corner of the church where he looked at a painting of Christ being tempted by the Devil in the desert.

"What's going on?" Kameron asked. "Why is it helping us?"

Celestial turned to the group. "You can thank Alex for his help."

Alex looked shocked. "Me? What did I do?"

"You showed compassion to him, something no one has ever done," Celestial pointed out to her.

Alex halfway shrugged her shoulders. "What? It was Christmas."

Kameron thought back to last Christmas realizing the Dark was at his home. At first he was angry but realized Alex had risked her life to save his family. He looked at her and mouthed, "Thank you."

Alex smiled back at him. "No problem."

Kale got agitated. "We need to find Anne." He stood up and headed out the door to see a girl standing in the doorway. "You look familiar."

The group of them looked at the girl. "I—I came to say I'm sorry," the girl said.

"Come my child," Celestial said. Ariel and Devine got back in front of Celestial.

"Who's this?" Agent Grossman asked Kameron. "Is she a demon or something?"

Kameron shrugged his shoulders. "She was on the plane with us, that's all I know."

Alex stood up and walked up to the girl and punched her across the face. "Father Tom is dead because of you!" The girl got up from landing on the pew, checking her face. The girl was lucky Alex was on church ground. She could only hit her with Alex's human strength. Alex shook her hands from the sting of the hit.

"I didn't kill him, he was a good person," she pleaded as she rubbed her face getting up from the ground. She turned to see Salamor floating in the corner and screamed. "You are all with him, I thought I would be safe here." She turned to run out of the church but was grabbed by Kameron. He had a hard time holding onto her as she was squirming to get free.

"We are not the Dark." Alex walked up to her. She grabbed her by the chin. "But it doesn't mean I'm not going to kill you for what happened here." Alex gritted her teeth out of anger squeezing her face.

"Alexandria," Celestial calmly said to her. Alex reluctantly backed down.

Kale walked up to the girl. "Do you know where they took my wife?"

"I do," the girl said with hesitation looking at Salamor.

"Well?" Kale said, getting more irritated.

"F.O.R. HQ, second to the top floor," she said.

Kale swallowed his pride as he saw the Shadow Myst still studying the picture.

"You have to protect me, please," the girl pleaded.

"What do we do?" Agent Grossman asked the group.

Alex looked to a cross hanging in front of the congregation. "I—I don't know," she admitted.

"I have an idea, but it's a long shot," Kameron said. They all looked at him. "But we need him." He pointed over to Salamor.

***

Gron looked over at Anne who came to them unmarked as requested. The provisionaries sat her down and tied her to a chair and slapped her across the face. They left the room as Gron motioned for them to leave.

"How are you doing, Anne?" Gron asked her, fixing himself a drink.

"What are you going to do with me, Roger?" she demanded.

Gron sighed at being called his human name. He turned around. "I heard that you and Kale got engaged, congratulations." He lifted his beverage as a toast.

"How about you let me go as an engagement present?" Anne said, trying to get herself free.

Gron came up to her and slapped her again across the face. "I can see Kale's arrogant attitude has started to rub off on you. You will show me some Goddamn respect."

"If you're going to kill me, then kill me, get it over with." Anne grit her teeth.

"I'm not going to kill you," Gron reassured her. "Can't." He shrugged one shoulder. "But someone I know wants to talk to you."

Out from the shadows came Vandor in his long greasy hair with white face. His blackened eyes stared at Anne containing her reaction to scream as he slowly walked up to her.

Vandor looked to Anne sitting there in her chair. "You are a pretty one," he said to her.

"Thank you," she softly said in return.

"And polite," he sneered. "You know you are going to die at my hand?"

"I know," she said. "I'm okay with the dying part, I'm just ashamed it is to feed you for another cycle."

"At least you know why you are here," he told her. "You have no idea what is on the other side."

"I don't need to, I have faith," Anne confidently told him.

Vandor was suddenly up her face as he licked her cheek. "Yum."

Anne shivered in fear and disgust.

"Who did you tell?" Vandor asked her.

"Father Tom," Anne truthfully told him.

Vandor stood up out of shock. Gron took his feet off his desk from amazement as well. "Wow, that much easier than expected."

Anne shrugged her shoulders. "I'm dead no matter what. You can't kill me until tomorrow night when the moon is at its peak, Father Tom was the only person I told and your team killed him; so, why not tell you the truth?"

Vandor studied her. "I like you." He opened his claws and swiped open one of her restraints on her arm. "You earned yourself a nice meal before you die."

Gron complied with Vandor's wishes. He called for another young girl to come in and take her order. "What would you like, Anne?"

Anne's was thinking of what her last meal would be and nothing sounded good. "I'm fine right now, thank you."

"Fair enough. It must be hard to think of that right now. I will have something sent to you upon request," Gron said. "In the meantime—" He motioned as a bunch of Demons appeared and picked her up, still sitting in the chair and took her out of Gron's office.

Vandor looked to Gron. "Make her comfortable, I like her."

"To your command," Gron said.

***

Anne got placed into a secured room. The door was a solid steel door. She knocked on it to see how thick it was. The small window opened to a pair of glowing red eyes. "What is it that you wish?"

Anne thought she might as well try it. "To leave?"

"We are here to serve you food and drink, anything else is not on the menu," the demon hissed.

"How about if I need to go to the bathroom?" Anne asked, looking around.

"The opening in the back of the room." The demon motioned.

Anne turned to gain a look at her cell. It wasn't that bad. There was a comfortable looking futon mattress on the floor. A TV with a cage was located embedded into the wall. She walked to the back of the room. The bathroom had no door but a working toilet and a hole in the wall with a button next to it. She pushed the button and water flowed from the hole. It fell onto the floor into a secured drain.

"Could be worse I guess." She walked to the TV and turned it on. She only had about 24 hours to live. She needed to pass the time, so she turned the channel to the news where the F.O.R. spokesman was talking about the positive actions of their organization in society. She shut the TV off and sat down on the mattress and fell asleep looking out the window.

***

Kale looked up to the night sky. The moon was bright, majestic, he couldn't help but think of Anne, as if they were connected at that moment. Throughout school, he never gave Anne a second

432

look before. She was cute, but he never thought of her in a sexual manner, let alone falling in love with her. He was startled when he turned around to see Alex staring at him with Komptin at her side.

"You scared me," he chuckled.

"You okay?" she asked him.

"I'm good," he falsely replied.

"Liar," she called him out. "It's okay to be scared, I'm scared every night I go out on a hunt."

"How do you manage it?" he asked her.

"I have faith," Alex positively said. She looked up at the bright purple star looking back at her. She smiled at it, wishing he were here.

"I always had a feeling of something, but could never explain it," Kale told her. "Getting off the booze, faith is one of the steps." He leaned over the railing looking down on the ground. "I never thought I would be hip deep in fighting demons to rescue my wife."

Alex smiled as she loved it, he referred to Anne as his wife even though they weren't technically married. "I've been there," Alex told him.

She walked up next to him as he turned around. She leaned back into his chest, and he put his massive arms around her as they did high school. "Kale, there's a good chance I won't make it through the night tomorrow."

Kale just squeezed his little sister tighter. "Yeah, you will," he smiled.

Alex just looked up and forced a smile at her big brother. She looked to see who was coming up the stairs. Kameron and Grossman were walking up the stairs carrying a couple of black duffel bags. "Hey honey," Alex said smiling at Kameron as he came up kissing as if they have been married for 20 years. It was just comfortable. Alex could feel herself blushing.

"What are you guys talking about?" he asked as he put down the bag. He rubbed his shoulder from the weight of the bag.

"Come on, let me help you with that, Grossman," Kale said, picking up the bag leading Grossman away from Alex and Kameron.

"Thanks man," Grossman said, as he walked into the church.

Kameron and Alex looked at each other. "Come here." She pulled him in and held him tight. He picked her up and placed her on the banister. Kameron thought she never looked so beautiful with the moon behind her and the stars twinkling over the city. The two of them just looked at each other.

"You know, there's no chance that we all make it out alive tomorrow night." Alex looked at him.

"I know," Kameron told her. He looked at her. "And I'm going to tell you something that you should know. You have completed my life and there's nothing, and I mean nothing, more important to me, than you." He smiled at her. "You hold on to the thought of us growing a family together, we'd have some place out in the country, I'll be working on some project outside while you are training on killing these dark bastards. You know, like every American dream." He laughed.

Alex gave him a little loving smile. "What about Komptin?"

"He'd be watching over our kids in the field," Kameron told her, brushing her hair out of her face.

Alex looked up with a worried look. "I physically can't have children."

"We'll adopt," he responded without skipping a beat. He smiled at her. "That thought, that inspiration, that way of life, is why I know we both are going to live tomorrow. You find something you want to hold onto and keep it here." He pointed to her heart. "And use that for that extra push to get you through what you need to do."

Alex closed her eyes imagining the life Kameron described. She smiled as she stared at him. "Come on," she said as she led him downstairs away from the church.

"Where are we going?" Kameron asked her.

"What I am going to do to you shouldn't be done on church property." She smiled at him as she led him to one possibly last night together.

***

"Everybody got the plan down, right?" Alex asked them.

Ariel and Devine looked to each other as they turned to look at Celestial. "We cannot leave her alone."

"Why don't you just go through the doorway while we do this?" Alex asked her.

"I cannot be that far without protection," Celestial pointed out. "It is a requirement."

"Okay, sis, gotta a motivating speech for us or something?" Kale halfway joked, covering up his nervousness.

"Yeah, don't die," Alex said, as she flashed her eyes. The group of them nodded as Kameron and Kale turned around to leave as Alex ran over to them. "Hey, you big ape," she said, punching Kale's arm.

Kale was scared to death, "Yeah," he said, chewing his gum radically.

"You got this," Alex said. "Just don't take any unnecessary risks."

"I'm going to get her out of there," Kale reassured her. He hugged her as he went into the car.

Kameron and Alex looked to each other, and they embraced in a passionate kiss. "Come back to me," Alex said to him.

"I will," Kameron said. "You be careful."

"I got this." She winked at him. "I love you."

"Love you, too," Kameron said as they parted ways.

Alex turned around to see Ariel and Devine looking at her with a teasing smile. "Shut up," Alex told them. Alex watched them drive off. She turned back to Ariel and Devine. "Well, I guess this is it."

Ariel and Devine just looked at her. They nodded as Alex thought they were fighting back tears. "Alexandria …" they both said softly as they formulated their words.

"Don't." Alex smiled at them. She turned to Celestial. "Am I going to go to Heaven?"

Celestial drew a tear. "If you fall using your powers, no," she told Alex. "You will join the others in the night sky."

Alex gut dropped. "Then do me a favor, please. Take care of Kameron when he crosses over."

"I will, Michelle and I will greet him on the plane," she assured.

Alex nodded, "Thanks." Alex gave a big sigh and turned to leave.

"You do not have to do this," Celestial yelled. "We can wait until the next cycle."

"And my sister dies," Alex told her. "I have to try to save her." She turned to Ariel and Devine, giving them one final wave.

Celestial along with her guardians watched Alex disappear into the darkness of the alley.

***

Anne looked at her watch knowing that she only had a few hours left before she would become Vandor's feast. She turned to the barred window and knelt to pray for Kale's well-being and the protection of all she loved. She started to regret that she will never have a future with Kale. Their kids would have been amazing.

She got up and turned around to see Roger staring at her. "You scared me."

Roger flashed his evil red eyes at her and smiled. "I never understood what you see in Kale."

He walked by her looking up at where she was praying and gave a scowl look up to the Heavens.

"He makes me laugh." Anne lavishly grinned. "The second we kissed, we both knew it would be forever. That connection is amazing. Didn't you feel like that with anyone?"

"No, not even Alex," Roger admitted remembering the night the two of them were making out at the party before Sara walked in.

"Then I will pray for you," Anne told him.

"Pray for me? I'm a demon. I don't need prayer, I can have any girl that comes across my path," he boasted. "And I had plenty."

"You just seem lonely, dark, and cold," she commented.

"I have power, fortune, and the ability to do what I want at will." He smiled. "You know Anne, I just wanted you to know. That night I beat the hell out of Kale."

"Yes." She remembered back then. Kale laying in her arms bloodied and beaten.

"I didn't want to kill you," he told her.

Anne looked up to him. "Oh."

"No, you always had a pure heart to you," Roger told her. He waived to the guards who were carrying heavy chains with bracelets. "And ironically, that is what is going to get you killed." He turned around and started to walk out of the room as the demons nailed chains to the wall which were no doubt for Anne.

***

438

Kale couldn't believe how calm Kameron was being as he watched over the building. He just stared as they stood a block down the road of F.O.R. Headquarters. He just confirmed over the radio that Grossman was in place. Kale looked to him. "We have to get Anne out of there."

"We'll do our best," he calmly said as he just stared at the building. He turned to Kale. "When this starts, we won't have long. Are you ready for this?"

"Sure," Kale said, as he nodded chewing his gum fast.

Kameron smiled. "We have an easy job, it's Alex that I'm worried about."

***

Alex walked with Komptin towards the F.O.R. building. She looked to the sky wondering where He would place her among the stars. She knelt down to pet her best friend before battle. "We're not going to make it out of this one."

Komptin morphed into his gargoyle state as he nuzzled up to her.

"I love you, boy," she said hugging him tightly. He gave her a loving growling snarl. She looked at him, "Ready to go to work?"

They both flashed their eyes as she lit her fists and walked towards the F.O.R. building. A small group of Provisionaries noticed Alex and Komptin walking towards them with her fists glowing. They got on their radios, no doubt informing the compound that the Sentry was coming.

***

"That's what I'm looking for." Kameron pointed to the guys running towards the other side of the building.

"Alex must be starting her fight," Kale said looking towards the direction the people were running towards. A body went flying out from the other side of the tree. "Yep," Kale said.

"You ready?" Kameron asked as he loaded his weapon.

Kale's eyes got big. "Yeah, let's do this."

Kameron and Kale got out of the car and snuck around to the back entrance of the F.O.R. building. They were hiding in a bunch of bushes looking at the entrance. Kameron just stayed there, looking at the door dead-faced. "What's the matter?" Kale asked. "The door isn't guarded."

"Yes it is," he pointed to two people taking post at the door.

"What are we going to do?" He asked.

Kameron looked around but frowned. "Damn it." He reached into his pocket and pulled out a silencer and placed it on the end of his weapon. "You may not want to watch this."

Kale's eyes grew big. "Are you going to…" Before he knew Kameron shot the two guards. The two of them hesitated before walking to the door. Kameron walked over the two bodies as Kale looked at their bodies not moving. Kameron took out his baton and smashed the windows to the door. The two of them entered the building.

"Elevator or stairs?" Kameron asked Kale.

"You're the expert," Kale said.

"Taking the elevator is faster, but we are confined if someone sees us, stairs give us more of an avenue of escape if need be. I would say the stairs, but I don't know how much longer Alex can distract them for."

***

Alex shot a Lite Beam at the closet Infiltrator because she knew she could take all the humans running after her. She punched the human closest to her as he fell instantly to the ground. Another managed to get behind her and put his arms around her.

She instantly smashed his nose with the back of her head. He let go of her to cover his nose as she grabbed him and threw him into an Infiltrator. The guy managed to get to his knees and open his arms towards the black beast.

"Absolute power." The Infiltrator jumped into the man as he rose with glowing eyes and turned to Alex.

"Uh OH," Alex said, as she watched him with the red eyes come after her.

The two of them began trading blows before Alex kicked the Demon in the crotch as he bent over from the pain. Komptin jumped on the

441

Demon's back and bit into the back of its neck ripping half the neck off and spitting it to the ground as the Demon dissipated.

A group of Infiltrators side tackled Komptin, knocking him to the ground with a subtle noise as the Infiltrators started digging into his side. He tried fighting them off but couldn't get a grip onto them. Alex shot her Lite Beam knocking one of them off as she ran tackling another one off. Komptin managed to grab the leg of the remaining Infiltrator and threw it into a group of a mixture of Demons, Infiltrators and Provisionaries running towards the two of them.

***

Gron overlooked the fight from up above on the balcony. He was amazed at how the Sentry was holding up. He took a sip of his drink. He felt the presence of Vandor behind him. "As you command." he bowed.

"She is fighting well," Vandor noticed. "Much better than expected."

"Yes, she would have made a fine warrior for you," Gron said.

He turned to look at Salamor who was overlooking the battle. He couldn't help but think he actually looked concerned over the battle on his expressionless face. He shrugged it off and turned to Vandor.

"It's almost time," Gron pointed out. "I'll go get dinner prepped," he said as he chugged the last of his drink.

Vandor nodded. Salamor turned to Gron and then glanced back down at the Sentry who was fighting a group of the Dark. Salamor turned and started to float away before Vandor spoke, "Where are you going?"

Salamor turned to Vandor. "Something isn't right," Salamor hissed. "I'm going to check the other entrances to make sure dinner isn't interrupted." Salamor disappeared through the floor.

***

Gron walked to the door. He waved off the guards and told them to go get Anne a flower. The guards looked confused, but they faithfully followed orders. Gron heard the chatter over the radio that the Sentry and her loyal gargoyle was starting to get closer to the headquarters building. Gron ordered more demons to the fight. The guard returned with a white daisy. Gron motioned for the guard to open the door.

He saw Anne was looking outside up at the moon. "Beautiful isn't it?"

Anne turned to Gron with her arms across her chest as if trying to get herself warm. "It is," she replied looking up at the moon not paying any attention to him.

"Scared?" Gron asked her.

She turned to him. "More of how bad it's going to hurt."

"It will be a sharp pain, for a split second you will see your heart in Vandor's hand before you die," he coldly said.

"Well, thanks for that." Anne shook her head in disbelief.

Gron walked up to Anne and handed her a flower. "This may make it a bit easier." He motioned for her to put in her hair.

She took it and she didn't want to admit but it did make her feel a little bit better. "Thank you."

Gron just gave a smirk as he motioned for the guards to shut the door. The slam of the door was darker and colder than Anne remembered. Anne looked at Roger as he sat down on the couch watching TV. It was a propaganda infomercial on the F.O.R. "We are doing good for the world," he said.

Anne looked to Gron in disbelief in what he just said, "It's all based on a lie."

"Ignorance is bliss," Gron said. "The people in F.O.R. don't fight, they are fed, they have a purpose."

"They are slaves and empty of His presence," Anne contradicted. "I fear for what happens to them in the end."

"What do you fear?" Gron looked up at Anne who was still standing.

Anne could feel tears start to form as she thought of her answer, "I fear the pain Kale will feel when I'm gone. I fear the regret of not starting a family with him. I fear the repercussions of my death because Vandor will not be vanquished, and I fear for you."

Gron chuckled. "You fear *for* me?"

"Yes, because sooner or later, Alex will get to you," she confidently said.

Gron could actually feel himself a little nervous about that. "I know our paths will cross again." He got up and joined Anne looking at the moon. "She had her chance to join us," he sighed as he looked to the stars.

Anne looked to Gron. "What happens to you if you fall?"

"Depends on if I achieve what the Dark requires of me," Gron said. "Failure is not an option."

"What do you get if you achieve it?" Anne asked.

He turned to Anne. "Power, power and the will to do whatever the hell I want."

"Better to reign in Hell than serve in Heaven," Anne paraphrased Milton.

"In high school, your kind never gave me a second look. I was an outcast, the dark, red-headed, drugged out little boy," Gron told her. "You know that night when Alex and I were making out was one of the only feelings I got like I was somebody. Here's Alex, a beautiful popular girl, choosing to make-out with me. I must be someone." Roger put his guard down.

Anne continued to listen to Roger as he went on with his thoughts.

"And when she told me it was a mistake, I had never felt so low, so worthless," he admitted to her. "I wanted her loyalty to me as she had with Kale. I hate him for that."

"You know they are brother and sister, right?" Anne told him. Anne could see that Roger didn't know that, but then he shook it off.

"When Vandor offered me absolute power, I couldn't pass it up," he told her. "The power he gave me showed me focus, confidence, and the absence of not caring what anybody thinks."

"That absence of not caring is only there because you don't feel God's love," Anne said. "When you know you are loved, you do things because you want to, you want to make them happy. You know you will be taken care of."

"Are you taken care of now?" Gron asked her.

"Yes," she said. "Maybe not in a way you see." She turned to look at him. "Roger, it is not too late. You can change your life around. You can help end this escalation. Let's get out of here together."

Roger looked to the moon as he saw a light flash in the corner of the window which no doubt Alex was fighting her way to the building. He stopped breathing for a second and let out a breath. "It's too late." With his glowing red eyes showed his decision. Forcefully grabbing her hand, he shackled her to the wall.

"Roger, you don't have to do this," Anne pleaded.

"Yeah, I kinda do," he told her as he locked her wrists to the bracelets.

"Promise me one thing, I beg of you," Anne asked him.

Gron turned to Anne. "What?"

"Please, please do not hurt Kale," Anne pleaded as she started to cry.

Gron turned to her out of disbelief. "Through all this, you just care about the safety of your boyfriend?"

"My husband," Anne corrected him. "Promise me."

"All right," Roger said as he started to walk away.

"Please say it," Anne asked.

Gron annoyingly turned to her. "I promise, upon your death, I will not hurt Kale Moler in any way." He looked at her. "When I return, I will not be alone." He knocked on the door for the guards to let him out. The sound of the cell door was even louder than before as Anne started to pray for her family.

Chapter 14

Alex got punched by a Demon and it spun her into a tree. She leaned on the tree as she kicked the demon in the stomach. It bent over from the blow. Alex took advantage of the weakness as she grabbed the head and snapped the Demon's neck. The crackling sound represented the Demon coming to a point where Alex could eliminate it.

Alex formed her Lite to a pointed knife and stabbed it in the back of the head. It howled as it disappeared into the ground. She took a moment to wipe some blood from her face as she looked over at her partner who just eliminated an Infiltrator. She leaned on the tree trying to catch her breath for the first time in a while.

"Komptin," she said to him.

He looked over at her in concern. He ran over to her to make sure she was okay. She noticed a couple of scratches on him and some blood dripping from his shoulder.

"I'm okay, you?"

Komptin flashed his eyes as they both heard the next wave about to show up.

"Let's rest up for a sec," she said.

She turned to lean her back on the tree. They watched the group form in front of them. The good news was that there seemed to be mainly Provisionaires, the bad news, there were a lot of them. She wasn't going to get through this without killing any of them.

448

"I hope they get to her in time." Alex got up from the tree as she lit her fists walking towards the group with Komptin at her side.

**

Kameron pushed the button to the elevator as he was listening to Agent Grossman on the other end. "Sounds like we're all good," he told Kale who was smacking his gum faster and faster. "You okay?"

"How are you so calm?" Kale asked him.

"Trust me, I'll be paying for it later if I make it through this," he said to him as he was analyzing the surroundings. The door opened as a man looked at them. He smiled with the glowing red eyes and sharpened teeth.

"Damn," Kale and Kameron both said as it lunged at them.

Kameron shot at it, but it just slowed down for a second before it grabbed Kameron's gun from his hands and threw it across the room. Kale ran off to get it but was tripped by the Demon. He landed hard on the ground as Kameron was taking his baton and started hitting him across the face as hard as he could. The Demon started bleeding black blood and was getting angrier as Kameron was hitting him. The Demon picked up Kameron and threw him over the information desk.

"I'm going to feel that in the morning," Kameron said to himself as he got up.

He watched the Demon grab Kale by the leg as Kale was kicking it as hard as he could. It didn't look as if he was doing any damage to it. Kameron acted quickly as he pulled out his knife from his vest and jumped over the desk onto the Demon to stab it in the back. The demon howled in pain as it flung Kameron off its back into the wall. Kale managed to break free from the grasp of the creature and helped Kameron get back up.

"How are we going to kill this thing?" Kale asked Kameron.

Kameron shrugged his shoulders. The Demon stood up and attacked the two of them. They just stepped to the side as the demon's head ran through the wall. Kameron went grab the Demon to see if it was dead and he reached out to grab Kameron's throat.

It squeezed as Kameron was losing his breath. "Get this thing off me!" He gargled, trying to pry its hands off his throat.

Kale quickly looked around for anything to help Kameron as he was starting to lose consciousness. He was getting frantic because he couldn't find anything. He found a utility closet. He hoped there was something in there he could use to help his friend. He opened it and found a set of chains that must have been used to secure some doors within the complex. He grabbed them and ran over to the demon. He wrapped them around its neck and pulled back as hard as he could. He could actually hear and feel the neck bones cracking as he pulled. The demon let go of Kameron as he dropped to the ground.

The demon turned around and swiped at Kale with its sharp claws. Luckily he dodged the claw before it connected. Kale stumbled backwards as the demon started to walk towards him with glowing red eyes showing his teeth. Kale's only regret before dying was that he was not going to be able to save Anne.

***

Anne tried to squeeze her hands out of the shackles, but they were too tight. She couldn't even get comfort by seeing the outside. All she could see was the door that once it opened, she would become the feast to Vandor.

She was okay with dying, but she regretted that she would help him survive for another cycle. She did hear some commotion going on outside as if something wasn't going to plan but she couldn't make it out. She couldn't help but think how long after the harvest moon had reached its peak before Vandor had to eat her. She knew it was getting close though.

"Historic heart."

Anne stopped as she heard a voice coming from the bathroom. It was a voice that she had heard before but couldn't quite place.

"In the dark," it whispered again.

Anne was afraid to look. She now knew it wasn't natural that was calling her. It was not something that should be of this world. She slowly turned her face to the bathroom where she saw a set of glowing eyes floating in the darkness. She could feel her stomach start to get nervous as she knew that shadow figure was only a prelude to Vandor coming to feast on her heart.

Then it said something Anne was not expecting. "Relax Historic Heart, they are coming to set you free."

Anne looked confused. "Excuse me? Who?"

"Your family," it hissed. It floated up to Anne slowly and met her face to face. "I shall try to stall my master," he turned around towards the door.

"What?" Anne asked in confusion.

It turned around with its glowing eyes staring at her. "The Sentry is coming, along with your husband." It started to float away. It stopped as it turned around to look at her one more time. "They have deep love for you."

Anne could feel a sense of hope as she remained shackled to the wall, helpless.

***

Alex grabbed the demon by the arm and swung him towards Komptin as he jumped in the air connecting with it to the ground. Komptin shredded the massive creature with a fiery set of claws into its chest. Alex ran by an Infiltrator jabbing her Lite Spear into its throat killing it instantly.

Two Provisionaries managed to attack her. She didn't want to kill them, but she was afraid it was going to be them or her. One of them looked at her. "Hey, aren't you Kameron's girlfriend?"

Alex knocked the second Provisionary with ease as she took the moment to catch her breath. "Yeah, why?"

"I like you two together."

"Ah, thanks," she said. Komptin came up behind her overlooking the area.

Alex noticed another group of people coming.

"You're not going to survive this, you should run, come back and fight another day," he told her.

Alex looked at him. She couldn't sense any Demon in him. She was really confused about his words and what he was meaning behind them. "My friend is in there."

"She needs to die," he told her.

Alex flashed her eyes as she saw a group full of Demons heading her way. The guy looked behind him at the group mainly consisting of Demons slowly started to walk her way. Alex could feel a deep dark sense in the air come over her. She knew she wasn't going to make it through this fight.

Alex turned to the man. "She is my friend, my sister, I have to try."

The man looked to the stars and Alex could have sworn it was a bit of a shock to his face. "I have to go." He turned around and went into direction away from the fight.

Alex was still confused as to who or what he was. She sensed nothing from him. Her thought was interrupted by the sounds of the group of Demons hissing and growling.

She looked over to Komptin. "I love you, boy."

She petted him behind the ears. Komptin nuzzled up to her knowing the both of them will join their brothers and sisters in the stars. They started to walk towards the group. The Demons started to run towards Alex and Komptin. The two of them just took a short deep breath and went running towards the group.

Lightening blasted the ground as a loud thunder overcame the sky and seemed to shake the ground. Alex looked up to see three figures falling from the sky. The group of Demons stopped out of fear. Alex just laughed as she saw Ariel, Devine, along with Malkaroy, in their full out armor land onto the ground indenting the Earth. Alex looked to Ariel and Devine in shock.

"Our little sister will not face death alone," Devine said.

"We will stand with you into the shadows," Ariel added.

Alex could help herself as she just hugged the two. They returned the hug and looked over to the group. "Shall we?" The two of them asked her they both cracked their necks looking over at the group of evil Demons.

Alex just nodded as she looked over at Malkaroy who she hadn't seen since Osiah's funeral. "What are you doing here?"

"Repaying a debt," he said as he formed a Lite Whip and Lite Sword in his other hand.

"Frankly, I don't care why." Alex laughed. She looked over at the Demons who were debating on attacking them or not. The demons looked to each other and started to charge them. Alex confidently looked at her team. "Oh, we got this."

***

Vandor looked over down at the window as he heard the thunder and flash of light coming from the night sky. "You wouldn't allow it, would you?" Outside the window were the Conduit's bodyguards along with a third angel standing with the Sentry.

Vandor squinted. "Salamor," he called for his Dark Myst. There was no evidence of his minion. "Salamor!"

Salamor floated into the room. "To your command."

"Where were you?" Vandor asked.

"Ensuring the Pure of Heart was where she was supposed to be," he admitted.

Vandor motioned over to the battle. "Is that Malkaroy down there with the Sentry?" Vandor asked him.

Salamor looked over to the battle. "It appears so my master."

Then Vandor saw something he was not prepared to see. He saw the twins fighting alongside the Sentry.

"GRON!" Vandor yelled.

Gron came into the room quickly. "To your…" He couldn't finish before Vandor interrupted him.

"Kill them!" Vandor screamed and pointed.

"They are trying, my master," Gron said. "I didn't want to leave holes in the perimeter."

"Kill them, send everyone! The Conduit is not protected! She must be nearby! Find her! Kill them! Send out everyone…. NOW!" Vandor commanded. Vandor gave a hateful scorn to the sky. "Now, I will show you how far I'm willing to go."

***

Kale knew this was going to be it. He silently sent a message to Anne apologizing for not being there for her. He wasn't going to give the Demon the satisfaction of him being scared. He looked at it right in the face accepting his fate.

The demon was about to strike until it stopped and took off out the door as if there was an emergency he had to attend to. Kameron got up from the floor shaking his head. "Oh man, that sucked." He looked around for the demon. "Where'd it go?"

"I kicked its ass, too bad you missed it," Kale said as Kameron helped him up.

"Come on, let's go get your wife." The both of them walked to the elevator and started heading up the floor. The door opened and both Kameron and Kale had their weapons pointed at what was on the other end. Two agents were next to a steel door with a small window. "She's gotta be in that one."

"Agreed," Kale said. "What do we do?" Kameron pointed his weapon at them to shoot but Kale stopped him. "What are you doing?"

"Neutralizing the situation," he replied to him.

"Do you know them?"

"One of them is a friend of mine," he said, raising the weapon.

"And you're just going to kill them, without even thinking about it?" Kale pleaded.

Kameron turned to him. "Look, I don't have the privilege of saving my friends and saving Anne. Those two know what they are into, Anne is innocent in all this, she's the one that needs protecting. She is the mission."

Kale was amazed how he could just push his feelings aside. Kameron had a deadpan face to him. He was callous in his thinking but logically speaking he had a point. "Do you think there might be...?" His thoughts were interrupted by two-gun shots as the two bodies fell. Kale's mouth dropped in shock.

"Come on, let's go." He motioned, keeping his gun up.

They walked through the hallway slowly and quietly. Kale was at Kameron's back. He could feel something wasn't right as he thought Kameron could feel the same thing since he was walking so cautiously. They passed a door as it broke open as a black creature with massive claws and red eyes tackled Kameron into a recreation room.

"Go Kale," Kameron yelled. "I'll buy you time to get her out of here." Kale ran to the door.

***

Gron turned to the door at the commotion outside the hallway. "I thought I heard gunshots."

Vandor leaned on the wall. His energy was depleting. He managed to look to the battlefield where the Dark Conduit opened. "I can't believe she's not protected. They better find her."

Gron looked at his watch. "Master, it's time."

Vandor looked over the battlefield as he could see the lights of the Sentry and Angels fighting his Demons. "I need to feast."

He bowed to the Dark Master. "To your command." Gron turned around and headed to the elevator.

***

Kale couldn't get the door open as it was locked. He was hoping the body of the guards had keys on them. He searched their bodies for a key. He found a card key and opened the door. He saw that Anne was locked up on the wall in shackles. "Kale," she yelled his name.

"Anne." He ran up to her kissing her.

"How'd you get here?" she asked him as he frantically looked for a key.

"We all came to get you, angels, Alex, Kameron." Kale looked around. "I can't find a key."

Anne motioned her head. "Kale."

Kale turned around to see Roger holding the key to the shackles. "Looking for this," he smartly asked with an evil grin.

Kale quickly drew his pistol and shot Roger in the head causing him to fall to the ground. "Man, that felt good," he said as he ran over and got the key out of his hands. He ran back to Anne undoing her cuffs. The two of them hugged and kissed each other in a loving embrace hoping they would never let go.

Anne whispered in Kale's ear, "I love you."

"Love you, too," he said as they turned around to see Roger getting up with blood dripping from his head.

Anne and Kale both looked at each other out of fear that they were not getting out of this alive.

***

Devine pulled her Lite Bō Staff out of an Infiltrator as she turned to Ariel who just killed a Demon with her sword. The two of them sat back watching the Sentry trying to fight her way to the doors of the F.O.R. Headquarters.

They smiled at each other out of pride for what she has become. Malkaroy finished killing a Demon by grabbing it with his whip and flinging it into Komptin as he clawed through the body. "She is quite the fighter. Osiah would be proud."

Devine looked to the rooftop of the F.O.R. Headquarters. "We need to get her to her friends."

"They will not make it out alive," Ariel added as she stabbed another Infiltrator and kicked it off her sword.

"I will take her," Malkaroy said. His whip dissipated and he spread his wings headed for the Sentry.

"We will maintain the battle here," they both agreed. They headed off to the fight.

Alex grabbed an Infiltrator in a headlock and turned it around as she stabbed it in the throat having it disappear into the ground. Blood dripped onto the ground when Alex realized it was coming from her nose.

"Damn it," she said wiping her face. She was scraped and cut in other places, but the majority of the blood was coming from her nose. She could feel bruises start to form.

Alex checked to see how Komptin was doing as he was busy taking on two Infiltrators. Alex looked around to see what was coming next. It looked as if they were winning this fight as there weren't many Demons or Infiltrators in the area. Just as she got some confidence, she saw a huge Demon was walking through the crowd.

"This isn't good," she said.

"Alexandria," Malkaroy said as he came to Alex. "We need to get you to your friends."

"Ya think," she said. "But we have kind of a 600-pound issue." She pointed over the creature who came out of nowhere. "What the hell is it?"

"A Caliginous!" Malkaroy looked at it with a dead stare but a look of concern. "Vandor must have opened a Dark Conduit to get it here. That must take a good amount of energy."

Devine was worried, "He will need to feast."

"She will not have much time," Ariel added on.

The two of them nodded at each other as the Caliginous roared with hate. "We got this." Ariel and Devine walked towards the creature. Their weapons flashed as they calmly walked to the creature.

"Can they beat it?" Alex watched out of concern as they walked towards the Demon.

"No," Malkaroy stated.

"Ariel! Devine!" Alex went running after Ariel and Devine to help them in their fight.

Malkaroy grabbed Alex. "We have to go." He spread his wings as he grabbed Alex with one hand lifting her off the ground and headed towards the F.O.R. rooftop.

"NO!" Alex cried for her surrogate sisters.

Ariel and Devine watched Malkaroy take the Sentry to the rooftop. Komptin was taking care of the infiltrators and demons that remained. There were no words as Ariel grabbed Devine's Lite Bo. Devine swung her Bō launching Ariel into the beast. The Caliginous swung its massive arms at Ariel but missed. She landed on its head stabbing it through the skull. It grabbed Ariel with his hands, crushing her. She pulled her sword out of its head as he was lifting her up to throw her. She continued to try to slice out of his grip.

Ariel was screaming as Devine ran full force swinging her Lite Bō across the Caliginous' stomach. It flinched a little as she quickly turned to stab it in the back. The creature let go of Ariel, dropping her to the ground. Devine quickly grabbed

461

her and got her out of the way before the Dark creature punched the ground causing an indentation in the ground.

**

Kameron could feel his face being crushed on the floor from the Infiltrator. For a split second he thought he could hear his skull start cracking as the Infiltrator was on top of his back. He heard Kale yell from the other end of the hallway, "Kameron, we need you."

"Busy at the moment," he tried to say.

He reached into his pocket and pulled out a backup pistol and shot the Infiltrator in the mouth. It staggered back from the blunt of the force, but it didn't seem to hurt any. He got up and ran to the other side of the pool table, creating some sort of barrier between. He had no idea how he was going to defeat this creature. The Infiltrator came to the table and chased Kameron. Kameron quickly counteracted by moving to keep the Infiltrator separated.

"Are we going to do this all night?" He laughed. The Infiltrator flashed its eyes as it swung downwards splitting the table in half. He looked back up at Kameron. "Crap."

**

Alex landed on the rooftop in a summersault as she stood up with fists lit ready for anything that

462

was about to attack. Malkaroy landed next to her in the ready position with his weapons in his hand.

"You never told me what Osiah did for you that you owe him so big," Alex said, surveying the land.

"He introduced me to my wife," Malkaroy said, as he walked towards the door leading to the downstairs.

Alex looked at him out of confusion and then chased after Malkaroy. "Huh?"

They entered the hallway from upstairs. They looked around. "Vandor is close," Malkaroy stated. "There is a powerful Dark Sentry at the end of the hallway and an Infiltrator just ahead."

"How do you know?" Alex asked him. "I can't sense anything because of how much darkness is in here."

Malkaroy sniffed the air, "I can smell them."

"The Dark Sentry… Roger." Alex started to get nervous as she walked down the hallway.

***

Vandor leaned on the wall as he tried to get up. Holding the Dark Conduit open to keep the Caliginous here was taking a toll on him. He needed to eat, he needed to eat quickly. "Salamor," he asked for.

"To your command," he appeared out of the shadows.

"Go tell Gron I need the Heart, quickly you slime," Vandor said as he dropped to the ground.

Salamor bowed his head as he left towards the Heart.

***

Alex and Malkaroy walked down the dark hallway. The light of the weapons were illuminating the hallway with the emergency lights. Alex saw a figure standing at the end of the hallway. She knew it was Roger. Alex started to head towards him when she heard a crash come from inside the room. She peaked inside the room to see Kameron being lifted by an Infiltrator by the throat.

Alex knew that look, it was about to lunge for Kameron's throat.

"Save Anne." She pointed to the end of the hallway. She shot her Lite Beam at the Infiltrator knocking it into the wall as Kameron fell to the ground trying to catch his breath.

Malkaroy ran full speed into the Dark Sentry as it was rising onto its feet.

"This day just keeps on getting weirder," Kale said as he saw an angel come out of nowhere to tackle Roger. Kale just sat there as he watched Roger fighting with an angel.

"Get out of here!" A dark shadow came from the bathroom. "Take the stairs to the right. Vandor is upstairs, if he gets his hands on your wife, all this will be for nothing. Get as much distance as you can away from him."

Kale looked at the shadow. Anne grabbed Kale. "Come on, Kale, I want to go home."

Salamor waved its hands telling them to go. Salamor floated by Gron as he was exchanging blows with the angel. Salamor floated by the fight to head back up to Vandor.

***

Vandor started to crawl up the wall. He was hoping to get to the Heart as quickly as possible. In his weakened state he was having a hard time maintaining his balance. He leaned on the wall. He limped over to the window to see how the Caliginous was doing. He could see the Conduit's guardians battling the creature, but still no word where the Conduit was hiding.

"Where are you?" he asked himself.

"I am right here," she answered as she walked up to him overlooking the fight.

Vandor looked beside him to see Celestial overlook the battle. She had much concern on her face and sadness as she was watching the humans and demons die. "Come to kill me in my weakened state?"

She just continued to look out the window. "I cannot hurt you no more than you can hurt me." She turned to him. "Is it not why Osiah was created, to do what you could not do?"

"I hate you," Vandor hissed.

"I know," Celestial said. "Hate is so cold, lonely."

"The humans embrace it," Vandor replied. "We will rule over them."

Celestial turned to him. "As long I exist, it will never come." She looked over to the battle.

"My Infiltrators will find every provisionary willing to become true power," he said. "The humans crave it. No one can stop them."

"The Sentry will," she replied to him. "I know you are scared of her. She is powerful." Celestial smiled as she said, "She has heart as rare as Blue Gold."

***

Alex ran after the Infiltrator. She quickly ran and slid underneath its massive claws as she quickly stood up and punched it in the side. The Infiltrator howled in pain as it turned and elbowed Alex in the side of the head where Sanah had scratched her. She screamed as she dropped to the ground. The Infiltrator swiped at her across the face, but Alex had time to put up her arms to block her face from being scratched. The force knocked her over onto the ground. The Infiltrator stomped on her side from where she was stabbed. She screamed in pain. The Infiltrator showed its claws as it was about to pounce on Alex.

Kameron jumped on the Infiltrators back with three pool sticks and used all his force to get it off his girlfriend. He screamed as he leaned back. The Infiltrator staggered back as he smashed Kameron against the wall. Alex took advantage of the situation as she formed a Lite Spear and shoved up through the bottom of its jaw. Her Lite Spear came out on the other end as it dropped to the ground disappearing into the ground.

"When we tell this story to our kids, can we say I got that one?" Kameron asked her.

"Of course, honey." She smiled as she kissed him and playfully slapped him on the cheek. "Let's go get Anne and Kale and go home."

***

Ariel and Devine continued to fight the massive demon. They were dripping liquid lite from cuts on their bodies. They continued to fight with the two of them knowing what each other's moves were in sync. The Caliginous was getting angry. He picked up a massive chunk of the Earth and threw it at Ariel. She sliced through it as she continued to attack the creature. Just as the Sentry does, Ariel slid on the ground between its legs on the other side of it. Her sister in arms jumped from half of the massive rock towards the creature and smashed its face with her Lite Bō as Ariel sliced the back of the creature's knees. The creature fell to the ground in a massive explosion that seemed to shake the Earth.

Devine landed on the ground and turned around to assess the situation. She saw Ariel jump on the creature's chest about to stab it when the creature grabbed her by the head. She screamed in pain as the Caliginous thrusted its hand into her chest. He stood up as he picked Ariel up as a rag doll and threw her into the tree.

"NOOOO!" Devine cried as she ran to Ariel.

Komptin came running over to help as he kept on jumping on the creature trying to distract him as Devine tended to Ariel.

Devine held Ariel's head on her lap looking over wounds. Devine had seen these wounds before, and she knew the outcome. "Do not look," she told her.

"Forgive me," Ariel pleaded.

"You fought with courage," Devine told her. She smiled as she wiped Ariel's hair out of her face.

"Please tell My Lady." She was holding on as long as she could. "Please tell My Lady I am sorry I will not be there."

"You will be remembered by being the brightest in the sky," Devine assured her.

Ariel smiled as she gasped one last time before dissolving upward to the sky.

***

"My lady," a male voice behind Celestial stated.

"You should not be here," another stated.

Celestial closed her eyes and shed a glowing tear as the sounds of those voices meant.

Vandor smiled as he turned to her new guardians. "We shall win this night."

Salamor floated into the room as the new guardians pushed back Celestial against the wall to

468

protect her. They ignited their Lite Swords to fend off the creature.

"Where is the Heart?" Vandor asked him.

"She is on her way," Salamor said.

"And to seal it, I feast." Vandor laughed.

***

Devine rushed after the beast as she and Komptin fought side by side trying to take it down. The beast howled in anger. Komptin grabbed it by the head, chewing. It flipped Komptin over its head and slammed him to the ground. Devine swung her Bō Staff into the stomach of the creature. Then she retracted as she spun around smashing it on the back of the head causing it to fall to the ground.

Both Devine and Komptin went on the offensive and started to attack the creature. The creature knocked Komptin off its back. It grabbed Devine by the leg and smashed her into the ground two times and howled in acceptance of its victory.

***

Alex and Kameron came out of the recreation room to see Kale and Anne getting out of the room as Malkaroy was battling Roger.

"Anne, Kale," Alex yelled.

"This way," Anne said as she ran towards the door.

Kameron heard put his hand up to his ear pierce. "Set it and go!"

469

Alex looked at Kameron. "You mean?"

"Yeah, Grossman set the charge, we gotta get out here," Kameron said as they ran towards the staircase. "We've got ten minutes before it all blows up."

Malkaroy turned to Alex. "Go!"

Gron took advantage of this as he took off to warn Vandor of his feast getting away. Gron knew he wasn't getting past the Sentry, so he took off in the opposite direction.

"Never mind him," Alex said. "Malkaroy, we don't have long, how many can you take?"

"One," he answered.

"Take Anne," Kale said as he shoved Anne into the arms of Malkaroy. He kissed her good-bye as Malkaroy grabbed Anne in his arm and jumped backwards out the window. He flew off to make sure Anne would be safe.

"Guys, we're on a time limit," Kameron reminded them. They headed out down the stairs to leave.

***

Vandor looked to Celestial. "You lost so much today."

Celestial wiped her tears. "Yes."

"And for what?" Vandor stated. "I don't think I'm going to have you killed. I'm going to take you to the Dark and watch what this world becomes at my hand."

Celestial turned to her new guardians. "Arome, Omiela, it is time to go," she stated.

"As you wish, my lady," the two stated.

"You can't leave," Vandor got agitated. "I want you to watch me feast on the Pure of Heart."

Celestial chimed in. "You mean that one?" She pointed to Anne flying away with Malkaroy.

Vandor turned to Salamor. "You lied to me!"

"To her command." Salamor stated as he flew away. He turned around. "You don't have much time."

She walked up to Vandor and placed her hand on his face. "Hate is choice." She smiled as she patted him on the face. "You never learned that." She walked away with her new guardians.

Vandor screamed as he knew he didn't have enough time to find another Pure of Heart. His weakness overcame his capability to prevent himself from getting thrown into the Dark Conduit.

***

Devine looked to Caliginous as it was about to strike. She would not give the satisfaction of showing the creature fear. She stared at it straight in the eyes. Pure hate filled the dark glare as it went to strike. Devine rolled out of the way, but the creature managed to grab her leg and throw her against a tree.

Komptin managed to get behind and bite the back of its leg, causing it to howl in pain. Devine was about to join her sister in the stars before something caught her attention.

"Lite Being," Salamor hissed.

Devine turned with disgust, "Come to gloat in my death."

Salamor hid in the shadow of the tree, "The Dark Conduit is closed. My Master is trapped. The Caliginous is no longer feeding. Now, you can strike."

"No Caliginous has been killed." Devine watched Komptin hold to its leg.

"Expose his black heart to the Lite," he hissed.

Devine looked to the chest of the beast. "Why are you helping?" But Salamor was no longer there.

Rushing the beast, she pole-vaulted into its chest, knocking it over. "We need to expose its heart." Komptin dug its claws into the chest of the Caliginous. With all his strength, he pulled back as hard as he could, exposing the black heart. Devine grabbed her Lite Bō and stabbed it into the heart. It screamed in pain before melting into the ground. Devine stood over her victory with Komptin being so weak he could hardly stand. She looked at Ariel's star and then watched as Malkaroy returned with the Pure of Heart.

Anne landed next to Devine as Malkaroy gently put her onto the ground. Malkaroy looked around and suddenly a look of sadness overcame him. "Ariel?"

Devine closed her eyes and pointed to the sky. "That one." She could feel Malkaroy put his hand on her shoulder in comfort.

472

"I am sorry," he said. "She was one half of the best."

An explosion startled Anne as they watched the F.O.R. building to burn to the ground. "Did they make it out?" Anne asked Malkaroy.

"I cannot sense them," Malkaroy informed her.

Anne started to fear the worst as Devine pointed to the rubble. "There are three figures coming out of the smoke and dust."

Anne smiled as she saw Kale running behind Alex and Kameron. She started to tear up as she went running towards Kale.

***

Alex had never been so glad to see Anne as she was running towards the group. Komptin as well was running with what energy he had left. She turned to Kameron as he was giving the update that Agent Grossman made it out okay. Alex grabbed Kameron's hand and looked at him. She had no words as she just was in pure bliss. He smiled back at her. They just started walking when they both looked at Anne who was in a dead stop. Her eyes grew big in a cold stare.

Both Alex and Kameron turned around to see Kale being held from the back with his mouth covered by Gron. Gron was hurt with blood dripping from his bullet hole in the head. Anger and heavy breathing with an evil smile overshadowed the fire of the F.O.R. Headquarters.

"Anne, you didn't keep your end of the bargain." Gron lit his fist as he shoved his fist through Kale's back coming out his chest. Gron pulled out his fist as Kale's body dropped to the ground.

Anne gave a blood curdling scream as Alex's body instantly covered in blue lite knocking Kameron onto the ground. She flashed her eyes as she attacked Gron with full force. She jumped in the air and punched him in the face. A fury of punches came from Alex as she screamed in anger. Gron screamed as he threw her off him.

He stood up as his body was now covered in a glowing red. The two of them started to punch each other. Alex ran at him. They wrestled but Alex got the advantage as she picked him up and threw him into the ground. Gron managed to shoot a Dark Beam at Alex, hitting her in the face. Her body spun around in the air before crashing into the ground.

Gron got up to continue the fight, but he saw two angels and a gargoyle run in his direction. "This was fun, but we will continue this another day." He turned and ran into the Darkness.

Alex got up, spitting out blood as she was about to chase him but was grabbed by Kameron. "Alex, Alex," he pleaded.

Alex screamed as she tried to break free of Kameron's grip. Kameron was losing his grip of her. Devine came to help restrain Alex as she continued to scream.

Anne slowly walked up to Kale's lifeless body. She stared at him as she dropped to her knees, crying holding his head. She felt a warm touch on her shoulders as she turned around to see a blonde angel with two identical angels in battle gear providing over watch.

"It should have been me, he wanted me. I made a deal with Gron," Anne said.

"My child," Celestial started to say.

Anne turned to her. "Don't, it's all my fault." Anne started to walk towards town.

Alex caught her breath as she watched Anne walk by not saying a word. She knew she had to go join her, but she couldn't bring herself to. What would she say? What could she do? Alex just sat there staring at her brother's body.

Celestial walked up to Devine and as the two embraced. "I am sorry, My Lady," Devine told her. "I am sorry."

"For what?" she asked her.

"She is gone," Devine told her.

"But not forgotten," Celestial told her, looking to the stars.

Devine just nodded as she walked away to look at the star of her lifelong partner.

Malkaroy looked over the devastation as Celestial walked by. "He will want revenge when he returns."

"Yes," she said.

"Do you think she will be up to it?" Celestial turned to the Sentry who was being comforted by Kameron. Malkaroy for the first time noticed something on Celestial that he had never seen before.

"I do not know," she said. "Vandor may be gone but a lot of Dark remains." She glanced over to dark alleyways. "The scale is still tipped in the Dark's favor, and I am afraid, Malkaroy. I am afraid for the Sentry." She turned to her guardians. She nodded as the four of them headed for the door.

Chapter 15

Alex just sat in the chair in her room staring at her outfit. She didn't want to put it on because that meant she had to go to the funeral. Her phone buzzed as a text message from Kameron came in telling her he will be at the church at 9:45 a.m.

She just replied with a simple "K." It was all she could muster to type.

Komptin jumped off the bed and nuzzled up to her as she petted his head. Alex just got done with Father Tom's funeral last week, and this week was her brother's. There were too many funerals in her life, Joseph, Sara, Osiah, Cardinal Frank, Father Tom, and now her brother's. Her choices brought them into this war, and now it claimed them. There should have been a way to hide them from this war.

Alex's family and Kale's mom flew in last night. A feeling of shame prevented her from approaching them. Tears were dripping from her face. "Damn it." She got out of the chair to ensure her makeup wasn't smeared after she finally found the will to get dressed. Osiah's flask was staring at her from the top of her dresser. The part where Osiah fused the rip from an Infiltrator cut her finger. She understood why he started to drink his pain away; if it didn't make her so sick, she would probably start. The flask was placed next to the picture of herself and Osiah, with Komptin in the background.

Alex picked up the picture. "I don't know if I can do this much longer." She placed the picture down next to a picture of Sara. Next to that picture was another one of Anne and Kale after he finished his Iron Man race. Such a happy time. The memory of Roger thrusting his fist through Kale's back coming out his chest flashed in her mind.

She closed her eyes as she tried to control her thoughts. After finding the strength to open her eyes, her eyesight was straight in line with the picture of Kameron and herself at Christmas. She slowly and reluctantly picked up that picture in fear of breaking it for some reason. She just stared at it. She swallowed hard, fighting the tears from falling again.

"Let's get this over with." She gently put the picture down and started walking out the door after she got dressed. Komptin slowly walked behind her in somber walk as he turned his head looking at the window.

***

Salamor watched the Sentry leave her room from outside the window of the rectory. Even though he had no power on this ground, his experience knew that the Sentry was in pain. He knew that once she stepped off church ground, he could influence her to either end her life or join the dark; anything to stop the pain. That would tip this war, maybe his master would forgive him for his betrayal. Forgiveness was not in his nature. Salamor

478

knew that once his master returns, he would hunt Salamor down and end his existence.

He floated to the rooftop on the other side of the street where he felt the presence of the Lite. He turned to see the living half of the former Guardian of the Conduit. "She is in much pain," he hissed. "She would be easy to influence."

Devine just stared down at the room where the Sentry stays. "You truly are pure…"

Salamor interrupted her, "I shall go, you will not hear from me again."

She looked over at the Dark Myst. "Where shall you go?"

"There is an abandoned church on the largest land mass, on the highest mountain. There I shall be hidden from my master." He turned and started to float away before he turned.

Devine turned to look at him.

"Be aware, Gron will search for the Dark Texts to bring my master back. The pages cannot be destroyed by anyone Lite."

"Then I will have the Pure of Heart destroy them," Devine calmly stated.

"No, any primate that destroys those pages will inhabit the evilness within the Dark pages. They will gain all its knowledge and power to tip the scale, they shall become Vandor's most loyal and knowledgeable servant."

Devine nodded. "I understand. Why are you telling me this? Why did you help?"

Salamor looked to the sun. "For the first time in my existence, I feel weak. It's the only thing I could do to make it go away."

Devine gave a small smile. "The pages shall be protected. Go and find your peace."

Salamor just nodded and floated towards the east.

***

Cardinal Joe flew in early to preside over the service for both Father Tom and Kale. He told the story of how he first met Kale at the hospital that night Joseph died. He reminded everyone how strong he was because of the people in his life, particularly Alex and Anne.

Alex couldn't bring herself to look over at Anne. She seemed so lost and stone-faced. She managed to be polite to all that came to pay their respects, but she was just going through the motions. Alex knew her too well; Anne was in deep pain.

The service concluded with a prayer, and everyone got up to head downstairs for the wake. Anne just stared at the casket with her head slightly tilted to the side. She cautiously walked up to the casket as she put her hand on it saying good-bye. She turned and watched the congregation leave the room. She even saw a couple of people laughing.

How could they be happy?

Her husband laid here murdered by the Dark. She placed her hands on the coffin and closed her eyes. She took out the flower out of her hair and placed it on the casket. She wanted the flower to be buried with Kale, but his body was too mangled for an open casket. Anne was approached by Kale's mom and put her hand on her shoulder. Anne flinched at her touch.

"Anne, honey, it's time," she softly said, trying to comfort her as much as possible.

"Give me a minute?" Anne asked looking down at the coffin. "I just need a second." She continued to look at the box where her husband laid resting.

***

Alex started to walk up to Anne but stopped. She stopped to look at Anne as she watched her calmly put her hand on the casket. Alex felt the presence of Celestial. Alex turned to look up on the second floor to see The Conduit with her new guardians. Celestial waved to her, but all Alex could do was nod in her direction with a somber look.

Alex looked down in the entryway to the congregation where Komptin and Kameron were down at the end aisle of the church looking over at Alex. Kameron stood so proper, so tall. He patiently waited for Alex to join him. She knew that he was wanting her to take her time. She turned to Anne again who now was crying with her head down on the coffin. Alex could see her tears drop on the casket and fall to the side. Alex couldn't stand it anymore.

Alex with tears running down her face looked over at Kameron.

He mouthed over to her, "I love you."

Alex just shook her head no as her tears started to fall. She looked to Komptin who started to walk towards her. She put her finger up to him to stay. She just shook her head. Alex turned to Anne one more time who was crying uncontrollably. Alex took a step towards her and stopped as she couldn't control her tears any longer.

She turned to Celestial up on the balcony. "No Alexandria, please," Celestial softly said to herself as she looked down at a tearful Lite Sentry.

Alex took off running out the side door as the last thing she heard was Kameron calling out to her as she ran into the depths of the city.

***

Kameron looked down to Komptin. "Can you track her? We cannot abandon her."

Komptin flashed his eyes as they took one step before Kameron felt a hand on his shoulder.

He turned around to see Devine preventing him from leaving. "We have to go after her."

"No, she needs to come to us," she said.

"But..." Kameron looked over at the doorway where Alex took off running.

Celestial joined Kameron down below as the two new Guardians stared at Kameron as they did not trust him yet. "Kameron, I have a message for you: 'Do not be a dumbass'."

Kameron turned and a laugh came.

"Patience Kameron, have faith." Celestial looked down at the Pure of Heart falling to the ground crying. "If you will please excuse me." She bypassed Kameron walking up to the front of the congregation. Her new guardians attempted to follow her, but she motioned for them to stay put.

***

Anne turned to watch Alex take off running. Anne started to shiver and tremble. She had never felt so cold. She held onto her crucifix, crying uncontrollably, falling to the ground. She felt a touch on her shoulders as Celestial bent down to her level. Anne, with her back leaning on Celestial, was shivering as the angel was trying to comfort her. Celestial's new guardians watched her drop a glowing tear from her eyes as the Conduit was trying to comfort her.

"Please, please tell me he is at peace, I beg of you," Anne cried onto Celestial's arm as she wrapped her arm around her from behind.

Celestial misty wings wrapped around Anne, comforting her as much as possible. "His love for you is so strong, you need to know that. He looks down at you now smiling and says he will always be with you."

Anne leaned into Celestial's chest looking up at her with her eyes. "I love him so much."

She smiled. "He knows, but he also wants you to live your life."

"I know time heals all wounds, but I—I don't…" Anne said to her.

"He wants you to be happy, that is how much love he has for you." Celestial squeezed her one last time before she stood up.

Anne followed suit as she leaned over the casket kissing it one more time. "I love you, Kale, I will never forget you." She turned to Celestial. "Thank you."

Celestial just nodded in return.

Anne looked over at the door where Alex took off running. "Will she be okay?"

Celestial looked to the sky with a worried look. "We will see."

***

Alex ran until she could not bear it anymore. She killed her brother, her choices in life killed him. She held her hand on the wall trying to maintain her balance.

"I killed him," she pleaded. She continued to walk down the street as she walked into a rustic rundown little diner where there was only enough room for a bar and stools to sit on. She bypassed the cook who just watched her head straight into the bathroom to wash her face.

The bathroom was pretty dirty, and she could barely see her reflection between the grime on the mirror. She wiped her face down and took a deep breath.

She walked out of the bathroom to see the cook staring at her. "Sorry," she said. "That was pretty rude."

"I deal with that day in and day out," the cook said, leaning on the cabinet next to the griddle. "You okay?"

Alex bit her lip and cried, "No."

"Sit down," the man suggested. "You look like you could use a double cheeseburger."

Alex smiled. "That does sound good."

"Mine are the best in the world," he said as he turned around to grab a handful of beef from a silver bowl in a small fridge next to the grill.

Alex sat down on a stool to watch him massage the meat into two balls of ground beef while mixing in some seasons before flattening the burgers onto the grill. The sounds of the grill caught Alex's attention as she watched him cook her double-burger. "So, are you going to tell me what is on your mind?"

Alex just shook her head no.

"I get it," the cook said. "Is there anyone you could talk to?" He flipped over the burger.

"No, there's no one who knows what I'm going through," she said.

The cook turned around. "I would not say that." He leaned on the counter. "There is always someone." He stared at her. "Thirsty?"

Alex said, "Yeah, what do you have?"

The cook looked over at his fridge. "The basic sodas, bottled water, Apollo Energy drink, Iced Tea."

Alex smiled. "I'll have an Apollo with ice."

"Sounds good." He walked over the fridge, opened it up, and poured into a cup of ice. He handed it over to her and saw her scars. Alex noticed him gazing at her scars. "Those look pretty bad, but not as deep as you are keeping inside," he said to her.

Alex dropped a tear from her eye. "You have no idea." She wiped her tears as she took a sip of her drink.

The cook turned his attention to the two patties and placed it on a bun. He turned around and gave it to her. "Tell me what you think."

She grabbed it and bit into it. "It's good, but I don't know if it's the best in the world." She tried to joke as she blew her nose into a napkin.

The cook studied her. "Ah, yes, of course, I forgot the secret sauce." He bent down underneath the counter and studied the bottle as he wiped some of the dust off.

Alex was starting to become leery of the sauce. "What are you doing?"

"Reading the directions, it has been a while since I have used this," he said as he studied Alex. "What are you? One hundred eighteen pounds?"

"Yeah," Alex said in confusion. Alex watched him put the sauce on her burger and then she took a bite.

"Tell me why you are running?" he asked her.

"What makes you think I'm running?"

"I am not stupid, Alexandria," he said to her as he leaned back on the counter.

"How did you know my name?" She looked up at him swallowing her burger.

"I need you to relax," he said as he grabbed an empty glass and put his hand over it. Alex watched as a soda with ice appeared in the glass as he took a sip. "So, there is no one for you to talk to?"

Alex shook her head as she thought her mind was playing tricks on her. "There's only one person who knows what I'm going through," Alex admitted. "But he's no longer with us."

"I've been with you since the beginning and will be until the end, Little Spitfire," a voice said next to her.

The diner got dark except a light shining where Alex was sitting. Her eyes got big as she turned to see next to her Osiah drinking from a golden flask. "It can't be," she said. "It can't be. Prove to me it's you."

"You still got my mop?" Osiah said, as he turned his body over to her. Alex jumped out of her stool and hugged Osiah, crying as she was squeezing him tightly. "It's okay Alex, please, get it all out. You'll feel so much better." Alex continued to cry into her former mentor's arms.

He squeezed her and Alex continued to cry. She pulled away to notice she left snot on his clothes.

"Sorry," she wiped her nose with a napkin. "I have a bad habit of that."

"It's okay," he laughed, as he wiped off his clothes.

"So much has happened since, since, you know," she said as she pulled herself apart from his

487

embrace. She sat back down onto her diner stool and took another bite of her sandwich.

"Since I got a fist thrusted through my chest. Not going to lie, it hurt."

Alex smiled as she listened to her mentor make light of the situation.

"Little Spitfire, I know what you are going through, I couldn't be prouder of you," he told her, taking another sip from his flask.

"How could you be proud of me? I killed my brother, Devine lost Ariel, and I almost got Anne killed," Alex admitted. "Some Sentry I am."

"You didn't kill your brother, Gron did," Osiah said. "You did not force anyone to join you in this war. All of them volunteered to help."

Alex just stared down at her burger. "So much death, pain; I brought this to all that I love."

"Take another bite," Osiah said. "All of them volunteered because of their love for you."

Alex took another bite and sip of her drink. "Their love for me?"

"Ariel and Devine pleaded to help you. Kameron, your boyfriend, to this day still blows my mind that you fell in love with someone who wears a suit," he teased her, punching her in the arm. "He would go to the depths of Hell for you."

She smiled at the thought of Kameron and then turned to a frown. "I'm afraid my lifestyle is going to get him killed."

"It may happen," Osiah admitted. "But it is nothing compared to what you will miss if you run, trust me on this. I know."

Alex turned to him with a single tear dripping from her eyes.

"The love he has for you equals my love for Celestial, and that is all that matters," Osiah said drinking from his flask. "How's the burger?"

Alex took another bite. "Really good actually." Alex turned to him. "What about Anne? I don't think I could face her."

"Her heart is strong, and she is extremely smart. She knows this is not your fault," Osiah said, taking another sip. "You know I'm right."

Alex shook her head. "You ever, you know?"

"Breakdown to the point of not knowing if I could go on?"

Alex embarrassingly nodded as she felt weak for being so emotional.

"More times than I can count, I was quite old," he said as he took a sip of his whiskey. "Finish up your burger."

Alex started to feel better. She felt she needed to fall to the ground to get back up stronger than before. She took her last bite of her burger and turned to Osiah. "This is a one-time visit?" she asked with a mouthful of food.

Osiah turned to her and slowly nodded his head.

Alex swallowed her food as a tear dropped from her eye and jumped out of her seat hugging him. "Then I'm going to enjoy this for as long as I can."

He smiled as he hugged her back. He gently put her back to her seat and wiped her tears from her eyes. "Rare as Blue Gold." He pointed to her chest.

"That was one heavenly burger," Alex joked.

"Thank you," the cook said in an echoing voice.

Osiah nodded. "I have to go. Give Komptin a scratch behind the ears for me. Tell Celestial..." He just looked away from Alex as she watched him wipe a tear. He turned back around. "Tell her, tell her that..."

Alex watched her mentor disappear. "Bye." She wiped her tears from her eyes. She took a moment before realizing what had just happened. She turned to the cook. "Who are you?"

"You know who I am," the Cook said.

Alex shook her head no.

"I am the dawn to your night, I feel your hurt with each scar, I hear your whispers when you scream," the Cook commented. The diner became clean and white, and the light brightened with silhouettes of numerous angels in the background. Celestial with her new guardians joined the Cook at His side. Devine and Malkaroy stayed by the doorway of the diner as if guarding it. "I am One who is most proud of you."

Komptin joined Alex next to her at diner stool in his gargoyle state. Alex stood up and fell to the ground in a bow.

"Alexandria, please, be on your feet." The Cook nodded. "There is much Dark roaming around my children," the Cook commented.

Celestial gave her a loving smile. "Alexandria, you have done well, maintaining the balance against tremendous odds."

"But the balance is still tilted," Alex continued. Alex fixed up her clothes, and cracked her neck, "You don't have to ask, I volunteer, if You will allow it."

The Cook smiled as he placed his gentle hand on her shoulder. He went on saying. "You will always have my support." He turned to the kitchen. "I have to get back to the kitchen." Everyone bowed as the Cook left to go behind some doors.

The diner returned to normal with all that remained was Devine, and Celestial with her guardians. Alex turned to Devine. "I am sorry about Ariel. She was truly amazing."

"She will be remembered with honor along with her brothers and sisters in the sky," Devine said. She walked up to Alex with her mystified wings and battle gear on. Her halo hovered above her head. "I shall be with you through this, Little Sister." She double tapped Alex's shoulder as she stood behind her.

Komptin's eyes flashed in agreement as Alex scratched him behind his ears.

Alex smiled as she turned to Celestial. "Can you please let me know where Anne and Kameron are?

***

491

Kameron walked into the lobby before entering the Cardinal's office. Megan sat at her desk talking on the phone, looking at Kameron with disappointment. "Good afternoon, Megan."

Megan just shook her head, "The Cardinal is expecting you," she said, covering up the phone. Megan spoke to Kameron before he knocked on the door, "She is no good for you. If you were smart, cut your ties now before something happens."

"I love her," he said, knocking on the door. The Cardinal invited him in as he entered.

Megan rolled her eyes and uncovered the phone.

"I don't know what the cardinal wants with Kameron. I haven't seen Alex since the funeral. Hopefully, she won't come back," Megan sat there listening to the other end of the phone. "I'll let you know what I find out, Roger, but Anne keeps her office locked up tight and it will take some time to get those texts." She listened some more, then smiled with a sneer. "Of course, I'll come over tonight, just as long as you show me those sexy teeth of yours with your mesmerizing red eyes." She gave a playful growl as she hung up the phone, staring at Alex's desk with disgust.

Kameron sat down with Cardinal Joe sitting across from him. He read over the report from his Administrative Priest. "Thank you, Father Richard, this is Special Agent Kameron."

Kameron shook his hand. "Nice to meet you."

The Cardinal started by saying, "Kameron, the Council cannot thank you enough for what you did to help Alex."

"It wasn't even an option not to help," he stated.

"Well, you have knowledge that most do not," Father Richard explained.

"I won't say anything," Kameron assured. "You have my word."

Cardinal Joe smiled. "I know that, Kameron. If Alex trusts you then that is all the assurance I need. She is a special girl."

Kameron smiled at the thought of her. "Yes, she is."

"Kameron, I'm in need of a bodyguard, and considering your security background and knowledge of the Council, the job is yours if you want it," Cardinal Joe asked him.

"Wow, wasn't expecting that," Kameron stated. "Sounds like a good job."

"We can match what you are making now, plus ten percent," Father Richard said.

Kameron took a second or two to consider it. "It sounds great, but I think I need to decline the offer."

Cardinal Joe sat back in the chair, "May I ask why?"

"The F.O.R. infiltrated the government with ease, we caused a major blow to them, but they are still more of them. I need to find them and help eradicate them," he said.

"It will look like you are betraying your government if you get caught," Father Richard interjected.

"I'll be saving it," Kameron said, getting up.

"I understand," Cardinal Joe said, getting up from his seat. He shook Kameron's hand. Kameron got to his car to see Alex leaning on it with Komptin sitting at her side. He slowly walked up to her. "You okay?"

She looked up at him shamefully. "I am." She looked away from him from embarrassment. "I'm sorry I ran."

"It's okay, I get it," Kameron assured her, putting his hands in the pockets of his trench coat. "Look, I know that you fear what your lifestyle will bring to the ones you love, but I'm not going anywhere."

Alex turned her attention back to Kameron. "And if I get you killed?"

"Then I die fulfilling life because life without you would be completely empty," Kameron told her. He slowly took his hands out of his pockets and placed one of them on her cheek and the other holding her hand. The two of them kissed.

"I love you, Kameron," she told him and then kissed him in return.

***

Anne sat on a rooftop of her apartment overlooking the city, wearing Kale's sweatshirt which he gave her down by the water. Anne needed

494

to sit on the rooftop. It made her feel a little bit more peaceful. Cardinal Joe gave her two weeks off to gather her thoughts and try to get back to normal.

The Council called her personally to ensure her that she would be taken care of financially and any other means. She didn't know what normal was going to be anymore without Kale. She hadn't heard from Alex since she took off from the funeral. Anne just stared into the setting sun over the buildings. She took a small sip of her wine while staring out over the city.

Anne saw movement next to her as Alex sat down next to her. The two of them just watched the sun going down. The two of them just sat there and then Anne leaned on Alex's shoulder. Alex put her arm around her, squeezing.

"I miss him," Anne told her.

"Me too," Alex said.

"I don't blame you," Anne told her, wiping her eyes.

Alex didn't know what to say, she just fought back the tears and nodded. "I need you, Anne."

"I'm not going to leave you, sweetie," Anne assured her.

Anne got up with Alex joining her as the sun finished going down. Komptin in his gargoyle state joined Alex at her side looking to the horizon. Kameron, wearing his suit and tie covered in a trench coat, came up behind Alex. Devine came on the other side of Anne in her battle gear with her misty wings and halo showing, holding her Lite Bō Staff.

Alex closed her eyes as she felt someone getting infiltrated.

"We have much to do." Alex lit her fists as Komptin's eyes began to glow blue before bellowing a massive roar into the distance.

THE END

www.ingramcontent.com/pod-product-compliance
Lightning Source LLC
Chambersburg PA
CBHW051936020726
47501CB00001B/147